IT AIN'T EASY, COMANDANTE

IT AIN'T EASY, COMANDANTE

The Cuban People's Struggle for Freedom!

A Novel

Caroll I. García

To Judy and Howard all the best.

Caroll

12/3/07

iUniverse, Inc.

New York Lincoln Shanghai

It ain't easy, Comandante
The Cuban People's Struggle for Freedom!

iUniverse books may be ordered through booksellers or by contacting:

iUniverse
2021 Pine Lake Road, Suite 100
Lincoln, NE 68512
www.iuniverse.com
1-800-Authors (1-800-288-4677)

Because of the dynamic nature of the Internet, any Web addresses or links contained in this book may have changed since publication and may no longer be valid.

This is a work of fiction. All of the characters, names, incidents, organizations, and dialogue in this novel are either the products of the author's imagination or are used fictitiously.

ISBN: 978-0-595-45114-2 (pbk)
ISBN: 978-0-595-89427-7 (ebk)

Printed in the United States of America

For the Cuban people everywhere.

"Peace and wealth come only through freedom"

José Martí

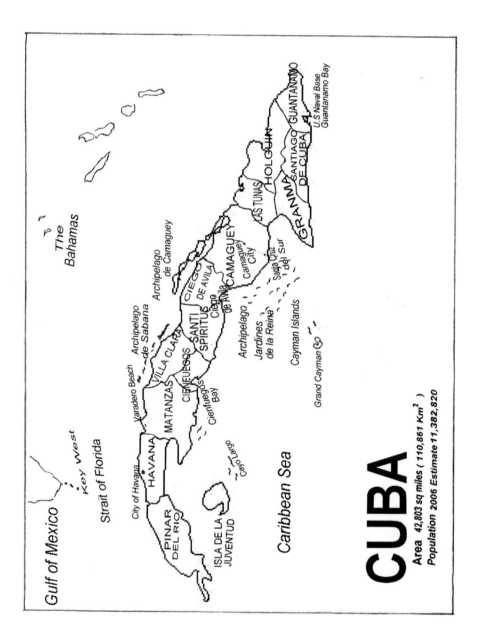

CUBA

Area 42,803 sq miles (110,861 Km^2)
Population 2006 Estimate 11,382,820

Gulf of Mexico

Key West

Strait of Florida

The Bahamas

Archipelago de Camaguey

Archipelago de Sabana

Varadero Beach

City of Havana

HAVANA

PINAR DEL RIO

ISLA DE LA JUVENTUD

Cayo Largo

MATANZAS

VILLA CLARA

CIENFUEGOS

Cienfuegos Bay

SANTI SPIRITUS

CIEGO DE AVILA

Ciego de Avila

CAMAGUEY

Camaguey City

Santa Cruz del Sur

LAS TUNAS

HOLGUIN

GRANMA

GUANTANAMO

SANTIAGO DE CUBA

U.S Naval Base Guantanamo Bay

Jardines de la Reina

Archipelago

Cayman Islands

Grand Cayman

Caribbean Sea

CONTENTS

PROLOGUE

▼

Near Santa Cruz del Sur, a small coastal town in the province of Camagüey on the eastern part of Cuba, two guys were walking down a sandy and muddy path along the shore. After a full day's work in *Combinado Pesquero Argerico Lara,* the state-run fish processing factory.

They were dressed in old, cheap jeans of unidentifiable color and dirty, sweaty T-shirts. Juan, who looked about fifty years old, was more than ten years younger than his friend Genaro. They both seemed tired and worn out by the hardship of their lives. Juan was married and had two daughters. Genaro never married, and his girlfriend was the widow of a soldier who was a friend of Genaro's brother Tito. The soldier was killed in Africa during Cuba's armed intervention in Angola. They were common people, the *Cubanos de a pie*, earning two hundred Cuban pesos a month—less than ten dollars U.S. They were living miserable lives and their future looked grim. Juan asked Genaro if he remembered the living conditions in Cuba before the revolution. Born in 1965, Juan knew only the life of poverty and Castro's struggle against the *Yanki* imperialists.

Genaro was ten years old when Castro came to power. His father was a *guajiro* with a small plot of land where he grew some vegetables and bred pigs and chickens that he sold at the open market in town. Genaro's mother was the schoolteacher. Genaro and his older brother Tito lived with their parents in a small house at the little farm twenty minutes from town. He remembered the good old times when the family enjoyed the fruits of his father's and brother's labor from their farm. He walked every day with his mother to school in town. Sometimes he helped his father and brother with chores, especially during harvest time.

Genaro said, "*Chico*, by any measure, we weren't wealthy, but we felt that we were owners of our life and enjoyed our family's simple life on our little farm. I remember those good times," he added, with a gesture of resignation.

Juan shouted, "Then, *coño*, what were the reasons for the revolution against Batista?"

Genaro had been young at the time of the revolution, but he remembered his father saying that the underlying motives of the revolt against Batista's illegal regime were to reinstate the Constitution of 1940 and to eradicate corruption in the government.

Juan interrupted, saying, "*Carajo*, why did the revolution establish a Communist system on the island? They didn't reinstate the 1940 constitution; neither did they clear the corruption in government. Instead they made a new *jodida* Socialist constitution and spread the corruption around the island!"

Genaro explained that Castro had lied to the people right from the beginning when he came down from the hills. The first thing he said was, "Our revolution is as green as our palm trees." Genaro also remembered what Castro said about Communism: "Nothing like that will happen in our country. Communism would not have here any justification and complicity with the government." Three years later, when Genaro was fourteen, he remembered his father telling his mother that Castro had declared himself a Communist, saying, "I always was and always will be, until the last days of my life."

"When the old man heard that, he didn't like it," Genaro said. "I remember that he told us that Castro had betrayed the revolution."

When Castro made the law of the Agrarian Reform a few months later, the government confiscated Genaro's father's farm and it became part of a large cooperative controlled by the government. By law, Genaro's father became a salaried worker on his own farm. Later, the family relocated to an apartment near town. The army recruited Genaro's brother and sent him to Angola, where he died from wounds received in combat. Genaro's father died of a heart attack, overwhelmed by sorrow, six months later and his mother followed three years later.

Juan, after listening Genaro's explanations, concluded, "*Chico*, then we were betrayed by that *cabrón*. I am able to survive the life in Cuba with my family because I receive the *remesa* from my brother in Miami, who as you know, fled the island in a small boat ten years ago. Nobody can feed a family of four with two hundred pesos a month. You know, Genaro," he added, "it ain't easy."

Then Genaro said, "Juan, do you want to leave Cuba? I am fed up; I can't live anymore on this rotten island. I might join four other guys fleeing the island on a boat sailing to the Cayman Islands. This is very confidential but I am telling you this because you are like my younger brother." He paused for a while and then continued, saying, "We are planning to leave very soon. The plant is sending me to Camagüey to bring some ball bearings for the factory, and I'm going to take that opportunity. Instead of going to Camagüey, I will take the boat to the Cayman Islands that night. If you want to go and if you have five hundred pesos, I think that my friends would take you."

Juan thought about the tempting idea for a moment, but he understood that he couldn't leave his wife and two daughters behind. He knew the dangers of the open sea voyage in a small boat with limited supplies and navigational equipment; he didn't even know how to swim. Flight wasn't his way out of his miseries.

He told Genaro that he wasn't interested in the idea because it was too dangerous to expose his family to such risky adventure. He also warned Genaro of the danger of the voyage and asked him to wait a few more days; maybe things in Cuba could change. Castro was sick, getting old, and his brother Raúl could come up with some good ideas, after all.

They continued the discussion until they got to town, where they stopped for awhile at the town's main square. A policeman making his usual rounds came close to them, trying to investigate the subject of the conversation. When Genaro realized that the policeman was close to them, he said, "You know my brother, it ain't easy."

The policeman asked what was going on. Genaro said they were discussing the upside break of the curve of the new pitcher of the *Industriales* national baseball team. The policeman, looking at them with scorn, said, "Keep moving, *bitongos*," and left them alone.

"It Ain't Easy, Comandante" is the name of this book, and it might sound too casual. However, "it ain't easy," it is one of the most common expressions on the island of Cuba. It is commonly utilized as a complaint against the regime, when the use of other—more specific—words could get you trouble, with the possibility of a trip to a Socialist prison.

Life in Cuba is difficult. The so-called *Cubanos de a pie*, or common people, suffer a lot of hardship and deprivations in their daily routine. Young people learn early in their lives that their future is gloomy. The Socialist government controls all aspects of the individual's life. There is no opportunity to live a private life in Cuba; you owe your existence to the revolution and to the struggle against ruthless capitalism—according to Castro's postulate in the *Proceso Histórico*. The antagonistic force against the freedom of the people is the government's corruption and the deception and betrayal of false leaders.

The protagonist of this story is the Cuban people in their long quest for freedom. Juan, Genaro, and many other characters participating in the story are nothing more than the voices of the people telling their own experiences. These voices create the story's plot as they endure usually common and sometimes memorable events over a relatively long period. They tell of many unhappy occurrences, but their stories are always full of heroic deeds.

The people found that the hope for a return to their constitution and free elections did not last long after the revolution's victory celebrations upon the downfall of Batista's dictatorship. Castro was turning the revolution—"as green as our palm trees"—on the path toward Socialism and away from democracy. Cuba was becoming a satellite of the Soviet Union, and the traditional alliance and friendship with the neighbor to the north—the United States—broke off. The island was making new friends with countries inside the Iron Curtain. The revolutionary government exhorted the Cuban people to sacrifice for the good of the revolution and to surrender individuality on behalf of the formation of "the new man."

Of course, the new doctrines were not well received by all Cubans. Many people decided to leave the island for a short time, until the situation was resolved. The majority thought the United States would not permit a satellite of the Soviet Union to exist only ninety miles from its coast. Others confronted the revolutionary government and revolted against the new Socialist regime. Many of the dedicated revolutionaries who fought against the Batista regime were fighting once again, this time against the Socialist revolution.

The new regime reacted violently, employing the repressive power of the state, imprisoning dissidents or executing them by firing squad. No one was safe; even cabinet members and rebel *comandantes* were targets of the firing squad, or they just disappeared in sudden "accidents" if they publicly disagreed with the direction the revolution was taking. The provisional president, Dr. Urrutia, was the first to go into exile, followed by cabinet members and highly placed government officials. Many others organized clandestine groups that conspired against the revolutionary regime. In rural areas, many peasants revolted and went to the hills to hide and fight against the government. At night, people living in urban areas could hear the blast of small homemade bombs; the rebel groups were arming. Again, the island was at war, this time against the Communist revolution, the betrayed revolution.

Two intense years of fighting ended with the frustrated Playa Girón invasion in April 1961. Once more, the Cuban people were betrayed, but on this occasion, betrayal didn't come from the Cuban Communist gang. The Kennedy administration withdrew the United States' promise to support the daring assaulting Brigade 2506, comprised of thirteen hundred exiled Cubans, after they had already disembarked on the beach. The clandestine armed groups on the island were never warned, so they were not able to coordinate urban and rural attacks in support of the invading forces. The invasion was a complete failure for the democratic movement—on and off the island—and a big victory for the new Communist regime. The ill-fated skirmish consolidated the Communist revolution and resulted in an embarrassing failure for the United States. The affair was a precursor, a few months later, to the October 1962 Cuban Missile Crisis.

The great setback weakened resistance on the island and practically silenced bellicose groups outside the country. The political problems on the island of Cuba transcended the internal affairs of the Cuban people; the incident gestated a new set of problems between the United States and the Soviet Union and contributed to the young Cold War.

The Cuban people felt frustrated after the United States seemingly abandoned them, and they came to believe that escape was the best solution. The massive exodus of Cubans through the ports of Camarioca and Mariel filled the front pages of newspapers throughout the free world. The regime was keeping under control what was left of the internal resistance, using its power to repress and fill-ing the jails with political prisoners. Cuban soldiers acted as a mercenary army in the warlike "internationalist" adventures in Venezuela, Nicaragua, Granada, El Salvador, Bolivia, and Africa. During those years, the island's population suffered the loss of their civil liberties and bore the miseries of a shortage of food and other necessities, even with the economic support of the Soviet Union. The living situation on the island was not easy to bear; the people survived the economic crisis, but the future looked grim.

After the collapse of the Soviet Union in 1991, the *Castrista* regime realized the Communist bloc had abandoned it and it faced an acute economic crisis. The Socialist government would call this crisis the *período especial* in an attempt to justify the poverty, the shortages, and the hunger suffered by the Cuban population after the suspension of subsidies from the Soviets. The regime tried to cover its failure to produce goods and services under the Socialist system and blamed the United States trade embargo for the difficult situation. The deterioration of the standard of living on the island drove the people to despair, which especially affected Cuban youths; their options seemed reduced to joining either the *jinetera prostitute* or the *balsero*, those who fled the island on small boats. Loss of faith in the system and the sense of helplessness limited their options to debasing themselves for survival or fleeing to escape from the Socialist inferno.

After abandonment by the Soviets and alienation from the United States, the regime, in its desperation, was able to find a new ally in Hugo Chávez and his Venezuelan oil. Once more Castro succeeding in finding a country to subsidize his failing regime, this time selling the services of Cuban physicians and the organization skills of state security teams to maintain repression in Venezuela. The delusional Chávez dreamed of being Castro's ideological heir upon the latter's death. The substantial benefits of a hundred thousand oil barrels a day, in part sold on the international oil market, gave Castro's regime enough income to be able to reject the help of European countries and to cancel some of the economic "reforms" undertaken during the hard years of the nineties.

Internal dissidence began in earnest during the *período especial*. This opposition differed from the one in the early years, as the new dissidents did not contemplate the use of violence to achieve their ends. Their objectives were non-violent and they sought to create and develop the country's civil society. This generation had known nothing but repression, having been born and brought up under the totalitarian system. The movement quickly spread through the island and to the Cubans in exile abroad; more than three hundred dissident groups were soon active. The regime could not permit this movement, even though it was not violent, and once more, the state employed force to stop the dissidents' activities. Many innocent people were sent to prison, convicted to long years of incarceration for nothing more than soliciting signatures, for possessing and lending certain books, and for asking for reforms that might help relieve the population's miseries.

However, with close to fifty years of revolution, *el Caballo*, a month away from the celebration of his eightieth birthday, began to lose his battle against age. Now, he was looking more like a *penco senil* after several emergency surgeries for intestinal bleeding. The news of his infirmity immediately unleashed celebrations in the streets of Miami, but Cuban exile leaders were cautious, calling for more time to analyze the situation.

Fidel, for a while delegated to his brother Raúl his functions as *"Presidente del Consejo de Estado, Comandante en Jefe de las Fuerzas Armadas Revolucionarias* and *Primer Secretario del Comité Central del Partido Comunista de Cuba."* This was the first time in forty-seven years of revolutionary government in Cuba that the "*Máximo Líder"* transferred power to anyone. The health of the "for-life dictator" became one great state secret.

After this brief introduction to the contemporary history of the Island of Cuba, we will continue our story, beginning with the day of the great rally in the Malecón, Havana's main avenue.

CHAPTER 1

▼

THE GREAT RALLY IN THE MALECÓN

Alex and Henry left the house accompanied by the president of the CDR and an agent of State security who was armed with an AK-47 assault rifle. They walked through the darkness to the middle of the block where a truck stood waiting. Ten people were already aboard the truck, and all looked agitated. No one seemed pleased to leave his home at midnight on a Sunday to spend the rest of the night at the Malecón, and then, after a sleepless night, go marching in front of a building for a cause that was not his own. The people in the truck already knew that the new leaders would demand more sacrifices of them, even after nearly fifty years of hardship and destitution. Now was the time of *planetary Socialism*, which Venezuela's dictator, Hugo Chávez, called *Socialism of the twenty-first century*. If anyone still felt any affection for the *Castrismo*, now they had to accept the fact that the idea had died, together with the illusions of the Cuban people, after the triumph of the revolution in 1959. The island was entering a new era, perhaps the age of the *Chavismo*. The Cuban Revolution was becoming the *Revolución Bolivariana*, and the great parade the next morning would be the official beginning of the new era.

In less than five minutes, more than twenty people had crammed themselves onto the truck bed—some young, others old; women, men, and even a couple of twelve-year-olds. All were standing together as closely as possible, like canned sardines. Soon another truck arrived, with five or six passengers already on, and stopped behind. One of the security agents spotted the arriving truck. He turned to the first driver and said, "Now you can leave for the Malecón." The driver started the motor and began to move the truck, but not before a uniformed agent with an AK-47 climbed into the passenger's seat.

The people in the truck had resigned themselves to being prisoners; they had been selected because they were not regime sympathizers. They were trapped. The whole island was nothing more than a great prison, the Malecón was in a way a concentration camp. Alex and Henry knew they would have to report to the authorities of the Ministry of the Interior, the MININT, on the following day. Henry knew they could not move from Havana, and it was impossible to leave the island. In order to escape from this hellhole, they had to throw themselves into the sea upon anything that would float. Henry felt very depressed—he had all but given up—but he didn't say anything to Alex; he preferred to keep his silence and pray for a miracle.

The truck turned right to take the Avenue of the Missions and wheel along the Park of the Martyrs until Plaza Thirteenth of May. To the right they could see the ancient Castle of La Punta, where Havana's Malecón Avenue begins. They joined scores of other trucks and *guaguas* that had come from other districts of Havana, converging along the Malecón like a funeral procession. All the passengers were quiet and motionless, as if they were shipments of rag dolls. Their faces were sad, like those of Alex and Henry—the faces of condemned people.

The truck continued very slowly along the Malecón and soon passed by the monument to General Máximo Gómez and the Park of General Maceo, where that famous general's bronze statue is located. From there, the passengers could see the powerful beacon from the lighthouse of the Morro Castle. The lampposts and the lights of innumerable official cars, trucks, and *guaguas* illuminated the avenue. It was a gigantic mobilization and a waste of scarce resources, all with the intention of intimidating the populace and showing strength to the rest of the world. "This is disgusting—a farce and a mockery," said Alex, through his teeth. "How long will the people put up with this?"

Finally, the truck stopped not far from the Maine monument. Alex remembered that, when the monument was constructed in 1925, it had the bronze sculpture of an eagle from the American warship that had exploded mysteriously in Havana's bay in 1898. The revolutionary government removed the eagle from the monument in 1961 after the Playa Girón invasion. The symbol of freedom had been another casualty of the current regime.

When Henry came down from the truck, Alex said, "*Mi hermano*, I believe you won't be able to leave by Pinar del Río. I feel sorry for you—what a mess I've gotten you into! The only way out might be through the SINA building."

The Embassy of the United States had been in that building before 1960, but now it was occupied by the Embassy of Switzerland in Havana and the U.S. Interests Section (USINT), called SINA by the Cubans.

"The problem isn't only getting into the building," said Alex, "but it's that you don't have your passport or any documentation that you can show to verify your American citizenship. Everybody thinks you're a Cuban named José Rodriguez Pantoja, and even that identification is fraudulent." Henry had already been disturbed, but upon hearing this, he felt much worse.

Then Alex told Henry he had a plan. "First, we're going to try to walk through this sea of human confusion until we get close to the SINA building." They could see the building less than three blocks away, and Alex added, "With God's help, some opportunity will come where you can go without being stopped and climb the building's fence. It won't be easy, but perhaps the chance will come." The way Alex spoke, it was as though Henry would be the only one who would be trying to get into the diplomatic building.

Henry said, "Well, we're going together."

Alex seemed to think about it for a moment, and then said, "Come on—let's start moving toward the SINA."

They started toward the building, slowly making their way through the crush of people with great difficulty. On every block a small wooden hut had been placed over the street's gutters as a makeshift public urinal. Powerful amplifiers lined both sides of the Malecón, continuously broadcasting revolutionary propaganda or the *26 de Julio* and the *International* hymns. Security agents walked the perimeter of the crowd, their AK-47s ready to quell any dissent. Almost everyone carried a plastic shopping bag from home containing a bottle of water and a hunk of bread or some other edible morsel, perhaps the only food the families had to eat. Nobody knew for sure when the state's stores would be open and what they would have for sale. Certainly, the faces of the people reflected their sadness and the anguish of the situation.

The two friends saw trucks pull up, full of flags from Cuba, Venezuela, and Bolivia. Groups of young people were sitting on the wall of the Malecón looking out to sea. Apparently they had been waiting for the truck because they jumped off the wall and jockeyed for position so each could haul out a flag. Other trucks arrived with big posters with the images of Fidel, Che, Raúl, Bolívar, and Martí. Many of the people who hoisted the posters were not Cuban; they had the features of South American Indians and wore the traditional dresses of Bolivian and Venezuelan Indians.

When the friends were a block away from the SINA building, they could see the huge luminous screen that the United States had erected atop its diplomatic mission in January of 2006 to display news, quotes from famous men, and passages from the Human Rights Declaration. The Cuban government considered the screen a provocation, so the regime had responded with what was known as the *mount*; underneath, almost at the height of the screen so that they blocked the view from the street, the Cuban government had erected one hundred and thirty-eight enormous black flags with white stars. The encounter had become known as the War of the Posters in the international press.

From the long, wide avenue of the Malecón, Henry and Alex could see the famous old National Hotel up on the hill. It, like all the hotels in Cuba, was only for foreign tourists; Cubans could not lodge—or even enter—the hotels.

As they approached the barriers placed by the government less than half a block from the building, Henry and Alex were able to read the news written on the giant screen. They could also see behind the barriers. When Henry spotted even more security agents with their AK-47s, his confidence faded even further. He said, "What are we going to do with so many agents in front of the building?"

"Let's wait for the right moment," Alex said. "We can read what's on the sign and kill some time."

"When the people lose their fear, the totalitarian regimes will lose their power," scrolled across the screen. Alex looked around and noticed the anguished faces of the people; in Cuba, he thought, there still was a lot of fear.

At 4:00 a.m., several modern buses arrived. They were not the local *guaguas* that Cuban people rode, but the type of buses used to transport foreign tourists. The passengers that poured out were not Cuban—it was easy to tell that by the way they were dressed. Soon the sound system blared that the foreign tourists had joined the grand parade "voluntarily" in solidarity with the "planetary revolution." From the buses' luggage compartment, the new arrivals began to pull out flags from Italy, Germany, Canada, France, Spain, and even the United States of America. Alex saw the American flag and said, "Let's try to get close to that group of American tourists."

After slowly working their way though the milling crowd, the friends finally were able to get to the group. Alex spoke with a young man—Robert—who said he was from New York City. Robert said the government's tour guide had encouraged them to come, because, he said, it would be the greatest parade ever held in Cuba.

"He said we shouldn't miss the opportunity to be a part of history," Robert said. "He promised us we'd be the guests of the government and dine in a beautiful restaurant on the outskirts of Havana." The young man liked the idea of an adventure and of a free meal, but he was especially glad he had taken the offer because those who had refused had been forced onto the bus anyway, after the authorities had confiscated their passports. After the parade, the unwilling marchers would be taken directly to the airport and sent back to their home countries. Robert pointed out a woman about forty years old who looked very upset and disgusted, and he told Alex she was one who hadn't wanted to come.

Alex said to Henry, "Let's stay here until we figure out what our next move will be." Henry glanced up at the luminous screen. "News Bulletin," it read. News had come from Camagüey: "Lieutenant Osvaldo Rodriguez Caso from the FAR has arrived in the city of Camagüey. He has accused the new government's leaders from the MININT of participating in the conspiracy of officers who raided the office of Comandante Raúl Castro. The lieutenant says he was able to escape by running down the service stairs to the underground garages of the Ministry building, stealing a car and driving it, nonstop, until he run out of gas in Camagüey. There, he was able to make contact with his friend and schoolmate, Lieutenant Iván Perez Vila from the FAR."

Upon reading the news, people began to shout, "Assassins! Assassins!" and an outrageous scandal developed. The news spread quickly through the crowd.

After few minutes, another "News Bulletin" appeared on the huge screen. It reported a rebellion occurring in the FAR in the provinces of Camagüey and Ciego de Ávila, but it didn't give any details. The second bulletin incited still more rage and shouting: "Assassins!" and *"Viva la FAR!"* The screen continued to scroll the bulletins, and with each one, the crowd shouted louder and louder.

Several minutes later, a third news bulletin started to scroll. This time it said that the rebellion of the FAR was spreading to the provinces of Sancti Espíritus and Villa Clara. At this point, the excitation of the people gathered in the Malecón reached an uncontrollably wild pitch. As the news spread from where Alex and Henry were, in front of the building of the SINA, up to the monument of Máximo Gomez more than a kilometer away, a wave of agitation seemed to move with the news, and the two men could hear shouting and cursing undulate with the news through the agitated crowd toward the monument.

As the crowd became increasingly agitated, a squad of about twenty State-uniformed agents, armed with AK-47 assault rifles, pushed through the throng toward the huge screen and lined up in a row in front of the barriers a short distance from the building on which it was mounted. At the orders of a captain, they raised their rifles and opened fire at the screen, volley after volley, nonstop, until sparks and flames lit the still-dark morning sky.

The people who had been near the barrier had fallen to the ground to protect themselves from the shards of glass and metal flying in all directions, while the state agents had thrown themselves to the ground to escape the shower of shrapnel from ricocheting bullets and the exploding electronics. Soon the squad reassembled in a row again—perhaps, the people feared, to initiate a second round of shooting.

The shots from the firing AK-47s and the explosions from the sign raised the agitation level of the crowd to the point of pandemonium. The confused and scared crowd began to attempt to flee, pushing one another toward the middle of Havana, breaking all barriers and leaving flags and posters in their wake on the pavement of the Malecón. The desperate multitude stampeded like cattle, toppling and destroying all sound equipment and crashing the public toilet huts to soggy, putrid splinters. Nothing or no one could stand in its path.

As the crowd crushed toward them, the security agents instinctively threw their rifles to the ground and raised their hands in surrender, but they immediately realized they were not the target of the human wave. They turned and ran, terrified, in front of the crowd to avoid being crushed by the panicking multitude.

Taking advantage of the mass confusion, Alex screamed, "Henry! This is your opportunity! Run with the American tourists to the SINA building; get in the gardens and don't go out!"

"Alex, are you coming?"

"No, my friend, I still have too much to do in Cuba."

Alex gave Henry a bear hug, and Henry sprinted off to follow the tourists. After allowing himself one more short glance at his friend, Alex turned his attention to a small group of other young men who, though caught up in the moment, seemed not to know what to do next. He shouted, "Guys! Let's go! Run to the Interest Section building before these assholes shoot us all."

The Americans, perhaps two hundred tourists, were running toward the diplomatic building behind the flag of the United States carried by Robert, the young New Yorker. The American guards opened the doors to the building's courtyard to allow the group into the garden, then closed the doors behind them and immediately mounted a guard so no one else could get in.

Feeling safer inside the diplomatic mission's garden, protected by a fence of iron grille, Henry peered out to the streets, trying to find Alex among the multitude that was running in panic toward the center of Havana. His friend was nowhere in sight. Henry suddenly felt very alone; he had to find his own way now, with no identification and no money in his pocket, and without knowing anyone in the diplomatic mission. Although his adventure on the island had become a nightmare, he took a deep breath and felt some of the tension and the anxiety drain from his body. At least he now had some hope of going home. He had escaped from the hateful hands of the Cuban security agents.

CHAPTER 2

▼

MEETING AND MEMORIES

Peter Jones was a graduate of American University in Washington, D.C., with a master's degree in international business. After his graduation two years before, he had gone to work for the State Department in Washington. Peter was from Miami, but he had fallen in love with the capital city the moment he first stepped off the plane. Washington, he thought, just might be the most exciting city in the world; the politics were always interesting and the city was full of pretty girls who came from all the states of the union to work in the various government agencies. Moreover, the parties never seemed to stop. The ones put on by the city's foreign embassies were particularly fun, and since Peter worked in the State Department, he usually was invited to them. But as much as he loved the city and as exciting as his social life was, after two years of pushing papers around, he had started to feel frustrated and bored with his job. For that reason, he had decided to take a job in the U.S. Interest Section in Havana. He had a good knowledge of Spanish, having learned the language in Miami when he was a youngster interacting with the neighbors and playing with his friends and schoolmates—sons and daughters of Cuban immigrants. Peter had arrived in Havana only a week earlier, and he was still living in the Diplomatic Section building.

Today—Peter's first real day of work after a week of orientation—was a very exciting day. It had begun with the early morning shooting of the luminous news board and the stampede of thousands of people in the Malecón. Peter was a people person; he loved to listen to people's problems and to help them, so he was in his element when he spent all morning interviewing U.S. citizens desperate to leave Cuba. During his lunch break he was thinking about his new job, feeling content, but he already was missing the pretty girls and the embassy parties in Washington. Then again, he thought, he would soon meet new friends and maybe start to get invitations to embassy parties where he could meet a beautiful *señorita* or maybe a statuesque Swedish blond.

Peter's first appointment after lunch was with a man who claimed to be an American citizen. He spoke English very well, but Peter could tell the man was Cuban by his accent, the kind he remembered from his Miami friends. Peter looked at the man's file and began the interview saying, "*Señor* Rodriguez, can you tell me why you are claiming U.S. citizenship, but have no papers to prove it?"

Rodriguez Pantoja insisted he was an American citizen. He stood up and walked to the window, with its view of the Malecón Avenue, and began telling a story explaining why he was in Havana without a U.S. passport.

"Mr. Jones, my history begins in Puerto Rico, in the San Juan Hotel, at eight o'clock in the morning, when I looked out the window of my cabana at the beautiful, sparkling azure of the Caribbean Sea and the gleaming white sand. The beach was surrounded by coconut palms with brilliant green leaves the color of a pool table's felt. The warm breeze and the scent of the sea intoxicated my senses. My mind traveled to happy memories of my youth on a similar island, with the same sea, sand, and coconut palm trees of the lavish tropical gardens of the Caribbean.

"My memories were pleasant and tender, like the caress of a mother, but, just as an orphan is, I am nostalgic at the loss of my mother country, my dear mother who has been violated and destroyed by a despot named Castro. The despot hides behind the names of justice and progress; he claims to work for the benefit of the oppressed and invokes Marx and Lenin as gods. For a fleeting moment, I felt my physical being shattered by the beauty of the scenery, which made me realize, once again, her loss. Her name was Cuba, of whom Christopher Columbus said, 'This is the most beautiful land human eyes have ever seen.'

"Excuse me, Mr. Jones, if I am emotional and my narration wanders, but I think it is important you understand my situation," he said.

The young diplomat looked at Mr. Rodriguez and said, "Calm down. That's fine—I understand, sit down. Please continue your story, but try to control your emotions."

"Thank you, Mr. Jones," Sr. Rodriguez said.

And he continued his story.

*   *   *   *

As I was gazing at the sea, someone banging on the cabana's door rudely interrupted my thoughts. When I opened the door, I saw a middle-aged man, a few pounds past his prime weight, but still with an athletic build, wearing a beach shirt with a brightly colored tropical design. His face seemed familiar, but I couldn't place him immediately. He had a few white hairs sprinkled through his full head of hair the color of old gold, and with his tropical-tanned skin, his clothing, and his physical condition, it had the effect of making him look younger than his age.

Without any hesitation, he said, "Good morning, *mi hermano*." In Cuba, you know, it is customary to call good, old friends "brother."

I was a little bit confused, but suddenly found myself saying, "Good morning, Alex!"

We hadn't seen each other in almost thirty years, and the last time we had talked was when Alex called to invite me to visit him in San Juan. In Puerto Rico, we had been co-workers when we began our professional careers after having completed our education in the United States.

Our friendship began in Cuba when we were a couple of adolescents enjoying ourselves with mutual friends, parties, and sports. We were living a beautiful and clean life, without worries, on a lovely island of natural beauty, among happy people and sensual music. Our idyllic lives were hiding from us the sad future of corrupt government and political dangers that our country would face. We were two young men who didn't know, at that time, that soon our destinies would take us to situations that required difficult decisions which would determine the course of our lives far away from the paradise where we were growing up.

While we were hugging, I said, "*Chico*, you haven't changed."

And Alex replied, "*Coño, mi hermano*, you are insulting me! We are a couple of middle-aged—almost old—guys, and I hope we were looking a whole lot better when we met last time!"

When Alex called me to come to Puerto Rico, he told me his wife Lorena had died a couple of years earlier, and he was very proud of his grown-up daughter and son; both were very hard workers and had done well for themselves. The daughter was an owner of a women's clothing chain with stores in Florida and Puerto Rico, and his son was a physician. Alex was living alone in an apartment in the Condado and had an apartment in Miami that he used when he visited his children.

While I was telling Alex the details of my own family, the room service waiter knocked on the door and delivered the breakfast I had ordered for us. We started with a tropical fruit cocktail with *guineos*, papaya, and mango. In Puerto Rico, bananas are called *guineos,* and papaya in Havana is called *fruta bomba*. The waiter also served us two glasses of fresh *jugo de china*, that in English is orange juice and in Cuba, *jugo de naranja.*

The waiter brought a small portable grill that he placed next to our table to prepare *tortillas*—what you call omelets—stuffed with ham, shrimp, and vegetables, very different from Mexican corn-flour *tortillas*. He also brought us a basket with a variety of breads, plenty of butter and fresh white cheese—*queso blanco criollo*—and to wash down the succulent feast, the waiter brought a hot pot of aromatic Puerto Rican coffee. The coffee production in Puerto Rico is very small, but very good, sold only in the domestic market.

We reminisced during the breakfast about our good times in Cuba, when we would go to the *fiestas de quince*—the fabulous parties that celebrated the fifteenth birthdays of Cuban girls. In the fancy ones, the *muchachos* dressed in tuxedos—*de traje informal*—with white smoking jackets in the summers. For the less-fancy parties, the invitations called for *traje de calle*, which meant that a suit and tie would be appropriate. The girls—*las chiquitas*—would wear beautiful long gowns. *Los muchachos* were invited to the party by the *chiquitas*, and they usually were a couple years older than the girls.

We talked about the *guateques*, a Taino Indian word for parties. For these parties, the *muchacho*s wore *guayaberas*, sometimes with a bow tie to complement the attire and to please the *chaperonas,* who were the mothers or aunts of the girls and always accompanied young couples to the parties to avoid inappropriate behavior. The *chaperonas'* vigilance used to make the parties more exciting; the little kisses and clandestine squeezes the young couples enjoyed took advantage of any *chaperonas'* distraction. The young girl always attended the big parties and the *guateques* in their best designer dresses and high-heeled shoes, white or black, depending upon the season.

"We always had Coca-Cola, beer, and Bacardi rum at the parties," Alex said. Bacardi is well known for the saying *sano, sabroso, y cubano*. With rum and Coca-Cola, they would make the famous drink called *Cuba Libre*, now called *mentirita,* after Cuba lost her freedom forty-seven years ago. At the elegant parties, White Horse Scotch whisky was always present. The girls never drank any hard liquor; they stuck to Coca-Cola, and the boys would each have maybe one or two *Cuba Libres*—that's why nobody would get *borracho* at the parties. Besides, *borrachos* were not well accepted by their peers, and any young man who became known as a *borracho* was taking the risk of not being invited to parties anymore. In Cuba, there was no legal age limitation for drinking spirits or beer. Maybe that was the reason young people were never very interested in drinking. Anyway, the young men always thought the parties offered greater challenges than drinking, like sneaking out of sight of the *chaperonas* and managing to kiss and fondle the girls. It was more fun to *hechar un pie*; you know—dance all night like a spinning top.

Alex reminded me that from the perspective of the young people, the music was the most important element of the parties; good music guaranteed a good time and a successful affair. Many popular musical groups played at the parties. At the fancy parties, you usually found the famous *Chavales de España, La Orquesta Riverside,* and *Fajardo y sus Estrellas*—a few that come to mind. They were first-class orchestras that left Cuba after Castro and continued to be famous abroad. Small musical groups entertained at *guateques* and the smaller parties, where you usually only heard popular Cuban music. But no matter what the size of the party or the notoriety of the band, you always heard the *guarachas,* the *cha-cha-cha,* the *danzones y sones,* the *mambo,* the romantic *bolero,* the typically Spanish *paso dobles,* the Cuban *conga,* and some romantic American melodies that were danced very tightly and slowly. At the end of the parties, the bands usually played an old romantic Cuban song, *En el Tronco de un Arbol.* This melody was very slow, and the couples would dance very close to each other. The last dance was always exciting and fast, the sensual Cuban *conga.* All the boys and girls made a *cola,* holding onto the waist of the person in front, while they danced and sang, "*Adiós mamá! Adiós papá! Que yo me voy con las bolleras.*" The music ended with a phrase that everybody cried out: "*Que ya esta conga se acabó!*"

Everybody enjoyed the good music and the parties in Cuba. Alex reminded me of the popular parties, open to all social classes, called *Verbenas de la Tropical.* Those parties were celebrated almost every Saturday in the beautiful gardens of the Tropical brewery company. The parties were open to the public, and the entrance fee for men was one Cuban peso. The ladies didn't pay; they had to be invited by their party partners. At that time, the Cuban peso was on par with the U.S. dollar. Since the revolution, a Cuban has to work three days to earn a dollar. Beer was sold for ten cents, and they usually served ham and cheese sandwiches for fifty cents. The bands that played at those parties were famous and very popular; one of them was the *Chapotin y sus Estrellas.* People of all ages attended the *Verbenas de la Tropical,* and, like the young people's parties, the atmosphere was always cheerful and festive. A popular saying in Cuba was "*La musica es el alma de los pueblos*"—"The music is the soul of the people."

I reminded him that the menu at the big parties usually included *arroz con pollo* or *lechon asado* in *mojo criollo* with *congri*. The salad usually was avocados and lettuce, dressed with olive oil and vinegar. For dessert, they always had chocolate or vanilla cake. At the *guateques* and other parties, they usually served *pastelitos de carne* and *cangrejitos de jamon*. Also, the menus always featured the famous *croqueticas de jamon*, usually the favorite of the *chaperonas*. If the *guateques* were celebrated al *aire libre*, they usually had an open charcoal barbecue to cook the *perros calientes*. I find it very curious that the young people didn't enjoy the food very much. They were more interested in the music, dancing, and laughing at funny stories. The *chaperonas*, on the other hand, always seemed to have big appetites and enjoy the menu.

So Alex and I laughed and agreed that everybody had a very good time, including the *chaperonas;* in addition to eating all the food, they usually spent their time *chismeando*—you know, gossiping about other people. In fact, the *chaperoneo* was the way they kept informed about what was going on in our social circle.

Mr. Jones told Rodriguez, "you really sure had a good time during your youth."

After reminiscing about the parties for awhile, we went on to talk about sports. Alex played basketball in school during the *bachillerato*, and I played the *pelota*. Before the revolution, all private schools had sports teams, one for those fifteen years of age and under, and the school team for those eighteen and under. All were very competitive, ready to face other schools in the leagues *Intercolegiales*. The public schools also had their own baseball and basketball leagues. Also, Cuba had many private clubs—for every social class and pocketbook—supporting competitive sports teams. The clubs' leagues usually included university teams, and in some sports, big corporations had teams participating. Alex used to row in shells for the club *Vedado* Tennis, while I rowed for another club, the *Habana* Biltmore. They were staunch competitors in the national regattas that took place in various cities on the island, like in the Havana Bay, in Cienfuegos, and at the famous Varadero Beach. Private clubs also organized their own regattas at the end of the season and invited other clubs. It was so exciting to compete against friends, and the camaraderie was excellent.

Alex remembered that I had been a fan of the *Almendares* Scorpions baseball team, while he was for the *Habana* Lions. Those two teams were the most popular teams in the Cuban professional baseball winter league. The other two teams in the league were the *Cienfuegos* Elephants and *Marianao* Tigers. The caliber of the teams in the winter league was a step below major league baseball in the United States. In fact, half the Cuban players would play in the majors during the summer. We both remembered some of the Cuban players like Orestes Miñoso from the Chicago Cubs, Pedro Ramos from the Yankees, Camilo Pascual from the Minnesota Twins, and Mike Cuellar from the Cleveland Indians—and some of the American players, like the famous Monte Irvin from the New York Giants, Don Zimmer from the Dodgers and a coach for the Yankees, and Dick Sisler and Lou Klain from the Cardinals of San Louis.

The winter league played first in the Tropical Stadium and, after 1946, in a new stadium named el Gran Estadio del Cerro. Alex's father and brother took him to the very first game in the stadium—when he was just a little kid—between the *Almendares* and the *Cienfuegos*. I asked Alex who had won that game, but he didn't remember, so I refreshed his memory. It was the *Almendares*, and the score was nine to one. The pitcher for the *Almendares* was Comellas. I knew that because I also went to that inaugural game. I remember the contention between the fans of the four teams; it was always quite intense and amusing. The stadium was sold out every day.

The delightful breakfast, the beautiful beach scenery that we could see through the cabana's window, the pleasant conversation about our youthful memories—all of it made us forget for awhile the chaos that had suddenly changed our lives after the Socialist revolution on the island. For a while, we became separated from the suffering of our Cuban brothers who stayed behind on the hellhole Socialist island.

Then, Alex changed the topic of our conversation by suggesting we take a walk around the *finca* to help digest our breakfast and breathe the fresh sea air. I didn't understand why Alex had used the term *finca*, but he smiled and clarified it: "*Chico*, what I mean is to walk on the beach and watch the pretty girls in the bikinis. That is where the good livestock graze."

I liked the idea, so I said, "Let's go to the *finca*! I am all for it!"

Chapter 3

The Cuban Exile and the Man with the Little Mustache

—Mr. Jones interrupted the story to answer a telephone call. After couple of minutes on the phone, he told Rodriguez to continue his narration.

We were walking along the beautiful Isla Verde Beach, which I consider the best beach in San Juan, looking at the *ganado* in their bikinis. When we stopped to look at a gorgeous *pollito* who crossed our path, I asked Alex, "Why did you ask me to come to San Juan?"

Alex replied, "*Mi hermano*, I am totally devoted to the fight for Cuban freedom. I want to talk to you about it, because I need your help.

"First, I want to discuss the crisis we are experiencing. There are many differences among the Cubans in exile. I believe the origin of the problems comes from the long time Cubans have been in exile, four decades—three generations—during which they have experienced distressing fundamental changes in their lives.

"The first wave of expatriates escaped in 1959 through 1961; the *Batistianos* were the first group to leave the island after the victorious revolution. That group was not very large, and eventually they didn't have much influence in exile. Otherwise, from 1959 through the first few months of 1960, the Cuban people enjoyed the gain of certain civil liberties that had been lost during the Batista years. But the good times didn't last too long in Cuba, and, in 1961, the fervor for the revolution started fading away. Many sympathizers and supporters became disillusioned with the bloody revolution and began the flight from the island; away from the 'righteous revolution.' Do you remember that at that time Castro used to say that the revolution was 'as green as our palm trees'? Very soon, the underground and the internal fight began against Castro's government and its attempt to communize the country. Many people who had participated in the fight against the infiltration of Communism into the revolution lost their lives, and others were jailed, sentenced to many years in prison.

"After that came the betrayal of the invasion of April 1961 and the loss of all hope. During that first stage, two generations fled into exile, which at that time wasn't easy—I know that from experience. But by God's grace, the pioneers of the Cuban exile succeeded outside their native land. The ones who made it to the United States found that 'the American Dream' was alive and well, and those who went to other free countries around the world found their ways to productive and enjoyable full lives. Those people were the foundation of the traditional exile; they were anti-Communist, lovers of freedom and of democratic principles."

Alex continued, "There are many happy stories of those in exile. Just to mention a few, I could remind you about the Cuban chairman of Coca-Cola, three well-known U.S. congressmen, two U.S. senators, and some members of the U.S. President's cabinet. In addition to those very prominent people, we know of a great number of professionals, entrepreneurs, religious figures, college professors, entertainers—many honest, hardworking Cubans who have contributed to society in their new country. Castro called them *gusanos* scornfully. And since most of them went to Miami, he called that city *la gusanera*."

We stopped briefly to watch another beautiful girl stroll by, and, after that, Alex continued his story. "The second stage of Cuban immigration took much longer, starting in 1962 and ending in 1984, while Cuban citizens worked as foot soldiers of the Soviet Union.

"Do you remember the October Missile Crisis, the warlike ventures and Communist infiltrations in Venezuela, Nicaragua, Granada, El Salvador, Bolivia, Africa, and many other places around the globe? During those years, the Cuban people suffered the loss of their freedom and endured shortages of food and other necessary items, despite the patronage of the Soviet Union. The situation on the island was not good, but the people survived and experienced hardships with very little possibility of any improvement in their lives.

"Because of the situation on the island, Cubans continued to flee abroad. Thousands left from the port of Camarioca, and many others tried any possible means to escape from the Caribbean hell. During the decade of the seventies, the United States established the *Ajuste Cubano* that, for a short time, gave legal status to emigrating Cubans and those already residing in the United States.

"In the early 1980s, enormous numbers of Cubans sought protection at several foreign embassies in Havana. At the Peruvian embassy, hundreds of Cubans entered the compound by force and stayed there for several weeks, begging for political asylum in Peru or any other country that might grant them visas. The regime reacted by organizing parades and protests against the people who desperately wanted to leave the country, but the government was unable to stop the exodus abroad.

"Later came the great escape from Mariel Bay, in the northeast of Havana province and one of the closest points to the Florida coast. With all the problems at the foreign embassies, Castro, with the consent of United States government, encouraged the Cuban exiles in Miami to go to Mariel to pick up their family members who were trying to flee Cuba. Castro took advantage of the situation and freed many criminals from Cuban jails, then forced them to leave for the United States in order to damage the reputation of the Cuban exiles. Thousands of Cubans traveled from the Mariel, waves of honest and professional people who were, unfortunately, infiltrated by criminals sent by Castro's regime.

"These new exiles were different from the first group; some were older people claimed by their children, and many were young people who had become disillusioned by the revolution. Their expatriate countrymen very well received the new refugees. They generally were not as well educated as the first group and had different ideology because of having lived more time under the Socialist system. However, this group also found success abroad, but perhaps in a more modest way. Castro identified all of them with the derogatory term of *gusanos*—for him all Cubans that left the island or did not sympathize with the revolution were classified as *gusanos*."

While Alex spoke, he sometimes stopped to gaze at the beach or to look at the traffic on Isla Verde Avenue. At times, he seemed to study the people who were walking on the sidewalk, entering the beach, or crossing the street, as though bothered by something happening around him; I noticed but didn't pay too much attention.

Alex continued to describe the exile situation. He told me that something very important happened between 1985 and 1989. During that time the Perestroika movement developed in the Soviet Union. Mikhail Gorbachev introduced the idea; it was the beginning of a revolution inside the Socialist structure operating around the world. The soviet leader pretended to redefine Socialist ideas in order to save the failing Soviet system. With his pragmatism, Gorbachev pretended to rehabilitate and revive Marxism and Leninism in such a way that people could consider it as a liberal or neo-liberal philosophy.

In fact, the Perestroika ideas also got to Cuba, said Alex. "These revolutionary ideas had a very positive impact on the young students of Cuban Socialism, born under the Socialist system created by the revolution. When Castro rejected the revolutionary new ideas that challenged the traditional concepts of Stalinist Socialism, the generation of the young students felt frustrated and became enemies of the old *Comandante*, even though they wanted to maintain the Socialist principles of the Great Cuban Revolution. Then, since most of those young people had been educated in the Soviet Union or in countries behind the Iron Curtain, they fled Cuba to reside in Europe in countries like Sweden, whose politics were oriented toward social democracy. Those young Cuban exiles called themselves the Rebel Sons of the Revolution, also known as the Red Worms, or Children of Perestroika.

"You can imagine, *mi hermano*, the impact that occurred when these Socialists found themselves among traditional Cuban exiles, the generation that not only hated Castro, but the whole damn Socialist revolution. This encounter produced a violent clash of ideas on dissidence that is very harmful for the cause of free Cuba.

"Even more, the dissidence in Cuba is not homogeneous; most of the liberal-democratic dissidents are in jail but they have the support of the traditional Cuban exile. Most of the dissidents with Socialist ideas are free, walking on the streets, of course, under the vigilance of the regime. In the same way, these Socialist dissidents have the support from the left-wing exiles and the self-proclaimed Rebel Sons of the Revolution."

I asked Alex the reasons for Castro's rejection of Perestroika. He told me that Castro saw in the new doctrine a threat to his business of exporting revolutions abroad, and he was concerned that the new doctrine could put in danger the economic aid Cuba was receiving from the Soviet Union. That aid was the umbilical cord that fed the island's economy, at least to a level of subsistence.

Alex stopped his story for a moment and said, "*Mi hermano*, I think we have a tail. Do you see that guy with the little moustache in the blue shirt and the khaki pants across the street? He has followed me since I came back from Miami, three days ago.

"I am going to take this opportunity to get rid of him. Don't worry about it, and don't do anything. I will see you in the cabana in a couple of hours." Without saying anything else, Alex left me standing, a bit confused, on the sidewalk in front of the beach. I didn't know what to do, so I decided to watch Alex's next move. I didn't have to wait too long; he walked right over to the man and grabbed him in a big, friendly bear hug. I was unable to hear the conversation since I was at some distance, but they spoke for at least a minute. Then Alex walked away, and the man with the little moustache started walking in the opposite direction.

A moment later, Alex stopped at a patrol car parked on the side of the street, leaned over, and spoke with the policemen in the car. He pointed to the man with the moustache, and then got in the patrol car, which drove toward the man with the little moustache. Just after the patrol car passed him, the car stopped and one of the policemen got out and walked over to talk to the man. Suddenly the man turned and ran, but the other policeman, who had also gotten out of the patrol car, was in the perfect position to lunge at the man and grab him, preventing his escape. Less than a minute had passed when a second patrol car pulled up and the two policemen pushed the man into the back seat. Alex was still in the first patrol car; both cars left shortly.

The whole incident lasted only few minutes, but it was long enough to draw a small crowd—some tourists and bystanders near the hotels, and two pretty girls in bikinis with their escorts. After a few comments, they all went their way, some into the hotels or onto the beautiful beach and others onto paths that led down to the light blue sea where they would lay on the white sand to enjoy the radiant rays of the tropical sun and the gentle waves of the Caribbean Sea.

I, though, was astonished and paralyzed with disbelief; I didn't know what to do. What had I just seen? What had Alex done? What kind of trouble was he in? After a few minutes of confusion and rhetorical questions, I decided to go back to the hotel and wait.

Back in my cabana, I gazed out the window at the people on the beach, still trying to make some sense of what I had seen. Why had the man with the little moustache been following Alex? Then I realized that Alex had talked a lot about the Cuban exile, but he hadn't tell me why he had asked me to come to San Juan.

About ninety minutes later, someone knocked on the cabana door, and when I opened it, there was Alex, looking quite calm and relaxed. He told me that everything was fine, and his suspicions had been correct; the man was a Cuban spy sent by Castro's regime. He had gotten into Puerto Rico illegally, traveling across La Mona Strait in a small boat from the Dominican Republic. Alex explained that this was quite common; taking a small boat across the strait was the easiest way for Dominicans to enter Puerto Rico illegally. Usually the illegal immigrants were deported when the local police found them.

"*Chico*," I said to Alex, "I witnessed the incident, but I don't know how you did it."

"Well," Alex said, "it was relatively easy. I went directly to the man and said to him in a heavy Cuban accent, 'Cousin Cheo! When did you arrive? I didn't know you were in San Juan. I am very glad to find you!' While I was talking and hugging him, I put this Rolex watch in his pants pocket. The man didn't notice anything and said I was confused, that he was not my cousin Cheo, and he didn't know me. I apologized and told him he looked just like Cheo. He seemed nervous and turned to walk away. That gave me the opportunity to go to the police car and tell them I was a tourist and the man with the little moustache had pushed me and stole my Rolex, then fled.

"The policeman ordered me to get in the back seat of the car so he could investigate. When we caught up with the man and the officer told him about my accusation, he said he didn't know anything about the incident. But instinctively, to prove his innocence, he put his hands in his pants pockets, and when he found he had the watch, he got terrified and tried to flee, but the other policeman captured him.

"As you saw, a few minutes later another patrol car came and took the man away as a suspected thief. When we got to the police station and the investigation continued, I identified myself as a tourist from Miami, visiting my daughter who's living in the Condado apartment. In reality the apartment is in her name—she uses it when she's in San Juan—so if the police investigate, they'll find my story is true.

"The man didn't have any identification and refused to give his address in Puerto Rico; that is what Cuban spies are instructed to do if they're captured, in order to protect the spy cells operating in the area. When they pressured him, the man said he was a Dominican who came across the La Mona Strait. The policeman returned my watch and said the authorities would take care of the suspect after further investigation."

I asked what would happen to the man with the little mustache. Alex told me, "Usually these illegal guys are booked and deported to the Dominican Republic. He was a Cuban spy who went to the Cuban embassy in the Dominican Republic as a clerk and, after awhile, he entered Puerto Rico illegally, where he stayed in a special house where spies or Communist sympathizers stayed with money handled by the Venezuelan Consulate."

Alex told me that the man would be deported; the Cuban embassy would claim him from the Dominican authorities, and, finally, he would go back to Cuba. There, Cuban state security would interrogate him and punish him for his failure in his international mission. Probably he would be sent to work in an agriculture labor camp far away from his family. Eventually the man would feel frustrated and would develop hatred for Castro. But, perhaps at the same time, he would maintain his *principios revolucionarios* and his admiration for the Socialist revolution. The man would be a good candidate for the Rebel Sons of the Revolution.

Then Alex said, "*Mi hermano,* don't think that I put on this act every day. This was only a dirty trick to get rid of that spy. These Cuban spies are sent to keep an eye on well-known Cuban dissidents and find out the day-to-day activities of the Cubans who live in Miami."

After Alex finished his story, I kept quiet for a moment. Then I burst out, "But Alex, you stood the risk of losing your valuable Rolex!"

Alex smiled. "Yes. It cost me ten dollars at the Stanley Market in Hong Kong."

—Mr. Jones listened the story and at the end just said, "tricky and handy friend, well done!"

C H A P T E R   4

▼

THE BATISTA ERA

—Mr. Jones offered a cup of coffee to Rodriguez and after serving it, told him to continue his story. Rodriguez took his cup, had a couple of sips leaned back into his chair and continued his story.

Alex looked at his now-famous Rolex, and said, "It is already 4:37 in the afternoon. How about if we go for a *chapuzon* at the beach?"

I liked the idea, because I knew that along the Caribbean beaches, after five in the afternoon, the sea is as calm as a plate and the water feels very warm and pleasant because the sun begins to lower on the horizon and the temperature of the air becomes lower than that of the water of the sea. We changed into our bathing trunks and headed out to the beach in front of the cabana. Indeed, the water was delicious and there were hardly any waves in the sea.

"*Mi hermano*," Alex said, looking out over the immense Caribbean Sea, "do you imagine how many Cubans have died, drowned and eaten by the sharks in this sea, trying to flee from the Socialist revolution? The poor *balseros* continue to try to escape because they cannot bear the misery and the repression of the Socialist regime. In Cuba, rights laws don't exist. The only choices of the Cubans are to live on the island illegally or to escape from her, also illegally. The Cubans feel like slaves of the State, without future for their families. The only thing they have to look forward to is the opportunity to get a boat and to find good weather. These poor *balseros* represent the last big wave of exiles. It is too early to characterize them, but generally, they are young and less educated than the other Cubans in exile. But they sure have a great desire to live in freedom."

Trying to change a subject that was really sad and stirring, I asked, "What was the problem you had during the time of Batista that almost got you killed?"

Alex said, "I am going to tell you the story of what happened to me on December 7 of 1956, hardly two weeks after the disembarkation of Castro in the Oriente province, from the boat *Granma*. "I was very young and without experience; it happened just after my freshman year in the university. I remember that I was taking a ride in my car with my friend Armandito. He was a student of architecture of the University of Havana who liked to paint landscapes. This young man was really talented in mixing the colors that he used to paint very pretty views of the Cuban fields. The story was that we were in the car looking for a landscape that could be seen from a street on a hill in Marianao. From there, you could see in the distance the Rancho Boyeros Highway to the José Marti Airport. From that point on the hill, not only we were able to see the highway, but also the forest of the valley framed by other distant hills. It was certainly an ideal site for a picture of the Cuban landscape, with its palms and leafy trees.

"The problem came because to arrive at that site we had to drive in front of the house of the chief of the national police—the home of General Rafael Salas Canizares. His house was a palace sitting by itself on a block of land of probably one hundred square meters. The house wasn't visible from the street because a wall ten feet high surrounded it. I was very familiar with the area because my family developed the urbanization, and during my childhood, I often walked around the area that was part of the property of my grandfather.

"A few years earlier, my father sold the land to the general and his brother Tino, who was captain of the police and was living in a nice, modest home a short distance from the general. My father knew them for that reason. He had spoken with the general a couple of times. He knew the captain a little better because he was the one who had taken care of the legal papers when the brothers bought the property. By the way, the general had a very bad reputation for being quite cruel with the people who opposed Batista's regime. He later was killed in a shooting when he entered the Embassy of Haiti without authorization, chasing a young man who was trying to gain shelter in the embassy.

"Capitan Tino was the confidant of his brother, the general, and people said he was in charge of collecting the money that the elements of the underworld paid as bribes to run the *bolita*. It was well known that the captain was not involved in the repression of the dissidents of the regime. By the way, he was lucky and had the opportunity to leave Cuba in 1959 after Batista fled.

"Well," said Alex, "the problem started when we were driving around the block, very slowly in the car and went twice around the general's house that was hidden by the wall. Apparently, the policemen guarding the place didn't like what we were doing. Our behavior must have seemed very suspicious.

"Two patrol cars full of policemen—we didn't know where they came from—stopped us and, with machine guns in hand, they searched our car and us. I did try to explain to them what we were doing and that I lived not very far away, but there was no way they heard us. They arrested us and took us in the patrol cars to a police station in the Calzada de Columbia in front of the Columbia military camp, not very far from the hospital of Maternidad Obrera. That was a public hospital for the labor class; its services were free for the humble working class, and it had a good reputation for the services rendered. There, they put us in two cells that looked like cages, where we were held for about forty-five minutes.

"Later, they took us to separate interrogation rooms, machine guns at our backs and our wrists in handcuffs. The interrogator told me that I was a revolutionary who was planning to attack the chief of police. The interrogation was getting a little ugly, because they put a pistol to my head. I imagined that Armandito repeated the same story that I told, about why we were on the street near the house of the general. After the interrogations, they returned us to our cages.

"Perhaps one hour later they removed us from the cages and said they were going to give us a *paseito* by the *laguito*. The site was very famous; it was in a residential area in Marianao called the Country Club. The place had a little lake with many leafy trees; it was a very dark place even during the day, and at night it was so dark than you couldn't even see your hands. In this tenebrous place, a year before, the corpse of a famous lawyer and politician named Pelayo Cuervo was found. The man was a leader of the opposition against the Batista regime. The man was killed during a *paseito* by the lake by Batista's henchmen, and the body was abandoned on the shore of the lake. Those killings and other outrageous acts were committed against the dissidents by a group of murderous policemen following orders from the regime's leaders. It was well known that it was not unusual to find corpses around the lake of unknown people who had been executed. The threat of the *paseito* worried us, and we tried, without results, to get them to let us call our families.

"When we were ready to leave the police station on our way to the macabre *paseito* by the lake, my brother José unexpectedly arrived. At that time, he was a university student with a couple more years of schooling until he would be physician. He worked as assistant physician in the Casa de Socorro in the city of Marianao. These Casas de Socorros offered medical emergency services to the population. They were free, maintained by the municipal government; they were an excellent place for medical students to learn and to acquire experience in their profession. Due to his work in the Casa de Socorro, José had frequent contacts with the police who brought in people wounded in road accidents, hurt in fights, or perhaps run over by the police forces. Luckily, the day of the incident, José was working. He didn't work every day—only two or three times per week.

"Well, the story was that he received an anonymous telephone call—maybe from a policeman—that told him his brother Alex was imprisoned in the police station and the situation was getting a little dangerous. Immediately, José called my father so he could call somebody for help. Since the Casa de Socorros was not very far from the police station, José went to the station. When he arrived and identified himself to the sergeant in charge, the sergeant ordered him placed in another cage as a suspect who would be investigated later.

"All the commotion delayed our departure from the station by ten or fifteen minutes. When again Armandito and I were walking—handcuffed and surrounded by four police, two armed with machine guns—the door of the station opened and two burly policemen burst in with a man dressed in a house gown and slippers. Immediately, all the policemen in the station seemed to become immobilized. The man in the house gown said in a clear and convincing voice, 'This is the General's business. Let them free and I will take full responsibility.' The man was Captain Tino Salas Canizares, the general's brother. Before we knew it, we all were set free, and Armandito and I left the station in a car with my brother José."

After a brief pause, Alex said, "Luckily, my father was able to contact the captain, who was at home watching TV. I never knew what my father said to him because the events and the experiences of that day were never a topic of conversation at home, but apparently the captain understood the situation and left in a rush for the station in his police car. I imagine my father sounded pretty upset, knowing the cruelty of the police during Batista's regime. I believe it was through Divine Providence that my brother José was working on that day in the Casa de Socorros, that a stranger identified me and called my brother, that my father could quickly communicate with the captain, and that the captain understood our precarious situation and took the time to help us. All these factors concurred in less than two hours and saved our lives.

"Remember, in Cuba the people used to have an expression: The one who has a godfather will be baptized. That's how it happened that this messy, dangerous situation was resolved. The same principle was applied on July 26, 1953, when Fidel Castro and a group of young people attacked the Moncada Fort. Batista's army killed many of the attackers, but the Bishop of Santiago de Cuba, Monsignor Perez Serante, protected Castro and saved his life. He was sentenced and sent to prison and, two years later, pardoned by Batista. The family of Castro's wife was very good friends of Batista and requested his release. In my case, my godfather was the Captain, and Castro's was the Bishop, the relatives of his wife and, ultimately, Batista."

Alex told me the incident had been a close call, with the violence and the terror; that wasn't uncommon on the island at that time.

"For that reason," he said, "my family sent me out of Cuba for awhile. I lived in Miami for about three months, returning to Cuba two weeks after the attack on the presidential palace in Havana that took place March 13, 1957. Do you remember that attempt to kill Batista? It was done by members of the *Directorio Revolucionario,* probably financed with funds originating from the exiled group from Miami, directed by the overthrown President Carlos Prio Socarras. My sour experience with Batista's regime opened the way to my dislike for the government and helped turn me into a sympathizer with the revolution. So during my stay in Miami, I made some contact with exiled groups that were fighting against Batista."

After a brief pause, Alex told me that he had realized his place was in Cuba, not in Miami, if he wanted to help in the fight against Batista's dictatorship.

"So I was able to convince my family," he said. "I told them I should return to Cuba with the excuse that I was looking forward to going back to the university to continue my studies," Alex said. "I complained that I was wasting my time in Miami doing nothing but reading novels and playing tennis."

I said to Alex, "*Chico,* I didn't know that story, but now I understand something, when in Varadero in the summer of 1957 during the rowing competition, I saw you wearing a red pullover with black lines—the colors of the *26 de Julio* revolutionary movement. Everybody looked at you and smiled, but nobody said anything. I imagine people didn't want to get involved or, perhaps, some people didn't recognize the colors of the *26 de Julio* movement."

I reminded Alex about the jokes and funny stories he used to tell to our friends whose parents were supporters of Batista's government.

"*Si, mi hermano,*" he said. "I remember one very funny story I used to tell them that happened during a convention of surgeons—specialists in transplants of organs and extremities. First, a French doctor said, 'In my country it was necessary to amputate both arms of a man working in a winery due to an accident, but I was able to transplant two gorilla arms on him, and after two years of therapy the man won the weightlifting championship in Paris.' The participants at the convention gave the French doctor a warm round of applause.

"A famous surgeon from Spain couldn't remain silent after hearing the French doctor's accomplishment and said, 'In Spain, the surgery is equally advanced or, perhaps, even more advanced. A train in Galicia cut off both of a man's legs, and I was able to transplant two powerful hind legs of a wild colt on him, and now that *"tio"* is the center forward of the Real Madrid soccer team.'

"The audience was very impressed by the stories, and stood up in acclamation to give a new round of applause for the two famous surgeons. After the commotion died down, a Cuban doctor stood up and said in a sarcastic tone, 'Very well, but that was nothing. During a hurricane in Cuba, a piece of zinc slab flew from a roof at a high speed and chopped the head off a man who was running away to protect himself from the wind and the rain. A Cuban doctor, who is a friend of mine, performed a very difficult surgery, where he transplanted a monkey head on the man, and now the man is the president of the republic.'"

Alex recalled he used to laugh his head off looking at the faces of his friends, sons of the *Batistianos* he had known since childhood. "I remembered that they used to tell me, 'Alex, *no comas mierda!* But it stopped there; their parents were doing business with the corrupt government, but they were not involved in any repressive activity, and, anyway, we were friends and the story was funny. I admit the joke was racist, but the dictator deserved it for his cruelty and lack of scruples, and I didn't have any intention to offend any race. What I was doing was comparing the dictator with an animal.

"Batista had led a military coup d'etat on March 10, 1952, a few months before the general elections," Alex explained. "The constitutional president in office was Carlos Prio Socarras, and he had to seek exile in the United States. He lived in Miami for the rest of his life. During the government of Prio, although he was rightfully elected president in free elections, the corruption and the poor administration of public funds was evident. But Batista, with the coup d'etat, turned the nation away from constitutional law, limited the citizens' liberties, and dismantled the process of free elections. That, without a doubt, provoked acts of revolt by the citizens and unleashed the violence of the repressive organizations created by the regime.

"Nevertheless, the country's economy grew substantially during the first six years of Batista's government. The general economic growth improved the standard of living of the citizenry and expanded the middle class. From 1952 to 1957, twenty-eight new hotels were built on the island, and the Cuban peso stayed on par with the U.S. dollar. Very important highways were constructed;

several airports were built, and three new tunnels, numerous bridges, new shopping centers, theaters, new modern means of transportation, and new hospitals operated by the government were all opened. Of course, the corruption and the dishonesty of the authorities within the government and the kickbacks and bribes from the builders and construction companies involved in those projects illegally enriched Batista and his associates and the corrupt government officials of the regime.

"As you well know, *mi hermano*," Alex said, "Batista had the support of the armed forces in 1933 during the days of the popular revolt against the dictator Gerardo Machado. He was the one who led the so-called 'Rebellion of the Sergeants' that overthrew Machado's regime. This gave the opportunity to the reformist politicians to restore the constitutional system with the new Constitution of 1940. On the other hand, Batista always had the support of the island's humble classes and most of the people of the black race. Batista was a mulatto, born in the eastern province of a humble farming family who worked in the field. Through his boldness, some good luck, and a desire to excel, he educated himself so he was able to enter the Army at the age of twenty, and, after working hard, he achieved the rank of sergeant major as a typist and office manager of the army's general staff. Later in life, his political ability and his impulsive desires for power led him to take extreme actions considered unacceptable in a civil and moral society. The fact was that the country's middle class, the traditionally well-off families, the intellectuals, the professionals, and the young college students never accepted Batista. He created a new class of rich people that benefited from government contracts of public works and the illegal businesses his associates were involved in as civil service employees."

Alex reminded me about Batista's association with organized crime members from the United States. He brought to Cuba a well-known mobster, Meyer Lansky, as an advisor for the state's gambling casino business. The casinos attracted tourists and high-roller gamblers, mainly from the United States, who were looking for a good time far from Las Vegas and the IRS. The casinos were well managed, and the games were conducted honestly. For the Cuban people, the casinos were not a problem and they offered new source of employment. Also, they offered the opportunity to the general public to enjoy spectacular, Las Vegas-style entertainment, with local and foreign artists, at a very modest price. Nevertheless, despite the advantages, it was disturbing to see the large number of underworld elements from North America who were connected with the island's gambling casinos.

The year 1958 was a sad year on the island, Alex said. "The economy stagnated; nobody was investing in new businesses. There were no more *fiestas de quince* celebration parties and *guateques*. The families worried terribly when their sons and daughters went out at night, because the repression was horrendous; many young people were arrested, jailed, and tortured. In the cities at night, you could hear the blasting of homemade bombs set off by the groups of urban resistance against the regime. The resistance's objectives were to keep the population in state of war against the regime and, at the same time, to keep the island's economy unbalanced. Bastista's regime was brutally fighting the violence in the cities through the national police, the *Servicio de Inteligencia Militar* (SIM), and the *Buró de Represión de Actividades Comunistas (BRAC)*.

"The Cuban people were losing their joy and the young people felt frustrated and threatened," Alex said. "During that time, our generation began to lose its innocence as we encountered the ugly face of crime and the oppression of a dictator."

Alex paused, deep in thought for a few moments, and then continued. "I believe that I have spoken too much, and, perhaps, it is time to leave, because it is already six-thirty and the exercise and sea scent have given me a tremendous appetite."

He reminded me that he had made reservations to have supper at eight-thirty in the Hong Kong Back Street, a famous oriental restaurant at the San Juan Hotel.

CHAPTER 5

▼

THE END OF BATISTA

Rodriguez had spoken a long time, and Peter Jones had listened quietly throughout. But at last he said, "Well, Rodriguez, your friend Alex had a very difficult experience during President Batista's regime. However, I still don't see the connection with you and your situation in Havana. Please continue, but be more specific about the reasons you are here without proper documentation."

Rodriguez began his story again.

*   *   *   *

I left the cabin and went to the lobby of the hotel to wait for Alex, who was due in the next ten or fifteen minutes. The lobby of the San Juan hotel looks sensational, particularly at night when all the lights of the chandeliers are burning. As I admired the majestic charm of the place, I concluded that the San Juan Hotel does not have anything to envy from any hotel in North America or in Europe. For my taste the San Juan is one of the best hotels in the world because of its sobriety and elegance. While I was waiting, I read the hotel's activities guide and discovered that the hotel has twenty-three restaurants, fifteen bars, and many nightclubs. The Gallery shopping center, full of elegant stores and with a very particular decoration, is in the basement. The hotel even operates a great gambling casino for the people who, having or not having a lot of money, like to lose it.

When I was reading the guide of the hotel, I saw Alex entering the main door of the lobby accompanied by a tall and attractive young girl. My first thought was that he was coming with his daughter, but then I thought, perhaps she is his girl-friend. The girl looked to be not more than thirty-five years of age. As soon Alex saw me, they hurried over and he introduced the girl as his niece Teresa. Almost without giving a second thought, I said half-joking, "Alex, are you doing to me what you did to the man of the small mustache?" That wise-man introduction "my niece Teresa" seemed very strange to me.

The girl immediately asked, "Who is the man of the little mustache?"

Alex answered, "Don't worry, Teresa, it is a joke of my friend."

Then the girl said. "I am the daughter of José, the brother of Alex."

"The doctor?" I asked.

"Do you know my father?"

"I don't know him personally but Alex has mentioned him to me," I said.

In order to clarify the situation Alex said that Teresa lived in Miami with her husband, who was French, and their three children. She was a language teacher who was in Puerto Rico at a teacher's convention. Teresa, born in Cuba, had come to the United States with her parents when she was eight years old. Because he was a physician, José had many difficulties in leaving the island. Teresa grew up in Miami and attended Miami University. Later she went to take a master's in language in France and there she met her future husband. They married and lived in France for more than ten years. For that reason, Teresa was able to speak per-fectly not only Spanish and English, but also French.

"She arrived a day early for the convention and took the opportunity to call me," Alex said. "I mentioned our dinner appointment and I took the liberty of inviting her to join us. Would you mind?"

Immediately I said, "Great, I am enchanted."

Alex then said, "Well, now we are the three musketeers."

From the lobby we walked through a wide hall to the restaurant at the end of the corridor that also leads to the gambling casino. The entrance of the Hong Kong Back Street restaurant is unique. First, it is necessary to cross a small wooden bridge over a little stream. Next we walked through a narrow alley. The peculiar thing was that after we passed the bridge and the alley, we could perceive a peculiar scent of a very exotic seaport. At the entrance of the restaurant, our host met us. She was a very interesting woman with Oriental features elegantly dressed in her *Cheongsam* of red silk. After Alex identified himself, we were seated in a large round table next to the little stream. The restaurant was luxuriously decorated in Oriental style. Really, for a moment I thought that we were in Hong

Kong, not in Puerto Rico. Our waiter, also with Oriental features and dressed in her yellow *Cheongsam*, asked us if we wanted to drink something before the dinner. Alex asked Teresa and she asked for a Coca-Cola. Then, Alex said to me, "*Mi hermano,* we are in the Oriental environment, but I am going to order a *mentirita.* Would you join me?"

I said, "Let's order two."

He turned to the waiter and said, "Bring us two Bacardi rums with Coke."

The menu was written in Chinese and for the people that didn't handle that language well, it also had mixed Chinese and English, like "Dim Sum Style Appetizers." Thank God, the ingredients of each dish were written in English. In this way, you knew that you hadn't asked for roasted dog. Alex suggested that we could share a Pu-Pu Platter to start. We agreed.

While we were waiting for our appetizer, Alex told us about his experience in a dim sum restaurant in Hong Kong. Out of curiosity, he had ordered the Century Egg. Alex said that the waiter brought him a giant egg the size of a grapefruit, which was cut in four parts. The outside was white and the inside was black with a scent of urine. He said that he watched it for a moment and said, "What in the heck is this?"

The waiter told him that it was the famous Century Egg. Then Alex asked how it was prepared. She, very politely, told him that a duck egg was placed in a substance for several months to cure. This substance was prepared with horse urine, dirt, ashes, lime, and straws from rice. The white outer covering was made with "congee of rice." Alex told us that he said, "Thank you very much for the explanation, but please take it away as my gift and enjoy it." The waiter took it, thanked Alex, saying that she would give it to her mother-in-law, and she went away.

Teresa looked at us, and satirically said, "Do you think that they serve *hamburgers?*" We spent some time, very carefully, studying the menu and finally each ordered a well-known Chinese dish, the type that you could call Chinese-American cuisine.

During supper, we talked about the exotic and elegant decoration of the restaurant and Teresa told us about the years she had lived in France and her experiences with Oriental restaurants. After the main dish, we had Chinese green tea, served by the waiter in an Oriental style porcelain teapot.

As we were sipping our tea, Teresa said, "Uncle, tell us about your stories in Cuba during the struggle against Batista." Looking at me, she said, "According to Grandfather and Grandmother, Uncle Alex always was in some kind of problem. He was first against the Batista government and later against Castro."

Alex said, "Do you remember, *mi hermano,* when we were walking today along the beach, before the incident with the man of the little mustache, when I was explaining to you the problems of the exile and the lack of unity between the Cubans?"

Teresa interrupted the conversation to ask, "Who is that man of the little mustache?"

Alex replied, "Don't worry about him, he went away." Then he continued. "I remember that during the fight against the Batista dictatorship, the opposition was also divided." He went on to explain the political situation at the time at some length, but Teresa and I were fascinated by this glimpse of history.

He told us that the players included the traditional politicians called *Autenticos* from the old Cuban Revolutionary Party. The deposed President Prio, exiled in Miami, led the *Autenticos* Party. This group wanted to recover its position of power on the island. College students and young members of the labor unions were in the *Directorio Revolucionario* that had been founded in 1955 by José Antonio Echeverria, an anti-Communist university leader. This group was fighting not only to overthrow Batista, but also to promote certain moderate social reforms. The other group was those of us in the *26 de Julio* movement, founded by Castro after the attack on the Moncada military fort in Santiago de Cuba. This movement also included the members of the old *Partido Ortodoxo.* Senator Eduardo Chivas founded the Orthodox Party, but he committed suicide, leaving the party without a leader. The Communists, represented by the *Partido Socialista Popular* (PSP), were the smaller group of the opposition. This group in reality never was an important factor in the fight against Batista. "Anyway," Alex said, "all these competing groups wanted to remove Batista from the power, but they competed among themselves and each had its own agenda, perhaps hidden, as history has proved the facts of that time."

He continued, "We saw the division between these opposition groups very clearly in April of 1958, when the Batista regime intensified the persecution of its opponents.

"At that time, the opposition fighters revolted violently, killing policemen and *Batistianos* accused of being *chivatos,* or people who acted like spies of the regime. During this period, Batista had suspended constitutional guarantees, governing under emergency laws and using all his power to destroy dissident groups. Under these conditions, opposition groups planned the execution of a general strike in the island. The idea was to paralyze the island's economy. The opposition hoped the strike would be supported by elements of the armed forces who were not loyal to the regime, and that they would form a military *junta* to remove Batista from office. Later, this *junta* would summon general elections. By then the United States had imposed an embargo on arms sales to Batista's government.

"Havana Province was selected as the main objective of the general strike. If the strike prevailed in Havana, the revolutionaries assumed that it would catch on in the rest of the island. This situation would allow Castro and the bearded, armed insurgents in the high ridges to fight more effectively against the demoralized forces of Batista. The group of the *26 de Julio*, represented by Faustino Perez, acted as coordinator of the strike. Its job was to provide the necessary arms and explosives for the urban resistance militia in Havana. The militia was made up of students, workers, and professionals from the *Autentico* party, the *Directorio Revolucionario,* and those of us in the *26 de Julio*. For this skirmish, Alex explained, they needed forty houses in Havana to store arms and to be used for meeting points of the conspirators. The strike was planned firstly for March 31. However, due to the shortage of arms provided by the *26 de Julio*, it had to be delayed until April 9. The night before the strike, members of the *Directorio* and the *Autentico* group complained about the plan drawn up by the *26 de Julio* and the lack of arms, dynamite, etc. The climate of the discussions between the groups got so hot that the *Autenticos* left the plan and it was not clear if the members of the *Directorio* would participate or not. The Communist members of the PSP stayed, as always, separate from this action. "All this mix-up created complete confusion within the dissidence, only a day before the strike," Alex said, frowning as he remembered the chaos that had led to disaster. "Something else happened, too," he continued. "The strike was supposed to begin at noon of April 9, but the armed groups of the *26 de Julio* received new orders by clandestine radio at 10:00 a.m. to begin the strike at 11:00 a.m. Without any justification, Faustino had suddenly changed the hour of the strike!" He shook his head in dismay, but continued with his explanation of the events.

The National Police as well the SIM seemed to be prepared to resist the strike, almost, Alex said, as if they were waiting for it. Commercial banks in Havana were closed and the stores were empty.

"I was with other students in the Universidad de Villanueva speaking with the administration of the school to convince them to close it in support of the strike," he recalled. When the action began, he told us how armed groups seemed to simply appear in the buildings and intersections of the main streets of Havana to block the traffic, and the forces of the government reacted violently, shooting and killing many of the revolutionary militants. In summary, the strike was a failure. The rebellious militants caused panic within the population, but they did not have the expected support. The workers didn't leave their jobs because they were afraid to go out where the shooting and the explosions could be heard loud and clear. A bomb blew up some power installations, leaving a sector of Havana without electricity. In other cities in the interior of the island, the rebellion also failed and never caught the popular support. "Nor did Castro and his bearded insurgents on the hills do anything," Alex said bitterly.

He paused, then said, "After this failure, analyzing all the errors committed, we felt that somebody had betrayed us. First, we thought that the Communist group of the PSP has betrayed us. The rumors were that the Communists had cooperated with the government in identifying the members of the urban rebellion and that they had given details of the strike. Many of the strike leaders had to flee into the hills where the rebels were operating. Castro seized the subversive movement after blaming all the leaders of the strike as incompetent fools and idiots. He named himself the military commander in chief of the rebel armed forces—including the urban clandestine militias and the secretary general of the *Directorio*. That reaction made us believe in possible treason on the part of Castro. But that possibility was very hard and sad to accept during the difficult times of the fight against Batista's regime. Perhaps we didn't realize that Castro feared that the urban clandestine militia had more power than him, with his bearded fighters in the hills. From that moment, Castro consolidated his power as the maximum leader of the revolution against Batista, which until then had been shared with the deposed President Prio and the leaders of the *Directorio*."

Alex stopped and looked at both of us to see if we were still following him. Teresa appeared fascinated by her uncle's story, so he continued. "As I mentioned before, many of the leaders of the clandestine groups fled and were able to join the rebellious forces that operated in the mountain range of the Escambray, in the province of Las Villas. Some, like Faustino Perez, were able to join the rebels in the Province of Oriente. Many remained in Havana and in other urban centers, but with very limited influence in the revolutionary process. The activities of the clandestine urban groups were somehow limited to support of the armed rebels in the hills. Perhaps this happened by design of Castro and his obsession with absolute power."

Teresa, who had remained quiet until now, asked him. "Uncle, what did the priests of the university say when you requested them to close the school?"

Alex told her that the president, Father Kelly, was an American priest of the Augustinian order. "He told us—and not in a very friendly way!—that the university would close the day that all the businesses in Cuba were closed. However, thanks to God, he never reported the incident to the government authorities. Nevertheless, I think the incident had been reported to the Embassy of the

United States, because Villanueva was an American school." Since that incident, Alex said, "The priests never were very fond of me. But I earned the respect and appreciation of the Cuban faculty that in its majority was against Batista."

Teresa said, "Thank God that the priests didn't report to the government. But, Uncle, what were the most important reasons for the revolt against Batista?"

Alex thought for a moment and said, "The fight against the Batista dictatorship was meant to reestablish the Constitution of 1940, to clean the republic of political corruption and dishonesty of the public fund administration, and to guarantee the individual liberties of all citizens. The people thought that Cuba could return to the democratic system if they could enjoy the virtues of the state of rights and liberties. This would lead to better distribution of social justice at all levels of society. These real objectives motivated the middle and the well-off classes in Cuba. Most of the intellectuals, students, workers, professionals, and businessmen considered Batista's regime as an illegitimate government that had arrived in power by the force of a coup d'etat. It was true that the overthrown constitutional government was also corrupt, but the Cuban people hoped to find a democratic solution to the state of prevailing corruption of the constitutional government in office; the presidential elections were only few months away when Batista took control."

After 1959, Castro gave other reasons for the revolt. I remember some of them, I told Alex and Teresa. The first to come to mind was the one for ending illiteracy in Cuba. The island, compared with the rest of Latin America, had an excellent educational system. Public schools were administered by the national government and the municipal governments maintained city schools. These schools represented the public elementary system of the nation. Attendance at elementary school was obligatory for all the children of the island and was funded by the state and the municipalities. The *institutos* handled the public high school program, the *bachillerato*, which young people attended for five years. The municipalities and the national government maintained the *institutos*. There was also a great number of private schools, some maintained by religious orders, and others, secular. These schools were not free and the students had to pay tuition. At the college level, there were three public universities in Cuba where tuitions were low, subsidized by the state, and three private universities. In addition, several schools taught the trades and arts; some were maintained by the state and others were private.

"Yes, the academic level of the education programs in the island was excellent, as was proved by the quality of the Cuban professionals and the technical preparation of the workers in the local business environment," Alex said.

"Other tales created by Castro were that the sugar industry was in foreign hands, but the facts show otherwise," he added. "In 1958, 60 percent of the sugar mills were in the hands of Cuban industrialists. This figure is very important to understand; it is necessary to remember that in 1902, when the new republic was established, the Cuban people didn't own any sugar mill operating on the island. All were in the hands of foreigners. The Cubans were completely ruined after the war of independence. Think how impressive it is that in only fifty-six years, they were able to control 60 percent of the industry! Castro said also that 90 percent of the power and telephone companies were the property of North American companies. This was true, but in Cuba before the 1959, there were no blackouts in the cities, as there were during the years following the Communist revolution, and the telephone system was the best among the Latin American countries. On the other hand, both the *Compania Cubana de Electricidad*, which was a subsidiary of the American and Foreign Power Company; and the *Compania Cubana de Telefonos*, that was a subsidiary of ITT, were famous for paying the best wages to their Cuban employees and for offering excellent social benefits. Everybody in the island wanted to work for these two companies."

Alex added, "Castro always spoke about the large estate owners in Cuba. He said that 2 percent of the landowners controlled 45 percent of the arable land on the island. However, he didn't mention that this was probably due to the type of agricultural products we grew." The main agricultural activities on the island were the cultivation of sugar cane and the breeding of cattle. These two industries require many acres of land to work efficiently. Cuba produced more than eight million tons of sugar per year before 1959. Now its production doesn't reach two million tons. The island before 1959 had more than six million head of cattle and the breeding was of such high quality that there was enough meat and livestock to export after the national demand was satisfied. "After forty-seven years of the Communist revolution, the Cuban people can't find beef to eat, and it is a crime to buy beef in the black market," Alex explained bitterly.

"Definitively, none of the reasons given by Castro motivated the Cubans to fight against the autocratic and dictatorial regime of Batista. All the reasons given by Castro were only but revisionist histories and myths used by the Socialist dictator to justify his errors and the crimes committed by his damn revolution. Castro betrayed us during the strike of April 1958 and has betrayed us after 1959."

After a brief pause in which he struggled to control his emotions, Alex continued his story. "The experiences in life have taught me that when lies are said a consistent way over some time, everybody begins believing the lie. Castro has mastered that art. *Mi hermano*, surely you remember when Castro brought Herbert Matthews, the journalist from the *New York Times*, to visit him in the Sierra Maestra mountain range?"

I turned to Teresa then, because I did remember the story. Castro had used Matthews to popularize his figure as a hero of the revolution with his bearded rebels in the mountain range. I said, "It was very deceptive how he tricked the journalist during the visit. Castro had the bearded rebels, who at that time were not many, walking constantly in front of the journalist to make believe that he had more troops than he really did. The troops pretended encounters and false battles against Batista's soldiers, making Matthews believe that the rebels dominated the region. Everything was a theater, all was a sham."

"Nevertheless," Alex joined in, "the journalist bit the bait and published in the *New York Times* everything he saw, giving to Castro credibility and the romantic popularity of the guerrilla fighting in the hills against the forces of a dictator.

"In reality," he added, "the government of the United States left Batista alone. They didn't sell more arms to Cuba; later the Batista government was able buy two helicopters and some arms from England. However, it was already too late; the army was very demoralized. The soldiers, called *casquitos*, didn't want to fight, the officers deserted, or they joined the rebel's forces. The chief of the armed forces, General Tabernilla, visited the ambassador of the United States a few days before Christmas in 1958 to negotiate the possibility of making a military *junta* headed by General Eulogio Cantillo. The ambassador was fearful because he knew that Tabernilla was Batista's intimate friend, and coldly said to him that he had to consult with Washington."

On the other hand, Alex told us, the rebels in the Oriente Province continued their advance. Castro didn't have problems of money and provisions. The Cubans exiled in Miami were able to raise funds and the well-off families on the island gave great sums of money to the revolution. Local businesses sent provisions through the urban resistance to the rebels in the hills. In Las Villas Province, the forces of Camilo Cienfuegos, Che Guevara, and those of the *Directorio* surrounded the city of Santa Clara that was finally occupied December 30, 1958, when they blocked parts of the main highway. The government removed the troops from the countryside and concentrated them in the defense of the cities. This allowed the free mobilization of the rebellious militia in the countryside, moving down from the hills where many peasants joined them. As a result, the number of the rebellious fighters grew and they went to the towns. "Of course, the chaotic warlike state that existed paralyzed the economy in the interior of the island and later in the country as well," he commented.

Alex explained that he had followed the struggle closely through the *Radio Rebelde*. "We used to listen to it every night looking for new orders," he said. The urban resistance in the cities had the mission to obtain and send supplies to the rebel forces and distribute pamphlets and propaganda against the government. The intention was to keep the population informed and the flame of the revolutionary struggle alive. Batista and his near collaborators realized their situation and began to prepare their flight quietly.

Teresa said that she had heard these histories at school, but never with so many vivid details. Looking at me, she said, "I told you; Uncle Alex was always in some kind of trouble when he was young." She then turned to Alex again. "Uncle Alex, what happened on January 1, 1959?"

Alex said, "Ah, that is another long story. But before going there, we are going to order some Oriental desserts!"

CHAPTER 6

▼

VIVA LA REVOLUCIÓN!

Peter Jones was so involved in Rodriguez' curious story that he was almost startled to realize they were still sitting in his office in the Special Interests building. He had heard none of these stories before, and for the first time the American began to understand the passionate hatred so many Cubans had for Castro. But he drew his professional persona over his shoulders like a robe. "Señor Rodriguez, please, you must remain calm. I still don't understand the point of your story—although I must admit, it is an interesting one. But I have many people waiting; you must get to the point."

"Ah," said Rodriguez. "I understand. But there is so much to tell, and I must make you see how it truly was." He continued his tale, and Peter sat, spellbound once more.

*   *   *   *

Oriental restaurants have a great variety of delicious and exotic meals, but when you look at desserts, they only offer fruits and fruit sherbets. I have always asked myself, where is the *crème caramel*, the *pastelitos*, and the apple pie? You can bet you won't find them in an Oriental restaurant. Under these circumstances, we three musketeers in search of something sweet after the exotic flavors of our Oriental cuisine had to accept sherbets of melon, mango, and of pineapple. When we were savoring the sherbet, Teresa said sternly, "Uncle, we are waiting for your story of January 1, 1959."

Alex slowly finished his spoonful of sherbet and then sat the spoon aside. "I haven't told this story to many people, because to certain point it is difficult for me to tell. It marks the beginning of a new phase in my life, and without doubt, a new phase of the history of Cuba as well.

"Let's see. As I mentioned before, the forces of Camilo and Che had surrounded the city of Santa Clara, and on December 30, they dominated it. The clandestine *Radio Rebelde* reported the good news and everybody in Havana was excited and full of hopes. The universities were closed because of the violence used by the repressive forces of the government and the insecurity in which the youth lived. In Havana, all types of rumors and conspiracies were going on. In the interior of the island in the provinces of Las Villas and Oriente the situation was much worse due to the advance of the rebel troops.

"Like other young university students, I was in limbo, with very little to do. Most of the time we were collecting and bringing supplies to send to the rebels in the hills, or distributing papers with the news of the rebels' advances and stories against the government, or asking for economic aid from our friends and families. Because not only did the rebels in the hills need to be taken care of, but the urban resistance underground needed help. The government transformed our activities into a civil conspiracy against it, and we knew we had to support the revolution or it would fail. Our activities were necessary to denounce the repressive measures of the regime and its policy against the values of the democratic principles and its violations of human rights. We were not violent, but we worked in the support of the rebels and our brothers of the resistance. Some groups within the urban resistance detonated bombs that accidentally caused physical injuries to innocent people. These, perhaps, had crossed the line of civil disobedience and might be called terrorists. Often, I thought that these acts were extremist and undesirable."

After a pause, Alex said, "Every evening after six, we tuned in to *Radio Rebelde* to learn what was happening in the interior of the island. We were always hoping for some signal that would tell us what we had to do. We knew that the government was severely wounded, that most of the people in the island didn't want Batista, and that he and his allies were a herd of thieves and assassins. The economy looked increasingly frail due to problems with the rebel-controlled highways in the interior of the island and the atmosphere of civil unrest in the cities. Tourism had diminished and none of us, none of the Cubans in Havana, went out at night to eat in restaurants, the theaters, or to visit the nightclubs."

Alex continued, "I imagine that Batista realized his regime was crumbling. The people didn't want him in power and urban resistance kept the citizenship in a state of psychological instability. The United States had abandoned him and wouldn't sell arms to him anymore, and the rebels in the hills were advancing towards the cities and blocking the highways, so necessary for the commerce and the industry of the island. His own army didn't want to fight because it was corrupted—in many cases soldiers and whole divisions of the army made deals with the rebels and many young soldiers, called *Casquitos*, deserted to join Castro." Alex shook his head sadly as he told us how the warlike state of affairs and the insecurity in which the people lived was driving the country to economic ruin. All these negative factors gave Batista reason to prepare his flight from the island. The dictator and his nearer collaborators already had accumulated great amounts of money in foreign banks abroad and he considered there was nothing left to rob in the island.

"Very discreetly, Batista began to prepare his flight. Apparently, he ordered secretly to have prepared three airplanes in the Columbia military base. These planes would be used to transport him and his family—the ones that were still in Cuba, because he already had sent to Miami his smaller children—and his near collaborators and friends. As part of the plan, he organized a New Year's party on December 31, 1958, at the Columbia military base. He invited the people whom he wanted to go with him in the airplanes. This select group of friends and close collaborators didn't know anything of the secret plan of the president and went to the great New Year's party to show the 'strong man' their loyalty and gratefulness.

"I don't think anyone in Cuba knew what he was plotting, though," Alex said. "Certainly I didn't know what was happening at the time. I only learned the story days later."

Alex recalled that he was living clandestinely at the time, as other young people did. It was better to be away from home, staying in friends' houses and continuously moving from one to another house in different neighborhood far from home. During this period he said, "I wasn't working or attending college, nor did I go to any parties or sporting activities. We were at war, working for the revolution, waiting for something to happen, and we were proud to be doing so—but in reality, we didn't know what was at the end of that endless waiting that was consuming our youth. No one did."

Again, my friend looked sad as memories of those hard times took over. He seemed to be reliving them as he spoke. "That New Year's Eve night, my friend Ernesto, *mi amigo* since school and all through college—we even worked together during the revolution—we were invited to supper in a house in the elegant residential neighborhood of El Vedado. This area of Havana, with its huge turn-of-the-century houses, represented Cuba's old money. The people who lived in these sumptuous homes were wealthy families who were not involved in politics. For that reason, Batista's henchman, executors of the regime's repression, generally didn't bother them. On the other hand, these families didn't get along with Batista because they considered him an illegitimate ruler and vulgar. For these reasons, these families usually helped the revolutionary young college students who saw them with certain affection. In many cases, we were college friends of their sons and daughters."

In Havana, supper was served generally at eight but since it was the New Year's Eve, supper was served around nine o'clock that night. "Dr. Gonzalez, the owner of the house headed the large dinner table, with his wife Raquel sitting at his right and his brother Leonel, an engineer, at his left, followed by his wife, Dr. Beatriz. Josefina, the daughter of Dr. González, was next to her mother and accompanied by Ernesto. I was sitting next to Mirian, the daughter of Dr. Beatriz. She was my college friend—and my girlfriend." He smiled at the memory before continuing his story.

"Just close to the end of the supper, around ten-thirty, the telephone rang. It was answered by one of the maids of the house; all of them were Spaniards who had worked in the house almost all their lives. They were considered part of the family. The call was for Dr. Beatriz. She was an intellectual who was a professor in comparative literature at the University of Havana. She was also our clandestine agent of contact with the *26 de Julio*. When she returned to the dining room, I noticed she was very excited and with great surprise, she announced that Batista had fled. I jumped off my chair and asked her for more details. She said it was the rumor through the underground and her contact had promised to call later to confirm it. We all remained excited with the good news—frankly, we did not know what to do.

"The night was bright and the sky was full of stars; the temperature was pleasant and the street was quiet, perhaps more that the usual. Ernesto and I wanted to go out to investigate what was happening, but Dr. Beatriz convinced us to remain calm in the house until we learned the truth of the rumors.

"We didn't have long to wait," Alex added. Before midnight, the telephone rang again. This time they all ran near the telephone, waiting for the good news. Dr. Beatriz spoke and everyone tried to interpret what she was saying. When she finished, she told them that everything was confirmed. Batista and his family and his close friends had fled the country in three airplanes from Columbia military base in Marianao; nobody knew their destination. Dr. González called one of the maids and ordered the opening of a bottle of champagne to toast the good news and to usher in a successful and happy 1959 in a Cuba free from the Batista tyranny.

Alex recalled that everything was so sudden and unexpected that they didn't know what to do. They made several calls to their contacts in the urban clandestine movement and everybody was like them, not a clue of their next move. They only confirmed that Batista went away and that General Cantillo had assumed the army command and had formed an exercise to control a temporary council governing body. Who was in that council? Nobody knew.

Ernesto decided to finish the night and go home. He thought his parents might be worried about him after his couple of weeks away. It was two o'clock in the morning and everybody in the house was looking a little tired. Alex thanked his host and hostess, gave a little kiss to Mirian and another to Dr. Beatriz, who said she would call him the next day with more information.

"Then, full of joy, I walked to the car. When I was going to start the engine, a white dove settled on the figurehead on the hood in front of my eyes. I said to myself, *From where this dove is coming?* I thought, *Well, she will fly away when the car begins to move.* However, she didn't!"

It took Alex about twenty-five minutes to travel from the house in El Vedado to his home in Marianao. His route went through a wide avenue called Calle Linea with many traffic lights. It was two o'clock in the morning but so much traffic made it look like it was five o'clock in the afternoon. Black and gray cars were running in all directions at high speed. The dangerous thing was that the drivers of these cars were members of Batista's regime who didn't obey the traffic signals. Alex had to make sudden stops to avoid head-on collisions with them. He said, "I still remember that within all this confusion I felt invisible, very calm and safe. Throughout all the way, the white dove stayed on the hood without moving. I didn't pay much attention to her; I was so concentrated in avoiding an accident with the cars that ran the lights that I didn't watch the dove. Finally, when I got home and parked the car in front of my house, I saw the dove fly away and disappear in the dark of the night."

He paused a moment, and I felt a chill of wonder shiver up my back. But he continued. "Frankly, at that moment I didn't give much importance to the white dove. I left the car and ran to the door of the house. When I got in, I realized that my parents were sleeping, but without thinking, I woke them up shouting, 'Batista went away! The dictatorship is over!' They rose and they embraced me, full of joy at seeing me well and, as it was said in Cuba, 'healthy and out of danger' after all the headaches I had given them during the struggle against Batista's regime. Then they told me to go to bed so tomorrow I could tell them more about this great news. But I could not go to sleep, I was very excited, so I went to the bar in the living room and open a bottle of the Spanish cider called *El Gaitero*. I served myself in a large glass.

"Seated on the chair in the bar, alone with my memories and drinking a cider, I was celebrating the great victory of the Cuban people against the dictatorship. I was remembering the bad time when the police took me to the station with Armandito, when by a miracle we left alive. The difficult moments lived during the clandestine activities and the good luck that I always had, to escape from all the dangers. The bad times and anguish that I gave my parents. When I was going to thank God for his kindness, the image of the white dove came to me. Then I thought, *Lord, was she my guardian angel, who took care of me during the struggle?* I then said, *Thanks, Lord. Please help the Cuban people in this new phase of their history in the same way that you have helped me. In You, I trust.* Then came to my mind a famous Spanish saying: God is not captain of bandits.

"I was drinking my sweet cider slowly without haste, without any desire to finish while I was enjoying my thoughts," Alex continued. "Well, first, I thought everything would return to normality in the country. The dishonest government officials would be disowned by society. The corruption in the government would disappear. General elections soon would be celebrated and I would vote for the first time in my life. My sacrifices and the one of thousands of other Cubans were not in vain. Then I stopped and said to myself, *Viva la Revolución!*"

Now Alex's main goal was to return to the university. If it opened again soon, he could finish in two years, maybe even less. Then he thought about what he would do after graduation. He told us, "For the first time, it came to my mind that perhaps I would like to go into the urban development business. My family was in that business and I liked it; it seemed to me very interesting and lucrative. The city of Havana and the town of Marianao were expanding together and new housing was in demand. On the other hand, I thought maybe I would like to continue studying two more years after my graduation, because Villanueva had an evening doctorate program in economics that seemed very attractive. I thought that perhaps I could study and work at the same time. I knew several people who were working and taking the program."

He spent the next thirty minutes or so simply enjoying the moment of victory, for the first time able to ponder a real future in a free Cuba. He savored his cider and his thoughts until nearly four o'clock in the morning, when he headed for bed with the thought that, in the morning, the sun over Cuba would seem more brilliant than ever.

At our table in the Oriental restaurant, Alex took a sip of water as he sat staring into a past neither Teresa nor I could see. Then he took up the tale again. "I woke up at ten-thirty in the morning. My parents were already awake and had had their breakfast. They thought that I had to be tired and they let me sleep until late in the morning. When I got in the living room, they were watching television; all channels were talking about the sudden departure of Batista and his collaborators. General Cantillo had assumed control of the armed forces and was trying to maintain order in the country. Later in the morning, all TV stations read a *Radio Rebelde* report from the mountain range of the Sierra Maestra. *Comandante* Fidel Castro had declared a general strike on the island. In the same statement, he asked the people to maintain calm and order. At the same time, he said that he had ordered *Comandates* Camilo Cienfuegos and Ernesto Guevara, who were in Santa Clara, to march towards Havana. Castro finished his official notice by vigorously denouncing the usurpation of power by General Cantillo as a military coup d'etat, shouting the motto, "Revolution, yes! Military coup, no!"

After this announcement, many people went to the streets in Havana and other cities in the island to loot the houses and businesses of members of Batista's government. Many of them had fled during the night and others were hiding, terrified, to save their lives from the enraged crowds. The result was that the furniture, television sets, and all articles of value were stolen from many houses and businesses. Many armed forces members took off their uniforms and burned them. Cubans who had been exiled in Miami began to arrive on the island. All the cities surrendered to the rebels and joined the general strike.

Realizing the seriousness of the situation, General Cantillo decided to bring another military man to help him to control the chaos and to appease the probable reprisal from the rebels. At noon, he ordered the release of Colonel Ramón Barquin from jail. The colonel was in a military prison in Isla de Pinos. He was a prestigious career military officer whom Batista had put in jail a few years before for his criticism against the regime.

Colonel Barquin arrived at the military camp of Columbia in Marianao in prison uniform with a "P" on his back. Other political prisoners accompanied him; among them, Armando Hart who was later named Minister of Education. The colonel immediately contacted Castro and called Dr. Manuel Urrutia, who was later named provisional president of the republic. Dr. Urrutia was the judge who refused to condemn Castro during the attack on the Moncada military post in 1953; for that reason, he had to go abroad in exile. The colonel ordered the arrest of General Cantillo and other military members of the tenebrous SIM. When the troops of *Comandante* Cienfuegos arrived at the Columbia camp during the night hours of January 2, Colonel Barquin understood that his position was very weak and that in fact he didn't have any power vis-à-vis the rebellious *comandantes* of the mountain range. On the following day, the colonel left the military camp. At the same time, *Comandante* Guevara seized the Cabaña Fort in Havana.

Meanwhile, Castro continued his slow march from the Oriente Province to Havana and the general strike on the island held firm. All stores and businesses were closed, nobody was working, and the people were waiting for their new Messiah. When Castro finally arrived at Havana at dawn on January 8, the people received him like the second coming of Christ. Everybody acclaimed Castro and his bearded rebels, repetitiously chanting, *"Fidel! Fidel! Fidel! Viva la Revolución!"*

Alex looked at Teresa and I and grinned. "I believe that I have strayed off a little from my story. However, I had to mention these historical events." After a brief pause, he continued his own story. "Early in the afternoon I called Dr. Beatriz and also I was able to talk with Ernesto. Neither of them had heard much more than what the radio and the television were saying. At about five o'clock in the afternoon, I got a call from Dr. Beatriz with a message asking me to go immediately to attend a meeting in a house in Miramar. As you all know, that neighborhood of Miramar had very nice homes constructed after World War II. I left immediately and got to the place in less than twenty minutes. The house was a mansion occupied by the revolution; it probably belonged to some *Batistiano* collaborator with the regime that fled the island. There were at least ten cars parked in the adjacent streets and the house itself was guarded by armed elements of the *26 de Julio* dressed in civilian clothes.

"I identified myself at the door and they let me in. The place was full of people walking around and talking; they looked like a pack of hens without heads. With so many people talking at the same time, almost shouting, it was difficult to understand what they were saying. Luckily, I found Ernesto, who said that Beatriz was speaking with Marcelo and Alarcón and that we had to wait. Marcelo Fernandez was an MIT graduate who, during the struggle against Batista, had returned to Cuba and had coordinated the urban resistance in Havana. Later he was appointed president of the *Banco Nacional de Cuba*, replacing Che Guevara, and in 1964, he was made Minister of foreign trade until 1980. Ricardo Alarcón was a student of the University of Havana. During the revolutionary period, he was the student coordinator for the resistance. He held several positions in the revolutionary government, among them, ambassador of Cuba in the United Nations. Nowadays he is the president of the National Assembly of the Popular Power. He considered himself a possible candidate to the presidency in the absence of Castro.

"While we were waiting, we introduced ourselves to several individuals; some were of the University of Havana and others from the labor unions. All were members of the resistance of the *26 de Julio*. Ernesto found Miguel, another student of Villanueva. We told him that we were waiting for Marcelo and Alarcón who had called us. He said that he also has being called and had just arrived at the house."

Alex said that, to kill time while waiting, he dedicated himself to listening to the commentaries of people in the house, all of whom had experiences more or less like his own. Some had had more serious problems with the police and were jailed for some time and mistreated by their jailers. After fifteen or twenty minutes, the doctor came and asked Alex and Ernesto to come along with her to the second floor of the house. Alex mentioned that Miguel had been called as well, and she invited him to come along.

"On the second floor we went to a room that looked like a library, where a man was sitting in a comfortable armchair behind a desk. He was not more than thirty-three years of age with black hair and a medium constitution, and he was dressed in civilian clothes. He greeted us very amiably and invited us to enter. Also in the room was a thin young man of about twenty-five years old. He was a little nervous and looked disturbed. The seated man identified himself as Marcelo and introduced the younger one as Alarcón. As he was finishing the introductions, the phone rang. Marcelo answered it and while he was speaking we, all kept silent. When he finally hung up the telephone, Marcelo told us, 'You are going to have to forgive me, but I must go immediately to the military camp of Columbia. Here I leave you with Alarcón, the student coordinator, and anyway, you are going to work with him.' He wished us good luck, stood up, and quickly left the room. I didn't see Marcelo again until the month of June, at a meeting at the University of Havana."

Once Marcelo left, Alarcón told Alex and his friends that members of the *Directorio Revoluvionario* had held up the University of Havana and that they had to go immediately to the University of Villanueva to occupy it before the *Directorio* or the Communists got there. It was very important that the *26 de Julio* controlled Villanueva. The young men all looked at each other, but they agreed on the mission. Alarcón took a paper from a pocket of his shirt and gave them a telephone number. "If you aren't able to find me at this number, then come here to see if you can find me here. However, the important thing is that you don't move from the university until the revolution determines what should be done next." He then left the room towards the stairs that went to the first floor.

Alex laughed. "We already had our orders: take over the university! How? With what? Until when? What for? What the revolution would do with the university? As usual, the revolution gave you orders verbally, never in writing. We didn't have any credentials identifying us as members of the *26 de Julio* movement, because it was an illegal, clandestine organization. Of course, we were all very young and pure, full of energy and with the desire to contribute to the construction of a better country, free of corrupt and dishonest politicians.

"I told Dr. Beatriz I would call her if we needed something and that Mirian could bring it to us. It was already seven o'clock when we left the house to fulfill our revolutionary mission to take over the University of Villanueva."

Alex paused, looked at his watch, and said, "Musketeers, my friends, it is eleven o'clock, and Teresa has to attend her meeting early tomorrow." Looking toward me, he said, "Tomorrow I am going to introduce you my friend the *mulato* Ernesto. We will be in your cabana around nine in the morning. If the hour, it is good for you?" I nodded, and it was settled. Teresa and I would have to wait for the rest of Alex's story.

We stood up from our chairs, left the beautiful restaurant, and walked down the corridor toward the lobby of the hotel, where I said goodnight to Teresa and Alex. They left together through the large door towards the dark of the night.

—Unbelievable story, Mr. Jones said. Please tell me what happen after. Did your friend was able to accomplish the task?

CHAPTER 7

▼

THE FIRST MISSION

After calling the hotel's room service to order a continental breakfast with a large pot of coffee to offer Alex and his friend Ernesto, once more the question came to my mind. Why did Alex ask me to come to San Juan?

Why did he want to introduce me to Ernesto? As I was thinking about this, I went to the front door and opened it as if I would find the answer outside the cabana. Of course, the answer wasn't there; nevertheless, I was able to enjoy a beautiful day with a bright sun and a smooth and gentle breeze.

Already there were mothers with their children swimming in the pool and beautiful young girls in bikinis toasting under the glittering tropical sun. A little beyond, behind the swimming pool and along the footpath surrounded by beautiful bougainvillea shrubs full of orange flowers, I saw Alex walking next to a quite short man with light bronze skin and black straight hair. I noticed the large contrast between Alex and his companion. Alex was tall with an athletic constitution and was dressed in a red golf shirt and khaki pants, while his escort was short, a little fat, and wearing a white *guayabera* and gray pants. Alex was walking at his normal pace, relaxed and without hardship, but his friend was working hard to keep the pace. Both were talking about something, but I was too far away to hear them. When they arrived, I was still at the door of the cabana; Alex greeted me and introduced Ernesto. As he used to say when talking about close friends, he said, "This is my partner, the *mulato* Ernesto."

I mentioned to Ernesto that Alex had already told me about their adventures during the struggle against the Batista regime. Ernesto immediately said, "We have been friends for years, since we were in school together." For five years, Ernesto had attended the free elementary school, *La Escuela del Niño de Belén*, maintained by the Jesuits in a building aside from the big school. He explained that this elementary school was for the children of low-income parents who couldn't afford the cost of the big private school. After they completed their preparatory education, without paying anything, the good students were accepted in the great private school called *Colegio de Belén*, also of the Jesuits. Ernesto told us that his father worked in the warehouses of the Polar Brewery Company and lived in a small house in a town called La Ceiba in Marianao, where the schools were located. Although the old man always had work in the brewery, the family didn't have enough money to spare after feeding four mouths in the house.

"When I finished my elementary education, the Jesuit priests gave me a scholarship to study at the *ingreso* and the *bachillerato* in the *Colegio de Belén*. It was there where I met Alex and where we were classmates for six years until we graduated. After our graduation from Belén, our friendship continued through college and still we are very close friends after many years."

Then Alex said, "We didn't live very far away from each other, either. Ernesto lived six or seven blocks from my home. I remember when the professional wrestlers were on television on Fridays at seven o'clock. I always went to Ernesto's home to watch. Ernesto, do you remember the Red Threat?"

"Of course, *mi hermano*," said Ernesto. "He was the dirtiest of all the fighters, the villain. However, no doubt he was the main attraction of the program."

"Do you remember Ricardito? The young guy who lived next to your house, who was one of the fighters?"

"Sure," Ernesto said. "Ricardito was strong like a bull, but outside the fighting ring he wouldn't kill a fly. He was a gentle, an amiable person, a very good guy." He added, "I wasn't very athletic. I liked to watch the wrestling fights and baseball, but never played. The athlete was my partner Alex, who liked to participate in sports." Then Ernesto, jokingly, said, "For that reason, Alex grew big and tall while I remained rather small."

Smiling, Ernesto said, "Alex, do you remember the *fiesta de quince* of my sister Guillermita? Your job was to take care of the door, to stop the party crashers. I remember that I told my old man, 'Don't worry, that Alex is big and no kid in the neighborhood will try to get in without an invitation.' I think that we were in our senior year then."

Alex laughed. "Yes," Ernesto said. "The old man gave a nice party for Guillermita. We had bread with roasted pig and *pastelitos de guayaba* from La Ceiba Bakery."

"The music was under my control, with my record player, my records, and the records that Alex had lent me. Everybody danced all night," Ernesto said. "Those were good times, my friends."

We heard the sound of little taps at the door and, presuming that it was room service, I said, "Here we have our coffee and something to eat." I stood up and opened the door so the waiter could enter with our breakfast.

When we were drinking our coffee and nibbling our toast and sweet breads, I asked Ernesto how he was able to go to Villanueva University since it was a private university and quite expensive. Ernesto said, "My father worked for long time in the Polar Brewery, which had a program of scholarships for the children of their workers. Since I always was a very good student, I earned a scholarship to go to Villanueva. The brewery paid my tuition until I graduated in 1960."

Then I asked Alex, "If you both graduated from high school together, why did Ernesto graduate in 1960, when you had at least couple of years more to go?" Alex reminded me that he lost more than a year of college when he had the problem with Batista's police and went to Miami. I had forgotten that.

Then I said, "Last night Alex was telling me that the seizure of Villanueva University was the first mission that the revolution gave to you guys, on New Year's Day of 1959."

Ernesto said that he remembered very well the adventure. "When we left the house in Miramar after speaking with Alarcón, we really didn't know what to do. Finally, Miguel came up with a plan that we all decided to follow. First, we would go directly to the priests' house at the school and we would try to speak with Father Kelly, the president of the university. We would try to explain to the priest that we were sent by the *26 de Julio* to protect the university property, and as the school's students and members of the *26 de Julio,* our mission was to avoid looting of school property by a rioting crowd that could come to sack the buildings of the university. We reminded Father Kelly of several regretful incidents in Havana where business were ransacked. It was true that some low elements of the society were taking advantage of the confusion of the moment and the general strike to loot and rob. The police were disbanded and dispersed and didn't dare to do anything in most of the cases."

Ernesto continued, "I remember we told Father Kelly that we would remain inside the university's campus in the main building and that we wanted to close all the other buildings' doors so nobody could enter without being seen. The school campus had six buildings of three and four floors, not counting the church in a separate a building. We told him that we would be in the university until the things were back to normal in Havana, once Fidel arrived."

Then Ernesto paused for a moment before saying, "The plan worked out perfectly. Miguel talked with the priest and explained our mission; he accepted our proposition, although not with great enthusiasm. We considered that under the circumstances, he didn't have any other option and we thought that at least he knew who we were and understood that we had a vested interest in the future of the university. He requested a daily meeting with us every evening after six so he could keep informed. Therefore, the Villanueva occupation began. We tried to call Alarcón to tell him that everything was under control, but the telephone number that he gave us didn't work. I had to return to the house in Miramar while Alex and Miguel remained in the school."

Alex said that he called Mirian to tell her the good news and to ask her to bring a flag of the *26 de Julio*. "This was very good idea. We placed the *26 de Julio* flag next to the Cuban flag outside the door of the main university building. I believe that this gesture gave the impression that the university was supporting the revolution. Father Kelly agreed, or rather accepted the idea, with certain reservations. Mirian brought us something to eat and to drink when she came with the flag and said that she was going to call some of her friends to keep us company the next day. Ernesto came back late that night and said that he had seen Alarcón and that he promised to pass by to see us; he never came, and I believe that after a short period of time he left the student group."

Ernesto said that he remembered Alarcón's last words to him: "Please, don't leave the university alone!" Well he recalled that they spent that night, like many others, sleeping on sofas in the students' lobby.

In the morning of the following day, Mirian came with two friends and later two or three other classmates came. Then, Alex said, "I thought we needed to get better organized because we didn't know how long we were going to be on duty in the school. We prepared a sort of a program where two of us would always be on the post, by ourselves or accompanied by any voluntary classmates. That gave one of us the opportunity to go home, take a shower, and to change clothes, etc."

Ernesto reminded Alex that he used to come in the afternoons after work. His dad had found him temporary work at the brewery so he could earn some money while the university was closed.

Alex said, "During the day we almost always had the company of student friends that left us before the six o'clock daily meeting with Kelly. Some of us used to go look for something to eat after the meeting and at night we used to watch television or listen to the radio, but we spent a lot of time discussing what was happening in the country. We watched Castro's arrival in Havana and heard his first speeches on TV. In reality, we were a little isolated from the rest of the population, locked up in the university. I believe that we were there for four or five weeks until the university was reopened."

The students took advantage of their free time to create a student association at Villanueva. Alex said, "Miguel, Ernesto, and I wrote the objectives and the bylaws of the association. My idea was not only to make the student association, but also to change the structure of the university, to make it more democratic and perhaps more Cuban."

Ernesto interrupted, "The University was run autocratically by the administration, which was composed of Augustinians priests, almost all of them from the United States, and maybe one was from Spain. The faculty didn't participate in any decision-making; the priests never consulted them. Of course, the students didn't have any representation. I thought that a committee composed by the administration, the teaching staff, and the students would better run the university. I always considered that the professional experience of the teaching staff was wasted. The university had excellent teachers in all branches of sciences and arts. Most of the professors worked in their own businesses or for prestigious companies; others were also teaching at the University of Havana. Most of them were coming to Villanueva to teach for the love of education rather than for the money. I thought that the teaching staff should have a voice in the direction of the university. On the other hand, the students were not organized and they needed an association that represented them. The idea was that if they had a voice in the direction of the institution, they would also have more responsibility, contributing to their professional and civic formation. We discussed all these ideas and the bylaws with the small group of students who visited to us during our watch."

Alex added, "Finally we were informed, through the official channels of the new provisional government, that Prime Minister Miro Cardona was going to pass a new law reopening all the universities of the island. However, the students of Villanueva and other private universities had to compensate the students of the University of Havana for the time they were open when the University of Havana was closed. This meant that by a revolutionary law the government would void a semester of our academic records."

"Immediately we, with the help of our teachers, prepared a document debating the law proposal," Ernesto said. "Our first argument was that the revolutionary government should not promote a division of the student class and that the idea wasn't the best way to unite Cuban youth. It was like saying that the thousands of students from private universities were *Batistianos* against the revolution, and they were now being punished for their transgression. Second, it was idiotic to suggest that the revolutionary government, by law, could make the students forget the courses already taken and approved. There was an important point to recognize—the University of Havana was closed by the students, represented by the University Student Federation (FEU), not by the Batista government that indirectly benefited from the closing because it eliminated a possible center of urban disturbances."

Alex said, "We reminded them that in the cabinet of the provisional government the Minister of Finance, Dr. Rufo Lopez-Fresquet, was a professor of Villanueva. That Raulito, the son of the Minister of State Raúl Roa, was a student of the university. The father of Pepe Llanusa, Havana's mayor, was Dr. Llanusa, a Villanueva teacher. Dr. Espinosa, a Villanueva professor, was the new treasurer of Havana's municipality. Like that, we were able to mention many other people from Villanueva who held new revolutionary government positions."

Ernesto added, "Our arguments were heard and the final approved law didn't contain the original discriminatory measures against the private universities. The new revolutionary law created the *Tribunales de Estado*. These tribunals, formed by public university teachers, examined private universities' graduating students. The idea probably came from the oral comprehensive test that graduating students take in many North American universities. This was a great victory for the students and the professors of private universities. This whole experience gave credibility to our idea of a greater participation of the professors and students in the university's affairs."

"A few days after the new revolutionary law was published, the university reopened," Alex added. "All the students were very glad to return and resume their lives in the new free Cuba. Nevertheless, suddenly outside in front of the university a group of at least one hundred protesters—not Villanueva's students—were marching and shouting, protesting the opening of the school and the law that hadn't punished the private university students. The priests were very nervous and they didn't know what to do. I don't know if they called the police, but if they did, the police never showed up."

Ernesto said, "Yes, and after so many days spent trying to avoid this type of problem, we felt responsible to resolve it. Alex and Miguel went alone to speak with the anxious crowd—all the students in the university watched. We were a little scared about the situation, so we watched from the windows of the buildings, along with the teachers."

Alex interrupted. "When we went to the street where the crowd was, I told them that I wanted to speak with the person in charge of the demonstration. When they took me to a young guy, maybe a little older than me, first I identified myself as a member of the *26 de Julio* and told to him that Alarcón had given me instructions to look after Villanueva's affairs. I asked him who he was, who he represented, and who had given him the order to make that demonstration. He said that young trade union members and perhaps some students of the University of Havana formed the group. Maybe they were sent by elements of the *Partido Socialista* and the *Directorio*. The important thing was that I apparently convinced them that I was following orders from the revolutionary government and that everything was under our control. In less than ten minutes all protestors disappeared in the same way that they came. All the students returned to their classrooms and the classes continued as if nothing had happened, and everything returned to normality."

The next day, Alex and Ernesto went to tell Father Kelly about their idea of creating a student association. Kelly was not friendly. He stared at them coldly and said, "I don't know you guys."

Respectfully, they gave the priest a copy of the bylaws and informed him that the next day they would have an assembly with all the students to explain the project. Later they would meet with the teachers to discuss the details of the project. The priest looked pale and sick as he said, weakly, "Leave me alone and go away."

Alex said, "That same day we distributed a notification to all students summoning them to the assembly that would explain the intention of the meeting and the objectives of the association."

"The results of the assembly were better than what we were expecting," Ernesto said. "All the students warmly received the idea, and many offered themselves as volunteers to help us. It wasn't any longer just our idea; now everybody worked in favor of the creation of the association. We had our meeting with the faculty; except for two or three of them, the rest of the teaching staff saw with good eyes and sympathy the project. The incredible thing was that we got a most favorable reception from everybody. It was like an ocean wave that couldn't be stopped. The administration didn't have any other choice than to accept the idea and to leave us alone."

A few days later the new association held an election to choose the representatives for the faculty; students voted for a president, a vice president, and a secretary of their faculty. The presidents of each faculty would be members of the student council; this council would appoint the president of the Association of

Students, a vice president, the secretary, and a treasurer. Within each faculty, several committees were organized to develop different activities.

The elections were celebrated with a great enthusiasm. Alex was elected president of his faculty and Miguel of his. Ernesto didn't run for office because he thought that he didn't have time; he had a part-time job and he needed to save money. He was looking forward to his graduation by the end of the year.

The student council named Alex as vice president of the association and the president of the faculty of architecture was appointed president. Miguel was the secretary of the association.

Alex explained, "I understood that the council gave the presidency to a student from the faculty of architecture because Miguel and I were very involved with the revolution and perhaps we were controversialists in our relations with the administration. The decision was good and well received by the students. The appointed president was a good guy, but I always believed that Miguel was the best candidate. He was a very bright young man and spoke very well in public."

Alex paused for a moment and then said, *"Mi hermano,* to make this story short, I will tell you that Father Kelly didn't last long as the university's president—I believe it was probably less than six months. The priest returned to Villanova in Philadelphia and was replaced by Monsignor Eduardo Bosa Mas Vidal, a bishop in Havana. This prelate was a great leader and a gentleman. He immediately earned the admiration and the respect of all of us, faculty and students alike."

During his tenure as president, Kelly had built a square in the college campus and named it the Plaza Kelly. The new university organization decided to change the name to the square to Plaza Espiralli and a bust of the famous priest was placed there. Father Espiralli was the famous Italian-American priest from the Augustinian order who had promoted the construction of the university and other schools and churches in Havana. He convinced the Arellano family to donate the land and was able to raise the money little by little to construct the buildings of the university. Father Espiralli was famous because after he finished his Sunday mass homilies in the church of San Augustine, he used to say, "I don't want any buffalos in the collection basket," meaning that he didn't want coins but only bills of high denomination. With his drive to raise money and his personal contacts with wealthy families on the island, he was able to make a great educational and apostolic work in Cuba. "We all agreed that Father Espiralli well deserved his square and his bust," Alex said.

Ernesto finished the story by saying that he completed his studies at year-end, and took the *Tribunales de Estado* test few weeks after, receiving his law degree.

Then he began to work in the legal department of the Cuban Telephone Company in Havana.

Alex continued his studies in Villanueva and stayed involved in the association, founding a newspaper and a fiscal committee formed by professors and students dedicated to study the new fiscal laws made by the revolutionary government. The committee discussed and published its commentaries on the new laws. The law and business schools used the publications as reference book.

"However, my normal life as a college student didn't last long," Alex said. "Several weeks later, I was called to my next mission."

CHAPTER 8

▼

TWO YEARS OF WORK AND HIGH HOPES

In his office, Peter Jones once again shook himself out from the spell of Rodriguez' story. "All this is very interesting," he said sternly, "but I still don't see the connection with your problem."

"Let me continue," replied Rodriguez. "This is just the beginning, where my problems began." He rubbed his hair and continued telling his story.

*   *   *   *

Ernesto looked at his watch, "Guys, I am very sorry, but I have to go. Since I took the day off from work, I promised Yolandita we would today have lunch together. How many days are you going to be in San Juan?"

I said that I was planning to go back home in a couple of days.

"Very well," he said. He shot a significant look at Alex. "Tell your friend a little more and tomorrow we could perhaps get together to talk more about the business."

I walked him to the door to say good-bye and noticed that the swimming pool was now full of pretty girls in bikinis, enjoying the radiating sun and the ocean breeze.

Alex had remained seated, looking at the ocean through the window. When I came back, he said, "Ernesto is very good guy. He and his wife have made themselves. He doesn't talk much of this, but the poor man was in Castro's political prisons for five years. After he was released, he remained for some time in Cuba and finally he could leave with his wife. She is a physician so she had problems in leaving the island. Castro wants to keep all the professionals he can find! When they arrived in Miami, Ernesto's wife immediately took the foreign test of medicine and passed it. She made her hospital residency in gynecology. Ernesto, during that time, worked in a 7-11 store and studied at night. When his wife began to work as an obstetrician, Ernesto left work and completed his requirements to take the American Bar Association test, passed, and become a lawyer in the United States."

Alex paused before continuing the story of Ernesto after he became a lawyer. Since he had worked with the Cuban Telephone Company, a subsidiary of the International Telephone and Telegraph Company (ITT), he got in contact with some old fellow workers. ITT offered him a job in the legal department in the Puerto Rico Telephone Company, which was also a subsidiary of ITT. When ITT sold the company, Ernesto kept his job in the legal department of the new institution. His wife worked in San Jorge Hospital in the gynecology department. She, who had brought so many babies to the world, had never had her own. They lived in a nice house near the neighborhood of Torrimar with Doña Josefa, a lady they brought from Cuba, and who became part of the family. She was in charge of the house and took care of them because both were always busy working.

I was listening Alex, but I couldn't stop thinking about Ernesto's last words before he left: "Talk more about the business." To which business was he referring? What did he mean? Despite my curiosity, I decided to wait for Alex to bring up the subject at its due time. I was aware that Alex had occupied a position in the temporary government at the beginning of the revolution in 1959, but I didn't remember it very well, so I decided to ask him how he got it after its experiences in the university.

It was easy to get him talking again. Two months after the reopening of the university, Alex said he got a call from Dr. Espinosa inviting him to participate in the inspection of the *Banco Nacional de Cuba*, the central bank of Cuba. The president of the bank was a well-known, distinguished economist, Felipe Pazos. He was one of the main participants in the civic resistance during the fight against Batista's regime and a member of the *26 of Julio*. Without a doubt, he was an honest and prestigious person with a very clear professional and political history in Cuba. Alex felt very proud for the invitation to participate in the team and accepted the job; Espinosa told him that it wouldn't take more than three months. In order to continue his school year, Alex had to change his schedule to evening classes. Alex said that it was hard to go to school after all day working, but he thought that it was only a temporary arrangement.

His job was to physically count, with other three people, all the monetary reserves of the country. These included dollars and other currencies and also gold bars and coins that were kept in the vaults of the bank. It was also necessary to count all Cuban bills held by the bank, including the non-issue bills and the mutilated bills ready to be destroyed. In addition, he had to count and to verify all domestic and foreign bonds in the vaults. All this was necessary to ascertain that all the country's reserves, bonds, and currency in the bank's vault agreed with the bank's book numbers.

"Mi hermano," Alex said, "the work was quite boring and tedious, and it was not very intellectually challenging. Soldiers armed with machine guns were guarding the vaults, and we were the only ones authorized to enter them. Well, I thought, somebody has to do it—it was necessary to verify the financial situation of the republic, after the dictatorship of Batista."

He told me that he learned that the *Banco Nacional de Cuba* was run with a high degree of professionalism. The reserves were well kept and properly recorded. He also learned that Cuba was the third country in Latin America in monetary reserves, after Brazil and Venezuela. It was for that reason that the Cuban peso was at par with the dollar.

"As you can imagine," he said, "my life was changing with the revolution. Between my jobs, my studies, and the work in the student association I didn't have too much time left for partying and sports. I didn't see Mirian at the university anymore and we didn't go out very often. Our romance soon ended in a friendly manner."

A few days after he had completed his mission in the bank, Alex got another call from Dr. Espinosa: "I would like to see you tomorrow in my office at the Havana's municipal building; I have something to tell you." What Alex didn't know was that the call was going to make his life much more complicated.

"In the morning I went to the Municipal Palace of Havana. The building was built during the sixteenth century to be the palace of the governor of the Island of Cuba, appointed by the King of Spain during the colonial time. Since Cuba's independence from Spain, during its republican time, the City of Havana had used the building. In front of the building, there is a beautiful park called La Plaza de Armas and to the other side of the park there is a small building, almost in ruins, called El Templete. That, as you know, was the place where the city of

Havana was founded in 1519. I never had been inside of the municipal palace. The building was made of granite, stone, and marble; it looked a little old, but solid and beautiful. The office of Dr. Espinosa was on the second floor; to get there I had to climb very wide marble stairs. When I was coming up the stairs, I saw, going down, Prime Minister Miro Cardona who was talking with two or three guys. When I saw him, I said silently, *Idiot, your idea of a law against the private university students made no sense.* I just looked at him, and then followed my way, looking for the office of the treasurer.

"Finally, I found it. The receptionist told me to sit down while she announced me to the director. Dr. Espinosa immediately called me in and, after greetings, he told me that he had a job for me in City Hall. The job was in the Department of Education of the Municipality of Havana and the title was sub-director—that means second in command of the department. The doctor told me that the municipality before the revolution had a quite good school system, but one that was limited in resources. Now the revolution had plans to expand the number of schools to the rate of opening a new school every two months for next the two years. The department also administered the municipal library and had under construction a vocational school of arts and trade. The project was planned to have thirty schools with an average of five hundred students per school. The number of students attending these schools would probably exceed fifteen thousand and the department would employ nearly a thousand people, between teachers and administrative personnel.

"The director of the department was Dr. Azela De los Santos, who had been the Minister of Education of the *26 of Julio* in the mountain range of Sierra Cristal, where Raúl Castro was in command. Dr. Espinosa told me that she would take care of the academic matters and the new position of sub-director would be in charge of all the administration of the department."

He would have to prepare new budgets; modernize the administrative and record keeping functions; and review and negotiate new contracts for the purchase of furniture and equipment, scholastic materials, and food supplies (the schools served breakfast and lunch to all the students). He would also approve all payments and coordinate the opening schedule of the new schools with the Public Constructions Department, in charge of the construction of the school buildings. The new sub-director would be responsible for the larger municipal budget and would work along with the other six directors of departments and the mayor of Havana. This group in fact was running City Hall. After the triumph of the revolution, the municipal councils were temporarily dissolved until future elections, as it was said and hoped. The mayor and the directors revolutionarily exercised the executive authority and legislative functions of the municipality. The same model was applied to all municipalities of the island.

"When I heard the proposal, which seemed to be really fascinating, apparently the doctor noticed a certain expression of astonishment in my face. He said, 'Alex, I know you well from being your teacher and I saw what you did and are doing in the university and your performance in the bank. The position requires, first, total honesty and a revolutionary spirit of sacrifice. You are the person the revolution needs for this position. I have the conviction that you can carry it out. I already spoke about you with Llanusa and Azela and they are waiting for you.'

"The words of my teacher and mentor gave me a lot of confidence and I felt motivated to take the next step—to speak with the mayor of Havana, Pepe Llanusa," Alex said. The mayor was the son of the Dr. Llanusa who had been Alex's teacher at the university. Llanusa had expended almost all the struggle against Batista in Miami raising funds and gathering supplies that were sent to the rebels in Cuba. Alex had known him very superficially during the time he spent in Miami. Like Alex, Llanusa was a civilian who worked in the resistance. "For those reasons I didn't feel very intimidated with his presence," Alex said. "However, I was very impressed when I met Dr. De los Santos. I didn't know personally any person so close to the Castro brothers who had been in the mountain range during the war against Batista. She was an intimate friend and college classmate of Vilma Espin, the wife of Raúl Castro, and was the sister of the rebel Comandante Rene De los Santos, who fought alongside Raúl in the mountain range of Sierra Cristal."

Dr. Espinosa went with Alex to the office of the mayor, who received them in a very friendly way. He didn't remember Alex from Miami, but he said that his father had spoken to him about Alex. After a short conversation, he called Azela and told her that Alex was with him and waiting for her. Llanusa was a young man of about thirty-five years; he was very tall, at least six feet, five inches. "Do you remember Henry, he played basketball in the University of Havana during his college years?" Alex asked me. I said that I did, and he nodded as if I now knew what the mayor looked like. Then he continued with his story. Dr. De los Santos was a tall woman with a very pretty face; she was pregnant with her first baby. She also appeared to be in her thirties. They both were extremely amiable as they talked with Alex about the department's program and the urgency to prepare the budgets and to reorganize the administrative functions. Suddenly they said, "Good. Tomorrow morning you begin to work with us."

"That was the way that things were done at the beginning of the revolution," Alex said, shrugging expressively. "It was a revolutionary call, and you had to comply with the order."

Alex went home and told his family about his new job, and was surprised when his father got very upset. He said Alex was the first person in family history to get involved with a political job.

"It's not a political job," Alex told him. "It's a good, challenging job where I will have the opportunity to meet many people inside and outside the government circle and where I will acquire a lot of professional experience, working with many of my college teachers." Alex explained to his father that it was a civil service position in Havana's City Hall. The job was without any military implications, not like the one that his friends the De la Guardia twins, Tony and Patricio, had taken in the new revolutionary armed forces. Perhaps his father got a little more comfortable when Alex promised him that he would always continue his college education. "I did it, because I continued attending the university night school until Castro's Socialist government in April 1961 permanently closed it," Alex said.

"I am telling you this story, *mi hermano,* so you understand me. I was feeling so motivated, the same as all professionals and college professors were. They all gave themselves to the revolution with the honest idea to save Cuba from the moral misery of the corrupted governments of the past. The situation was the opportunity we all were looking for, to build a new Cuba, like once Jose Martí described: 'With all the people and for all the people.' I almost didn't care about the good salary that I was making, nor the car with driver they gave me. These material rewards were secondary to the pleasure of serving the community and the revolution."

After a brief pause, Alex continued his narration. "The work, as you could imagine, was very intense. I had two secretaries, one in the office and another who accompanied me outside the office when I went to visit schools and for meetings with suppliers. I always had a lawyer from the department helping me. Administrative honesty was the norm during the temporary revolutionary government. I was very careful and always was accompanied by another person when I was discussing contracts with companies or people that we were doing business with; my dealings were always clear and transparent."

On the other hand, Alex reminded me of what had happened in the year 1959 in Cuba. The economy grew at a very brisk pace. The companies and the workers cooperated with the revolution with great donations of resources and working hours. In summary, the nation began to wake up after the nightmares and tribulations of the dictatorship. However, the people were watching and criticizing the executions of hundreds of people who the authorities of the Rebels Armed Forces identified as criminal supporters of Batista's regime. These executions took place after short criminal trials, called Revolutionary Trials, made in dark military quarters. Alex explained, "These events generated many doubts in our minds, but we had the hopes that perhaps these mistakes would be surpassed in the near future. On the other hand, the provisional government, of which I felt to be a small collaborator, didn't present any obstacles to the growing activities of industry and commerce, which bloomed by the febrile economic activity in benefit of all the citizens. We also saw through our work that the economic progress of the country fomented a better distribution of social justice in sectors of the society previously marginalized.

Alex reflected, "Perhaps we were so involved in our work that for awhile we didn't face the reality. That was that Castro wanted to gain absolute control of the country with the intention to betray the true objectives of the revolution. Castro hid his sinister intentions to us, in order to create a totalitarian Socialist system on the island of Cuba. You remember his famous words during the early days of 1959, 'Our revolution is as green as our palms trees'?"

I nodded and Alex continued his description of his life as a member of the revolutionary government. His department opened ten schools in a year; prepared the budgets; modernized the bookkeeping system; inventoried the warehouses; renegotiated all contracts with the providers; inventoried all properties and equipment of the department; and reorganized the administrative functions. Everything was running well and the teachers and administrators of the schools were satisfied in their jobs. The department enrolled five thousand new students in the schools; the majority of these students came from the national public schools system. Azela had her baby and was out of the office for two months. Two doctors in education who worked with Azela took care of the academic issues while she was on maternity leave. Azela and her assistants could dedicate all their time to scholastic matters while Alex was in charge of the administration; they coordinated their activities quite well. "My work offered a great satisfaction to me," Alex said. "I was very happy to serve the community and at the same time, I saw my progress and professional development at a very early age."

However, something was happening. Alex noticed that, very quietly throughout the year, little by little, most of the departments' directors resigned. The first one was Dr. Espinosa; later the architect from Public Works followed the one from the Cultural Department. "All came to me to say good-bye and discreetly let me know about their frustrations with the Cuban Revolution; nobody complained about the mayor," Alex said. "They all had a great affection and respect for Llanusa. The problem was what was going on on the island. The City of Havana, the largest on the island, was running well in a corporate style. I only listened to their frustrations, but I didn't comment on my own doubts. I only told them I was going to miss them and I wished them luck, but I was a little scared." The only two directors who didn't resign were Azela and the rebel captain Dr. Machado Ventura from the Department of Health. Machadito, as everybody called him, was a reserved man who spoke very little. Years later he got to be the ideological head of the Cuban Communist Party, third secretary of the party, and second vice president of the council of state.

The exodus of coworkers and friends, all supporters of the revolution in the past, made Alex reflect a little more about what was happening in Cuba. He said, "I discovered the Communist infiltration in the Revolutionary Armed Force (FAR), the Ministry of Justice, and the labor unions. Then, I decided to read about Socialism and Communist ideology, to be able to understand what was happening." He acquired a series of books translated to Spanish, published by the Soviet Union to explain the origins and the utopia of Socialist thought. He read *Das Capital* by Karl Marx and the *Communist Manifesto* of Marx and Engel. "This one I read three times to be sure of its meaning," he said. "After having a much clearer idea of what Socialism and Communism were, I realized what was being developed in Cuba. *Fidel Castro was betraying the revolution.* However, Havana City Hall had not been seriously infiltrated by Socialist influences. Llanusa, the mayor, never seemed to me to be a Communist. Nevertheless, I could identify two or three Communist administrators in the schools and I realized that Azela and her two doctors assistants were also of Socialist ideas.

"I felt sad and disappointed because the revolution was becoming Communist. The economic growth and the improvement of the standard of living of the population gained in 1959 were losing their impetus."

Then Alex reminded me that President Urrutia and the members of the provisional cabinet left the government in April of 1960.

"I felt uncomfortable working with the government," he said. A little bit later the Revolutionary Militia began to be organized. Nobody understood what the militia was. What was the purpose of this new organization? What was its function? Was it military or for civil works? At the same time, Castro was drifting apart from the United States and approaching the Soviet Union. Anasta Mikoyan, Deputy Premier of the Soviet Union, visited Cuba in February of 1960 and signed a commercial deal with Castro. During his visit, he placed a floral offering at the statue of Jose Martí and a group of anti-Communist college students removed it. The government reacted violently and detained some of them. A few days later, three of them were executed by a firing squad in the Cabaña Fort.

"I knew Tapia Ruano, called Tapita, who was one of them," Alex said. "These young men were innocent—never committed any crime—but the revolution murdered them. I didn't believe in the revolution anymore and wanted to resign my position.

"My problem was how to resign without being labeled as a counter-revolutionary. I felt that I had the responsibility to fight against the Communist revolution that had betrayed us, but it was not wise to resign; there was the possibly that I would be imprisoned, or I'd have to flee to a foreign embassy and request political asylum, as many people whom I knew did. Finally, after several months, an idea came to my mind. I spent two or three months preparing it, looking for the opportunity."

"What was it?" I asked, thinking that at last I might find the secret to my friend's mysterious invitation.

"In the month of July of 1960, we had already almost finished, ahead of time, the program of construction of new schools and there weren't talks to continue the expansion. There, I saw my opportunity. I told Azela that my work was nearly completed and that I would like to go to work in the Ministry of Finance. It was in reorganization with a new Minister. I suggested a substitute for me in Azela's department. He was a school administrator who was a member of the Communist Party. She then sent me to speak with Llanusa. I told the mayor the same story and I asked his help to get me in the Ministry of Finance. Apparently, my arguments were very convincing, because Llanusa called the new Minister, Diaz, and said that I wanted to see him because I was very interested to work with him. Minister Diaz gave me an appointment to see him in two weeks, on a Thursday at 10:30 in the morning. He told me that he had an open position in the corporate tax department. That same week I resigned my position in City Hall."

Alex laughed. "I never took the position from the Ministry of Finance and in order to cover up my decision, I invented a new excuse: *'For the benefit of the revolution I must concentrate my energies and complete my college education and perhaps enter the Revolutionary Militia.'*"

I asked, "Well, what did you do after leaving your job in City Hall?"

Alex thought for a moment and told me, "Well, I dedicated myself to my college studies and again to conspire, now against the Communist government, what I am still doing until Cuba is free and democratic. I never again worked in Cuba after I left the City Hall job."

"How you were able to leave Cuba?" I asked. I knew how difficult it had been even in the early years of Castro's rule. "I left when my uncle in Miami sent us the visa 'waiver' so I went with my family in December 1960 to Miami."

Alex looked at me and said, "*Mi hermano,* my case was a little more complicated. A few months after the Playa Girón invasion in 1961, I was able to have a secret meeting with CIA agents in Havana. They told me that I couldn't enter the United States, because I had been a member of *26 de Julio* and according to their record, I was an enemy of the United States with my Communist ideas, even though I was out of the government. At that time, I saw that many of my clandestine friends detained and put in prison. I realized that my clandestine activities were less and less effective and meaningful inside the island." After a pause, Alex said, "Honestly, and against my better desires, I decided to leave Cuba before spending the rest of my life in prison or getting killed by a firing squad.

"However, I found myself in a dilemma. I could leave illegally in a small boat to the United States—that probably was easy, but I feared that the U.S. authorities would send me back to Cuba. Then where I could go? I reached the conclusion that there was nowhere, and as I told you before, I never liked the idea of going to an embassy to ask for political asylum, because I didn't trust the diplomats. The only solution I had was to leave illegally, but with a legal appearance.

"For this purpose, I made contact with a young Spanish sailor who came with the crew of the Spanish boat *Marques de Comilla.* This young sailor in fact was fleeing from Spain because he was against General Franco, the Spanish strong man. When he arrived in Cuba, he didn't want to return to Spain. I bought his passport and working papers as member of the crew working on the boats of the Spanish shipping company the *Trasatlantica Española,* which operated the boats. I used these documents to embark as a crewmember of the Spanish ship called *Virginia de Churruca,* which was returning to Spain."

Alex laughed again. "I never thought to go to Spain. That would mean ending up in a Spanish jail. The boat made several stops to load coffee along its way to Spain. The first stop was in Puerto Limon, Costa Rica, and later we stopped in Cartagena, Colombia. When the boat docked thirteen days later in the port of La Guaira in Venezuela, I disembarked and requested political asylum as a Cuban citizen fleeing from Communist repression. At that time, the president of Venezuela was Don Rómulo Betancourt, the great democrat and anti-Communist. He was an enemy of Castro and a good friend of the Cubans' cause."

Alex told me how he had lived for a year in Venezuela and finally, after many interviews and conversations, he was able to clarify his situation with the Embassy of the United States in Venezuela. Finally, by the end of the year 1962, they gave him a visa to travel to the United States.

He said, "*Mi hermano,* my exit from Cuba was not easy. However, with my desire to live in freedom and with the help of God, I finally made it. Nevertheless, here I am, as always, fighting for the freedom of the oppressed Cuban people."

—Very well Rodriguez, said Jones, your friend really had the ability to survive and elude the early Castro's repression moves. However, I don't see the connection with your situation, those events had happened long time ago.

—Be patience Mr. Jones, said Rodriguez.

CHAPTER 9

▼

THE PROPOSAL AND THE PLANS FOR THE FUTURE

Alex invited me for dinner that night at his apartment in the elegant residential area of the El Condado, on the outskirts of San Juan. I took a taxi for the fifteen-minute ride from my hotel. The taxi driver charged me eight fifty and I gave him a ten-dollar bill and told him to keep the change.

The apartment building had seven floors and Alex's apartment was on the last floor. At the front door of the building, I found the doorman, uniformed with a white suit and a cap that seemed like the one worn by an admiral of the English fleet. I told him that my name was Henry González and that I was coming to visit the gentleman in the penthouse. The elegant porter got the telephone and made a call to announce my arrival; later he led me to the door of the elevator and he himself pushed the button of the seventh floor and told me to have a good time with my friend.

*   *   *   *

"Wait a minute, Rodriguez," said Peter Jones as the words broke the spell of the story Rodriguez was weaving around the state department official. "Why did you use the name Henry Gonzalez?"

Rodriguez smiled gently and said, "Well, that is my real name, Mr. Jones. You could call me Henry from now on that is what everybody usually calls me. Please allow me to continue my story."

Jones frowned, contracting his eyebrows darkly, but he waved a hand and said, "Go ahead, Mr. Gonzalez." So, Henry continued his tale.

*   *   *   *

Alex was waiting at the door of the elevator to welcome me. The first thing he did was to take me around the apartment for a small tour of his gorgeous place with its great view of the sea and El Condado. After the tour he said, "Now I am going to introduce you to Doña Josefa, who is preparing tonight her specialty for us, black rice with seafood, thanks to Yolandita who lent us her tonight. I asked you to come early so I could talk to you before Yolandita and Ernesto come to join us later for supper."

We entered the modern kitchen and met Doña Josefa. She was a woman of an average height and physical constitution with gray hair carefully piled up in a bun. Alex introduced her as his aunt, Doña Josefa, "the best looking female that has come from the Iberian Peninsula."

She smiled. "This Alex and his flattering remarks!"

Doña Josefa probably was seventy years old, but she was moving around as if she were fifty. She had a joyful expression on her face and spoke to us in her acute Castilian accent in a tender, but at the same time authoritarian way, as usually do mothers to their children.

Alex asked her how the *paella* was coming along. Doña Josefa told him that she wasn't cooking *paella*, that she was preparing black rice with seafood. Then she opened the kitchen door and told us that she would call when dinner was ready and said that we could take the *croqueticas de jamón* that she prepared for us.

Alex playfully said to me, "From better places I have been thrown out; let's go to the terrace to have a drink."

We then went to sit on the terrace, enjoying the soft marine breeze and the blue sky adorned by a few white clouds that seemed made of cotton, and we began to eat the *croqueticas* of Doña Josefa and to drink the *mentiritas* that Alex had prepared. The friendly atmosphere gave me the opportunity to ask Alex what had been in my mind for a while.

"Why did you ask me to come to San Juan, Alex? What did Ernesto mean, 'with the business?'"

Alex gave me a long, hard look before saying, "Yes, *mi hermano,* I believe that we must talk of that now." He then continued. "Since I resigned my position in the revolutionary government in 1960, I have dedicated a great portion of my life to the fight against the Communist dictator and his collaborators that ruthlessly have destroyed the Island of Cuba. During the struggle, we have used many methods, some violent and others non-violent. We have used international diplomacy and even the Pope has intervened. We have countries that are allies and others that are enemies. We have received help from some nations, the treason of others, and the apathy of many. All these have contributed to form us in the fight and to give us the experience that today we have."

After a brief pause, he continued. "Castro has tied up the future of Cuba with the international Communist movement. The bloc of Socialist countries always has maintained the economy of the island artificially. The failure of the Communist ideas and the disappearance of the Socialist bloc have had great moral and economic meaning in Castro's plans to perpetuate his power and his Socialist ideas in Cuba. Castro has lost some power and prestige, and from been called *el Caballo,* now he is called *el Penco Senil.* His health has led him to delegate provisionally all the powers to his brother Raúl. Of course, he remains in the background backing Raúl's authority among all other heirs. But, the people are tired of the *Fidelísimo* and the *Raulismo* political and economic systems. The lies that they have repeated for so many years, nobody believes. The myths of the great education and health service are vanishing. The differences between the life full of deprivations and necessities for the Cuban people and the ways that the foreign tourists live, with all types of comforts and abundance of food, is corroding the nationalistic fiber of the Cuban society.

"Still more, the differences between white and black Cubans are something noticeable. The black Cubans aren't working in tourism and great majority don't receive the dollar *remesas* of economic aid from their relatives outside Cuba, like the Cubans of the white race. Castro promised that the revolution would eliminate privileges and social classes and now the people see that the differences of classes on the island is more visible than before the revolution. On the other hand, the youth would like to have a better future than the one than the revolution is offering; they can see the misery where their parents have raised them. This makes them to think that while the *revolución* stays in power, they won't have the opportunity to improve their living conditions and won't have a future.

"The only alternative is to leave the country legally or illegally in a boat, which is very dangerous. In order to leave Cuba legally, first the Cuban has to win the so-called 'lottery' from the 'big drum' to obtain the U.S. visa. Every year more than a half million Cubans apply to the lottery for twenty thousand U.S. visas. Those that win have to pay two thousand dollars for the expenses that the Cuban government has imposed. You have to remember that the average wage in Cuba is ten to fifteen dollars per month. The first requirement, if you win the lottery for the visa, is to resign to your job. That means that the money to pay for your visa must come from relatives or friends abroad. So to leave Cuba legally is very expensive and difficult. The people are desperate, particularly the youth."

On the other hand, Alex explained, "The international community has arrived at the conviction of the necessity of a free Cuba. The European countries finally have reached the conclusion that Castro's regime has betrayed its people and it has condemned them to misery due to the economic failure of the Communist system. In order to condemn the repressive wave of the spring of 2003, European intellectuals and political leaders created the International Committee for the Democracy of Cuba. The committee supports initiatives to promote the respect of human rights in Cuba and tries to create a common approach in Western Europe toward the Cuban problem. Another significant change took place when the European Commission decided to postpone indefinitely the request of Cuba to participate in the Cotonou Agreement, the agreement of preferential commercial treatment. We can see that the European countries are implementing measured pressing for a change of regime on the island."

Alex explained that, like the European allies, the United States is ratifying its support to increasing civil liberties in Cuba and the development of a free society that would make Cuba a participating asset to the Latin American community. Paralleling the decisions taken by the European countries, the United States created a Commission for Aid to a Free Cuba. For the first time, the positions of the European countries and the one of the United States are very reconcilable. Both agree that Castro brothers, either *Fidelísmo* or *Raulismo,* are enemies of democracy and the economic progress of the region.

During Alex's exposition, I silently listened to him and occasionally sipped my drink of *mentirita*. His arguments seemed to be very convincing and interesting.

He concluded, "I think that we could say that we are at the end of our long struggle for the freedom of Cuba. However, there are still dangers and obstacles that I will mention later. However, this is the opportunity that we were waiting and have worked toward for a long time. Our plan isn't warlike; we do not need arms or training camps. *What we need to succeed in our quest is a little bit of money, a few volunteers, and the will of God.* The last one, I believe we have, because we trust him; the Cuban people are ready for the change. The money is the most difficult part, but we would manage to raise it."

Alex told me that later he would disclose more details of the plan. First, he told me a story that he heard from a German who was in Berlin in 1989, when the misery and desperation of the Berliners got to the point where the only solution was a radical change or to live life on the brink of madness. In the same way, that it is happening now to the people on the island of Cuba.

A civil movement initiated by a small group of brave citizens took place in Berlin; they went out and stood in front of their respective homes, challenging the Soviets. The people stayed a short distance from their homes, always watching the movements of the police and soldiers so, if they saw them coming, the only thing they had to do was to return to their homes to avoid violence. When the police left, the people would go out again. Neighbors were spreading the strategy and gaining confidence that continued growing as more people went out, up to the point where the city became paralyzed. The people got bold after sensing their success, and in a few hours all arrived at the Wall, where the border patrols didn't know what to do, so the repressive forces didn't do anything. The story ended when the first person, a woman, walked away freely towards West Berlin. When she was free across the Wall, she said, "*I am not a prisoner anymore.*" With only empty hands and a deep desire for freedom, the Berliners decided to challenge the infamy of the Soviet regime.

Alex believed something similar could happen in Cuba. "When the Cuban people realize that they are millions against a handful of traitors at the service of Castro's regime, the people will decide to take the streets." He said civil disobedience already existed in the island and was part of daily life. The so-call *jineterismo* on the island was just the reflection of civil disobedience—the corruption and theft in companies run by the government, and all the petty immoralities used by the Cuban people to survive the misery of life in Cuba and the abuses of power of the state.

Then, Alex said, "However, *mi hermano,* how are we going to mobilize the people so something like this could happen?"

He answered himself. "Our work is to take these concepts to the Cuban people and to help them to lose fear of the state. The Cuban people want to return to democracy and capitalism, to the *Cubanidad,* you could say. They see it from the capitalist countries from where the tourists privileged with dollars and euros come. I believe the time is ripe for a change."

He said the first steps were already being taken, adding, "But I won't tell you more about this plan until I explain what we want you do and you accept the mission. I am doing this for your own benefit so that you won't commit yourself before hearing my proposition."

I asked, "Which group are you representing?"

"Very good question, brother. Our group does not have anything to do with any exile organization or with the CIA. It doesn't belong to the Left or to the Christian democracy and we don't have anything to do with the *Batistianos* or to any group of the so-called extreme Right. Mainly, intellectuals, professionals, and businessmen in exile compose the group. In Cuba, we are working with students, workers, honest members of the armed forces, and humble people in the cities and in the countryside.

"If you want to mention the common denominator of the group, you could say that it is made by Cubans who are not in agreement with Socialist ideas, nor Communist, nor Fascist, and that we don't believe in the approach of engaging in a dialogue with the tyrant. What we want for Cuba is a democratic republic with a liberal political system and private enterprise and market economy as the economic system. Most of us outside of the island don't have the interest to hold any official position in the future government of Cuba. What we would like is to be part of the constitutional process. Cuba needs a new constitution prepared by a constitutional assembly with the participation of all Cubans. The contribution of Cubans outside the island in this process is fundamental. You have to remember that the Cubans living on the island have been educated in a totalitarian system that has kept them marginalized and in ignorance of what citizen's rights are. They don't know how to protect themselves against the abuses of the state. A new constitution is the essential requirement of the new republic as it re-enters the civilized world. The new constitution unconditionally shall grant freedom to the Cuban people under a multi-party system to elect their government officials in free elections. The Cuban people wish to live under a state of laws where all citizens can enjoy and express without fear within a climate of economic prosperity. The new constitution would limit the powers of the state and would affirm the principles of individual liberties and right to private property."

I said, "Alex, I have so many questions to ask you that I am going to leave them aside for the moment. First I would like to know what you think are the main problems that the new republic would have to solve. How would your group solve the problem of the confiscated industries and businesses?"

"On that issue we have thought that the goal of the new republic is to foment a society where each citizen benefits and enjoys in fullness the fruit of his own destiny protected under a state of law. In this case, we don't have any other alternative than to recognize without hesitation that private property must be the cornerstone of the system where all Cubans could enjoy without restrictions their human liberties within a climate of economic prosperity and justice. Based on this concept, the new republic shall have to recognize that the Socialist government committed an illegal act when it seized, without paying compensation, all the private business on the island. Individuals, domestic and foreign corporations, all of them, as legitimate property owners, must have the right of ownership of these illegally confiscated businesses.

He explained that the infrastructure, physical and managerial, of the industries and businesses on the island were in very poor shape and needed to be modernized in order to operate in more efficient and competitive conditions. This would require the investment of great sums of money, which the Cuban people don't have. "The country is totally ruined and undercapitalized by the disastrous Socialist economic system and the embezzlement of large amounts of hard currencies deposited in government officials' personal banks accounts abroad," he explained. "We reached the conclusion that capital for the island would have to come from abroad."

A privatization program could be combined with the efforts of recapitalization of the private enterprises. Each business would prepare a budget program of renovation and modernization. This would include a working plan and the schedule for its implementation. The legal owners would have a reasonable time to implement the plan and would have the responsibility to raise the required funds. The original, lawful owners would have the option to implement the plan and to operate the enterprise; in the case that they were not interested in continuing the business, the companies could be sold in auctions so individuals or corporations interested in investing the required capital for the renovations could acquire them. The buyer would pay the auction price to the state, which would then pay to the legal owner compensation in cash and government bonds for the equivalent to the value of the company in 1960. The residual funds, after compensating the legal owners, would be utilized to amortize the legal external debt of the nation.

I asked, "What would be done with the confiscated residential houses?"

Alex explained that respect for private property was the indispensable cornerstone to reach justice and well-being for the citizens within a society that wishes to enjoy human liberties. The people who live in houses that were confiscated from their legal owners without compensation would not be evicted; the current occupants were paying rent to the state. The state had created legal limitations that impair the occupants' rights in the exercise of the property ownership, like the freedom to sell, rent, remodel, destroy, and reconstruct the property. In reality the revolutionary government has maintained control of the properties and never has completed the transfer of the properties to the occupants, although it has always told them that they were the owners.

"Legally, in a state of laws, these houses belong to legitimate owners," Alex said. "The revolutionary government took the possession of them, illegally, under coercion, and without paying compensation to its legal owners. Fairly and reasonably enough, the people who live in these houses should continue living in them and paying rent to the legitimate owners, with the option to buy the houses if they have the desire. On the other hand, the legitimate owners would have the obligation and the responsibility to maintain and remodel the properties. Therefore, if the owners invest in the remodeling of the properties, it would be reasonable if the rent of these properties increased proportionally."

Ticking the items off on his fingers, Alex said, "These measures would provide manifold benefits to the country. First, the occupants of the houses continue living in their houses and have the options to rent them or to buy them. Second, the properties are given back to their legitimate legal owners. Third, the program provides incentives for the owners to maintain the houses in good conditions; fourth, the quality of life of the population would improve because they would live in better houses; and fifth, the concept of private property and the state of laws would be certainly confirmed. Of course, these measurements would not apply to properties used by prominent members of the regime, collaborators, and leaders of the Socialist government."

Alex said the same principles would apply to Castro's so-called agrarian reform with its inefficiencies, errors, and injustices, which brought food shortages and misery to the island. The new republic would have to recognize the legality of private property and denounce the abuses committed by the Socialist government. The only variant on this subject would be the cooperatives. In this case it would be reasonable to leave the farmers who have been working the lands as partners of the legal owners of the farms The owners would have to make capital investments to modernize the agricultural equipment and the houses of the workers, stimulating investments on the island. The farmers as well as the owners would have a voice in choosing the administrators, the gains would be proportionally distributed according to the work, and capital investments made. The cooperatives would work independently, without government intervention. Their common interest would be to run the cooperative efficiently and profitably; all would win if harmony existed and all would lose if they couldn't do it.

I took the opportunity to ask Alex about the future of the foreign investments made on the island during the Socialist regime. Alex said that the foreign investments on the island would be respected, except those made to purchase confiscated companies, taken without compensation by the revolutionary government. These would have to be treated like all confiscated companies. "What I mean," Alex said, "is that these non-scrupulous foreign investors could probably lose their investments because they were made to buy stolen properties."

In the case of foreign investors that concurred in the practice of labor exploitation Alex said, "I think they would have to compensate the workers for the difference between fair wages and the wages of misery that they paid. In the case that the foreign companies refused to do it, the government would have the right to auction the companies, to pay the compensation money to the workers, with any surplus balance left to be given back to the foreign company. These companies would be prohibited from investing in Cuba for a period of ten years."

Alex sat back in his chair and stretched as if a long, difficult task had been completed. "Well, these are some of our political and economic ideas for a new Cuba after the nightmare of Castro's Socialism," he said. "The people, particularly the youth, don't want any more Socialism; it has led the country to economic ruin and has deprived them of their individual liberties. The revolution has been a failure. It wasn't possible to improve the well-being of the citizens by implementing a dictatorship. It wasn't possible to feed the people and to offer them a successful economic system by transferring the ownership and control of the economy to the state. It wasn't possible to give the people a free health and education systems by paying wages of ten dollars per month. It wasn't possible to promise social justice to the people by taking away their freedom in return. These truths, my brother, are the most powerful arms that we have against Castro's regime."

Alex paused. He glanced at me. "Do you understand what I have said or does it sound to you like a mermaid's mythical song?"

I didn't know how to respond him. All I could say was, "Well, it sounds very interesting."

Alex grinned at my confusion. "I understand, my brother, that what I just told you isn't easy to assimilate. You need some meditation. I haven't even mentioned the details of the operation and your mission in the struggle for the liberation of Cuba from the claws of Castro's Socialism."

Alex continued, "Later I will give you more details of the operation, but your mission is to raise money in the northeast of the United States. You would have to pay for your own expenses—everybody in our organization does it. We send all the gathered money to Cuba to cover direct expenses related to the shipment of goods and to finance the activities of the people within the island. In our group, bureaucracy and titles don't exist; we all have our functions, and each person is responsible for its obligations. What unites us is a deep love for Cuba and our conviction that freedom is the hope of all human beings, because God gave it to us at creation."

Now, Alex had really put the ball in my court. Again, there was a prolonged silence as if he was waiting for my reply. This time the only thing that came to my mind was to ask him, after taking a sip of my *mentirita,* if Ernesto was doing that type of work in the group. Alex replied, with a quite dry tone, that more or less that was Ernesto's job, among other things. However, I realized that he didn't want to go any deeper on the subject. After this dry and sharp response, I didn't know how to continue the conversation.

Fortunately, the doorbell rang. Alex stood up and said, "I believe that Yolandita and Ernesto are here," and he went to open the door for them.

Indeed, they were at the door. I was relieved and took another sip from my *mentirita* as I said to myself, *well, at least for the moment the bell saved me.* This interruption would give me the opportunity to prepare my questions and arguments before committing myself to such complicated and dangerous task. Nevertheless, I knew that I had to make a decision and give an answer to Alex soon. But I had so many doubts in my mind.

Soon, Alex entered the terrace accompanied by Yolandita and Ernesto. He introduced me to Yolandita, who had a very pretty face. She was not very tall, and she seemed to be five to seven years younger than I knew she was. When she spoke to me and smiled, I realized her affability. It seemed like she had known me for a long time. I greeted Ernesto, who asked me, as a joke, if Alex was treating me well. I responded that I already was into my second *mentirita* and that we had eaten the *croqueticas* made by Doña Josefa.

Alex offered a drink to Yolandita, who said, "Thank you, Alex, but I had better go see Doña Josefa in the kitchen to see how the cooking is going."

Ernesto served himself a *mentirita,* seated himself next to me, and lit a cigarette.

Without much hesitation, Ernesto asked Alex if we had spoken about the business. Alex said yes, but told him that we hadn't discussed the details and that we hadn't arrived yet at any conclusion.

Ernesto said, "Think about it. I will be always available to help you in everything that I can."

Alex very calmly said that the decision was mine, but that he understood that I might need a little more time to make up my mind. "The mission is very important, the job is very difficult, but the satisfaction of having fulfilled a duty is greater that everything else," he said. No sooner had his words fallen from his lips than Yolandita entered the terrace with the good news. Dinner was ready!

CHAPTER 10

WAS ALEX A TERRORIST?

Peter Jones leaned forward, at last they seemed to be getting to the heart of the story. "Well, Henry, your friend made you a proposition. Did you finally accept?" Jones asked.

Henry didn't answer directly, but he told Jones that he had many doubts about his friend Alex's activities.

"Mr. Jones, let me continue my story. It will explain my doubts and concerns about Alex's involvement in violent activities during the early struggle against Castro's regime."

*   *   *   *

I came back to my cabana with a full belly and a joyful heart. The black rice with seafood was delicious; it was no doubt that Doña Josefa cooked very well. During the supper, we spoke of the tasty and hearty dishes from Spanish and Italian cuisines. I believe that I had gained some weight since I arrived in San Juan; the food had been plentiful and excellent, first Oriental style and tonight the Spanish banquet. While we were enjoying our meal, we all had a wonderful time telling and listening to stories of our youth in the Cuba of yesterday (BC, Before Castro).

Well, thanks to the aftermath of the sumptuous eating and the good wine, I forgot for the night my commitment to give Alex a reply to his proposal and simply went to sleep a few minutes after I got back to the cabana; it was close to midnight.

Around six o'clock in the morning, when the tropical sun began to come out on the horizon of the Caribbean Sea, I woke up and immediately it came to my mind that today I would have to talk to Alex about his proposal. Things weren't as simple as to say that I accepted his proposal or that I didn't want to or couldn't do it. The reason for my indecision wasn't that I didn't go along with the noble cause of helping the Cuban people to free themselves from their miseries and sufferings. I had always been against the Communist dictator and his Socialist system. I knew that I could fulfill the mission Alex proposed. I had extensive contacts with many Cubans of comfortable economic position who were full of desire to see a change in Cuba. In addition, I knew many Cubans in New York, New Jersey, Washington, and Virginia that had relatives in Cuba and were sending money to them every month. I could not continue sleeping and I decided to prepare myself for the meeting with Alex.

In fact, I had not been completely sincere and honest with Alex. In our conversations, he had mentioned his friend Armandito, the one that liked to paint rustic landscapes, who was arrested with him in 1956 by the guards of Salas Canizarez, the chief of the National Police Force. Alex didn't mention his name again, but I knew that Alex and Armandito were comrades in arms during the warlike resistance underground against the revolutionary government of Castro during the years 1960 and 1961. I knew Armandito and had spoken with him a couple of months before he died in exile as a consequence of the bad treatment he had received in Castro's prisons over his sixteen years of imprisonment. Armandito had a great affection for Alex and he always spoke of him with great admiration. When he learned that I was a good friend of Alex, one day he told me some of the stories of the dangerous urban guerrilla warfare in which both participated during the clandestine fight in Cuba.

I had always thought that some of these actions might be considered as terrorist acts. If they weren't, they were very close to being so. *Was my friend Alex a terrorist?* I asked myself.

The story that impressed me most was when Armandito and Alex, together with two other men and one young girl, went in April 1961 to pick up a truck with two tons of explosives and weapons. The action took place only a few days before the Playa Girón invasion. The truck was loaded with high-power explosives with detonators, hand grenades, bazookas with projectiles, machine guns, and ammunition. The vehicle was parked in a street in Miramar, a residential area of Marianao, close to the shore. The lethal cargo had been dropped in the shallow waters of the coast by high-speed boats that came from abroad to support the clandestine resistance. How had the truck gotten there? Armandito never mentioned the detail to me, nor did I ask him. The beige truck didn't have any identification or logo; an olive green canvas covered the deadly cargo load.

Armandito told me that one guy and the girl stayed with him in the car parked a block away from the truck, while Alex and a young skinny fellow named Nelson went to get the truck. First, they looked at the cargo area and grabbed four hand grenades from an open box of grenades and then they got inside the truck. Since they didn't have the truck's key, they made an electrical bridge with the starter cables to start the engine. The young Nelson remained lying on the floor of the truck holding the hand grenades while Alex was driving. The grenades were their defensive weapons in case the security forces stopped them.

Armandito told me that they followed the truck at a short distance; the girl was driving the car while he and the other guy were armed with two Browning .45 pistols for protection in case the government forces stopped them. Alex was driving the truck to a house located near the Villanueva University, in the residential district called Biltmore. On their way, the truck had to go through an area called Marianao Beach that had two traffic circles. When the truck was going to pass the first one, Armandito saw a column of five military trucks full of soldiers with machine guns approaching the circle from the left side, only a block away. Armandito told me that they thought that it was an ambush and instinctively they were prepared for the worst. However, the surprise was when they saw Alex calmly waving the first military truck of the column past and placing his truck at the end of the military convoy. He continued there for two or three miles until they got to the other traffic circle. When the trucks of the military column were taking their turn on the second circle, Alex took the first exit of the circle, leaving the convoy line. The military trucks continued their way in a different direction without noticing Alex's truck.

Then Alex continued for five or six more miles, followed by the escort car with Armandito and his companions. The truck stopped in front of the gate of a house fenced with a six-foot wall. Two young guys came from the house and opened the gate. The truck entered the driveway of the house, followed by the Armandito's car, and the two guys that opened quickly closed the heavy gates.

The events of the story made me think. Could we catalog these actions as terrorist activities? The truck was parked in a residential zone with many people and cars around. If that truck had exploded when Alex made the connection of the wires to start the engine, the explosion would have been awful, like a small *Cobra*. The cargo ship *Cobra*, loaded with armaments, had exploded accidentally in the port of Havana in 1960 and cost a great number of lives. Sure, this explosion wouldn't be of the same magnitude, but it could have destroyed a block of houses and caused the death of many innocent people walking on the street.

The story didn't finish there. Armandito told me that when he entered the patio of the house where the truck was parked, he saw Alex with a black beret like the one used by Che Guevara, and with a red handkerchief on his neck; he was disguised as a militiaman. Armandito told me that he asked Alex where he got them, and Alex smiled and replied that he had gotten them from his guardian angel. Suddenly it began to rain very hard and Alex said, "This is our opportunity to distribute these arms and explosives and get rid of this truck."

They put the weapons in several cars to take them to safe houses. These weapons were for the urban underground militia to support the awaited invasion from abroad. The explosives, composed of bricks of plastic with their detonators, were loaded in two cars. With these explosives, the urban resistance would maintain the hope of the people, reminding them of the struggle against the Communist revolution. Every night, the residents of Havana could hear twenty explosions or more. However, it was true that these never caused any injury or death; they only made a lot of noise.

I asked myself if these violent activities were terrorism. Were these nightly explosions detonated to intimidate the population? People used to confuse them with the famous "cannon shot of nine o'clock" and for that reason they looked at their watches in confusion.

These stories made me fearful to associate myself with people that might be involved in terrorist activities, despite the fact that their intention to release the Cuban people from the odious Communist dictatorship was good.

Due to my friendship and respect for Alex, I didn't dare to tell him my doubts when he made his proposal. Now had come the moment when I had to be sincere with Alex and reveal my doubts and my conversations with Armandito.

I waited until eight-thirty in the morning to call Alex. When I got him on the phone, first I thanked him for the delightful night and then I told him that I wanted to see him. Alex told me that he would come to my cabana around ten o'clock in the morning.

I had a light breakfast and I kept preparing myself for what I would say to my friend. He arrived at the cabana a few minutes after ten. We cordially greeted each other, and without any hesitation, I told him that I had met his friend Armandito and that we had spoken of the clandestine activities of the years 1960 and 1961. I excused myself to Alex for not mentioning it when he spoke to me about Armandito, and without any vacillation, I asked him, "Alex, do you consider that your clandestine activities during those years were terrorist?"

Alex looked at me and said that he had been waiting for my revelation. He told me that Armandito had told him a few days before his death that he had mentioned their past activities to me. Alex admitted that he had found it somewhat strange that I hadn't said anything of my friendship with Armandito when he and I had spoken of his old comrade. "I am glad that you told me about it, and this proves your honesty and our friendship," he said. "In reference to your question, I would define terrorism: It is said to be the succession of acts of violence executed to instill terror, a violent form of fighting meant to destroy the established order or create a climate of fear and insecurity, with the purpose of intimidating the adversaries or the population in general. And of course it is the domination of people through the employment of terror and fear."

He stopped for a moment and said, "I agree that certain of the acts committed during our clandestine activities were violent. However, they were not committed to instill terror within the population. The explosions of homemade bombs every night were a way to keep the people aware of the existence of an active popular dissident movement that wasn't in agreement with the way the Communist traitors had changed the revolution. The proof that they weren't meant to intimidate the population is that never were people hurt or killed. Those that handled these explosives were instructed, very clearly, never to place them inside iron tubes or with shrapnel. You remember that at that time, political parties didn't exist anymore and all the mass media was under the government control. The nightly explosions were the only source of information for the people, letting them know that the dissidence was fighting a desperate war for freedom because all the peaceful means had been exhausted. The freedom fighters' objective was to guide the nation toward a legal state of rights, and they didn't try to rule using terror as the revolutionary government was doing.

Additionally, he pointed out, "The freedom fighters never used weapons against the population. If our intentions were terrorist, probably it would have been more effective, for publicity, to detonate the entire load of the truck. Certainly, this would have given a powerful psychological blow, but it would have cost many innocent lives. We kept the weapons to support the invasion that all the people were waiting for. *Mi hermano*, I understand that a delicate line separates the violent acts executed and directed to instill terror and to intimidate innocent citizens, and other actions, also violent, which are committed with the objective of defending the rights and the freedom of the citizens against totalitarian governments. In all cases, the first do it to dominate the people with terror, while the last ones do violent acts to release the people from the terror and the domination of the first. The objective of the freedom fighters wasn't to do violent acts against the population, but against the dictators and their militia. I have never accepted the argument that freedom fighters are terrorists for the other political group. That, *mi hermano*, is a fallacy; *a terrorist is a terrorist because his objective is to intimidate the citizens in order to exercise dominion over them.* The *Mambises* that fought against the colonial Spanish Crown for the independence of the island were patriots, not terrorists."

Alex paused before continuing. "I mentioned yesterday that our plans are not warlike, nor do we need armaments. The primary target is to promote the development of Cuba's civil society. This movement is already underway; it is happening every day in the hearts and minds of the Cuban people that demand their citizens' rights and the power to decide their own future. The people want to finish with the system of state terrorism. The state directs the economy and education is the state indoctrination system. The state imposed an inadequate and unfair health system. The state is the only employer and controls the labor unions; the miserable level of wages paid to the workers is a state mandate. The state has established an apartheid system between Cubans and foreigners.

"We want to return respect for human rights. Our strategy is concentrated in helping the internal dissidence and supporting the sprouting of a civil society. This tactic will eventually promote civil disobedience of the citizenship in every corner of the island. When Cubans feel they are no longer prisoners of the state, they will see themselves as free people, no longer under the Socialist dictatorship. At that point, the regimes will self destruct from its own weight of contradictions and wickedness."

Alex's arguments were so clear and convincing that I didn't have any other choice but to apologize for having distrust and doubts about his activities in Cuba during the years 1960 and 1961. After his statement, I felt obliged to accept his proposition. Nevertheless, I still had my doubts and I didn't stop thinking about the idea of terrorist activity. I was trying to postpone my final decision. I felt that I couldn't say that I was not interested in his proposal, because in fact I considered that the cause was noble and good. I was convinced I could help the Cuban people in the struggle for freedom.

In the middle of my indecision, Alex said, *"Mi hermano*, what do you need to reach a decision?"

Again, I didn't know what to say. The only words that came to my mouth were to say that the idea and the cause were good, and that my conscience forced me to accept the proposition.

Then Alex told me, "I believe that your fear is to associate with a group that could have terrorist tendencies. I understand that. However, I consider that your contribution would be very important for our cause. For that reason, I am inviting you to come along with me on my next trip to Cuba to see for yourself what are we doing. Our group is fighting against state terrorism and it doesn't employ terrorist tactics."

I thought immediately that Alex had put again the ball in my court: *Touché.* Then I said, "Do you think that to go to Cuba is somewhat dangerous?"

Alex, with a smile, told me, "Well, we have a better security record than NASA does in its space flights." Then he added, "Our group sometimes does more than six trips to Cuba per month. We have an efficient network on the island, right under the noses of Castro's security system."

"But Alex, how are we going to do it!" I exclaimed.

He calmed me down, saying, "Don't worry; you don't have to make any arrangements. Next week, you will receive a telephone call from Alberto Federman inviting you to join him on a fishing trip in the Cayman Islands. A few days later he will mail you some advertising catalogs for electronic equipment, like screens and telecommunications systems, etc. He is a large electronics equipment distributor and usually he invites his clients on fishing trips on the high seas, departing from his home in Grand Cayman. Please accept the invitation and follow his instructions."

Alex ended by saying, "I must leave tonight on a trip, but I recommend you call Ernesto and speak to him. The advice of Ernesto could be useful in your mission. Don't initiate yet any activity related to your mission and don't speak with anybody about your impending trips to the Cayman Islands or to Cuba. If you must justify your absence to somebody, you could say that you are going to investigate the possibilities of a telecommunications equipment dealership with a distributor that has invited you to the Cayman Island for a presentation."

Alex rose from his chair and shook my hand, while at the same time saying, "Welcome to our group; you are fulfilling your call to duty. Be patient that everything will be fine, with the help of the Lord." And without saying anything else, he left the cabana.

I remained seated alone in my cabana for few minutes, thinking about my conversation with Alex until finally I felt the urgent need to call Ernesto for help. We agreed to get together that night at eight in the cabana. I also called Continental Airlines to confirm my return flight for the next afternoon. It was already close to noon and I decided to go to the beach to enjoy that tropical sun and the sea breeze that only can be found in the Caribbean Sea. My head was spinning and I felt very excited for the adventure that I was getting into, and at the same time, I felt that I was fulfilling my duty. Perhaps I needed the challenge. I was feeling rejuvenated and full of energy.

At eight o'clock Ernesto knocked at the door of the cabana. I offered him a drink and he said that a *mentirita* would be great. I had a bottle of rum and several cans of Diet Coke in the cabana, the perfect ingredients for preparing two *mentiritas*. While we were sipping our drinks, I told him that I had accepted Alex's proposal to work with them and that Alex recommended that I talk with him. I didn't mention anything about my trip to the Cayman Islands, and Ernesto, if he knew, didn't mention it to me. His advice on how to raise funds and to serve as conduit in the shipments of money sent by Cubans in the United States to their relatives on the island was invaluable. We spoke for two hours, but neither of us mentioned anything about my impending trips.

I was learning that sometimes you have to listen and keep quiet. Ernesto, with his great experience in all this type of activity, had been very discreet in what he told me about the operation. I thought that Ernesto didn't need to know that I was going to the Cayman Islands and Cuba. I thought that possibly Alex hadn't mentioned it to him. Perhaps, he only mentioned that I had accepted the mission and that I needed some help to perform it. I was proud of myself for my shrewd behavior in keeping a secret.

When Ernesto left, I kept thinking about everything that I had done in three days in Puerto Rico. Everything was very interesting and stimulating. It was a good trip. My next trip looked to be still more exciting.

✳   ✳   ✳   ✳

"Now I am beginning to understand your problem," said Jones. "You came to Havana with your friend Alex. He was trying to show you that his activities in Cuba weren't terrorist that he was trying to develop Cuban civil society through peaceful means. But things got out of hand. Okay, tell me the rest. How did you do it? Where did you get the name Rodriguez Pantoja?"

CHAPTER 11

▼

MY TRIP TO GRAND CAYMAN ISLAND

When my wife picked me up at the airport in Newark, the first thing she told me was, "Henry, I believe you really liked the food in Puerto Rico."

"You're right; in less than a week I gained five pounds!"

"What about Alex? How did he look? Did he look old? Was he fat? Is he dating somebody I know?"

I told her that Alex was looking good and answered no to all her other questions, laughing at her curiosity. Her last question was the most difficult.

"Why did he want to see you?" she said.

I had prepared an answer to this question during my return flight, and I told her, "Alex found out that I had left my investment banking career on Wall Street and he wanted to speak to me of the possibilities of entering into a business with him."

Natalia immediately asked, "What type of business?"

"Sales of telecommunications systems."

"What do you know about that business?" she asked.

"Not much," I admitted, "but I will learn if there is some opportunity to make some money."

On the following day, I was again enjoying the ocean view, this time from the window of my home in Point Pleasant, a small town on the Jersey Shore. I was trying to compare the view of Point Pleasant Beach, with its white sand, with the one that I saw from my cabana in Isla Verde, Puerto Rico. The two beaches both have very beautiful sand, but the difference was in the vegetation. The beach in Puerto Rico, with its palms trees and flowers of bright colors, has a seductive, tropical atmosphere. The beach in Point Pleasant is perhaps longer and wider, but without trees. Its beauty is in its dunes that have only a little vegetation. However, the big difference is in the temperature of the ocean water. The ocean temperature in Puerto Rico is 86 degrees, perfect for swimming; New Jersey water is 68 degrees.

No idle thoughts could separate me from my conversations with Alex and Ernesto. My wife continued asking me about my trip and I told the same stories to her. I was waiting, impatiently, for the call from Alberto Federman. Perhaps I was fascinated by the adventure or I was excited to be able to help the Cubans' cause. I could not tell which reason was uppermost in my mind. I repeatedly reminded myself that I had to deal this matter with discretion.

Three days later, I received a call from Federman. He told me that our friend Alex told him about my interest in the distribution of telecommunications equipments. He was calling to invite me to a presentation in his home on Grand Cayman Island and taking advantage of the occasion to take me on a fishing trip. He suggested that I take the United flight that leaves Newark at eight o'clock in the morning and arrives at Grand Cayman at 1:04 p.m. I should leave from Newark on Tuesday, May 17, with a return on the following Tuesday, May 24. The return flight leaves the airport of Grand Cayman at 3:00 p.m. and arrives at Newark at 8:57 p.m. He also indicated that he was sending me a letter formalizing his invitation, along with pamphlets about the telecommunication products he distributes. He also said that he would send a car to the airport to pick me up. The tone of the conversation was formal and concise.

Well, now I had to give Natalia the news about my next trip. I was thinking how to break the news without upsetting her too much. It was difficult, because I had just come home from Puerto Rico and now I would be going to Grand Cayman Island. The island has gorgeous beaches and is known worldwide as a fishing paradise, but I wasn't worried that she would ask to come along. Natalia is a professor of mathematics at the University of Monmouth in New Jersey and she was busy with a research project now. Still, it was necessary to sweeten the news to her so she wouldn't ask many questions and I wouldn't bother her much.

When the letter and the pamphlets arrived two days later, I showed them to Natalia. She didn't like the idea and said that my friend Alex was getting me into a business that I didn't know. Nevertheless, she quieted down when I told her that I was preparing a trip to Italy with her in July after she completed her project. She took the opportunity to remind me again not to get involved in a business that I didn't know, and I said I would consider it seriously before making any commitments. If only she knew what I was really up to!

I made my reservations as Federman had instructed. Since I didn't know much about the Cayman Islands, I decided to read a little about them. I discovered that there are three islands, Grand Cayman and two smaller islands named Cayman Brac and Little Cayman. They are four hundred and eighty miles from Miami in the Caribbean Sea. Cuba, to the north, is less than one hundred sixty miles away. Politically very stable, they are part of the British Overseas Territories, so a visa isn't required to enter the islands. Tourism is their main industry; visitors go to enjoy the sun, the beaches, and the deep-sea fishing. In addition, with no direct taxation, the islands are a prolific offshore financial center. I was unable to reconcile my destination with my trip to Cuba, but everything still seemed exotic and exciting.

On May 17, I took my plane and five hours later, I landed in the airport of Owen Roberts in Grand Cayman. When the plane flew over the island, I got the impression that it was quite flat. From the air, it was possible to see the islands' beautiful beaches and the clear turquoise waters surrounding it. I quickly went through immigration and gathered my suitcase. Then I went to the main lobby of the terminal, where there was a little confusion of passengers looking for their local transportation. Immediately, a man cut me off, saying in Spanish, "Welcome to Grand Cayman, Mr. Henry."

The stranger added, "I am Ramón, and I work for Mr. Federman." Ramón was a man of medium height who seemed to be about sixty years old. He took my suitcase and we walked quickly to a Range Rover parked near the exit door of the terminal. I noticed that the steering wheel of the SUV was on the right side of the vehicle, following the British custom of driving on the left side of the road. I always have the impression that they are driving on the wrong side—well, that is only my feeling and habits.

Ramón amiably told me that the house was not very far from the airport, and reminded me that on this small island everything was near by. Then he asked, "Mr. Henry, have you been to Grand Cayman before?"

"This is my first visit," I told him.

Ramón very politely asked me if I would like to learn the important points on our way to the house. I said yes, because I wanted to know more about the island.

He explained that we were going to the southeast of the island and that the capital, George Town, was just west of the airport. A few minutes after we passed a shopping center, he pointed towards the right and said, "In that way is the so-called South Sound." Later we passed two small towns named Prospect and Savannah; in this last one, Ramón recommended the restaurant James Castle, which was located on the shore. A few minutes later, we passed near a town called Beach Bay. Twenty minutes after we left the airport, Ramón stopped in front of the entrance of a white painted fence of about six feet in height. He told me, "We are home; the town is about five minutes away, and its name is Budden Town."

He pushed the button of the remote control and the gate opened. The house was visible from the entrance less than seventy-five yards away. To get to the house we went along a car path bordered with palm trees, tropical shrubs, and flowers, and the surrounding area was covered with a beautiful green lawn dotted with some trees. Ramón followed the path until stopping in front of the house. The house two-story brick house was trimmed with wood painted in white. Red Spanish tiles covered the roof. The front had large spacious windows on both floors and it was possible to see the bright colors of the curtains in the interior of the house.

Ramón took my suitcase and told me to follow him to my room. We entered the house and went through a large vestibule, the walls covered with wallpaper printed in gold and white and accented with the image of a pineapple hospitality symbol. The pink tile floor gave a special freshness to the place.

After we crossed the vestibule, we entered a full inner courtyard with many large red and green flowerpots with palms trees and tropical flowers. The atrium had rattan furniture with cushions upholstered in fabric printed with colorful flowers and palm trees. The prevailing colors of the furniture and the wallpaper of the entrance were white, gold, pink, and dark green. At the end of the atrium, I noted that I could see the light blue ocean through several large windows that almost touched the floor. Large terra cotta colored slate tiles covered the floor of the inner courtyard. The stairs to the second floor swept up from both sides of the courtyard; Ramón invited me to take the near stair on the left side of the atrium.

The second floor had a wide U-shaped hall around the inner courtyard of the first floor. The courtyard side of the hall had the same dark green iron railing of the stair handrail, and the other side of the hall had several white doors. Ramón opened one of them and invited me to enter, saying, "This is your room."

It was quite spacious, with two windows overlooking the sea. They were accented with curtains that blended with the room's decorations of palm trees and pineapples. The room had a large queen bed covered by a comforter printed with the same colorful images. On the other side of the room, there was a chest of drawers, a small desk with a chair, and a comfortable armchair with cushions upholstered with the same fabric of the comforter covering the bed. The desk had a flat TV screen, a small box of controls, and a wireless desk phone on top. A door opened to a private bathroom, with shower and bathtub enclosed by sliding crystal panels. Several pictures of boats and nautical motifs covered the white walls of the room.

After opening the windows, Ramón told me that Mr. Federman was with the other guests in George Town's warehouse; they would return at four. He informed me that I was invited for cocktails in the courtyard at four-thirty and later for supper. He also mentioned that I would meet the Browns and the other guests there. When I was in front of the windows looking out to sea, Ramón told me that he had forgotten to mention that the swimming pool was there to my right behind those trees, shrubs, and flowers. He said, "You just have to follow that narrow stone path to the pool," as he pointed it out. I looked but didn't see much, then I looked at my watch. It was two-thirty in the afternoon and I realized that I had two idle hours before the cocktails.

First, I thought to take a walk to the beach, but I decided to stay in my room to rest a little before showering and preparing for the activities of the evening. I gave thanks to Ramón for his kindness and I asked if I had to wear a jacket for the evening activities. He told me that it was not necessary and, as a commentary, he told me that in the Caribbean islands, comfort dominates dressing. When I asked his country of origin, he told me he was from Santo Domingo, and then he left.

When Ramón went away and closed the door, I opened the suitcase and put my clothes in the drawer and inside the closet. Later I went to the windows to look again for a while the radiant blue colors of the sea. I always like to compare ocean views with my own home view of Point Pleasant Beach. Afterwards, I sat in the armchair and looked up to the ceiling where I found a lazily moving ceiling fan. The temperature of the room was very comfortable even with the air conditioning off, because the cool breezes coming from the ocean and the ceiling fan did their jobs.

Suddenly I remembered what Ramón told me and I began to ask myself who the other guests might be. Who were the Browns? Who was the owner of this beautiful house? Who was Alberto Federman? What had all these people to do with Cuba? Even Ramón didn't sound to me very Dominican. The most important question was, where is Alex? Nevertheless, the armchair was very comfortable and I felt pleasantly intoxicated with the sea breeze; the combination made me go to sleep for a while.

When I woke up and looked at my watch I realized that I had less than half an hour to get ready for the evening affair. I rose quickly and ran to take a shower.

I left my room at 4:35; I didn't want to be the first person arriving, not knowing what to do if nobody was there yet. I walked to the hall railing and looked down to the courtyard where I saw several people standing and talking. Therefore, I thought that it was time to go downstairs. I took the same stair that I had gone up with Ramón and when I arrived at the bottom, I had the great luck of meeting Ramón, who was coming with a tray full of small sandwiches. When Ramón saw me, he put the tray on a table and said, "Mr. Henry, let me take you to Mr. Federman."

I followed Ramón across the courtyard until he stopped in front of a tall, quite bald man that looked to be less than sixty years old. He was dressed in a white beach shirt printed with green palm trees, and he wore white pants. Ramón told Mr. Federman that I was his guest, Mr. Henry Gonzalez.

Federman immediately cut off the conversation with the other two gentlemen, welcomed me to his home, and affectionately shook my hand. Next he introduced me to the other two men, Señor Bravo from Colombia, and Señor Veira from Brazil. Federman mentioned that both were associated with him in their business of telecommunications in their respective countries. Of me, Federman told them that I was interested in the business of telecommunications systems for the Puerto Rican market. In a joking tone he said, "Henry lost the opportunity to be a member of the crew who hooked the three-hundred twenty-five pound blue marlin that we caught yesterday. Too bad that he was late." Bravo and Veira smiled and I only shrugged my shoulders because I didn't know what they were talking about.

Ramón asked what I would like to drink. He suggested a rum punch in the style of the Cayman Islands and I accepted. Federman and the other guests were already sipping their rum punches.

The conversation on the catching of the blue marlin followed its course for a while, until a man, quite tall with an athletic bearing and black curly hair, came down from the second floor. He looked about thirty, and he was wearing a white *guayabera* and dark pink pants. When he finally joined the group, all greeted him in a very friendly way and called him Manny. Then, Federman introduced the newcomer to me as Manny Brown, his right hand in the business. Ramón, without asking, brought him a rum punch. Manny took the glass and gave thanks to Ramón.

The conversation between Manny and the guests changed to business matters for a while, with sporadic interventions from Federman. This one, looking at his watch asked Manny, "Hey, where is your sweetheart?"

Manny said, "Alberto you know how long they take to get dressed. She told me to come down first, that she would come in five minutes." Then Manny looked up to the second floor and continued talking with the guests. I was listening to the conversation as if I knew about the subject, and on some occasions, I nodded in affirmation.

Five minutes later I saw coming down the stairs a gorgeous, tall young woman of less than thirty years of age, wearing a long white dress, almost to her ankles, with a tropical motif in brilliant pink, gold, and green. The white background of her dress gave a darker tone to her light milk chocolate skin. I watched her as she began coming down the stairs until she got closer to our group. I was asking to myself. *Who is it that this woman looks like?* Suddenly I realized that she reminded me of the famous film actress Halle Berry.

I believe that Manny realized my indiscreet curiosity and went ahead, taking her hand, to introduce her as his wife, Julisa Brown. She greeted and congratulated the two guests for being part of the crew who caught the great blue marlin and kissed Federman on the cheek. Ramón repeated the same ritual that he had with Manny, only that this time he brought for Julisa a glass of white wine.

Everything happening in this gathering was very confusing to me. The subjects of the conversations jumped from technical telecommunications problems to economic situations in the different countries in Latin America and their political ramifications; sometimes they even discussed the economic policies of the United States, Europe, China, and Japan. My interventions were brief and I only made comments on the United States' financial and economic policies. What surprised me was that Julisa spoke of technical problems in telecommunications with apparently great dominion on the subject. Another thing that I didn't understand was whether Julisa and Manny were also guests like Bravo, Veira, and I. If they were, why did Ramón know what they liked without asking them?

After a couple of rum punches and tasty snacks, it came dinnertime. Ramón told Federman that supper was ready. Federman said, "Lady and gentlemen, we are going now to taste the blue marlin."

Julisa looked at me and said, "I hope that you eat fish, Henry."

"It is my favorite meal," I said. "However, I have never tried marlin."

"You are going like the way Doña Ramona prepared it."

I followed the small procession toward the dining room in the right wing of the house. The dining room had quite a long table that could seat twelve. The table, the glass display cabinet, and the chest of drawers used as a server were very well placed in the room. Over the table, a candelabrum of dark metal hung from the ceiling, its design contrasting nicely with the nautical illustrations on the wallpaper. Several pictures and paintings of boats hung from the walls. The decoration seemed to be sober but made with very good taste. Again, I observed that the colors of the tablecloth, the covers of the chairs, and the curtains were white, gold, pink, and dark green.

On the table were six small place cards held by porcelain figures of stingrays. Federman sat at the head of the table with Veira at his left, followed by Manny, Bravo on the right side next to me, and Julisa. The seating positions at the table emphasized that the guests were Veira, Bravo, and I. The host of the house was Federman, and Julisa and Manny were considered as members of the household.

Ramón poured a glass of chardonnay for each of us to make a toast. Federman raised his glass and again welcomed the three guests. He said, "May the worst day of our future be like the best day of our past! *L'chaim.*" After that toast, he told Ramón to bring Doña Ramona and Ramonita. In less than a minute the two women came. One seemed to be about fifty-five years old and the other was a girl, quite attractive, less than thirty years of age. Federman rose from his chair, embraced them, and kissed them. Then he said, "I have the pleasure to introduce to you Doña Ramona and her beautiful daughter Ramonita who, along with Don Ramón, are responsible for our comfort in this house.

"Now we are going to savor the delicious meal they have prepared for us this evening. Also, I want to congratulate our friends Veira and Bravo for their contribution to this supper, for supplying the blue marlin that we are going to enjoy tonight."

The supper began with a very spicy fish soup, Caribbean style, and a very exotic tropical salad with lettuce and small pieces of pineapple, avocado, and banana. The blue marlin steaks were delicious, accented with a seasoning that I had never had before. The meal was a banquet.

During dinner we spoke about fishing in the islands; they have a fishing zone of two hundred nautical miles around them. Federman mentioned that the best fishing months were May, June, and July. The most abundant fish during those months are the yellow fin tuna, the dorado, the bonefish, and the blue marlin. He mentioned that the wahoo was very abundant from December to March. He pointed out that the *Caymanians* enjoyed one of the highest standards of living in the world; they could find all types of foods and household items to make life pleasant. Although the islands don't have any water source, drinkable water necessities are satisfied with the stagnation of rainwater. Unemployment in the islands is very low, less than 4 percent. The fiscal advantages that the islands offer, since there is no income tax, have attracted many foreign financial institutions; more than forty thousand companies are registered in the islands. The tourist industry represents 70 percent of the GDP. With a certain tone of pride, Federman said, "There aren't many poor people on these islands. This is a paradise. Telephone communications are very good and we have four cable television stations; of course from the satellites, we can receive all channels available." When this topic was brought up, all the guests began to speak of their telecommunications businesses in their countries. I took the advantage of the occasion to speak a little with Julisa, who had been very quiet during supper.

In order to break the ice, I asked, "Do you and Manny live near here?"

She smiled and said, "Henry, we live here in this house. Alberto doesn't live here all year round. He lives in Santiago de Chile with his wife, Julia, and his two daughters. They come every year for three months during the school vacations. Nevertheless, Alberto comes almost every month for business. Manny is an electrical engineer who specializes in designing telecommunications systems for Alberto's company. I met Manny at MIT in Massachusetts when we were attending college."

While Julisa was talking, I was looking at her beautiful black eyes; they were as black as the night without a moon. Although I was paying attention to her, I imagine that she noticed the ecstasies of my eyes and the indulgent expression on my face. Suddenly in the middle of the conversation, she asked me, "Henry, are you married?" It took me a few seconds to come out from my trance before I said yes. I spoke a little about Natalia and where we lived. Later we continued talking about the islands and the beaches. She told me that they had come to Grand Cayman to work with Federman four years ago and had fallen in love with the island. Then I asked her what she was doing with her time on the island. She told me that she helped Manny in his work. She graduated from MIT in computer science and she was doing other things that kept her very busy. We also talked about the beauty of the house and its magnificent decoration. She asked if I had seen the swimming pool and enjoyed the views from the cliff behind the house. I told her that I hadn't. She told me that tomorrow she was going to give me a tour of the house and its surroundings. Federman had asked her to take me to George Town and show me the island. She suggested we should go early, after breakfast, about eight-thirty in the morning.

We finished our supper by savoring a delicious coconut custard and espresso coffee. Federman, looking at his watch, said, "The night is young; it is only eight o'clock. Do you young men have any plans for the night?"

Bravo and Veira looked each other and said, "Somebody told us that we couldn't leave Grand Cayman without seeing the Chameleon Club. They told us that it has a good show of typical music and dances of the Caribbean islands."

Federman said, "Yes, it is a good place. Who will join these two young men?"

Julisa and Manny immediately said they'd go, and Federman apologized for not accompanying them, but said that he would have a busy day in the morning. Then he asked, "Henry, are you also going?"

I thought about it for a moment and excused myself from the evening's fun. I said that I had had a very pleasant day but that I was feeling a little tired. Federman reminded the night owls that tomorrow their flight departed at 9:00 a.m. Bravo and Veira said that they didn't see any problems; they would fall asleep on the plane.

Before leaving the dining room, I thanked Federman for his hospitality and the delicious meal. Julisa and Manny said good-bye to me, and Julisa remind me that we had a date the next day for breakfast. I said good-bye to Bravo and Veira, and they wished me luck in my new business and offered to help me in case I needed it. Manny told them that he was going to get the car and Julisa went with the guests to the front door a few minutes later.

When everybody was gone, Federman told me that the next day he would tell me when we would go fishing. Meanwhile, he told me to enjoy the tour of the island. He said, also, that I should consider myself at home. If I needed anything, I was to speak with Don Ramón. Then he said good night and climbed one of the stairs, I imagined to his room.

I went to the large windows at the end of the courtyard but I couldn't see anything. The night had already fallen and the moon was not out. The darkness of the night reminded me, for a moment, of the loving black eyes of Julisa Brown.

A few minutes later, I went to my room and turned on the television. First, I watched the local channels for a while and later those via satellite. Federman's comments were right; the reception was very good. I got ready to go to bed and was sitting in the armchair watching television when suddenly my mind aroused, full of concern and questions. What did all these people have to do with Cuba? Nobody had mentioned anything about Cuba all night. Nobody mentioned the name of Alex. Where was Alex? I hadn't come here to go fishing. Soon after, I fell asleep, still seated on the armchair in front of the flat television screen, until I roused enough to go to my bed.

—Henry I think that you strayed away from the issue, said Jones. The Grand Cayman Island is far from Havana. Please, could you be a little more focus in your story.

—Well, believe me Mr. Jones my trip to Grand Cayman was my first step in my journey to Cuba. Let me continued telling you what happen the next day, said Henry, after sipping some coffee.

CHAPTER 12

▼

GOING FISHING IN THE EVENING

Around eight in the morning, I went downstairs and entered the courtyard. I thought that breakfast would be served in the dining room so I was walking in that direction when I saw Federman through the large windows. He was seated at a table outside on the terrace reading a newspaper with a cup of coffee in his hand. I got closer to the window and realized that breakfast was outside underneath a green awning. I changed my direction and walked to the terrace where Federman sat. When he saw me, immediately he rose, greeted me, and asked me to sit next to him. Before sitting, I took the opportunity to look around and enjoy the gorgeous view of the Caribbean Sea. Distantly I spotted the silhouettes of boats moving on the horizon. Small white clouds were floating in the sky and moving like the boats. Then, Ramonita came and kindly greeted me and asked if I would like to have coffee or tea. I told her that black coffee would be fine. Federman told me that Veira and Bravo had already gone away to the airport, accompanied by Manny.

As Ramonita was serving the coffee, Julisa entered the terrace. She looked radiant in a white sundress printed with flowers of dark pink. She walked to the table, greeted us very warmly, and then seated next to me. She appeared to be very happy. Federman looked at her and said, "Looks like you had a good time last night in the Chameleon. Manny already told me that you didn't stop dancing all night."

She simply said, "Yes, it was good." Ramonita brought a pitcher of fresh milk and a pot of coffee, pouring a little of each into Julisa's cup for a *café con leche*. She placed a full basket of muffins and breads on the table. When we were talking, Ramonita came again and asked if we wanted something else. Julisa said that she would like to have a little orange juice and she asked me if I wanted some. I said yes, and we continued talking about the wonderful weather and about the interesting places on the islands.

While we were talking, the cordless telephone next to Federman rang. He answered and listened for a while, and then he said, "Very well. We will be there at five-thirty this afternoon." Federman hung the telephone; he looked at us and said. "We are going fishing in the evening. Captain Bogart said that everything is ready."

I didn't know what to say, so it only came to my mind to say, "Wonderful."

Julisa stood up and said, "Henry, I believe we must begin our tour around the island so we can be back in time for your fishing trip."

Federman, with an affirmative gesture, said that was a good idea and reminded Julisa to be back in the house at four-thirty. Julisa, with a smile, answered, "Yes, Daddy!" Federman looked at her very seriously and went away. After he left, Julisa, still smiling, told me, "Sometimes, I believe Alberto thinks I am his daughter." After this comment, we walked towards the ocean side of the yard.

We walk for approximately fifty yards, stopping at the top of a cliff. The ocean waves were breaking against the rocks about thirty feet below us, producing a rhythmical melody. The wind was waving the silky and shining black hair of Julisa and fluttering the white dress that was squeezing her body hard. She looked like a figurehead of a goddess on the bow of an old ship. I could not turn aside my eyes from such a beautiful figure.

She continued talking and pointing at the different points of interest that could be seen from the cliff. We were there for a few minutes and then we followed a different path to the swimming pool.

Shrubs and fragrant tropical flowers of very bright colors surrounded the pool. Between the swimming pool and the house was a lawn of well-mowed grass of a brilliant green. Several majestic shade trees, which Julisa told me were called *casuarina*, marked the lawn. The water of the swimming pool was very clear and clean with an aquamarine color. The water came from the ocean, brought through a pumping system. Salt-water swimming pools need less chemical agents for their purification and are very pleasant. Around the pool on the deck was some furniture to sit or to lie down on and take the vibrant Indian sun of the Caribbean. On the left side of the deck, I saw a barbecue and a bar. The place was splendid and with the beauty and grace of my hostess, it felt heavenly.

We sat there for a while talking under an enormous pool umbrella that protected us from the rays of the hot tropical sun. The subjects of our conversation were varied, pleasant, and innocent. Julisa treated me as if I were an old family friend.

We were talking by the pool maybe for ten minutes when Julisa told me, "Let's move on, we don't have much time. I am going to take you to the west side of the island to a zone called Seven Beaches, an area of white sand on the shore that has several beaches. The people here claim that they are the most beautiful beaches of the Caribbean."

When I heard that statement, I asked, "Do you think that they are prettier than the Varadero beach in Cuba?"

She looked at me curiously and said, "I never have been in Varadero. My parents, who are from Cuba, have told me of the extraordinary beauty of it. But I was born and raised in New York City."

"Then you are Cuban," I said.

She responded, "Well, that was what my girlfriends said when I was a little girl. When I grew up they said that I was a Cuban-American like you."

"But I was born in Cuba," I said.

"Well, it is more or less the same. I kept Cuba in my heart." Then she took the stone path that lead towards the garages; I followed her behind like a little dog.

We entered the garage through one of the three doors. Inside was room for three cars, but only one bay was occupied. It contained a small two-seat sports car painted canary yellow. Julisa asked, "How do you like my little car?"

"Very pretty and appropriate for the owner."

She opened the door and sat on the driver's side, telling me, "Henry, get in."

I didn't recognize the make of the car, so I asked her. She told me that it was an Aston Martin DB9 made in England. I realized that she was very proud of her car and was taking good care of it.

We drove through the front driveway to the highway and opened the gate. Then Julisa took the same road that Don Ramón used to bring me from the airport; the only difference was that now we were going in the opposite direction. Later Julisa changed to the highway that ran along the shore. While we were driving, I began thinking about Julisa's revelation. I said to myself, *well, already I found out the first mystery of the Browns; she is a* Cubanita.

Then I took a glance at the beautiful legs of Julisa that carelessly moved when she changed from the accelerator pedal to the brake or pressed the clutch to change speeds with the manual transmission. She continued showing me the important points of the island, but I could not take my eyes off from her legs until I made an extraordinary effort to look at the landscape.

A few minutes later, we entered George Town. The convertible top was down, the sun was very hot, and apparently, Julisa saw that my face was getting red. She asked if I wanted to put the top up but I told her that I was fine. We drove through the town's historical zone for few minutes until she stopped the car in front of a department store. "Let's go to see the store," she said, hopping out of the car.

I immediately thought, feminine weakness. They are all the same. How they like to buy things!

The store was well stocked. It had a ladies' department and another one for men, and a cosmetic and perfume section. We went to the men's department and directly to the hat section. Julisa chose a hat, the Stetson Airway Panama Outback with a wide brim. She put it on my head and said, "Henry, you need this hat. Your face is getting very red with the sun." Smiling, she said, "It goes very well with your face. I want to give it to you as a present."

How I could say no to this beautiful creature who was worrying for me? I gave her thanks for the hat and put it on. After a brief walk around the store, we returned to the car, where I thanked her again for the hat; she just smiled and looked at me fondly.

We left George Town and took a highway to the north of the island. This highway bordered the famous Seven Mile Beach to our left. The beach was pretty, with very white sand, and full of coconut trees, palm trees, and *casuarinas*. Along both sides of the road we could see luxurious homes, condominiums, and hotels. We passed through small towns with their typical houses surrounded by gardens full of tropical flowers. Some of the towns were very bustling, like Treasury Island and Regal Beach; both had many stores and restaurants where we saw many people walking on the sidewalks and going in and out of the stores. They looked like tourists and *Caymanians* that enjoyed the high standard of living on their island.

Next Julisa took the highway in the direction of the Hyatt Hotel. There we took a ferryboat to cross the North Sound to Rum Point. The North Sound is like a large shallow bay. To our left we could see a small island called the North Wall and a larger one called Cayman Kai.

The ferryboat trip took us more than forty minutes, and during this time I took the opportunity to talk with Julisa in a little more relaxed way. She asked me about my wife, Natalia, and I took the opportunity to learn more about the Browns. Manny was the son of a girl who left Cuba with her parents in 1965, when she was only twenty years old, during the exodus of Camarioca. After living in Miami for awhile, they moved to Trenton, New Jersey. Two years later, she married Thomas Brown, a young U.S. Air Force officer who was serving in McGuire Air Base, not far from Trenton. Manny was born in New Jersey and, like all military families, they moved around quite often to many bases in the United States and Europe. Manny's better memories were when they lived in Puerto Rico for five years during his years of adolescence. Since he always was a very good student, he earned a scholarship to MIT, where he graduated with a master's degree in electrical engineering. It was there he met Julisa.

When I asked her how she went to MIT she told me that she was lucky to gain a scholarship and get a student loan. This was quite common in families of moderate income, she told me. She then said, "Everybody has a chance to study in the United States, if they seriously want it and work hard at it."

I looked to her eyes and said to her, "I congratulate both of you; what a beautiful couple you make."

Julisa's face got a little blush, and then she kissed me on the cheek and thanked me. After that, I was the one to blush.

After the ferryboat docked at the Rum Point station, we took the car and continued driving along the north beaches of the island. This area was less populated and it is a little more peaceful. Their beaches, like Azure Breeze and Coco Kai, are good but not as good of those of Seven Mile. Not far from the shore, we could see the reefs that protected these beaches from the beating of the waves. All along the highway, we saw typical *Caymanian* homes placed close to the ocean and surrounded by coconut trees, palms, and commercial areas full of restaurants and stores. We continued our way, bordering the north of the island towards the east, until we arrived at Gun Bay.

It was already two-thirty in the afternoon and I thought that it would be a good idea to stop to eat something. Also, I wanted to speak more with Julisa and ask her about Federman. With great diplomacy, I told her, "Listen; did the ocean breeze make you a little bit hungry? I would like to invite you to eat something."

She immediately replied, "Henry, that is a very good idea. Not far from here is a typical *Caymanian* restaurant called Arlain's. Let's go there."

Indeed, a couple of minutes later we were parking the car in front of Arlain's, only a hundred yards from the ocean. We sat at a table and ordered our lunch, and then Julisa ordered two Stingray Darks. This is the most popular beer of the Cayman Islands; it has an orange-copper color. Its taste is unique, very different from the beers we are accustomed to drink in the United States.

While we were sipping our beer and waiting for our food, I took the opportunity to asked Julisa about Federman. "Alberto is a good man," she said. "He is very discreet and careful by nature."

"Is he Chilean?"

Julisa looked first around us as if she feared that somebody could be listening to our conversation. "His wife is Chilean and he lived in Chile for many years," she said, again looking around furtively. "But he was born in Cuba. His parents went to Cuba in 1942 from Belgium, fleeing the persecution of the Nazis against the Jews. He grew up in Havana. His father had an electrical appliance store. The family left Cuba when the revolution confiscated their business in 1961, when Alberto was only seventeen years old. Since they were Belgian citizens, they didn't have too many problems in leaving the island. When they left Cuba, they went to Chile and there the father opened a new business and Alberto continued his secondary education. Then after, he went to Loyola University in New Orleans and when he completed his studies, he returned to Chile to work with his father."

"Then he is Cuban," I said.

Julisa said, "Yes, but he never speaks about it with anybody." In an almost imperceptible voice she added, "Henry, in the Cayman Islands arrive many *balseros* from the south coast of Cuba. It is necessary to be alert, because there are many of Castro's spies here. It is for that reason that Alberto doesn't like to speak about Cuba. He wants to keep his house safe, without suspicions of any activity related with Cuba."

I only shook my head in affirmation, while I was saying to myself, *Well, I didn't expect this story*. Since Julisa had been so honest and open with me, I asked her, "Julisa, do you know Alex?"

She looked at me with those beautiful black eyes and said, "Yes, I do. But Alex never has been here in the Grand Cayman house. Henry, I am telling you these things because I trust you. I believe that if Alex sent you here, he must have absolute confidence in you. Alberto was worried when Alex told him about your mission; he told me. I believe that he is still worried. But the friendship between Alberto and Alex comes from Cuba. You know how convincing Alex can be."

I was listening and thinking how delicate and complicated was this entire affair. Then Julisa said, "Henry, I beg you not to mention anything of this conversation to Alberto. Please continue doing what he says so that everything will come out well, God willing."

I said, "I imagine that Don Ramón, Doña Ramona, and Ramonita must be a trustworthy family. Don Ramón told me that he was Dominican."

Julisa smiled and said, "They are Cuban. They came on a boat from Cuba about ten years ago. Alberto found them and they have been working with him since. He trusts them completely; they are very discreet and know that they must be very careful." She told me not to talk about this with any of them.

"Do you know where Alex is?" I asked.

She said. "I don't know, but we will soon see him."

The food came and we changed the subject to favorite local dishes and island customs. Julisa interrupted the conversation to call Manny. He said that he was in the warehouse with Alberto and that they would be leaving for the house in the next fifteen or twenty minutes. She told him that we were having a bite at Arlain's and that we would be at the house before four-thirty.

To please my curiosity, I asked her about the telecommunications business. She said that the business was going very well. Alberto was very astute business-man who knew a lot about the Latin American market. Manny complemented Alberto's market savvy with his technical knowledge. Julisa was helping Manny in the programming of the systems. Both expended long hours in the warehouse preparing the equipment and installing the parts that came from the United States and Japan. "Here in Grand Cayman we pack and ship the complete systems to the projects in different Latin American countries," she explained. "When Manny travels to supervise the projects, I go to the warehouse to take care of business. Manny and I love our jobs."

When I asked her if Bravo and Veira were really distributors, she said yes. "They are good distributors in their countries. Alberto invited them to come to the island to go fishing, as he did with you." Then she smiled and said, "But you didn't fish the blue marlin, because you came two days later. However, tonight we are going to give you another opportunity."

I looked at my watch and said, "Julisa, it is four o'clock."

"We must go; the house is half an hour away. However, in my Aston Martin it will be a piece of cake."

We got in the car and took the highway toward the west. It bordered the ocean. We passed the East End and later Frank Sound with its reefs. Julisa was telling me where we were going, but now she was paying more attention to the road because we were going quite fast.

Again, my eyes were struck by her beautiful legs and the silky black hair that, unruly, fluttered with the wind. But my admiration for Julisa and her husband made me turn my eyes aside and made me think on the things that Julisa had revealed to me. I had the impression that there were more secrets to discover yet. I thought about Alex and our friendship and the trust he had in me.

Well, at 4:28 p.m., we stopped in front of the house. We entered and walked through to the courtyard where Alberto and Manny were seated. Julisa stood in front of them and said, "Here we are, a minute before four-thirty." Alberto asked me if I liked the tour. I said that I did like it.

"The island is very pretty and seems to be very prosperous. The tour director was sensational, also—I gave her a good tip." Then Alberto told me that the hat was looking good on me, and that I would need it for our fishing trip.

Looking at his watch, he said that he was going up to change his clothes and suggested that Julisa and I do the same. When Alberto left, I asked Julisa, "What do you recommend me to wear?"

"You are fine with those white pants and the beach shirt but change your shoes to sneakers so you won't slip and fall in the water." I thanked her and left the Browns alone.

In less than half an hour, we all met again in the courtyard. After Julisa kissed Manny, he wished us luck, and then we walked outside where Don Ramón was waiting for us with the Range Rover. Alberto sat with Don Ramón in the front, while Julisa and I were in the back seat. Julisa had changed her clothes and now was wearing white bell-bottom pants with a dark green blouse. She also was wearing a white baseball cap with the blue marlin image and her hair was coming out from the back of the cap in a ponytail. As always, she looked gorgeous. I noted that she had a large black canvas briefcase that she placed behind her seat.

Don Ramón took the same highway that Julisa and I had taken to return to the house, only now we were going east. There was not much conversation during our trip, with the exception of sporadic comments made by Julisa to Alberto about the new constructions of hotels.

Twenty minutes later Don Ramón left the highway and entered a parking lot through a gate that had a poster that said "Captain Bogart's Fleet," and, in smaller letters, underneath, "Private Fishing Charter, Night and Day." Don Ramón stopped in front of a wharf next to a small bay; three yachts were moored in the wharf. We left the Range Rover and walked to the office, which was in a small house situated at the end of the wharf.

Through the large glass window, I saw five people seated at their desks speaking on the telephone and working their computers. At the end of the big office room, I saw two men with yachting caps seated in front of a large desk speaking; they looked really busy.

Alberto told Julisa to remain with me outside of the office and he went inside. Through the window, I saw that he was speaking with one of the guys with yachting caps and after few minutes, he walked out of the office with them. Both men continued speaking and I could hear one say to other "Captain Nautilos, I will be leaving in the next ten minutes in the *Liberty*. Your group must arrive in less than twenty-five minutes; the *Hope* is ready. Tell Captain Kit to prepare the *Humanity* for the group that will go tomorrow early in the morning. I will see you here tomorrow before noon."

The other captain replied "Yes, sir, Captain Bogart," and went back to the office without speaking to us. He seemed to be very busy.

Alberto introduced me to Captain Bogart; later Julisa greeted him and gave him a kiss on the cheek. Captain Bogart was a tall, slim, quite athletic man. His skin was quite dark and he had a short white beard and white hair. Perhaps the color of his hair and the beard made him look older than his age. He seemed to be in good physical condition for a man in his sixties. The captain took us to the *Liberty*, one of the yachts in the wharf. While we were walking on the wharf, I looked at the names of the other two yachts; one was *Hope*, and the other, *Humanity*. Then I realized what the captains had been speaking about when they left the office. I thought that the yachts had very original names.

When we all boarded the yacht, Captain Bogart said that he wanted to show me the location of the life jackets, the dinghies, and the emergency equipment. He mentioned that all this procedure was routine but necessary. Then he told me that the boat was a Magnum 60 with twin diesel engines with over a thousand horsepower. The yacht could push forty-five knots. The boat was well rigged, full of electronics including radar, GPS, sonar, and telecommunications equipment. He showed me the helm station, which had three screens and the rudder, and we went under the deck to a quite large area. Here I saw the galley with the refrigerators and kitchen and a round table with seats. In addition, there were three doors; two of them opened to cabins and in one was the bathroom. The captain showed me where the life jackets, the dinghies, and the emergency package were located. After that, we went back to the deck where Julisa and Alberto were talking.

The captain sat in the armchair in front of the controls, began starting the engines, and gave some orders through the phone. I imagine that he called the wharf control because a guy immediately came to cast off the boat ropes from the wharf. We sat in the back of the main cabin on the deck behind the helm; when I raised my eyes I saw the fishing poles placed to both sides of the main cabin of the boat.

We left the small bay and went through a water channel between the shore and the reefs that protected the bay from the waves. When we got to the ocean, the boat turned left and for some time the reefs and the coast could be seen; later only the coast was visible, and soon Grand Cayman Island seemed like a large boat floating on the sea until it disappeared over the horizon.

Then, I could only see the vast ocean and some other yachts in the distance. The sun to our left side indicated that our course was north. The horizon was dyed red and gold until the ball of fire submerged into the sea. After the last rays of light, the sea and the sky began to darken from gray to black. It was black like Julisa's eyes. She watched the horizon in silence while Alberto spoke with the captain. The immensity of the ocean, the silence, and the prevailing darkness restricted my faculty to speak. I was only thinking and asking myself. *Where are we? Where do we go? Where is Alex?* Our lives were in God's hands and our world was the vast ocean and the boat.

CHAPTER 13

▼

RENDEZVOUS IN THE
QUEEN'S GARDEN

Peter Jones cleared his throat, jolting both him and Henry back to the uncomfortable present in the small immigration office. "Are you telling me you came to Cuba illegally from Grand Cayman?" Jones asked. "How were you able to land without the Cuban coast guard noticing your boat? How did you manage to avoid the Cuban security forces?"

"You'll see," Henry returned, as he began to weave his magic story once more.

*　　　*　　　*　　　*

All was darkness around us, total darkness. The moon was absent and we could only see a black sky full of stars. The screens at the helm where the captain sat tenuously illuminated the interior of the cabin. It had been two hours since we left the wharf. Since we didn't have any reference points, it seemed that the boat didn't move, it only swung rhythmically like a rocking chair. We could only hear the sordid roar of the engines and the crack of the waves against the bow of the boat. The night was calm.

When Alberto was talking with the captain, I again took the opportunity to get close to Julisa and whispering, I asked her about Bogart. She told me that he was a Cuban, graduated from Annapolis Naval Academy. After twenty-five years in the U.S. Navy he had retired with the rank of captain. After his retirement, he and his wife moved to Grand Cayman to open the fishing boat business. "He is very anti-Communist and an enemy of Castro's government, like all of us dedicated to the cause of Cuba's freedom," she told me.

Alberto stood up. "How about if we eat something?" he said jovially. "We still have three hours more to go. Do you want a sandwich, Bogart?"

"Sure," said the captain laconically. "How about chicken salad? One of those made by Doña Ramona."

"Do you want something to drink?" Alberto asked him.

"No, thank you, I always bring my own coffee from home," the captain said.

We all went down to the galley where Julisa opened the refrigerator, took out two bags of sandwiches, and said, "Doña Ramona prepared sandwiches for a battalion, as always." Then she told me to take whatever I wanted. Alberto took one and sat at the table. I did the same. Julisa took two sandwiches and one Diet Coke and said that she was going to the helm to keep the captain company.

Alberto and I remained seated, eating our sandwiches and drinking our Diet Cokes. Alberto made some comments about how powerful and comfortable the yacht was. After we finished our sandwiches, he asked me to follow him as he opened one of the doors of the galley. When we entered the cabin, I saw three identical cardboard boxes and another smaller box. "This is our cargo," he said, gesturing. He opened a box, took out a book, and gave it to me. The title was *Como llegó la noche*, and it was written by Hubert Matos. I had read the book and I knew that it was prohibited in Cuba. Alberto opened the other two boxes and removed other two books from them. One was a book written by the deceased Cuban writer Guillermo Cabrera Infante, titled *Mea Cuba*. This book is satirical and criticizes the Cuban situation and the revolution. It was also prohibited in Cuba. The other book was by William Korey, titled *NGOs and the Universal Declaration of Human Rights*. Alberto said to me. "Can you imagine that the reading of this book is prohibited in Cuba? As you know, Cuba is one of the signatory countries of this document."

For the first time I saw Federman speaking about Cuba. What surprised me more was the enthusiastic way that he spoke. He then told me, "Henry, the books in these boxes are going to be distributed to the *Bibliotecas Independientes* in Cuba. These small libraries are located in private homes with collection of three hundred books minimum, to the service of the neighbors, friends, and any person who wants to read them. They have books on all subjects. Many of these books aren't in the public libraries because the revolutionary government prohibits possessing and reading them. The libraries lend the books to the users like traditional libraries. Frequently, security forces seize the books, close the libraries, and send the people living in these homes to prison. Nevertheless, there are so many on the island that they represent a problem for the revolutionary government that wants to maintain the control of information in the country."

I looked at the smaller box, and asked, "Do you have more books there?"

Alberto said no. He opened the box and I saw that it was full of manila envelopes. He opened one and took out a bundle of bills in the denominations of one, five, ten, and twenty dollars.

"This box contains fifty thousand dollars. Some of this money is destined to help the dissidents in Cuba and the other portion represents the remittances that the Cubans abroad send to their relatives on the island, the so-called *remesas*. You can imagine that no one can live on the ten dollars a month they earn from the state-owned businesses! All Cubans have rationing notebooks where the government indicates to them what they can buy with Cubans pesos in the state stores. These stores have very few products to sell, and of course, the scarcity creates poverty and economic dependency on the government. The remittances and the money we distribute in small amounts of fifty to two hundred per month to thousands of families in Cuba in order to break their dependency on the government."

After a pause he continued, saying, "With these dollars, the lucky ones to receive the *remesas* buy foods and other articles in the black market and in the special stores, where only is possible to buy with dollars or *chavitos*. This economic independence not only solves the nutritional problems of the people, but also is like a ray of freedom that maintains the hope of the people enslaved by state terrorism."

I didn't know what to say. I was so surprised by the fervor of Federman's words that I could only nod my head in affirmation. Federman continued, saying, "Henry, I know that you are a very good friend of Alex. But I don't know if he mentioned that our group is made up of men and women who accept great personal risks and economic sacrifices to fight against an evil monster. The Socialist system enslaves eleven million unfortunate people on the island of Cuba. These men and women work in secret, employing non-violent fighting methods, and in many occasions in anonymity with no other desire than to reach the freedom of the Cuban people."

I said that I recognized the great work and the courage of all, and that I felt proud to participate in the fight and in the search for the freedom of the Cuban people. Federman then told me, "Henry, in few hours you will illegally enter

Cuba. Be very careful because the regime and its surveillance system are very dangerous. Don't trust anybody and never mention the way you entered the island."

He took an empty manila envelope from the box and said, "Henry, for your security, it is better that you place here everything that you have in your pockets including your ring and watch." Federman closed the envelope and placed it on the table. He took packing tape and began closing the boxes; I helped him with his work.

When we finished, he took the envelope with my personal belongings and we went up to the helm. The captain was looking at the screens with his hands on the rudder. Federman went to Julisa, gave her the envelope with my things, and told her to save them in her bag.

We spent the next two hours talking about the poor conditions of the country and the suffering and hardships of the Cuban people. They made some comparison between the standard of living in Cuba and the Cayman Islands. Federman said, "Life is good and normal in Grand Cayman; in Cuba it is miserable and abnormal."

Later, Julisa removed from the bag a laptop computer, a little antenna, and a telephone. Alberto asked the captain how much farther we had to go. He said that we were about ten miles from the archipelago of the Jardines de la Reina.

Julisa asked him if she could begin communication. The captain said yes. Julisa turned on the laptop, called up a program with the mouse, and took the telephone. She pushed some buttons and began to speak. Her first words were, "Socialism or death." The answer from the person with whom she connected was, "Mierda." We all smiled a little. Julisa told them that we were about ten miles away and that the captain was going to give them the coordinates. The captain, looking at his screens, gave the coordinates and told them that we were going to call again in twenty minutes.

I asked Julisa what kind of telephone she was using. She told me, "This is a STU-III encrypted telephone that communicates by way of satellite. The conversation on this phone can't be intercepted; it is completely safe."

Twenty minutes later, the captain told Julisa to call because he had had the others on the radar screen for a while. He told Julisa to mention that we were going turn on the spotlight. Julisa did and they answered back that they could see the light. The captain stopped the boat; we could only hear the roar of the engines running in idle. Julisa said that they had already thrown the rubber boat into the water and they would be here in two minutes.

Indeed, a few minutes later, we heard a noise as if somebody was striking the hull of our boat. A human figure suddenly was climbing the vessel near the stern;

a few seconds later another figure appeared. Alberto went ahead to meet them and I followed him. The first person that I saw was Alex. He greeted me with a slight nod and at the same time that he said, "Good evening, *mi hermano*," Alex greeted Alberto, and introduced us to Genaro. He was a man of medium height that looked to be near sixty years of age. Alex went to Julisa and gave her a hug and a kiss on the cheek. The captain greeted him very affectionately and said that the execution of the rendezvous was getting better every time they did it. It was a perfect boarding in the middle of the ocean.

After the greetings and welcomes, Alberto said, "Let's go down to the cabin to bring the boxes." The captain and Julisa remained at the helm while we all went down to the galley. Alberto opened the cabin where the boxes were and Alex checked the boxes and told Genaro and me to move them out of the cabin up to the deck. After we completed our mission, he told me to exchange all my clothes with Genaro, including the shoes. "Nobody in Cuba has clothes like yours," Alex said. Genaro's height and constitution was very similar to mine; only the shoes felt a little tight.

When Genaro saw himself in my clothes and my Stetson hat, he said that he was dressed as a tourist. I was feeling like a beggar in his old rags. They consisted of a dirty white T-shirt with a revolutionary motto, quite faded, that said, "Van Van." The pants were a pair of old cheap blue jeans and a dirty red baseball hat completed the outfit. But the worst thing was the shoes; they were made of canvas with a piece of truck rubber for a sole, and they were stitched up with a heavy, coarse thread. When I saw myself in the mirror, I said to myself, *I am dressed as un Cubano de a pie.*

Back on deck, Alex said good-bye to everybody and I did the same. Julisa came to me, gave me a kiss in the cheek, and wished me luck. She also told me that they would see me in two or three days. The captain turned on a light on one side of the boat and Alex went down through the gangway to a rubber boat floating in the water. He told Genaro to lower the first box. Alberto and I helped to lower the other three boxes. Alex placed them in the middle of the rubber boat on the dark ocean water. Finally, after he completed his task, he told me, "*Mi hermano,* come down now."

Alex started the small electric outboard motor and we moved away from the *Liberty*. Suddenly I saw a spotlight fifty yards in front of us. Alex steered the rubber boat in the direction of the light that seemed to be floating in the dark. In about a minute, we came near the light and I realized that it came from a large boat.

Alex fastened a rope from our rubber boat to a small gangway hanging from the larger boat and told me to climb up through it. When I got on the deck, I found a young man there. He said amicably, "*Bienvenido, compañero.*" I greeted him and helped to raise the boxes from the rubber boat. Finally, Alex came on board and we all helped to lift up the rubber boat, stashing it on deck near the stern. After we completed our job, Alex introduced me to Vladimir.

The fishing boat was smaller that the *Liberty* and it looked a little bit old. We finally accommodated the boxes and covered them with an old dirty canvas.

We all walked inside the small cabin, where we found a man seated on a bench in front of the boat rudder, a panel of registers, one screen, and couple of joysticks. The cabin didn't have any light; it was dimly illuminated by the reflection of the control panel. Alex introduced me to Captain Pombo, whom he called the sea wolf; he was a young man in his thirties.

The captain said, "Welcome to the *Trocha*." Then I realized that he was looking at a computer laptop. In his hand he held a telephone similar to the one that Julisa had. After he briefly spoke with Alex, I saw him making another call, saying, "The merchandise and the passengers are on board. Good night, darling." Then he pushed one of the levers and the boat began to move.

So far, I had done everything that I had been told to do and I was feeling a little bit confused. I asked Alex, "Listen, where are we?"

"We are fifteen kilometers from Santa Cruz del Sur on the southern coast of Cuba. We are crossing the archipelago of the Jardines de la Reina." He warned me that we wouldn't see much around us because there was no moon and the night was very dark. "I can tell you that in fifteen minutes we will pass near Cayo Cabeza to our left and Cayo Pilon to our right. This archipelago has hundreds of uninhabited islands of all sizes. Its navigation is quite dangerous. That is why the government doesn't maintain good surveillance of these coasts. But don't worry because Captain Pombo knows all the channels and the locations of the islands—besides, he has a GPS. Anyway, we have two more hours left before arrival at our landing point; let's go down to the galley—I want to give you something."

We walked down several steps through a narrow stairway to the galley. On one side there was a kitchen and a refrigerator; on the other side were a few bunks and one door. The life jackets and other emergency equipment were stored behind the stairs. Alex got an envelope that was on the table and opened it. He got a card from the envelope and told me, "This is your identity card." I looked at it and I recognized my photo, but the name was Genaro López Marrero. Then Alex asked, "How do you like your new name. Señor López?"

The only thing that came to my mind was to say that the name was very appropriate for a farmer, a *guajiro*.

Then he gave me another card saying, "This is your identification from your workplace. You work in the *Combinado Pesquero Argerico Lara* in Santa Cruz del Sur. This boat is part of the fishing fleet that berths at the wharf of the processing plant. This letter from the plant authorizes you to go to Camagüey to get some spare parts for the plant machinery."

I looked at the documents and read the letter. Alex was looking at me as if he was expecting some questions. I only said that all seemed to be all right. What else could I say? I had to trust my friend and carry on with the adventure. Of course, my legs were shaking and I felt cold and my body was shivering.

— Peter Jones interrupted the narration and asked Henry about the name Genaro López. Henry, what happen to that name? Why did you changed?

—Henry told him that he would explain later about that, and continued his story.

Alex asked me if I had any type of identification or articles in my pockets. I told him that I had left everything with Julisa. He said that the documents he had just given me were very important; I should keep them at hand. Then he gave me five Cuban ten peso bills (equivalent to less than fifty cents U.S.), and a blue rationing notebook, called *libreta*, with my new name. All Cubans, employed or unemployed have a rationing notebook issued by the Oficola, that is, the office controlling the distribution of food supplies. He told me that with the Cuban pesos and the *libreta* I could go to a state store to buy what was allowed in the notebook. The only problem was that the stores don't have merchandise to sell. People must be very alert when products arrive at the store and then make long lines (*colas)* to buy what is available. Cuban workers were paid in Cuban pesos but most of the products, other than the staples, were only sold in convertible pesos called *chavitos*. These replaced the dollar and were equivalent to a rate of exchange that oscillated between twenty-five and thirty Cuban pesos for one *chavito*. With them, you could buy food and other articles of first necessity in the *tiendas especiales*, but these articles were marked at very high prices.

Alex said, "Never mention to anybody the way you got onto the island. Be very careful with the so-called *cederistas*. These are the members of the *Comité de Defensa de la Revolución* (CDR). As you know, there is one on almost every block on the island. Also, remember that *La Policía Nacional Revolucionaria* (PNR) is an incredibly repressive organization whose motto is that all Cubans are suspicious and criminals except the ones integrated with the revolution. In Cuba, the

Ministerio del Interior, MININT, directs all the brutal repression in the island through the state security agents, *Agentes de Seguridad.*"

In this manner, he continued preparing me for my adventure on the Socialist island of the Castro brothers. I listened to him and realized that my visit to the island wouldn't be a pleasure trip. My only comfort was that Alex was going to be with me. I had a lot of confidence in him and his ability to survive in the underground.

The plan for my trip to Cuba was to go to the city of Camagüey, about seventy-five kilometers from Santa Cruz, to meet with members of the *Bibliotecas Independientes*. Later we would meet with a representative of *Las Damas de Blanco* and if it was possible we would try see an officer of *Fuerzas Armadas Revolucionarias* (FAR). We would return in two days to Santa Cruz del Sur to be picked up on the coast at dawn of the third day by the boat *Trocha* and transferred to the *Liberty* near the archipelago of the Jardines de la Reina, in a way very similar to how I came to Cuba. Genaro, who had impersonated me for the return of the fishing trip, would come in the *Liberty* from Grand Cayman with Alberto and Julisa on the second fishing trip. I would again exchange identity with Genaro, who would return to Cuba in the *Trocha,* and I would return to Grand Cayman in the *Liberty.*

Everything until now had been running very well and I was expecting that it would continue. On Tuesday, I would be back in my home in New Jersey and would raise money for our cause with far more enthusiasm after I had seen the pathetic reality of life on the island.

Alex asked me if I was tired. I told him that I was so excited that I couldn't go to sleep. We took four cups of black coffee and we went back to the helm. I gave one to Vladimir and Alex gave his to the captain. We couldn't see anything outside—it was very dark and the sea was calm. We could only hear the roar of the boat engine. Captain Pombo's eyes were glued to the GPS screen and his hands didn't let go of the rudder.

One hour later Captain Pombo told Vladimir to call the shore with the STU-III phone and tell them to turn on a flashlight; he would like to see a light to locate them on the coast. A few minutes later, a tenuous light was seen at quite a lot distance. The captain said, "There they are." He told Vladimir to call them again to say that we saw the light so they could turn it off and put it on again in ten minutes.

The captain changed course a little and reduced the speed of the boat. Ten minutes later, the light was in front of us again, this time much closer. Again, the captain told Vladimir to phone back and tell them to leave the flashlight on until the rubber boat got to the shore. Vladimir repeated everything that the captain said. He then told us to help him lower the boat to the water. We threw the rubber boat, which was tied to the gangway, into the sea. Alex went down the gangway and immediately Vladimir and I lowered the boxes to him as he stowed them in the rubber boat. When we finished this operation, I said good-bye to the captain, who told me that he would see me soon.

Then I went down to the rubber boat. Already Vladimir was inside arranging the boxes. The surge of the tide wasn't strong but I felt it was dragging us towards the light. Alex put on the small electrical outboard motor and the boat start moving. The light began to look closer until it was right in front of us. When the boat hit against something hard, Alex cut the engine and told me to throw a rope to the light. I could see the silhouettes of three people and the light of the flashlight that illuminated our boat. I realized we weren't landing on a sandy beach, but on the reef of the shore.

I jumped out of the boat onto the reef with the aid of one of the guys on the shore. Vladimir and finally Alex jumped out onto the reef. We all pulled the cord to remove the boat from the water and placed it on the reef.

Alex was the first person to speak; he ordered two of the guys to carry three boxes to a truck that was parked close to the shore. Vladimir helped the guys take the boxes away. Alex told the other man to take the smaller box to a car parked next to the truck. The complete operation didn't take more than two minutes. Vladimir came back to us and said good-bye. We again put the boat in the water and pushed it out. Vladimir put on the outboard electric motor and with the sound of a bee it disappeared in the dark of the sea in the direction of a small light from the *Trocha*.

When I looked back to the truck and the car, I saw Alex speaking with the two guys. The truck was not very big and it was loaded with boxes that were half covered with a canvas. The night was very dark and I couldn't read the sign on the door of the truck. Anyway, the truck started moving right away when the two guys got in. Alex came back and said, "Let's go. Juan is waiting for us."

We got in the car. It was quite old, of a make unknown to me, and it sounded like an old piece of junk. First, we took a dirt road for about ten minutes and then we turned right onto a narrow paved road full of potholes. The road didn't have any illumination but from the headlight of our car, and that was not very strong; I could see that we were going through high scrub grass. Some parts seemed to be neglected sugar cane fields. I was sitting in the back seat and Alex was seated next to the driver.

Alex asked the driver if there was any news. The driver said that the government austerity programs kept the population very *jodia*. He continued, "The state wants that we do more with less, to live without food, without water or light, and without clothes. It ain't easy, my friend. Around this area, the government has closed many sugar mills; well, you can see the abandoned sugar cane fields around us. The people don't have work. The *periodo especial* have never finished for us, not even with the aid of Venezuelan oil and with Raúl's temporary succession; we are in the same *mierda*. The repression is stronger, mainly in the towns." Then he repeated again the slogan, "It ain't easy."

Alex, trying to lift the spirits of the driver, said. "Well, Juan, for that reason we are here fighting for the peoples' freedom. We are helping the good citizens who endure the misery that this Communist dictatorship has imposed on them by force and with lies and deceits." They continued speaking the rest of the way about the desperate Cuban situation. I didn't say anything; I was only listening to the conversation.

Fifteen minutes later, we took a dirt road until we stopped at an old wood barn. It seemed derelict and deserted. The driver got out of the truck and opened the large door of the barn, returned, and drove the car inside. After he closed the door, he turned on a flashlight and took us to a room inside the barn. On a table were two candles. He lit them and said to us, "We are going to stay the rest of the night here."

Alex looked at his watch and said the time; it was 3:20 a.m. "We'd better get some sleep. We leave for Santa Cruz tomorrow at six-thirty in the morning." In the room there were three or four canvas camp beds; each of us took one, and the driver extinguished the candles.

The room was dark and smelled bad, as if something was rotten. I was sweating a little; I didn't know if it was due to the heat or to my nervousness. I was trying to sleep but I couldn't, due to noises that we heard from the walls. In the dark, I heard the voice of Alex saying, "*Mi hermano*, don't worry; those noises are from the rats running inside the barn. Tomorrow, with the light of the sun, everything will look better."

I thought, *well, at least I will be able to see the sun, because so far, I haven't had the opportunity to see anything and I don't know where I am!*

CHAPTER 14

▼

THE MORNING AFTER

While Henry talked, Peter Jones had pulled out a map of Cuba and quickly looked for Santa Cruz del Sur on the southern cost of the island. When he found it, he commented that the province of Camagüey was a long way from Havana. "How did you come to Havana."

"That is coming in due time," Henry said.

Jones offered him a fresh cup of coffee. "I'm anxious to learn what you did in that small town of Santa Cruz del Sur and how you traveled to Havana. You have opened many questions. First, you were Genaro, but at some point you changed your name. I would like to know more about that; go ahead on your story."

Henry took a couple of sips of his coffee and continued.

*　　　*　　　*　　　*

In spite of the anxiety and confusion, I was able to sleep for couple of hours. My rest was interrupted by the voice of Alex, who shook me, saying, "Wake up, *mi hermano,* it is already five-thirty in the morning."

I opened my eyes and found myself in the same room without windows, illuminated only by the two candles. The first thing that came to my mind was, *Where is the morning, where is the sun?* I noticed that Juan wasn't in the room and I asked Alex where he was. Alex said that he had gone to the bathroom.

"Where is the bathroom?" I asked.

Alex looked at me with a smile and said, "Go outside the barn and look for some nice bushes and there is your bathroom."

I grinned. "This is a first class hotel with a garden in the bathroom!" I had to pee, bad. I left the barn to find a suitable bush to go behind. When I went out, I found Juan coming back. He recommended some good bushes nearby.

When I came back to the room, I saw Alex and Juan opening the box we had brought from the Cayman Islands. From the box, they took several envelopes and two bags made of canvas. One had the logo of *Combinado Pesquero Argerico Lara* and the other said *Comité de Defensa de la Revolución, Ciego de Avila*. Alex opened the last one and pulled out a small laptop that looked like a portable DVD player, and a cellular telephone. The equipment was very similar to the STU-III phones of Julisa and Captain Pombo; the only difference was that it was smaller. Inside the bag, there were papers with letterheads of the CDR of Ciego de Avila with programs of revolutionary activities of the CDR.

Alex removed all this material and placed it on a table. Then he opened a secret compartment at the bottom of the bag, selected some envelopes, and placed them inside the secret compartment together with the laptop and the phone. He then closed the secret compartment and filled the bag with the CDR papers of revolutionary activities. Then he opened the other empty bag and placed the rest of the envelopes inside its compartment, except for two. He gave me the bag with the fish processing plant logo and told me, "In this bag, you will carry the spare parts."

After he finished, Alex put one envelope in his pocket and gave another to Juan, telling him, "This is for you and your people." Juan took the envelope, thanked Alex, and left the room. When we were alone, Alex told me that now in Cuba he was using the name of Armando Santana Lara, and he asked me to remember it because all his documents had that name and most of the people knew him by it.

We took our bags and got into the car where Juan was waiting. When we were leaving the barn, we saw the first rays of sunlight, meaning that the new day had arrived. We took the road to Santa Cruz del Sur. The road was full of potholes and on both sides of the road, we could see neglected sugar cane plantations and marshes with mangrove swamps; the landscape wasn't pretty. We didn't see anybody on the road—no traffic at all—and twenty-five minutes later, we were entering the town.

The town was small and it seemed very calm. It had some stores on one side of the only square in town. A sign advertised *Coppelia* ice cream and another said *Pizzería*. The town didn't have a beach and the ocean water was quite cloudy and contaminated. Not very far away, we could see the islands of the Jardines de la Reina; they seemed to be floating on the ocean. In the distance, we could also see the building of the fish processing plant *Argerico Lara*.

Alex told Juan to maintain contact with Captain Pombo to coordinate our return in two days and asked him to drop us off at Aníbal's home. Juan said he had to hurry a little to return the car, which he had borrowed from the plant's garage. Then he said, a little worried, that he had to be in the parking garage before the *pincho* arrived.

We stopped in front of a house that had a signboard that said *Comité de Defensa de la Revolución*. We said good-bye to Juan and got out of the car with our bags.

The house from the outside seemed to be large but quite old. When I saw the sign, I said to Alex, "Are we in the right place? This is a CDR, one of the main surveillance organizations in Cuba!"

Alex smiled. "Only in appearance—don't worry."

We knocked at the door and a woman in *chancletas* opened it. She seemed to be about thirty years old, and she was dressed in an old ragged muumuu with a discolored flower print and with her hair piled in a bun. She briefly welcomed us and without wasting any time, she shouted, "Aníbal, here is Armando." Immediately came a man in a T-shirt with olive green pants, also in *chancletas*, a little fat; like the woman, he seemed to be in his thirties. The man very affectionately greeted Alex and said that he was waiting for him. Alex introduced me as Genaro and told me that the woman's name was Maritza. The man looked at me and said to Alex, "*Oye, el compañero*, Genaro is looking a little bit fleshier!" That reminded me that I was using Genaro's papers and identity.

Aníbal, trying hard to show his hospitality, said that we came in at the right time for breakfast and shouted, "Maritza, bring two more *café con leche*." We walked to the dining room and sat at the table. The decor was hideous, nothing coordinated. The dining room table didn't match the chairs and the living room consisted of multiple pieces of furniture without any balance or coordination. The living room had a Panda television set, a short-wave radio, and on the walls there were pictures of Fidel, Che Guevara, and Raúl. The outside of the house needed some painting, and the inside walls peeled. I thought that with a coat of paint the house would look better.

Maritza brought three glasses of *café con leche*, a couple of pieces of bread, and a small bar of butter. I asked Aníbal if I could go to the bathroom to wash my hands before breakfast. He pointed the way, but told me that the faucet didn't have water so I would have to use the water in the bucket close to the toilet. I went to the bathroom and washed my hands and face without soap. After, I came back to the table and tried the *café con leche*. It tasted like watered down milk with sugar and just a trace of coffee, but since there was no other liquid available, I drank it to help me swallow the piece of old bread and butter.

Aníbal, with great pride, said that the butter and powdered milk were from the agricultural cooperative of Santa Cruz. He bragged that, thanks to his good contacts, we could eat them. He had obtained them through a swap with a friend who worked in the cooperative. Aníbal gave him cans of fish from the processing plant in exchange for the powdered milk and the butter. Milk consumption in Cuba is restricted only to children under seven years of age. The rationing notebook doesn't allow milk purchase for anybody older than that. Butter is a luxury item almost never seen in the markets and it isn't in the quota of the rationing notebook. The bread came from his friend the baker, to whom he also gave fish. Well, I was starving and as the saying goes, "When there is hunger, there is no hard bread." I ate everything and Alex did the same.

Just after we finished our breakfast Maritza came with two children dressed in olive green uniforms with red handkerchiefs on their necks and red berets on their heads. "These are the *Pioneros*," said Aníbal. "The school is not far, but Maritza walks them to there just in case some *elementos antisociales* bother them on the way."

Maritza added, "Also to keep an eye on the town people."

The children looked at us and both at the same time shouted, "We will be as Che!" They left with their mother. I remained speechless when I heard their good-bye. Aníbal apparently noticed my face for he said to us, "You see, this is the indoctrination they give in the schools." He told us that after school hours the children must clean the school or work on a small farm. The crops they produce go to the state stores that sell the products to the town people through the *libreta*.

Then he continued, using the comment we had heard so often before: "The life in Cuba, it ain't easy. Everybody must follow the rules. If my children weren't *Pioneros* and working as volunteers for the revolution, the poor kids never would have the opportunity to go to the university. You know the slogan, 'Education is only for the revolutionaries.' When they grow up, they must show that they are citizens socially aware of the *proceso histórico* and they will have to do volunteer work in the labor camp on weekends, to perhaps be members of the Youth Communist Union. This will serve them as a shield to obtain social respect, making use of the *doble moral* that exists in Cuba to survive the misery in which this country is."

After a brief pause, he continued, saying, "Listen, *compañeros,* Maritza and I are in the same boat. Here in Santa Cruz there are six CDRs. I am the coordinator of all the CDRs in town. I know that the other *compañeros,* presidents and secretaries of the CDRs, are involved in the black market, illegal activities of all types of articles and products, as I am. But we all quietly *'Hacemos de la vista gorda,'* saying nothing. Nevertheless, we all are very active preparing the *actividades revolucionarias* to maintain the town in *jaque* and under pressure. Because, *compañeros,* in Cuba *hay que resolver.* Do you think that somebody can live with the wages that the state company pays? I work in the fish processing plant and I am the union representative at the plant. I make two hundred and fifty pesos per month (twelve-fifty in U.S. dollars) and Maritza works in the plant and makes a hundred pesos per month (five dollars U.S.). With that misery nobody can live. With the *libreta,* we can buy very little. It is necessary to go to the special stores or the black market to buy most of the food and other things that you can't find in the state store."

Alex said, "But Aníbal, you and Maritza don't go very often to the fish processing plant. You guys are always here in the house or around the town."

Aníbal answered, "Well, Maritza always is watching the neighborhood, but I, at least, go twice per week to see how things go on and to pick up my fish cans so I can exchange them for anything available. These help us to solve the problem of food. You know, Armando, that is business."

Then Aníbal said, "I am going to tell you the way the state companies work in Cuba. For example, the plant produces fifty boxes of fish cans per day and we report forty-five. The bosses keep the unreported boxes for their business and give some to their loyal workers in the plant, so they can make their own businesses. That is the way that the cooperative conducts business and it's the same in all the companies run by the state. The problem used to come when the plant didn't have electricity to run the machinery. Then there wasn't any production and the situation was bad. But we have learned that when we have electricity, we have to produce a lot of ice to keep the fish fresh until the electricity comes back. If it takes too much time to come back on, then we eat the fresh fish or swap it for other products and we report that the fish rotted. Because, *compañeros, hay que resolver.*"

After he finished telling this story, Aníbal asked Alex, "*Compañero,* do you have something for me on this trip? The children need new shoes and we can only buy them with *chavitos* in the Special store."

Alex gave him an envelope, saying, "This is for you and your family."

Aníbal thanked Alex and, looking at me, said, "Genaro, that T-shirt you have is old and looks *churrosa*. I am going to give you a shirt that I have here that I took away from a *bitongo*; it is too small for me." He left and came back with a white shirt with blue lines that was far better that the faded dirty old T-shirt that Genaro gave me in the boat. I tried it on and it fitted me well. Then I thanked Aníbal.

Alex told Aníbal that we were going to Camagüey for a couple of days and that he would like to take the first *guagua* that left Santa Cruz. Aníbal said that the *guagua* was coming from Camagüey around eight in the morning and it was supposed to leave at eight-thirty. However, he said, "You know how the schedules work in Cuba. Always there is a delay." He said he was going to take us to the station in case there was any problem. To give us more confidence he said that he knew the driver and the policeman that came to verify the papers of all the passengers. "I go there every day to see who comes to town and who goes to Camagüey. That is part of my job as coordinator of the CDRs of Santa Cruz del Sur. So there won't be any problem, *compañeros*."

It was still early to go to the station, so we stayed talking with Aníbal for a while, hearing his complaints of how bad life in Cuba was. He was telling us about the frustration of the people and the incapacity of the revolution in developing the economy and the government errors in handling the crisis. The blame of everything wrong on the island, according to the government, is due to the imperialistic blockade. Aníbal, with his resigned face, said to us, "Is this *el Caballo's* fault? Maybe it was the fault of the Soviet Union and its final disaster. I don't know. But the reality is that we are very *jodidos*, with Fidel as *el Caballo*, with Fidel as a *penco senil*, and now with Raúl as the new *máximo líder*."

To survive the *proceso historico* on the island, they had to make believe that they were good revolutionaries and militants.

I listened to him, asking myself. *How can Alex trust this guy?* Then I thought that after all, I didn't have any other alternative but to follow ahead with Alex's plan. The reality was that Alex had bribed Aníbal with the dollars in the envelope. Aníbal needed the money to support his family and I didn't think he would denounce us to the Cuban authorities and lose the opportunity to make some more money to get by on.

We talked for a while longer until Aníbal said, "I believe that we should leave now for the bus station." He left us alone for a moment and came back with a medium-sized ball bearing part. He said, "Genaro, put this machine part in your bag."

"Go ahead, that it was a good idea," Alex said, and we all left the house with our bags. I noticed that Aníbal also brought a bag very similar to the one Alex had. It seemed to me strange but I didn't make any comment.

We walked a couple of blocks to the omnibus station. The station was only a small shed with a door and a window where a man was selling the bus tickets. We bought our tickets for five pesos each, about twenty-five cents in American currency. The city of Camagüey is only seventy-five kilometers from Santa Cruz, but the trip takes two hours due to poor road conditions, Aníbal told us.

Standing next to the ticket shed, we saw twelve people, four men and eight women, who were there waiting for the bus. We stopped in line next to them and Aníbal went to speak with them. He began asking questions like, "Why are you going to Camagüey? When will you return? Who are you going to see in Camagüey?" He reminded them that they had to attend the events programmed by the CDR on their return. He also wrote down their names in a notebook that he carried in the bag. I realized that the idea was to keep them under pressure and to show his authority as president of the CDR.

We waited in line for about forty minutes. The heat wasn't very bad because the sky was cloudy. Finally, a truck came with a wood framed cargo box covered with green canvas. The truck was our bus; the cargo box had two wood planks at each side of the box, used as benches to seat the passengers. Six passengers came off the truck from Camagüey, and quickly they were interrogated by Aníbal. He looked at their identification cards and other documents and he wrote down their names in his notebook.

The passengers in our line began to get on the truck. They gave their tickets to the truck driver and presented their identification cards to the policeman who came in the truck. The policeman looked at the identification cards and requested the documents authorizing the trip. Aníbal came to us and said in a very low voice that he didn't know the policeman that came today with the *guagua*. "But don't worry," he said. "I will identify with him."

I looked at Alex, a little scared, and he told me to keep calm; Aníbal would solve the problem. He also told me that I wouldn't have problems because I had the letter from the plant authorizing me to go to Camagüey to look for spare parts.

Aníbal approached the policeman, spoke with him, and showed his ID card. Then he looked at Alex and called him. I saw Alex give his identification to the policeman and remain standing with Aníbal next to the officer. The passengers in line continued to get on the truck without any incident until a woman in front of me gave her ID card to the policeman, but could not produce any documents authorizing her trip. The policeman asked her again for the documents and she said that her mother was in a hospital in Camagüey and that she was bringing her a bar of soap and vitamins that the hospital didn't have. The woman began arguing with the policeman; when Aníbal heard of the problem between the woman and the officer, immediately he intervened.

First, he greeted her and asked about the health of her mother. The woman was looking nervous and agitated and Aníbal tried to calm her down but she started crying. Then he told the policeman that the woman was an active *compañera* that cooperated with the CDR and participated in all the revolutionary activities and that he would vouch for her. The policeman looked at her again and seemed to be thinking about the situation. Then Aníbal opened his handbag and took out two cans of fish and gave them to the officer telling him, "*Compañero*, I want to give you these fish cans produced here in Santa Cruz in the *Combinado Pesquero Argerico Lara* where I work with the husband of this *compañera* and where I am also the labor union delegate."

The police said, "*Compañero, cederista*, if you *avala* her, it is good. But, *compañera*, always remember to have your documentation because the revolution must be vigilant of the *elemento antisocial* and the *escoria*." Then he looked towards me and asked for my papers. I gave them to him and when he saw my letter he said, "*Compañero*, I see that you also work in the *combinado*."

Aníbal told him, "Yes, *compañero*, Genaro works with us."

The police told all passengers to move into the truck, so Alex and I sat at the end of the box looking at the road. We were fourteen passengers, seven on each side, seated on the wood planks. It wasn't very comfortable, but the trip wasn't very long. The policeman jumped in the crew cab next to the driver and told him, "We must go now before the rain because the road is full of potholes filled with mud."

The truck left the town and took the road towards the city of Camagüey. Indeed, the road was full of potholes and the truck couldn't go very fast. It jumped like a goat. Fortunately, the road wasn't very busy; we only passed two or three trucks from the agricultural cooperatives. The passengers were very quiet; some had their eyes closed, and others had their open in a blank gaze. Somehow, we seemed like a group of prisoners transported from jail. The first part of the way when we left Santa Cruz we went through marshes and swamps, but later we saw some cattle grazing in poor grass fields and neglected sugar cane plantations.

Far away at a distance, I saw the silhouette of two sugar mills against the horizon, probably closed. The government closed in the year 2002 more than seventy sugar mills, which represented half of the mills operating in the country at that time. In the year 2006, only forty-two sugar mills were working. Some of the mills closed were dismantled and the machinery parts were used to repair the few mills that continued operating. In the year 2005 only one and a half million tons of sugar was produced. The island before 1959 produced more than eight and a half million tons.

The revolutionary government divided Camagüey Province in two provinces, Ciego de Avila and Camagüey. Camagüey province, before 1959, was the largest producer of dairy products in Cuba and famous for its cattle herds. It was the richest province on the island. It was famous for its Holstein cows and its modern dairy farms with their milking machines. The Socialist projects of *Unidades Basicas de Producción Agropecuarias* (UBPA) created the collective property that it is for all, but in reality, no one is in charge of it. Aggravated by management corruption, the outlook for the province has become hopeless. Its vast grazing plains of high quality pasture have been transformed into leafy fields of *marabú*. The great cattle facilities have disappeared from the landscape. The cows of the neglected cooperatives do not give milk, but inspire pity.

As I was watching that devastated landscape and thinking what it had been before the revolution, the woman with the mother in the hospital tried to establish conversation with me. First, she said that she thought it was going to rain. Later she began to complain about the truck seats. I was trying to cut her short, but she insisted on chatting. Finally, she asked me if I was *cederista* like the guy seated opposite to us. She discreetly pointed to Alex. I told her that I wasn't. Then she asked for my name, saying, "Because your face isn't familiar."

I didn't know what to say to her, but I decided to follow the game plan so I told her that my name was Genaro Lopez and that I worked in the plant. She looked at me and told me, "I am Ines, the wife of Otilio Martinez, and I believe that he has mentioned your name." She added, "I am not from Santa Cruz; I am from Camagüey. I have been in Santa Cruz for less than a year, since I married Otilio. That's why I don't know all the people in town."

I breathed deeply, thinking that I was very lucky that she didn't know the real Genaro Lopez.

Apparently, Genaro didn't have a reputation in the plant of being very strong government sympathizer, so the woman continued complaining about the health system on the island. She told me that her mother was admitted to the hospital in Camagüey and that the patients had to bring their own soap, towels, and bed linen because the hospital didn't give them. She said that her mother had high blood pressure and she was anemic. She needed vitamins that don't have potassium, which the hospital didn't have. The mother need to take Enarapril for high blood pressure, and when she went to the state pharmacy with the *tarjeton* to buy the medication, the pharmacy simply told her that they didn't have any. They told her that apparently the government had sent many medications to Venezuela for the program *Barrio Adentro*. Her cousin Gladys, who lived in Miami, had sent her a package with Enarapril, vitamins, and a bar of soap. As soon as she received the package—thanks to God, the government didn't open it—she went to take the *guagua* to Camagüey. That was the reason why she had forgotten to request permission from the CDR.

The woman, with her face full of resignation, said, "Well, thanks to Aníbal *que me tiro la toalla,* I was able to take the *guagua*. But from now on, he is going to *joder,* forcing me to participate in all *actividades revolucionarias* of the CDR. You know life in Cuba, it ain't easy."

During the trip, Alex didn't speak to me. He only watched me and smiled when he saw me talking with Ines. I imagine that he was enjoying the predicaments that I had with her. The two hour trip, watching the misery of the once prosperous land and hearing the sad stories of Ines, served as prelude for what I was going to endure during the next days in the Socialist Cuba of the Castro brothers.

CHAPTER 15

▼

CAMAGÜEY, THE CITY OF THE TINAJONES

Jones pointed to the map and said, "Now I'm beginning to follow you, Henry. Here is the city of Camagüey. It's the third largest city on the island; I know that because I have some good friends from Miami whose parents came from there. They used to brag about the enormous wealth of that area."

"You are right, Mr. Jones; Camagüey is the third largest city in Cuba, with more than two hundred and seventy thousand inhabitants. The city is full of old squares and it was famous for its traditional *tinajones*. It is smaller than Havana, but its colonial architecture is very beautiful and of an elegant simplicity. Before the revolution, the Province of Camagüey was probably the wealthiest province in the island."

Henry sighed. "Mr. Jones, now I come back to my story, picking up the thread of my tale in downtown Camagüey."

✳   ✳   ✳   ✳

Downtown was full of foreign tourists who were walking around the narrow colonial streets and squares of the city. Some were coming in and out of the foreign-only currency stores for the tourists. Between them in the corners of the squares, I noticed the famous *jineteras* mixing with the tourists, hunting for foreigners who would trade sex for money, food, and even bath soap. These poor souls worked like this only for necessity to help their families and to survive the misery in which they live on the island.

Our truck stopped at the local bus station called the Terminal de Municipalidades, to the northeast of downtown. Since we were coming from the south along the street called Republica, I had the opportunity to see parts of the center of the city. It was already eleven-fifteen in the morning and the traffic was light. What caught my attention were the so-called *bici taxis*—modified bicycles with a sidecar for a passenger and a trunk for the baggage. The passengers of these vehicles were foreign tourists sightseeing in the city. The exteriors of the hotels and tourist restaurants were rather well conserved, in contrast to the houses and stores for the Cubans, which looked neglected, with the outside walls peeling off and some propped up to avoid cave-ins.

As the truck was going through downtown, I could hardly recognize the place. I said to myself, *This city is not the Camagüey that I knew during my youth.* It was the image of a city in ruins with superficial make-up to satisfy the curiosity of the foreign tourists during their brief visits. The place looked dirty and derelict, the people were sad, and nobody was smiling. Then I asked myself. *What has became of the elegant beauty of the Camagüeyana woman, now turned into a jinetera by the miseries of the Socialist revolution?*

We passed in front of the train station and the Ignacio Agramonte museum and finally we arrived at the Terminal de Municipalidades. The station was full of people waiting for transportation to the towns within the provinces of Camagüey and Ciego de Avila. The people were poorly dressed and with anguished faces, standing in lines with their canvas bags, very similar to the ones that Alex and I had. Alex had explained to me that in Cuba it is very common to see people with canvas handbags. They are very useful for carrying any type of food or articles that one can buy during the day. Another reason was that the state stores didn't provide paper or plastic bags.

When we came down from the truck, I noticed that the station was full of the feared state security officers and *cederistas*, some in uniform and others in civilian clothes. They were walking around and looking at the passengers' identification cards. Suddenly a man dressed in civilian clothes requested our documents. I gave mine and after checking it, he ordered me to go ahead. He did the same with Alex. I saw that Alex said something to him before he walked away, but I didn't pay any attention to it. The fact was that Alex left the station very quickly, walking in front of me without saying anything to me.

I followed him for two blocks until he stopped in front of the Ignacio Agramonte museum. He glanced at the outside of the building, then turned to me and said, "Here comes the car to pick up us."

When I looked at the street, I saw that Alex opened a car door and entered in it. I, without thinking, did the same, sitting in the back seat of the car. When I looked at the driver, I realized that he was the same guy that had looked at our documentation at the station. Nobody said a word for at least a minute. Finally, Alex said to the driver, "Norberto, drop us off in the Agramonte Square."

The driver said, "Very well, Armando. I will be waiting for you tonight at home. Raúl is going to speak today at a convention of the Cuban Women's Federation, all the *empachaos* are going to be watching the television, and nobody will see you guys coming into the house. We are expecting to hear something about the health of the *penco senil*."

Ten blocks later, the car dropped us at the famous Agramonte Park at the center of the city. The park was full of foreign tourists, drivers of *bici taxi*, Cuban *cuentapropista* selling tobacco and any other things to the tourists, and by all means the famous *jineteras*. I also saw several policemen walking around the square very discreetly without speaking to anybody, only watching and frightening the people with their look. We took a walk around the square and crossed in front of the famous La Casa de la Trova, which was fairly well conserved for foreign tourism. Later we walked in front of the library building and turned left to Martí Street. In the next block in Lugareño Street, we saw the birthplace of the poet Nicholas Guillén. There we stopped for a while, watching the outside of the house which is a museum that tourists visit. At the door, we saw two policemen guarding the place.

Then, Alex said, "In that small house less that half a block away, we are going to visit Leonor Correa. She is my clandestine contact with the *Damas de Blanco*. She works in the *Ministerio del Interior* (MININT) as a radio dispatcher of the patrols; her husband is a drill sergeant in the *Fuerzas Armadas Revolucionaria* (FAR). He is away most of the time, only comes home every two weeks and spends three or four days in the house. In the Ministry, she works from four in the afternoon until midnight, receiving notifications by radio and sending orders to the patrol cars. For the average level of income for Cuban families, this couple is doing well. Between the two of them, they make nine hundred pesos per month, about forty-five U.S. dollars. However, she doesn't agree with the drastic government punishments given to the dissidents. She quietly, in secrecy, works with the *Damas de Blanc*o."

He paused and told me, "You can see, Henry, her case is completely different from Aníbal in Santa Cruz. Leonor cooperates with us for her convictions and Aníbal for necessity."

He said, "Our secret signal is that when her husband is home, she leaves that window open. It isn't that her husband is a *comecandela Fidelista*. But she doesn't want to jeopardize and destroy his military career, so she keeps him away from her clandestine activities. They are in their thirties and don't have children. Both have a reputation of being very good revolutionaries, like Aníbal and Maritza. As you already know, everybody has to fake it in Cuba to survive the outrages of the system."

We walked towards the house and saw that the window was closed. Alex knocked at the door and a woman quickly opened it and immediately invited us to come in. She greeted Alex and he introduced me as Genaro from Santa Cruz del Sur. I could see that Leonor was an educated woman. The house was humble but very clean and the inside maintained well. She was dressed in a light blue blouse and dark blue skirt and her black shining hair was neatly arranged.

Leonor invited us to sit at the dining room table to have lunch with her. She told us that usually she took her lunch a little bit later because she began work at four in the afternoon. She had prepared a plate of rice with *picadillo* and boiled *malanguitas*. She apologized for the menu, but with the rationing notebook called *libreta*, not much could be bought in the state stores. She told us that they usually didn't buy anything on the illegal market due to the nature of her job in the Ministry and her husband's career in the FAR, although she knew that almost everybody in Cuba did. She ended by saying, "Well, you know that the life in Cuba, it ain't easy."

During lunch, we talked about how the movement of *Las Damas de Blanco* began three years ago on March 18, 2003, the date known as the Black Spring of Cuba. On that day, the government unjustly jailed seventy-five peaceful opponents for the crime of defending their rights to the freedom of expression, for wishing the well-being of the people, and for loving their country. The majority of them were independent journalists and writers. Among them was also included a woman, the economist Martha Beatriz Roque. They were convicted to prison sentences from six to twenty-eight years. Fifteen of them were released little by little from April 2004 to December 2005. Then the fifteen were jailed again, but due to their poor health, they were released again few days later.

Motivated by these events of massive abuse of power, the movement of *Las Damas de Blanco* arose. The spouses, sisters, and daughters of the prisoners integrated the group which, every Sunday after Mass was celebrated in the church of

Santa Rita in Marianao, met and peacefully marched in silence in the street, challenging the Communist dictatorship. They only asked for the freedom of their loved ones. The movement had grown, and now this ritual was being observed in every corner of the island. It now included the participation of thousands of women. Due to their courage and dignity to fight pacifically for the freedom of the political prisoners, the movement had obtained the Andrei Sajarov Prize from the European Parliament in 2005.

Leonor proudly said that the arrogance and the cruelty of the Communist regime saw itself helpless in front of the courage of these women who demanded the immediate and unconditional freedom of the sixty people who remained in prison. Alex interrupted the conversation to remind Leonor that *Las Damas de Blanco* should also request the freedom of all Cuban political prisoners, who number in the thousands, for those that have been in prison for years, just as for those that have been taken recently and haven't been put to trial yet.

Moreover, Alex continued, "Leonor, you know how they mistreat and abuse those prisoners. They find themselves hopeless and they go on hunger strikes for many weeks until they almost die. And remember, the government refuses to provide medical assistance for them. It is unbelievable, the repression and the harassment from the security of the state to all the relatives of the political prisoners." He commented on the precarious prison situation in which was Dr. Oscar Elías Biscet, a prisoner of conscience and president of the Lawton Foundation for Human Rights.

Leonor, with an affirmative gesture, said that it seemed fair to her and that she would discuss the matter with the leadership of the group. She continued telling us about the new programs and meetings planned by the group. Alex said that the movement was expanding around all the free countries of the world and that our group was raising resources to help the political prisoners in Cuba. "Our group sees in *Las Damas de Blanco* a women's movement with great courage and with a noble cause that we want to continue supporting."

We were more than one hour speaking with Leonor and at the end of the conversation, Alex gave her an envelope with five thousand dollars to aid the prisoners and their relatives. Leonor said, "Armando, I am going to repeat the question that I always ask. Are you sure that this money doesn't come from the *Yanki* CIA? Because if it does, I can't accept it. That is what Fidel said, that the CIA finances the dissidents in Cuba."

Alex told her, "You can be sure, Leonor, that this money comes from the Cubans in exile and their friends who want the freedom of Cuba. I can tell you that our group infringes the laws of the United States and takes great risk to send this money to their brothers in Communist Cuba's political prisons. Leonor, I trust you and know that you are an honest woman who fights in silence for the freedom of the Cuban people."

Leonor took the envelope and said to us, "This generous sum of money, which we deeply appreciate, will be used to buy food, medicines, and other needed articles for the political prisoners in Cuba. It will also be used to help the prisoners' families to survive while their spouses and children are in the jails."

Then she asked, "Armando, from which group could I say this money is from?" Alex told her that it came from the heart of the Cubans in exile, for their brothers in prison as reminder that they were not forgotten, to help them maintain their faith and confidence that their sacrifices wouldn't be in vain.

We said good-bye to Leonor and when we were leaving the house, a policeman was passing by. I imagined that since our faces were not familiar, he stopped and asked Leonor if there was any problem. She very naturally said to him that there wasn't any, that we were from Ciego de Avila and came to Camagüey for a few days for assigned tasks from the CDR and that we had brought her a letter and photos from her cousin Rina from Ciego. She then said, "Thank you, *compañero,* for your revolutionary vigilance."

We took Lugareño Street towards the south to go to our second appointment on 24 de Febrero Street, only four blocks away. While we were walking, we briefly compared our impressions of the meeting with Leonor. I told Alex that she had made a very favorable impression on me. Alex said that Leonor was a good example of a Cuban disillusioned with the revolution and in search of a right and rational system. Alex pointed out that she and her husband were born and brought up in a Socialist system and knew very little of other political and economic systems, only what the regime had taught them. Nevertheless, because they were honest people, they could see the injustice, the corruption, and the repression that the regime maintained to control the population.

Alex said, "I don't know if she understands what democracy and the free market economy are. But, because she has honesty and human sensitivity, I can assume that her mind is open to accept and to learn new political and economic models. For that reason, she got involved with *Las Damas de Blanco* in quiet, secret protest against the injustices of the regime. This is her objective. I don't believe that she has in mind any other intentions, so far. But remember, *mi hermano,* not everybody has the same fighting objectives. I believe that the love of freedom is the common denominator of the people of good faith."

Our next visit was with two men related to the *Bibliotecas Independientes* movement. He said, "This group has dedicated itself to the peaceful job of keeping the people informed that there exists another world outside the isolation produced by the sugar cane-chaff wall that the regime has constructed in Cuba. The Socialist government controls all news, radio, and television programs, education curricula, books, and newspapers that the Cuban people can access. The function of the *Bibliotecas Independientes* is to provide the citizenship with all types of information that can't be found in the public libraries. They try to satisfy the diverse interests and needs of their users who go to them to solve scholastic tasks, to investigate scientific subjects, to watch videotapes, and to hear music CDs. They have books by authors prohibited in Cuba, and magazines and newspapers from other countries. In addition, they offer diverse cultural activities like exhibitions and conferences that promote civil society and improve the educational level of their users so that the people have the judgment necessary to decide the way the Cuban nation will go in the future. Their work is very important."

He added, "We give books and other cultural materials to them and we are helping them economically. Many organizations and countries also help them. The government persecutes them, harasses their members, closes them down, and seizes their books. Nevertheless, they reopen new libraries in other locations. It is a great movement to develop civil society in Cuba. Currently, there are eighteen librarians in prison under the criminal charges of *peligrosidad social.* Some fulfill sentences up to twenty-five years."

When we were close to our destination, we saw a policeman coming toward us. Alex said, "Don't look at him. These guys usually only follow orders from their superiors. They operate like robots because they want to do the least work possible. If they do something, it is for their own benefit. You saw the one that asked Leonor if there was any problem. The policeman knew that she works in the MININT and he wanted to demonstrate to her that he was a good revolutionary in case he needs her recommendation for a better job." Indeed, the state security agent continued on his way after taking a good look at us.

Alex stopped at last. "That is the apartment house on 24 de Febrero Street." The apartment house had two floors with only one entrance door to the street. Our meeting was in apartment number four. Alex told me that he never had been in this place. "We are going to proceed with caution and follow this strategy. First, go around the block while I walk in the front of the door of the building, see the distribution of the apartments, and confirm that the door of the building is open. I will see you on the other corner and then I will tell you what are we going to do. While you walk around the block, look around to see if you see any strange movement on the block behind the apartment, like cars of the state security or groups of people waiting for somebody."

When I saw Alex again a block from the apartment, I told him that I hadn't seen anything unusual. Alex said, "Apartment four is on the second floor so we will have to climb the stairs. I will go first while you remain here. When you see the window of one of the apartments on the second floor close, that is my signal that you can enter the building and go up the stairs and knock at the door with a single blow."

Alex walked towards the building, entered, and in less than two minutes, I saw a window on the second floor was closing. I entered the lobby where there were two flags painted on the wall; one was a Cuban flag and other one was the *26 de Julio* flag. Above them a signboard read, "This is Your House, Fidel." I watched this display of *Fidelismo* with indifference, and I thought that I was already getting used to all this propaganda. I immediately climbed the stairs to the second floor, where there were two doors, one to the left and another one to the right. I saw that the door on the right was number four, so I gave it a single blow and immediately Alex opened it.

The apartment was neat and tidy, although the furniture looked a little old and out of fashion. The living room had a Panda television set and a short-wave radio. The walls were decorated with old photos of *tinajones* and landscapes of the countryside *Camagüeyano*. As apparently in all the houses in Cuba, the walls needed a fresh coat of paint. In summary, the apartment had seen better days, but now it needed some remodeling.

Two men were with Alex. They seemed to be in their fifties. One was called Erasmo and the other was Gerardo. They said that they worked in state companies and began very early in the morning so they had free afternoons. When Alex asked them who the neighbors of the apartment were and if there was any *chivato*, both smiled and Erasmo said that there wasn't a problem. The owners of the apartment were his parents, who lived in one of the apartments on the first floor. The parents of his wife lived in the other and Gerardo was married to his sister, Carmen, and they lived in apartment three across the hall. The two families were very good friends and they had moved together to this building during the first years of the revolution to avoid the government's confiscation of the apartment house from them when the revolutionary government made the law of *Reforma Urbana*. Erasmo proudly said, "Our old men had a good idea. Here, we all live together to survive the *mierda* of this revolution. Because, *compañeros*, "it ain't easy."

Erasmo thanked Alex for the economic aid and for the books and materials that Alex's group regularly sent to the libraries. Alex reminded them that all this operation was clandestine and executed under great risk of loss of life or imprisonment. Erasmo said that even though the state's censorship and repression was applied every day with more force, the *Bibliotecas Independientes* project had opened more than fifteen libraries throughout the island in the past three months, thanks to the support received from groups outside of the island.

Alex mentioned that he had heard of the idea to celebrate in Cuba a National Congress of Independent Libraries, which would be summoned by the *Aamblea para Promover La Sociedad Civil.* He said that he didn't like the idea. Alex explained to them that, under the current situation of threats and repression from the regime, defying it just to defy it could put in danger the existence of one of the most serious and successful programs of civil society. The *Bibliotecas Independientes,* with their limited resources, had broken the state monopoly, providing the Cuban people with the truth about a civilized society. The destruction of these libraries, resulting from irresponsible decisions, would mean a hard blow to the fight for freedom.

Erasmo and Gerardo said that they understood Alex's concerns and that they considered it was very important to discuss more on this subject. They suggested that, taking advantage of our visit to their house, they perhaps could ask a clandestine representative of the *asamblea* dissident group to come to the house to talk about this issue. Alex thought a little about it and finally agreed with the suggestion. "That wasn't in our program," he said, "but it seems very important." Erasmo called a man named Roberto and invited him for dinner and to hear Raúl's speech. Roberto accepted the invitation and said that he would be in the house around six-thirty.

Later, Gerardo told us that the issue of our discussions with Roberto could be elevated to the leaders of the dissidents and the librarians. He added that it has always seemed to him that the odd habit of making assemblies has been inherited from the Communist regime. "Frequently at all these meetings, nothing is solved," he said.

Alex, Erasmo, and Gerardo were busy preparing a list of the books that the libraries didn't have and noting which libraries needed books. While they were working with their list, I was getting drowsy and had to make an effort to stay awake. The day seemed very long, even if it had been stimulating.

After an hour of work I saw that Alex gave an envelope to Erasmo and told him, "Here you have twenty-five hundred dollars for the librarians, to help them in their work." Then Alex asked about a man called Pepe Herrera and Erasmo said that he was in prison waiting for a trial. The state security had arrested him two days after the *acto de repudio* in his home with the illegal confiscation of his short-wave radio and typewriter. The authorities accused him of *figura delictiva de peligrosidad social.* I found out that Erasmo and Gerardo were Pepe's replacement at our meeting.

We continued talking about the precarious situation that the Cuban people live under in the Socialist regime and as an example Gerardo told us that many post offices in different municipalities were being closed due to the little mail they had to handle. The island had come to a complete standstill; people were sad and simply trying to survive the shortages and the misery of their life. The youth, as always rebellious, understood that they had no future in Cuba.

It was already 6:25 p.m. when somebody knocked at the door. We all stopped talking and Erasmo rose and asked who was it. From the other side of the door a voice said, "It is I, Roberto."

Erasmo opened the door and a young man came in, not very well dressed, of probably less than thirty years of age. He greeted Erasmo and Gerardo. Erasmo introduced us only as Armando and Genaro. Then Erasmo explained to him that we didn't belong to any political group of the dissident movement, but that we were helping economically the *Bibliotecas Independientes* with resources raised abroad. He told us that Roberto was one of the coordinators of the dissidents' *asamblea* group in the province of Camagüey.

The young man looked at us with certain indifference. We all noticed his attitude, but nobody said anything. Erasmo was the one that continued, saying, "Our friend Armando has expressed his concerns in relation to the idea of celebrating a Congress of Independent Libraries summoned by the *asamblea* of dissident groups. He considers that the gathering now could be a dangerous move. It represents a challenge to the regime without any intention other than to defy it. This act could place in jeopardy the existence of one of the most effective projects of civil society."

Before the young man spoke, Alex said to him, "It is very commendable, the assistance of the dissidents' *asamblea* on education and the information of the public opinion and the stimulus to citizen participation in the work of the dissident organizations. We agree with the determination to articulate a peaceful social movement that allows preparation for the change to democracy. The formation of a democratic culture in that process is very important, which has been the work of the libraries. I consider that the objective of the gathering is to improve the program. However, the libraries don't need to improve, because they are doing their job very efficiently. We don't need more martyrs—already too many Cubans have died. We need all honest men and women in Cuba to work in the construction of a democratic society." He concluded, "The independent journalists and the libraries are the most active and consistent sectors of civil society on the island. Their success is, among other factors, their detachment from political parties and their independent attitude."

The young Roberto looked, as he didn't know what to say. Finally, after thinking for a while, he said, "The dissidents' *asamblea* is a civic communitarian group of parties with the objective of developing and promoting ethical and patriotic principles. We employ all the efforts and resources we have to help the work of the *Bibliotecas Independientes* to extend them through the island and made them more reachable to the common citizen."

He then paused, and added, "I will speak with the director in Camagüey, and perhaps you, Armando, can offer your observations to the *asamblea* leaders in Havana."

Erasmo realized that Roberto could not solve much more, so he decided to change the tone of the conversation, saying, "*Caballeros,* I believe that we need to eat dinner. My parents have promised to prepare something to offer Armando and Genaro." Jokingly, he added, "We'll add a little more water to the soup for Roberto." Gerardo stood up and said, "I am going down to see what has been done."

When Gerardo left, we kept speaking of the success of the general meeting of the dissidents' *asamblea* that had taken place the year before on May 21. They were saying that government repression had increased against not only the dissidents and members of the civil society, but against all the population. The MININT and the PNR handled the repression while the CDR, *Partido Comunista* (PCC), and other groups organized by the labor unions kept the population under pressure. While this was happening, the FAR was invisible. With all the force that this institution had, it didn't get directly involved in repressive acts. The generals and colonels lived very well, dedicated to lucrative business activities of industry and commerce with the tourists and the special stores that only sold in hard currencies. Rumors were that the FAR wasn't prepared for an effective defense of the island in case of a *Yanki* invasion, due to the lack of spare parts, resources, and military training.

Suddenly Gerardo entered the room followed by two women who brought two trays with five plates of food and place settings. Gerardo carried another tray with glasses and a pitcher of water. Erasmo briefly introduced the women as "my wife Hilda and my sister Carmen." They greeted us and went away immediately. The plates had *picadillo*, rice, and boiled *malanguitas*. I took a glance at it and said to myself, *Close your eyes and swallow.* Erasmo told us that the state store only had that available that week. The good foods are only available in the special stores that only now accept *chavitos*. He ended saying, "Friends, the life in Cuba, it ain't easy."

After we finished the dinner, Alex said we were already a little behind schedule so we had to go. We said good-bye to all and went down the stairs. When we got out in the street, we realized that it was raining a little. Alex said, "I am glad that it is raining; it is already dark and we must walk more than eight blocks. When it is raining the policemen don't go out because they don't like to get wet!"

The streets were dark—not a single streetlight illuminated them. Only the reflection from the dimly lit windows of the houses could be seen. We walked quickly, like two shadows, through the desolated streets of the city. We didn't see anybody on our way; we only had the company of the spring drizzle that fell on our caps.

Ten minutes later, we stopped in front of a house that bore a poster with Cuban and *26 de Julio* flags painted on it. It read, *Comité de Defensa de la Revolución*. Alex told me, "We are going to spend the night here."

CHAPTER 16

▼

THE CAPTAIN AND THE LIEUTENANT

"All these clandestine meetings with Cuban dissidents—you and your friend Alex were really looking for trouble," Mr. Jones said. "But why didn't you go back to Grand Cayman as you planned? How did you end up in Havana?"

Henry explained, "I am going to tell you what happened that night that made Alex change his plans. It was quite an experience. That was one of the reasons that I am here in Havana. If you think that we were playing with fire, wait until I tell you what happened the next day, Mr. Jones."

*   *   *   *

The familiar face of *compañero* Norberto opened the door of the house. He said he was waiting for us and asked how our day had gone. Alex just answered, "Fine." Alex had told me to refrain to make any comment about our meetings. Norberto didn't need to know what we did during the day. His function was only to facilitate our transportation and lodging. Immediately Norberto's wife, Gloria, came into the room. They seemed to be in their late fifties, and they had two grown children; both these boys were soldiers in the FAR. The house was not very big, but for them it appeared to be comfortable. It had two rooms; one for them and other that was shared by the two sons when they lived at home. The living room had, like the one of Aníbal, the famous Panda television set, the short-wave radio, and the photos of Fidel, Che, and Raúl, the new temporary *máximo líder*. The furniture didn't match, just like in Aníbal's home. It seemed to me that this design was very common in CDR houses. The television set had on the only show of the night, the Federation of Women Convention.

We didn't pay much attention to the television because Alex wanted to call Juan in Santa Cruz to prepare my return. We went to our bedroom, which obviously was the boys' room. Alex pulled out the STU-III phone from his handbag and checked for messages. He found that Julisa had called that evening at seven o'clock. While he was dealing with the telephone, Gloria knocked at the door asking if we wanted to eat something. Alex thanked her and said that we already had eaten. Gloria told us that she had rice with *picadillo* and boiled *malanguitas*. That it was the only thing that the state store had this week, a good week, she said, because usually they don't have anything to sell at all. Alex thanked her again and playfully said, "Save me that for another day."

We closed the door, leaving Gloria and Norberto watching the television in the living room. Alex called Julisa and she answered immediately. I noticed in the face of Alex that Julisa was giving bad news to him. Alex told her to continue looking for him, that it was very important to find him, and to call back in two hours because he had to make a decision tonight. When he hung up the telephone, he told me that Genaro had disappeared in Grand Cayman. This was a very serious problem. There were several probabilities. Maybe he didn't want to return to the island after seeing what life without the miseries of Cuba could be. Another possibility was that he had contacts with some *balseros* who were living in Grand Cayman. However, the worst thing would be that he had contacted Castro's agents in Grand Cayman. This last possibility could put in danger the group that worked with Alex in Santa Cruz, including Juan, Captain Pombo, and Aníbal. He stopped for a moment to think, and then told me that my identity of Genaro Lopez was not safe. Neither was his own. If they couldn't find Genaro tonight, our identities and documents would have to change.

We went to the living room where Gloria and Norberto were watching television. Alex sat next to Norberto and asked him, "When does the train for Havana leave?"

"The Number Thirteen usually leaves about eleven at night," Norberto said.

Alex didn't say anything; he stood very quietly, thinking. Then he asked, "Norberto, do you think it would be possible to find two ID cards, documents authorizing the trip, and two tickets for that train to Havana?"

Norberto looked at him in surprise and asked, "How soon do you need all that?"

"Tomorrow," Alex said.

Norberto jumped from his chair and said, "For tomorrow!"

Alex told him, "Well, it isn't for sure yet, but I will know more in a couple of hours."

Norberto said, "Well, you know, Armando, that in Cuba everything is possible when there are dollars on the table."

Then Gloria said, "Listen, guys, the new leader, Raúl, is going to make his speech." We took advantage of the event to keep our minds away from our unexpected trip to Havana and what we would have to do if Genaro didn't turn up. We all sat down to watch the television for a while.

Raúl began his speech by bringing back the old stories of the glories of his brother and the revolution. Gloria said, "The good thing is that this *comemierda* speaks shorter that the *cabrón* brother."

Suddenly, Norberto asked Alex, "Armando, when do you think that you are going to know that you need these things? Because tomorrow is Saturday and the CDR has several activities programmed."

Alex only answered that soon he would know.

When Norberto and Alex were talking, Gloria shouted, "Listen what the *comemierda* is saying." Raúl was saying that he had mobilized thousands of the military, including retired soldiers, and turned them into detectives to investigate the corruption that was expanding like a mortal cancer on the island. We all stopped our conversation and watched the television. Raúl Castro, the provisional president of the council of state, commander in chief of the armed forces, and first secretary of the central committee of the Communist Party, continued, saying that the six thousand active military and two thousand retired, working in pairs, had discovered that the situation of the country was much more serious than its leaders had imagined. Raúl was heading a national commission against the corruption and illegalities created in the last three years by the Communist Party. Gesturing at his chest with his hands, he added, "The metastasis of this mortal cancer is being transferred from the knee up to here."

Norberto said, "It is incredible that the number two in the hierarchy of the regime could say that. Something big is happening in Cuba—corruption is not a new phenomenon on the island. Fidel will never yield complete control and never will yield the power. Perhaps Raúl wants to consolidate his power because the *penco senil's* health must be very *jodida*."

The rest of the speech was rather routine, with the same revolutionary slogans, but with a less aggressive tone against the traditional enemies. It seemed peculiar that Raúl didn't mention Hugo Chávez, the Venezuelan dictator, and the *Revolución Bolivariana* in his speech.

We all talked about the speech for quite a long time. Norberto was looking worried as he repeated that something big was cooking in Cuba. The next day he planned to learn more about the situation. "The reality is that the people can't put up with it anymore—life in Cuba is a hell of violence, shortages, deficiencies, and annoyances arbitrarily imposed by an incompetent bureaucracy."

With a sad face Norberto added, "The system doesn't work because it is bad and in opposition to reason, not only for the stupidity of the administrators of this tragic comedy of intrigue. Here everybody must have two faces to be able to survive this *mierda*. We make believe that we are *Fidelistas* and we keep watching and *jodemos* the people. On the other hand, we don't like the regime and we commit all types of illegalities, because, *compañeros,* it is necessary to find a solution daily to be able to live here. The life in Cuba, it ain't easy."

Around ten o'clock Julisa called from Grand Cayman to tell us that Genaro was still missing. Alex told her that we had to make changes. They should continue looking for Genaro, but I couldn't return to Grand Cayman through the same route I came to Cuba on. He asked if Alberto was in the house. Julisa said that he was out with Manny, looking for Genaro. Alex said that he was going to call him the next day, and he told Julisa that they had to be cautious because they all were in danger if Genaro made contact with Castro's spies.

After he finished with Julisa, he immediately called Juan, who also had a STU-III security telephone. Juan answered immediately. Alex explained the situation to him and told him that he should alert first Captain Pombo, and then mention it to Aníbal the next day. All those in the Santa Cruz group were in great danger if Genaro made contact with the *balseros* and Castro's spies in Grand Cayman. He told Juan that he and Pombo should bury their special telephone. They would maintain contact through other people in the region. He ended the conversation by telling him that all arrangements for my return were cancelled.

Alex told me that Juan was very upset with Genaro. He was the one who recommend Genaro for the mission. Juan could not believe that Genaro was a spy. However, he knew that he was desperate to leave the island. He understood that Genaro maybe wasn't the right man for that job, and he was very sorry.

Then Alex made another telephone call with the STU-III. I realized that he was preparing my new way to leave Cuba. When he finished, he told me, "*Mi hermano,* you are going to have to leave from the south coast of Pinar del Río to Yucatan. First, we must prepare our trip to Havana for tomorrow night."

He didn't give me time to answer—he stood up and went to the living room where Norberto was listening to *Radio Martí.* Gloria had already gone to sleep in her bedroom. Alex took a seat in front of Norberto and told him that we needed two ID cards, letters justifying our trip to Havana, and two tickets for tomorrow night's train to Havana. Norberto's first reaction was to ask what had happened. Alex told him, "Don't worry, this is a precautionary measure."

"Well, tomorrow is Saturday, but that is perhaps better for us, because on the weekends the CDRs have many *actividades* and the *empachaos* are all in them."

"How much do you think all this will cost?"

Norberto thought for a moment and said, "At least eight hundred dollars U.S. I need to talk with Gloria so she can cover me in the *actividades* that CDR has programmed for the weekend. I need to dedicate all my time to arranging your trip."

Alex told him, "Tomorrow we have to go to several places in town. Could you drive us to town around eight-thirty in the morning? We would see you at the train station later in the evening, about ten-fifteen."

Norberto nodded. "You'll need photos for the ID cards. Before dropping you in town, we can stop at the house of a friend of mine who is a photographer."

It was almost eleven o'clock and the electric lights began to blink until they went away totally. Norberto lighted several candles and said, "You see, this is happening almost every night. Now for a while, we will have running water in the faucet, which we didn't have during the day. Now, the people must gather water to have it tomorrow. The electricity might return tomorrow in the morning, but then the water goes away again. This, *compañero,* is the *mierda* where we live."

When we heard that there was tap water, Alex asked if there was enough for us to take baths. Norberto said yes, but we should do it quickly because sometimes the water goes away again. He gave us a little bar of soap and two small white towels and told us, "A friend of mine that works with tourism gave me this soap and towels when I fixed his refrigerator. These are luxury articles in Cuba. Only the special stores have soap and towels." He also gave us two shirts that were old but clean. He told us that he confiscated them when he made inventories in the houses of people leaving the country, and added, "Where do you think most of this furniture comes from? My friends, they are coming from those *gusanos'* houses."

After taking a short cold-water bath, we went to bed. My mattress was worn out and it felt like the springs were nailed into my back, but it was far better than the camp bed of the night before. Although I was very tired, it took me some time to fall asleep for the anxiety that I felt. I had left New Jersey four days ago and it seemed that a month had passed. I was asking myself what Natalia would be doing. When she sees that I wouldn't return Tuesday, she is going to worry. I suddenly realized that I had to call her to tell her that I was going to Mexico and that I wouldn't be back, at least, until Wednesday or Thursday. Then I thought that I should speak with Alex on this subject. The trip to Havana was still not a sure thing. The train trip worried me; we had the risk of been discovered and captured by the state security agents in the train station. I saw how Alex trusted Norberto, but he didn't give me much confidence. Everything that he did was because Alex gave him money, not from his own patriotic conviction. The fatigue, the tiredness finally won, and I fell asleep.

It was already daytime and the sun's rays were entering through the blinds of the window when Alex shook me and said, "Wake up, Henry, we have much to do today."

"What time is it?"

"It's 7:00 a.m.," he said. "Hurry."

I went to the bathroom and got dressed quickly. Alex did the same. Then I saw him making a phone call with the STU-III phone. He talked for about five minutes, giving me the impression that it was with Alberto. When he hung up, he told me that Alberto was very upset at Genaro's disappearance and that he feared the worst. For that reason, he was taking emergency measures for protection. Alex told me Julisa would travel to Yucatan to bring my passport and my personal belongings. If everything came out well, I would be in Yucatan by Tuesday.

Then I remembered that I had to call Natalia to tell her about the itinerary changes. Alex told me that I could call her with the STU-III, but he advised me not to tell her any details. He said, "Tell her you are going to stay a couple of days more, but don't mention that you are going to Mexico. She probably is going to worry more and ask all types of questions." I thought that Alex was right, but I decided to call her later because Saturday was the only day that she didn't work so she usually slept the morning away.

We went to the living room where Norberto was already waiting. Gloria came and told us to sit at the dining room table so she could bring in some breakfast. As we were waiting, Alex gave an envelope to Norberto. He said, "Here you have a thousand dollars to pay for what I asked you last night. If you have something left after you pay for all expenses, it is for you." Norberto thanked him and, very excited, said that after breakfast we would go to the house of his friend the photographer.

Gloria came with four glasses of *café con leche* and a few pieces of bread. I thought that perhaps this *café con leche* was better than the one at Aníbal's house in Santa Cruz. However, it was the same watered milk with sugar and a trace of coffee. Norberto proudly told us that they always had powdered milk because he fixed the 1954 Chevrolet that a friend who worked in a special store had. Since I was hungry, I drank my *café con leche* with a small piece of bread. While I was having my breakfast, I thought about the wretched way of living in Cuba in contrast with any other place that I had ever been.

After we finished our breakfast, we thanked Gloria, took our canvas bags, and left the house with Norberto. I realized that Norberto's car was a different color than the one we took yesterday when coming from the bus station. Out of curiosity, I asked him, "Norberto, this isn't the same car you used to pick up us from the bus station, is it?"

"You are right, this is another car. I am a mechanic for the *Ministerio del Interior* and when I need a car, I take the one that I am repairing. We are going to my friend Virgilio's home. He works in the Ministry as a photographer and in the archives. He keeps identity cards from people that have gone away from the island or have died, and I'm sure that he should have two that we could use, changing the photos. We are going to see how much money he wants for them. He is a very discreet man and I have confidence in him."

In the streets, I saw few trucks with people and quite a lot of people walking. Norberto told us, "These people go to the *actividades*. They could be military maneuvers or voluntary work in the fields. All these *actividades* are controlled by the CDRs and the *Milicias de Tropas Territoriales* (MTT). I left Gloria in charge of that today."

Ten minutes later, we stopped in front of a three-story apartment house. The walls of the building were peeling and needed painting, like all the other buildings around. Norberto told us to stay in the car so he could speak first with Virgilio. We saw him enter the building. While we were waiting, I took the opportunity to mention my concerns for Norberto. Alex told me, "Don't worry, because he needs the money to live. Although at the beginning he got along with the revolution, he now feels deceived and frustrated by it."

Ten minutes later, Norberto returned and told us to follow him. We climbed the stairs to the third floor and knocked at apartment eight. A quite short, thin man with bulging eyes opened the door. Norberto introduced us to Virgilio and then told him that his friends needed two identity cards for today. Virgilio first said that it wasn't so easy because the Ministry didn't issue ID cards on Saturdays. Then Norberto said, "Virgilio since they are really in a hurry, do you think you could use two of those identification cards that you keep for emergency cases?" Very slowly, as if he were analyzing the possibilities, Virgilio told us that it was possible. However, those were scarce and cost a little more. Norberto asked him, "Virgilio, how much?"

"Three hundred fifty each, American dollars," Virgilio said.

"Virgilio, would you do both for six hundred dollars?"

He looked us over and then said to Norberto. "Well, for being friends of yours, I will do it." Then he took our pictures and said the IDs would be ready after two o'clock in the afternoon. Norberto told him he would come back with the money. After saying good-bye, we all left and went back to the car.

Norberto seemed to be very excited and told us, "Well, Virgilio did it. Don't worry because he is a good men and discreet. Now after I drop you guys I must go to the train station and speak with a friend of mine to buy the tickets for tonight. The regular price is five hundred seventy-five Cuban pesos each, about twenty U.S. dollars. However, I am sure that for tonight it will cost double."

Alex told him to drop us off at San Martin Street and Lugareño. He reminded Norberto that we would see him at ten fifteen at the train station. "Don't forget to bring all the documents."

Norberto said, "Don't worry, Armando, that all is under control." A few minutes later, he dropped us off and drove away.

We walked a couple of blocks until we stopped in front of a house in the Santayana Street. The place was a one-story colonial style home; it seemed that once it had been a nice house, but it now looked derelict and uninhabited. I noticed that the roof needed many tiles and that the outside walls and windows were peeling. We knocked at the door and, after waiting for almost three minutes, a quite thin old man with white hair, at least seventy-five years of age, opened the door. Alex greeted him and called him Captain Rolo. The inside of the house seen to be neglected, full of old furniture covered with dust. Alex introduced me to Captain Rodovaldo Rodriguez Mira, a retired officer from the *Fuerzas Armadas Revolucionarias* (FAR).

Alex said that the captain had been in the Sierra Cristal mountain range with Raúl Castro during the war against Batista and that he had gone to Angola and Nicaragua with the FAR before retiring after more than thirty-five years in the army. The captain told us that he had lived in the house for more than thirty years and that his wife died two years ago. The captain gave us to understand that his health was not very good and he complained about the poor medical attention that old people received in Cuba. He told us that there were no medications and that the hospitals were a disaster. These were dirty and they didn't have the necessary equipment to take care of people. He also complained about the pension that he was getting from the FAR; it was not enough to live on. He survived thanks to the *remesa* that his brother sent him from Chicago. Alex opened his bag, pulled out an envelope, and gave it to the captain saying, "Here is two hundred dollars that your brother sent you this month."

"Thank you, Armando. I had received a letter from Roberto, my brother, saying that he had sent it." Drawing us into the room, he added, "I would like to introduce you to Lieutenant Iván Perez Vila from the FAR, who should be here in about ten minutes. Lieutenant Perez Vila was under my company command for a long time, until I retired. The lieutenant, like me, isn't a member of the Communist Party so he didn't receive promotions in the army, in the same way that had happened to me. We are called the *plantados*," he said. "We are army career man with great respect for the FAR. However, like all young people in Cuba, Vila is very frustrated with the revolution and doesn't know what to do. For that reason I told him to meet with you, Armando, my friend."

The captain added, "The lieutenant, like me and most of the young officers of the FAR, fears what is going to happen on the island the day that Fidel dies. In my humble opinion, within the structure of the government, there isn't any other person like Fidel who could use so effectively the power to inspire as much fear—not even his brother Raúl." He ended saying, "There are so many ambitions repressed between the groups that compose the regime, aggravated by Hugo Chávez and his *Revolución Bolivariana,* that at the disappearance of Fidel, eventually these could end in a fight for power. On the other hand, the people, controlled by terror for such a long time, could rush to the streets to release their frustrations and find revenge."

Then he paused and told us, "When this happens, who are they going to call to put order on the streets and to kill people? The men and women of the FAR. We are in the armed forces to defend the nation and the people, but the FAR's objective isn't to harass and to kill Cuban citizens. *Compañeros,* the situation, it ain't easy."

When he was saying that, somebody knocked at the door of the house and the captain slowly stood up. "That must be Lieutenant Iván Perez Vila." He opened the door and a quite young man dressed in a military uniform entered the house and very respectfully greeted Captain Rolo. The captain introduced us to the lieutenant and we all moved into the living room, brushing the dust from the sofa as we sat.

First Captain Rolo told Lieutenant Perez Vila that we were not from the *Yanki* CIA nor did we belong to any dissident group; we were only interested in helping the Cuban people to develop a civil society and democratic principals. For that purpose, we were economically helping many people on the island. At the beginning, the lieutenant looked afraid to express his feelings and only listened to Alex and the captain. However, as the conversation developed openly, we all accepted that the regime was deeply unpopular and stayed in power by means of repression and the fear that Castro inspired. The lieutenant began exposing his frustrations and worries of how the people would change their opinion of the FAR if it attacked them.

The lieutenant said that the generals and colonels, all members of the Communist Party, had become a class apart. These high-ranking officers managed the mixed commercial companies in partnership with foreign capital, enjoying all type of privileges and living the great life while the captains, lieutenants, and the troops served in the companies and were exploited like slaves in jobs outside their military duties. The FAR had equipment and obsolete arms and it was probably not ready to stop an invasion from abroad. Many of the tanks and airplanes were worthless for lack of spare parts. Troop training was limited due to the shortage of resources and because the soldiers were working in the fields or transporting tourists. Then he added, "Can you imagine that the air force doesn't fly at night to save fuel? The pilots of the Russian MIG-29s aren't authorized to fly maneuvers or air combats drills for fear of accidents and airplane losses!"

Concluding his thought, he said, "We didn't choose a military career to protect a failed and unjust government. We aren't in the army to beat dissidents, neither to harass defenseless *Damas de Blanco*, nor to fill the jails with people who look for signatures requesting a referendum or lend books they keep in their homes as independent librarians. The FAR has a glorious history. It defeated the tyrannical Batista regime and the Playa Girón invasion; it fought in Africa, Nicaragua, and in many other parts of the world. We can't permit these corrupt military mobsters to discredit our prestige by converting the FAR into an oppressive army hatred by the Cuban people. Most of my friends in the FAR shared my worries and beliefs."

He added, "On the other hand, the hierarchy of the FAR is static; the seniority of the chiefs in their positions is the longest one in the world. The last appointment of a general in the army occurred seventeen years ago, on the occasion of the crisis with General Ochoa. We have the oldest active generals in the world. There are no opportunities for young people, especially if they aren't members of the Communist Party."

The lieutenant realized that he was getting very excited and said, "I am sorry, Captain, but you know how I feel and the frustration that I have with this government." The captain looked at him and said, "I understand you, Iván, because I happened to go through all that, and you have seen how they have treated me, after dedicating almost all my life to the revolution."

Then he asked us, "What do you think about Raúl Castro's speech last night?" Quite upset, he answered himself: "Now he has discovered that corruption is expanding like a mortal cancer. *Compañeros*, corruption isn't a new phenomenon on the island, already for years it has been present. Who do you think supported and maintained it? The government bureaucracy, the Communist Party, and the generals in the FAR! I believe that Raúl is going to blame some people and get rid of them in the same way he did with General Ochoa and his assistant Captain Martinez, Colonel De la Guardia, and Mayor Padron. You know, this regime uses you for awhile and when they no longer need you, they throw you to the *mierda* or they execute you."

Captain Rolo interrupted the conversation to calm the lieutenant down, as he was getting very agitated. Then he told Alex, "Well, Armando, tell us your opinion on this situation."

Alex began by saying that he understood very well the lieutenant's frustrations and fears. Nevertheless, he recommended patience and care in the decision-making process. The lieutenant's reasons were certainly reasonable, and he suggested several things to help him to find a solution for the situation that has developed in Cuba.

"First, you must be very careful in the selection of people that you speak with about this matter," Alex cautioned. "Before sharing a view on this matter, be sure that they are sincere and that they are looking for a long-term solution and not simple cosmetic repairs. Don't expose yourself so openly, and never trust members of the Communist Party. Second, don't change your daily activities—this would include your professional and family life; continue living a normal life. Never speak of this subject with your family. Third, think what would be necessary to make contact with civil dissidents. To succeed, any movement of the armed forces would need the support and acceptance of the people. Otherwise, it would be seen as merely a change of oppressors, hated by the people. Associate with the more democratic civil dissidents and avoid the ones with Leftist tendencies or Socialists that are only in search for power. These only want a *Fidelismo* or *Raúlismo* without the Castro brothers. They only want a change of commanders with the same corruption, not a change of direction. Beware of the reformist dissidents. These only want to make cosmetic changes to the Socialist constitution and probably eliminate the FAR and leave only the *Milicias Territoriales* as a populist move."

Alex concluded, "I am going to put you in contact through the captain with a person from our group who can help you to establish these relationships. I would like to stress the importance of handling these activities very confidentially, for the security and well being of all parties."

After a brief pause, Alex told the lieutenant that all these conversations and contacts represented the beginning of a seditious movement that was very delicate and confidential. "Once it begins, it is no longer possible to stop it until it reaches the climax of victory or a tragic ending of defeat. You will need the unconditional support of your colleagues and the troops to be able to bring forward the popular support of the Cuban people."

Captain Rolo said, "Iván, are you aware of the seriousness of this matter? I am a little bit old, but I am willing to help you in everything, for the freedom of the Cuban people, as I did against the dictatorship of Batista. The imposed forty-seven years of Socialist regime in our country has only served to lay down the foundations of state capitalism with its corruption. The ideology of this system has failed miserably and all the people's liberties have been denied. Iván, I believe that the hour has arrived, once again—the FAR is ready to say, 'Here we are to free the Cuban people.'"

The lieutenant listened without saying a word to both Alex's advice and the intervention of the captain. When they finished, he said, "Armando, I thank you for your good advice. I believe that I am going to follow it." Then he looked at the captain and said, "Captain, you know that I respect and love you as if you were my own father. I am determined to fight the corruption and I thank you for your support. I can give you my word that what I am going to do is for my children's future and for the future of all Cuban youth. The cause is very dangerous, but it is the only way to reestablish sanity in this country and eliminate the corruption in the government."

I didn't say anything, but I realized that I was witnessing a very important and very dangerous meeting. I hadn't expected to hear a conversation like this. Certainly, I was nervous, but I was also delighted. I never thought that my trip to Cuba would be so exciting or that I would meet people who might change the history of the island.

We spoke for about ten more minutes, preparing the groundwork for the next meeting. Then Alex said that we had to go. We all shook hands and said good-bye and left the house. When we were walking towards our next meeting, I asked Alex, "Listen, what do you think about the lieutenant?"

"He seemed disillusioned with the revolution and worried about his future and the future of the FAR. There is no doubt that the FAR is on the way to becoming a repressive organization hated by the people; eventually it might even be destroyed and accused of supporting a dictatorship."

Then Alex added, "*Mi hermano,* my feelings are that with dissidence like there is in Cuba, employing only peaceful methods of protest, it will be difficult to reach a change of regime without the intervention of the armed forces." He also pointed out that an insurrection of the armed forces, without an alliance with the civil opposition, never would obtain the support of the people or receive international recognition. "History has taught us that when a military movement overthrows a dictatorial regime which only offered miseries to the people, it is usually well received as a liberator."

Since there were not many people walking on the streets, we were able to speed up enough to make one last meeting in Camagüey before we boarded the train for Havana.

CHAPTER 17

▼

THE COLAS AND THE
CALDOSA

During Henry's last narration, Peter Jones hadn't said a word. He was excited and amazed with the story he was hearing. At last, he couldn't help himself; he burst out, "Do you realize you are involved in a secret conspiracy against Castro's regime?"

"I'm very aware of it," Henry replied calmly. "I was an eyewitness to the beginning of the conspiracy, although I felt removed from the actions of the conspiracy. Alex was always the brains of the affair."

"Please, Mr. Gonzalez, continue your story," Jones said.

*   *   *   *

Alex and I walked a few blocks and stopped in front of a *bodega* called La Mina, where there was a *cola* of people waiting in line at the door. It was a state store where people came with their rationing *libreta* to see what they could buy with Cuban pesos.

"My friend Benito works as manager of this store," Alex said. "He is my contact here in Camagüey for the distribution of *remesas* from abroad. I have complete confidence in him; he discreetly and in silence helps everybody. In addition, he maintains contact with the dissident groups like those of the *asamblea*. All his family left Cuba several years ago, but he refuses to leave the island. He thinks that his place is here, and that somebody must fight for the freedom of the Cuban people. He practiced law here in Camagüey before the revolution. He has great talent and political ability that allows him to move among government sympathizers and the dissidents."

There were only twelve people in the *cola*. Alex told me, "I believe it is better if we stand at the end behind that lady who seems to be the last one in line. If we try to enter the store without getting in line, the people are going to protest. We must avoid any argument that can attract the police."

So we joined the line. I noticed that there were more women than men and I realized that everybody had *jabas* in their hand. These *jabas* usually are of vinyl and they sold in the black market for three for one Cuban peso. They are used because the state stores don't give any type of wrapping or bags to carry articles bought. Some people had canvas bags very similar to ours, where they put their *jabas* with items bought. Everybody in line had in the other hand the *libreta*, a light blue notebook of six by four inches. This notebook indicates the staple foods and other articles of first necessity that can be bought monthly and the quantity the state allows for each person in relation with the number of people living in the home. This doesn't mean that the store has those articles available all the time, just that if an item is listed in the *libreta*, the state has authorized its sale in Cuban pesos when these items are available. The clerk who takes care of the store must mark the notebook to indicate that the person bought his or her monthly allotment. This rationing system was instituted in Cuba more than forty-five years ago.

The store had two doors but only one was used to enter; the other was used as an exit. The building had only one floor and it didn't have windows. The woman in front of us seemed to be more than sixty years old, and she was very carelessly dressed, wearing rubber slippers. She was talking with a woman in front of her who seemed to be much younger, but also was dressed in very poor apparel. When we stopped behind them, I noticed that they stopped talking. A couple of times they looked at us with certain fear. In order to calm the apparent tension, Alex told the woman, "Thank heavens the *cola* is moving so fast, because the sun is burning!"

She looked at him and said, "Yes, it is moving quite fast; that means that there isn't much to buy in the store. Listen," she added, "you two aren't from around here, because your faces aren't familiar." Alex said that we were from Ciego de Avila. She immediately said that why we seemed strangers to her. Then she asked, "What are you guys doing in Camagüey?" Alex told her that we had come for matters related to our Centro de Trabajo and we were taking advantage of the opportunity to visit the store's manager, who was a relative. Immediately the woman said, "So, you are relatives of Benito, the administrator of the *bodega*. I have known Benito for thirty years, since we moved to this *barrio*. Listen, it isn't because you are his relative, but Benito is a very fair and good person. You know the *bodega* has little to sell, but when something good comes, Benito always informs the neighbors so they can take advantage of it."

The woman turned to the younger woman and said, "These *compañeros* are from Ciego and are relatives of Benito, the administrator." The woman slightly smiled at us.

After this introduction, the women continued *chismeando* about the other neighbors and the problems with the tap water and the blackouts. Among other things, I found out that they had come because somebody had mentioned the *bodega* had *malanga por la libre*. This means that the state had authorized selling an item over the quota allocated in the notebook, only for that week. This rarely happens, but it could be that they had a very good harvest of that product or that they had to sell quickly before it rotted.

The line moved, but more people continued arriving and we were now fifteen. Of course, now we only had five people ahead of us. Suddenly I saw a woman of about thirty years of age come to the door. She said to the person standing next to the door, "Excuse me!" as she showed a notebook and cut in line. The rest of the people who were in the line made faces, but they didn't say anything. Our friend told us, "That young woman had the *plan jaba*. I believe that she is from the CDR of her block and has priority to buy in the *bodega*. Do you think that is fair? The *bodega* has little to sell and these privileged people take it all." Alex shook his head and shrugged his shoulders in a gesture of resignation.

Finally, after forty-five minutes in line we entered the store. The store had a counter of greasy scratched white Formica; on it sat an old scale that in its good times had been painted red. The walls had several unpainted, worn wooden shelves, which were almost empty. There were only five cans of something, three packages of noodles, a large can with coffee, one dozen eggs, and yellowish pink bars that I imagined were laundry soap.

Behind the counter was a man in his sixtieths and a younger woman. They greeted the clients by name and took their rationing *libretas*. The clients requested their allowance of rice, noodles, or other items. The man and the woman behind the counter first checked the *libreta*; if the notebook had that item open, they served the quantity allowed into the plastic bags that the client brought. The client then could pay in Cuban pesos.

When the man behind the counter saw Alex, he immediately came to greet him. Alex introduced me to Benito while the woman behind the counter took care of our friend from the line. She wanted to buy *malanga,* and asked if it was *por la libre.* The store clerk said that the *malanga* wasn't available for sale outside the quota of the *libreta.* The clerk looked at the notebook and told our friend that her *malanga* quota was already consumed.

Benito walked away from us to help our friend from the line, telling her, "Doña Jimena, the *malanga* isn't open, but today we just received a large can of coffee. I believe that you have it open in your *libreta.* If you want it, we could fill your quota."

The woman said, "Please do it and I want to have my sugar quota." Then Benito told the store clerk to take care of Doña Jimena, that he would be back shortly.

Benito took us to a room in the back of the store. The room had a wood table, four metal chairs, and a medium-sized refrigerator. On the floor, there were three one-hundred pound bags with rice, beans, and sugar, and one box with several pieces of *malanga.* The room had a small window almost at the level of the ceiling; an iron grille protected the window frame. Benito told us, "The food situation in the town is getting worse; what you saw outside in the store and what there is here is everything I have available until the end of next week. I don't know how the people are going to survive these two weeks."

Alex said, "Benito, I have a lot of things to tell you, and I must go to Havana tonight. When do you think we can talk? Also, I have to give you the *remesas.*"

Benito looked at his watch and said, "It is already twelve-thirty and the store will close today at four. We could talk here in the *trastienda* then. Can you wait for me here? Are you guys hungry? I could offer a piece of bread the baker gave me when I gave him a little more *malanga.* In the refrigerator, which doesn't work very well, I have some *pasta de bocadito* that I received yesterday and a pitcher of water—the water is good, I boiled it." Alex told Benito we would wait for him there in the *trastienda.*

When Benito left us, Alex said he could use the time to make some phone calls through the STU-III. First, he called Julisa to see if they had found Genaro. Julisa told him that he was still missing. He mentioned to her that tonight we were leaving for Havana and that if everything went well we would be at Cancún on Wednesday. After he finished with Julisa, he made another call that I imagined was to his contact in Havana. With these, he was more than five minutes speaking. When he finished, he told me that his friends in Havana didn't know what was happening in the government, but the MININT had doubled the security guards at the foreign embassies. There was a surprising silence in the circles of the regime's power after Raúl's speech the night before. The rumor was that Fidel was very sick, perhaps close to death.

Later Alex asked, "Do you want to call Natalia in New Jersey?" He reminded me not to tell her about my trip to Mexico and not to speak too loudly even though the door was closed and the only window of the room was very high; it was necessary to take all precautions.

When I called home, Natalia was having lunch and she was very happy with my call. However, when I told her that I was going to delay my return three or four more days, she didn't like it. Immediately she began asking questions and blaming Alex for my delay and complaining about my trips. I followed Alex's advice and tried to be brief and I didn't say where I was or where I was going. I ended up telling her that I would call later with the details of my return.

When I hung up, Alex said, "*Mi hermano*, I feel sorry to put you in this complicated situation. But you are the right person to raise money for the Cuban cause and I have complete confidence in your loyalty and talent. I believe that now you have seen for yourself that the dissidents employ only peaceful methods and that we are not terrorists. The terrorist is the corrupt and abusive Communist regime that badly governs Cuba." After a pause he added, "I think that in the way that things are in the island now, my presence here is necessary. I believe that we are at the end of the fight. I can't leave it now. You already know how many of our activities work; when you return to New Jersey, get in contact with Ernesto in Puerto Rico and Julisa and Alberto in Grand Cayman. They are going to help you in your very important job."

I told him that I found Cuba much worse than what I was expecting. People live badly and without a future under a repression that inspires terror. The corruption had reached all levels of society. Furthermore, I believed that the prevailing system of living had institutionalized corruption not only within the government but also in the population. For that reason, we saw the illegal markets, the *jineteras*, the thefts in the state industries, the state apartheid between Cubans and the foreign tourists, the crimes and the abuse of the power of the regime. The island needed many changes, both political and economic. Nevertheless, the more important necessity was the recovery of the moral fiber of the nation.

"Therefore, you can count on me, *mi hermano*," I told Alex. "If before I had my doubts about your activities, now I am convinced of the purity of your intentions and the great sacrifice that all the people in the group make in their fight for the freedom of the Cuban people."

With a smile on his face Alex said, "*Mi hermano*, are you hungry enough to try a piece of bread with the *pasta de bocadito?*"

I thought for a moment and said, "Well, I am going to try."

We took a piece of bread and spread it with the paste. The paste had a disagreeable scent and indeed, we could verify that its flavor was even worse. We put away the *pasta de bocadito* and only with the piece of bread, we killed the hunger at least a little.

When we were experimenting with the horrible *pasta de bocadito*, we heard a very loud discussion in the store. We never went outside the back room, but we could hear the shouts and the bad words. Apparently, a woman wanted to buy two pounds of rice and her *libreta* indicated that she already had bought all her quota for the month. Well, the police had to come and take her away; she was shouting at full voice, "These *cabrones* Communist are killing us of hunger," and "*Al carajo* with the revolution!"

At four o'clock in the afternoon, the clerk left the store and Benito closed. When Benito came to the backroom he said, "These incidents are happening almost every day and the police have to come." With great pain, he said to us, "That woman will be probably sentenced to a year in jail for disrespect to the revolution. What can I do? I always try to help everybody, but with the shortage of food, it is impossible to feed and to satisfy the necessities of the eighteen hundred people in the neighborhood that the store has to serve. When the government allowed the so-called 'farmers' markets', the people were doing a little better because they could buy some agricultural products that the farmers brought from their small farms. However, the government changed the laws and prohibited them, because they said the farmers were becoming rich. Only the people who receive *remesas* from their relatives abroad can buy the things in the special stores."

He told us that people were waiting for their *remesas* and he asked Alex if he had brought them. Alex told him that they were in the handbags. Benito said, "Let's do that first. I want to put them in my safe box because I must begin to distribute the money tomorrow."

Alex took the canvas handbag that I had brought, opened it, and removed all the envelopes from the secret compartment. He gave all to Benito and said, "Here is the list of the people who must receive the remittances their relatives have sent them. Also, here is the remittance that your family sends you." Benito took the envelopes and, with the aid of Alex, confirmed that the list and the money agreed. There was nearly twenty-five thousand dollars that would be distributed among more than three hundred families. Those were some of the lucky people in Camagüey.

Raúl Castro owned a company that also made these shipments of money. Naturally, they charged for their service, and in many cases, the money got lost. The regime now charged 20 percent if the remittance was in dollars; Alex's group didn't charge anything for its service.

After he finished counting and checking, Benito moved the refrigerator from its place and raised several slabs that covered a hollow in the floor. He took all the envelopes, placed them in the hollow, and put the slabs and the refrigerator back in place. Smiling, he said, "The money is in the safe box. Well, Alex, what have you to tell me?"

Alex first said, "My friend, I believe that we are at the end of the Castros' dictatorship. The current economic, political, and social situation of the country has taken the population to the point of desperation. They understand that civil disobedience is the only solution. For that reason the regime has increased repression; it doesn't respect the private life of any citizen on the island. It has been snatched with the *actos de repudio*. These are violent acts committed by nothing more than rogue crowds organized by the regime, all with the objective of terrifying the civil population. On the other hand, the dissidents have used very effective, peaceful methods, like the *Bibliotecas Independientes, Las Damas de Blanco* and the *Asamblea para Promover la Sociedad Civil.*"

Benito said, "The five hundred and fifty-four prisons on the island are packed with prisoners. The situation of the prisons couldn't be worse. Beatings, abuse, and inhuman treatment are the norm. These situations provoke hunger strikes of the inmates. Here in Camagüey we have two of the worse prisons on the island. One is the Ceramica Roja prison and the other is the so-called Kilo 8. The political prisoners are forced to work without pay under terrible conditions."

Alex said, "On the other hand, the novel thing is that Fidel has admitted for the first time that the generations born under Cuban Socialism have a conduct deviation that places in danger the *logros de la revolución*. Raúl Castro has denounced the corruption like a 'cancer mortal.' The words of these two authors of the Cuban disaster can only represent their recognition of the moral defeat of the imposed Socialist system in Cuba."

However, he added, "While they have Venezuelan aid from Chávez, the regime feels able to survive by exerting more and more repression on the dissidents and requesting more sacrifices from the people, with slogans without sense—like *convertir reveses en victorias*. But the fatigue and the weariness of the people might go the way of a popular rebellion after the death of Fidel. Nevertheless, it seems that Fidel, even after death, has plans to leave Raúl governing the country without a dose of common sense."

After a pause, he added, "But if this popular rebellion explodes and Hugo Chávez and the Cuban *inmovilistas* try to contain the people using the FAR military force, I believe that they aren't going to bring out tanks and shoot the people. I consider that the armed forces would respond negatively to this order. They don't want to be remembered in history as an oppressive force, hated by the people. The young officers, like all youth in Cuba, feel frustrated and worried about the uncertain future the regime offers to them."

Alex continued explaining, saying, "It would be very difficult for the civic dissidents by themselves, using peaceful methods, to change the regime in the near future. On the other hand, a military coup by itself would find it very difficult to gain the support of the people or obtain international recognition." Then Alex, looking to Benito, said, "For that reason we must put in contact the civil dissidents with the young military officers. I believe that both groups would complement each other."

Benito replied, "Alex, your ideas made a lot of sense. But how can we make contact with the military?"

Alex told him that he had already made some contact and he thought that Benito could prepare a meeting between the two groups. He told Benito of our meeting with Captain Rolo and Lieutenant Perez Vila. Alex said that the problem was that he had to take the train tonight; he wouldn't be back in Camagüey until Wednesday, at best. But there was no time to spare. He told Benito to make the first approach with the captain tomorrow.

Benito was extremely excited at the idea and said that he had once met Captain Rolo and that sometimes he came to the store to buy toothpaste when he heard that the store had some. Alex gave the address of the captain's home and Benito said that the house was only few blocks from the store.

There are many groups and tendencies of Cuba's dissidents, Benito said. He almost knew them all. Nevertheless, he preferred to make contact with a representative of the *asamblea*. Dissident groups with tendencies that were more democratic and had better contact with Cubans abroad composed this movement.

Alex said, "Benito, I have a great confidence in your ability and discretion to make these contacts. But I want to warn you that these activities are extremely dangerous. I already have mentioned this to the military, the delicate nature of this process. You must explain very clearly to the civilian dissidents the situation. The minimum indiscretion by any side would be a fatal blow for our fight and would cost many lives." Alex asked Benito to call him using the STU-III phone as soon as he made contact with the captain. Benito nodded. Then they continued talking about all the details of the process.

It was already near seven-thirty and Benito said that he had to go to an *actividad* organized by the CDR of the neighborhood. The activity was called a *caldosa*. This consisted of cooking in public in a big pot of food called *ajiaco*. Attendance at this *actividad* was compulsory for all the neighbors. Each neighbor paid five Cuban pesos to cover the expenses. Since he was the administrator of the state store, commonly called a *bodegero*, it was assumed that he would bring some vegetables to throw in the pot. The butcher could bring some bones or any other piece of meat that he had left. In the past, Benito used to bring two bottles of rum or a box of beer, but now those were luxury articles. Since so many sugar mills had closed, rum production was small and everything was exported or sold in the hotels to the foreign tourists, and beer no longer could be bought with Cuban pesos. People missed the rum and the beer, but they attended with quite good spirit to be able to eat something that wasn't subject to the rationing notebook. In addition, they took advantage of the occasion to meet and to speak badly of the government, things that were prohibited by revolutionary laws.

Benito told us, "I know that the train to Havana leaves about eleven o'clock. Would you guys like to come to the *caldosa* with me? It starts at eight and finishes, like, at ten. I don't see any problem because I am bringing half a box of *malanga* that I kept for tonight. The president of the CDR is a friend of mine and he won't care if I bring two guests. I am going to tell him that you are my relatives from Ciego de Avila that are here in Camagüey in some type of labor union activity."

Then Benito, with a broad smile on his face, said, "If you feel hungry you could fill your bellies if you hurry up, because on the train you could maybe only buy a sandwich with *jamonada* that, as my friend Pancho says, doesn't have any ham."

Alex thought for a moment and then asked me, "What do you think?" I told him that it was fine with me if there was no problem with the CDR people.

Benito then told us, "I am going to give a last check to the store, and we can go." After few minutes, he returned and said everything was well. He grabbed the *malanga* box and we left through the back door.

We walked two or three blocks arrived at a *solar*, an empty lot in the middle of the block, surrounded by houses of one and two stories. All the houses seemed neglected and in need of a fresh coat of paint. Some tile roofs needed repair and I imagined that their residents were getting wet with the rain. In the lot several men and women were placing pieces of wood on a bonfire where there was a big pot mounted on few old bricks and iron bars. When we got near the bonfire, I realized that the lot was empty because the house that had been there had collapsed. The iron bars, bricks, and the pieces of wood came from the pile of debris accumulated on one side of the lot.

One of the men working with the bonfire came immediately when he saw Benito arriving with us. He greeted Benito in a friendly manner and Benito gave him the box of *malangas*. The man then thanked him, called another man, and told him to clean the *malangas* and drop them in the *ajiaco*.

Benito introduced us to the *compañero* Vladimiro, and he told us that Vladimiro was "the president of the best CDR of Camagüey, where the neighbors can always find support to maintain the exaltation of the fatherland's values." With that kind of flattery, the man was so proud of himself that without a doubt *no le cabia un comino*. Benito also told him we were his relatives from Ciego de Avila, who were here in *actividades* of the labor union, and if he didn't mind, he had invited us so see the best *caldosa*. The man looked at us with his best expression and said that we were welcome.

An hour later, there were almost one hundred people in the place. Some were inside the lot and others were standing on the street talking. The street was closed for traffic and there weren't any vehicles parked on it. The guests brought from their homes plastic bottles of water, metal or plastic containers, and soupspoons. Benito gave to each of us a bottle of water and a plastic container with the spoon.

The people looked at us with scared faces, but nobody said anything until the woman we had met in line at the store walked near us. Alex saw her and said, "Good evening, Doña Jimena."

She smiled and told the woman who was speaking with her, "Fela, these are Benito's relatives, they live in Ciego. It is good that Benito brought you to the *caldosa* so you can meet his neighbors and friends." When the people around us found out that we were relatives of Benito, the administrator of the state store, everything changed. The people saw themselves at ease; they greeted us and smiled.

This change of behavior gave me the opportunity to hear about what the people were talking. The terrible economic condition was the main subject. People complained that they didn't make sufficient money to live. The state stores had very few items to sell. One of the most common complaints was the situation of black families in Cuba. Most of the people who had been able to leave Cuba were white. They sent the dollar *remesas* to their relatives in Cuba who, with those dollars, bought *chavitos* to pay for food and articles of first necessity in the state special stores. They could use the dollars to by food and other items illegally on the black market. Most of the black families didn't receive *remesas* and only could go to the state stores to buy what the rationing notebooks allowed them. The revolution always had said that one of its objectives was to attain racial equality. The colored people didn't believe it. They said that now it was worse than before the revolution for them.

Most of the people complained about the national health system. There was a big scarcity of medicines and only a few doctors. Cuba had fourteen thousand doctors in Venezuela in the program *Barrio Adentro*, but none for the people at home. The blacks were at a disadvantage there as well, since white people received medications from their families abroad.

Education had become indoctrination and to go to the university, young people had to work as "volunteers" for the state and belong to Communist Youth. As it is said in Cuba, "Education is only for the revolutionaries."

One thing that caught my attention was that there weren't any young people at the gathering. When I asked Benito about it, he told me that the youth generally showed defiance by not attending these activities. In addition, many were fulfilling their compulsory military service or hustling as *cuentapropistas* and *jineteras* with the foreign tourists in search of dollars. Still others had escaped from the island as *balseros*.

I listened to a story that I considered incredible. In Ciego de Avila, a group of deaf and mute people who lived in extreme poverty with very little aid from the government decided to make an organization to help themselves mutually. They called it the *Asociación de Sordos Independientes de Cuba*. State security took prisoner the founder of the association and locked up him in a narrow and dark dungeon without water or electricity—but with plenty of cockroaches and other insects. This torture chamber was famous in Ciego de Avila, well known as the place where "everybody sings." What cruel irony—only a terrorist regime like the one in Cuba could have done such and evil and stupid thing.

The sun disappeared from the sky; only the bonfire now illuminated the lot where the big pot cooked the *ajiaco*. In front of the *solar*, a streetlight illuminated part of the street gathering. All the ingredients of the *ajiaco* had been placed in the pot. The butcher had brought a piece of meat and bones, neighbors who had worked that day in the fields brought two or three bananas, Vladimiro brought a piece of pumpkin, and by all means, let's not forget the *malangas* from Benito. The broth already gave off the aroma of *salcocho de viandas* and meats. People were hoping anxiously for the *ajiaco* in the twilight of the dusk.

Suddenly a voice was heard saying, "*Compañeros*, I have a message from the *cederista* family." Vladimiro was speaking through a portable battery loudspeaker.

"I am going to refresh you on several dispositions approved by the *Asamblea Nacional del Poder Popular*. All citizens of legal age have the obligation to give to the authority any raw materials produced in their houses; to pay the monthly dues to the CDR; to participate in the cleaning and the beautification of the *barrio*; to participate in voluntary works and political-ideological activities; to donate blood to state institutions; and to register in the military service those of military age. Also, I want to remind you all that it is prohibited to participate in games of chance, to use satellite antennas at home, to sell or to buy houses, to rent houses without state authorization, and to incorrectly use household electric appliances sold by the state."

After finishing his message, which the people received with great indifference, Vladimiro said, "The committee has a surprise tonight. There will be a piece of bread for each person. It will be distributed with the delicious *ajiaco* that the kind revolution has prepared us tonight. *Viva la Revolución! Viva Fidel! Viva Raúl!*"

Men, women, and children began to make a line in silence in front of the pot. Everybody knew what they had to do to receive a few ounces of broth and a piece of bread. Perhaps many hoped to find a small piece of meat swimming in the broth. With hunger, poverty, and terror, the state dominated the will of the citizens in the totalitarian regime. The individualism of the human being was given to the state. The life of these people was in the hand of the corrupt administrators of the state. *Poor Cuban people,* I thought!

Despite of the fact that throughout the day I had eaten very little, I no longer felt hungry before the pathetic spectacle that I had witnessed. Then Alex said, "*Mi hermano,* let's get in line." I told him that I wasn't hungry. Alex replied, "Better have something to eat, even if it is a piece of bread. We are going to take the train at midnight and who knows when we will have the opportunity to eat again." I thought for a moment and decided to follow the advice.

After waiting in line for almost half an hour, we took our broth and the piece of bread and sat with Benito on the curb of the street to eat. People ate in silence, looking towards the pot; others ate quickly and walked around the pot to see if they could go for a second time or if there were some bones left at the bottom.

When the streetlight went off it was nine-twenty. "The blackout came a little early tonight," said Benito.

Alex said, "I believe we should go now."

"That's a good idea," Benito said. "The train station is approximately fifteen minutes' walk from here." Alex reminded Benito to call the captain and said he would probably see him on Wednesday. I wished luck to Benito and we left.

The city of Camagüey was completely without light; we only saw in some windows the reflection of a candle. Luckily, the night was clear and the light of the moon illuminated our way to the train station.

CHAPTER 18

▼

THE DEATH OF THE TYRANT

"Aha," said Peter Jones, "Therefore, you came by train to Havana with the false "documents that you got in Camagüey. Henry, you and your friend had courage to get involved in something like that, with Cuba's tight internal security system!"

"Mr. Jones," Henry said, "we didn't have any alternative. Alex has a lot of experience in the clandestine business and he has an extensive underground network in Cuba. He is full of resources and the imagination to survive the state's repressive conditions on the island. Now I will tell you about our train trip."

*   *   *   *

We arrived at the station five minutes before ten o'clock and decided to wait at the corner half a block from the doors of the station. There was no light in the street so we could only see the shape of the people entering the station. The doors of the station were open and glare was coming from the inside. Alex showed me three state security agents guarding the entrance and pointed out the patrol car parked on the street at one side of the building. He said that the number of guards seemed normal considering the conditions of the hour and the blackout. However, he said that we must remain hidden there waiting for Norberto because they might ask us for identification and the train tickets at the door. "Open your eyes and be alert," said Alex, "because we must identify Norberto in the dark."

There we waited for more than ten minutes, which seemed to me eternal. The few people walking toward the door all looked like Norberto to me. When I realized that each one wasn't him, I felt afraid that we would never going to recognize him in the dark. Suddenly Alex said, "There he is. We are going to intercept him before he enters the station."

When Norberto saw us, he immediately stopped and went with us to our spot in the dark. Alex pointed out the three security agents and the patrol car guarding the door of the station, saying that he feared they would request tickets and identification. Norberto said that was probably true. He suggested that we follow him to his car, parked only a block away. Inside the car, he told us, "I will give you everything and then I will drive you to the station in the Lada. When the guards see you guys coming out of this car from the MININT, they are going to think that you are two *pinchos*—perhaps they won't even request your documents. If they do, it is to show what a good, vigilant job they are doing."

Three minutes later, we were inside the car. First Norberto gave us our new identification cards. My new name was José Rodriguez Pantoja and Alex was Manuel Jiménez Colón. In addition, he gave us two letters from the CDR authorizing our trip to Havana to prepare us for some type of "ideological cultural activities." Then he said he had a surprise for us. I didn't like that; I was scared about everything, and it probably reflected on my face. Alex just looked at me first and then told Norberto to go ahead. Norberto told us that he had managed to get us better seats on the train. He immediately added, "Not in the tourist wagon with air-conditioning, because those only are sold to the foreign tourists. It is in the wagon where the members of the CDRs, the lower officers of the MINFAR and the MININT, and other government officers travel. I assume that it is quite a bit better than those where the common people go. In addition, in this car they are serving breakfast and *merienda*. The train should leave Santiago at 4 p.m., arriving at Camagüey about eleven that night. The trip to Havana is thirteen hours. If everything goes well and the train doesn't have any problems, you will be in Havana Sunday at noon; here are the tickets."

Norberto told us about the rumors that *el Caballo* was dying. He said, "Apparently, Raúl is going to speak on radio and television to the people. When? Nobody knows. With this rumor and what Raúl said last night, *A mi me da muy mala espina,* something big is happening in Havana. I believe that the *fifo* is dead. We are going to see what Raúl says; couldn't be worse that what we have now."

Alex told him that he would probably be back Wednesday when he would call him. Then he thanked Norberto and praised him for the good job done.

Norberto stopped the black Lada in front of the train station and we walked in the direction of the door guarded by the security agents. We quickly climbed the four steps were ready to enter the station when an agent said to us, "*Compañeros,* with your permission, could you show me your identity cards? We pulled out our cards and showed them to the agent. He looked at them and said, "*Compañeros* Jiménez Colón and Rodriguez Pantoja, you understand that I must fulfill my vigilant job by requesting your ID cards, because, as you know, it is necessary to protect the revolution from the *elemento antisocial* that wants to destroy our great revolution. Please go ahead with your duties."

Alex replied, "Very well, *compañero,* you are fulfilling your revolutionary duties."

The lobby of the station was full of old wood benches where many people sat waiting for the train. The place was illuminated by three portable oil lamps that produced a bright light that was enough to see what was going on in the room, but not sufficient to read a newspaper. Most of people were quiet, as if they were dozing, except for a group telling stories and laughing quite loudly.

Alex told me that he was going to look for the bathroom and asked me if I needed to go. I said that I did. We walked a little around the lobby until we found the door of the bathroom; the sign said, "Closed for Repairs." Alex pulled out from his pocket several keys, with one of them opened the door, and entered. I followed him behind. When we were inside the room I told Alex, "Listen, did you see the sign on the door?"

He replied, "Don't worry, the sign will make our job easier." He closed the door with the inside latch. The place was very dark and smelled very bad. Alex removed from his handbag a flashlight and the telephone STU-III and said to me, "Go and do what you want to do while I make a call to Havana." I wasn't able to avoid listening to Alex's conversation while I was doing my necessities. It seemed to me that he was asking about the rumors of the death of Fidel and making the last arrangements for our arrival in Havana. Later he made another call, which I imagined was with his contacts in Pinar del Río, to prepare my exit from the island. In five minutes, more or less, when we both had finished with our necessities and had dried our hands with the *Granma* newspaper that, due to lack of sanitary paper in Cuba, is used as toilet paper, Alex opened the door very carefully, threw a glance to the lobby, and said to me, "Let's go—everybody is sleeping or talking and drinking rum."

When we left the bathroom, I realized that four guys with their bottles of rum were chatting and telling stories in quite a festive tone. All had sport shirts of different colors and gray khaki pants and wore military boots; their olive berets were lying on the benches. The group was so involved in their conversation that they didn't realize from where we had come. Alex said, "We are going to sit near these security agents from the MININT; with their shouting, we can speak without fear of being overheard."

When we sat, I asked Alex what he had heard from the people in Havana. Alex told me that the rumor seemed to be certain because many government cars were seen running the streets and his contacts noticed more policemen than usual. The main rumor was that Raúl was going to speak the next day. Then Alex told me, "Your trip is prepared for Tuesday at dawn. I will take you to Pinar del Río, leaving you with the people who are going to take you to Yucatan. I'll leave immediately for Camagüey. The moment of great changes in Cuba seems to have arrived." He apologized several time for not being able to accompany me to the shore where I was going to take the boat. I told him that I understood the situation—after so many sacrifices, they couldn't waste the opportunity of the moment. Fidel's death could open the doors to fundamental changes within the island.

Alex thanked me for my words and my support. He said, "There are two great questions on this subject. First, what will be the reaction of the people and will they accept Raúl as the definitive successor? The government officials know that people are very displeased with the way of life they have. The new leader must come making changes to improve the standard of living of the people. The second question is what will be the reaction of the FAR in front of a new leader. The FAR is at the service of the generals and their personal businesses and every day it is more business oriented. Could the new leadership try to utilize the armed forces against the people if they protest and run wild on the streets?"

He pointed out that the Cuban people always have been waiting for something. First, they waited for many years for the revolution to fulfill its promises. Later, after the fall of the Soviet Union, the regime began the *periodo especial*. The people hadn't seen the benefit of this program. Life became more difficult every day and the future more uncertain. Now the people, in spite of the respect that Fidel inspired, were waiting for his death. The problem was aggravated by the fact that the people didn't know what was going to happen the day after Fidel's death. But they were waiting, as always, waiting for changes without knowing what those changes would bring.

On the other hand, Alex said, "There is no doubt that the regime has close to a million Communist militants who are well trained and supported by international accomplices. The Communist Party of Cuba had infiltrated Cuban society, the FAR, the universities, and even the internal and external dissidents. The depth and penetration and the espionage of the Cuban Communists has reached the Pentagon in Washington. Remember, *mi hermano*," he said, "criminal regimes never stop their actions unilaterally. The changes must come from above and be supported by a very strong will. Any change whose first step isn't the overthrow of the arbitrary political, economic, and social order imposed by force by the Communist government would not be morally acceptable."

We continued talking for a while; the station's lobby was quiet and nothing important was going on. Suddenly, five minutes before eleven, several policemen and state security agents in uniform came into the lobby. They went to the two doors that gave entrance to the train platforms and stood in front of them. One of them spoke through a portable loudspeaker, saying that they were going to start checking ID cards and travel documentation and recommended that passengers have train tickets ready.

The ten or twelve foreign tourists entered first. Three tour guides, possibly soldiers from the FAR in civilian clothes, accompanied them. The guides had all the documentation and train tickets of the tourists. The tourists were carrying their own small suitcases. All went quickly through the door and walked left toward the end of the platform.

Then the announcer called for all government officials, members of the CDRs, members of the FAR, MININT, and the *Milicias de Tropas Territoriales*. We and seven other passengers were in this group, including the four guys that were drinking rum in the lobby. The agents at the door checked our ID cards and our documents, as they did to the other passengers of our group. We didn't have any problems. We entered the platform and stopped about fifty feet away from the tourists.

When we were walking onto the platform, I heard the announcer call all other passengers, who were the larger group. Perhaps around twenty or twenty-five people formed a line in front of the door. The security agents were checking ID cards and trip documents for more than half an hour; during that time, I could hear their discussions with more than four passengers. The state security agents didn't allow some of them to go on the train and the policemen took two of them into custody. When they finished the inspection, this group was placed on the right end of the platform away from the tourist group and us.

The three groups stood on the platform waiting for the train; it was already 11:45 p.m.; walking around us, the policemen and the security agents maintained their vigilance over the three groups. Finally, at 12:05 a.m., the train arrived. The tourists were the first to get on their air-conditioned wagon. Next, we were allowed to get on ours and I imagine that the rest of the passengers in the third group did the same.

Our wagon was quite old; it didn't have air-conditioning, the seat cushions were worn out, and the lining material had grease spots all over. The carpet was gray and had visible coffee spots. There were no reserved seats and when we got on the wagon, the passengers coming from Santiago de Cuba occupied more than half of the seats. The inside light of the train was very tenuous and it wasn't possible to read by it. Nevertheless, all the passengers had copies of the newspaper *Granma* in their hands. Another thing that caught my attention was that through the intercom of the wagon I could continuously hear the "tick-tock" of *Radio Reloj*, a radio station giving news and government propaganda. After every minute, it said, "*Radio Reloj da la hora*," and gave the time.

After a short walk down the corridor, we found two empty seats behind the guys who had been drinking rum at the station. The hour was 12:22 a.m., according to the monotonous and boring *Radio Reloj*. Ten minutes later, the train began to move and everybody placed the newspapers open over their faces to cover their eyes from the dim light of the wagon and, I imagine, protect themselves from the cockroaches that flew over their heads.

The train was moving slowly and it creaked as if it was ready to derail. Alex told me that the trains were old, made in Russia during the good old times of the Soviet Union. The railroad lines weren't well maintained due to lack of resources. The foreign tourists usually didn't use the trains so the government didn't see the need to fix them. The FAR and the Communist Party maintained a good fleet of buses for tourism. The farmers in the interior and the common people generally were the ones that used the rail service.

Most of the passengers were sleeping, including our neighbors, who were *durmiendo la mona* after all the rum they had been drinking. Everything was calm; you could only heard the train creaking, the far engine roar, and *Radio Reloj*. I looked at Alex, who seemed to be sleeping as well, so I decided to try to do the same. The train already had been delayed for more than an hour, and who knew what could happen on the long way to Havana? I was thinking that if I was planning to leave Cuba on Tuesday at dawn, I night not get any sleep until arriving at Yucatan.

Well, finally, I fell asleep. I only opened my eyes twice due to the abrupt movements of the wagon. Once I realized we were very slowly crossing a bridge. Most of the time, the train didn't go too fast, but when it crossed a bridge, it moved like a turtle.

When the first rays of light entered the window, I awoke, and *Radio Reloj* said the time was 5:45 a.m. I looked through the window and saw that the fields were still a little dark. I tried to sleep a little more, but I believe that I was too nervous, or perhaps I was feeling hungry so I couldn't sleep any more. Alex was sleeping, like most of the passengers.

At 6:00 a.m. *Radio Reloj* announced that Comandante Raúl Castro would speak to the people on television and radio with very important news.

When hearing this news, I instinctively woke up Alex. The few people that were awake in the wagon began to speak all at the same time. The argument was that Fidel had died and that his brother Raúl was going to give the news. Most of the passengers were looking worried at the news, others were nervously laughing. Alex then said, "I now believe that probably we will learn about Fidel's death on the train; let's see how these regime sympathizers react."

Every five minutes *Radio Reloj* repeated the same news without any comments. Fifteen or twenty minutes later two girls came with a black coffee canteen and pieces of bread. They poured the coffee in cardboard cups and gave a piece of bread to each passenger. The coffee seemed to be very weak and had too much sugar; the bread was old and hard. Nevertheless, I was hungry and ate everything very quickly. That was the breakfast that the train gave to the passengers who worked in the government and were sympathizers of the regime and the revolution. I don't know what they gave the tourists; I imagine it was something better. The other passengers, the common people, got nothing; they had to bring their own food to eat.

Later I needed to go to the bathroom so I went in search of it. A policeman was standing outside the door of the wagon and the passengers could go only to the wagon's bathroom. Nobody was allowed to go to another wagon. The bathroom was dirty, without toilet paper. Next to the toilet on the floor were a large number of copies of *Granma* newspaper. I thought, this government newspaper isn't read by anybody, but there is no doubt that is well used by the people.

At seven-thirty in the morning, we arrived at Santa Clara. The train stopped in the station, some new passengers came in, and some left. Several peddlers came aboard selling candies, lemonade, cigars, and bottles of rum. These last two articles could only be bought with dollars. In addition, two girls came in selling small shots of black coffee from a canteen. The peddlers did very well; most of the passengers bought something. We bought some candy. Our neighbors bought several bottles of rum, lemonade, and a few cigars.

The candy tasted hideous, but it was useful to kill my hunger. As we were sucking our candies, I said, "Listen, the sale of almost all these products is illegal."

Alex said, "Yes, like the rum and cigars."

"These peddlers must know that this wagon is for the government people—how is that they dare to come in to sell illegal products, some even for dollars? The most interesting fact is than these officials are buying from them and they don't say anything to the peddlers!"

Alex looked at me and said, "*Mi hermano*, that is the problem. The regime is corrupt and has corrupted the people. That is the system of the *doble moral*, the one that everybody must employ to survive in Cuba, where what is said and done means diametrically the opposite. The laws aren't respected because they are illegal and they are capriciously imposed to maintain the people oppressed and the regime in power."

After awhile, the atmosphere of the wagon became more festive as the passengers took their refreshments and the rum. Our neighbors ahead of us began to talk louder and we were able to hear an innocent confession from one of them. One man said to his three friends, "At heart, I am a good man. You know, we believed that we were doing the right thing, we were convinced then. We had never heard about the *mierda* of human rights, and they were the enemy." He stopped to take a sip of rum and then said, "Many atrocities were committed. The revolution was going forward, the wheels were caught up with them, and we were the wheels. It was said that they took them to retrain them, but we all knew that was pure *mierda*, we knew well what it was." After another drink, he added, "The *cabrones* worms died of typhus, diarrhea, hunger, shots, and blows. Torture? Well, there was a lot of imagination and we were bored. Some we buried in the earth up to the neck, without water. They lived a day or two. Others were tied up naked with barbed wire. The mosquitoes bit to death the *cabrones antisocial*." After a long pause, he said, "Sorry? No, then, we thought that it was the right thing to do and we were following orders."

The confession of this executioner left me disturbed. I asked to myself. *How can a human being do so much injury to another human being in name of a so-called revolution?* I said to myself, *there are no doubts that any process of reconciliation and establishment of a democratic system must include the application of justice before the law.* These types of murderers must be brought to justice under all the guarantees that can be offered in a state of rights. Without this process, there couldn't be justice and couldn't be a real reconciliation between Cubans.

The passengers seated behind us were trying to find a logical answer to the sudden announcement of the news on *Radio Reloj*. One said to the other, "I believe that Raúl is going to speak again on corruption and, possibly, he is going to designate somebody to control it."

The other said, "Fidel's doctors said that Fidel was going to live a hundred and forty years."

The first woman said, "Perhaps you are right, but all this gives me *muy mala espina*."

All passengers in the wagon were talking and discussing the situation without end. I got so tired of hearing so many idiotic speculations and arguments about the news that I decided only to think of my exit from Cuba, which was getting increasingly complicated. Alex, on the other hand, was very quiet and seemed to be somewhat worried. The train slowly continued its way through the fields and the sun was already burning the mist away so we could see the majestic palm trees in the distance of the beautiful countryside. The dark red of the soil contrasted with the green vegetation and the blue sky was adorned by small white clouds floating in the heights.

I believe that I slept for a while, until Alex woke me up to tell me they were going to serve the *merienda*. The same two girls that had brought breakfast were now distributing a *bocadito de jamonada* and a bottle of warm soft drink called CuCola. The bread of the *bocadito* was *zapatúo* and the so-called *jamonada*—well, it wasn't made from ham, God knows what it was. However, hunger won again and I ate it all.

The next stop was in the city of Matanzas, at eleven forty-five in the morning. The same ritual followed: some new passengers came aboard and others got off, the train was invaded by peddlers selling the same stuff as before. The passengers that hadn't bought before did it now. However, this time we didn't buy anything.

The new passengers came with fresh news and speculations about Raúl's message to the people. In Havana, the streets were deserted; everybody was at home waiting for the message. All cultural, political, and recreational activities and voluntary work was cancelled. The guards in the embassies and hotels were reinforced, as well as in the special stores and in all government offices. The train had left the station and was on its way to Havana when *Radio Reloj* said the time was 12:05 p.m. After giving the time, it broadcasted the message of Comandante Raúl Castro, provisional president of the Council of the State, directly from the Ministry of the Revolutionary Armed Forces in Havana.

First, Raúl Castro announced the death of the *máximo líder*, his brother Fidel, and informed us that he was next to his deathbed until the end. After acclaiming the life and figure of Fidel, and what he had represented in the history of the nation for more than fifty years, he requested five minutes of silence in memory of the *máximo líder*.

All the passengers stood up and remained in silence. I don't know if the five minutes were obeyed out of politeness and respect for Fidel, from fear, or from simple paralysis produced by the news. The news, long awaited by many, finally had arrived. Alex and I glanced at each other, but we didn't dare pronounce a word. At the end of the five minutes, all the passengers began to speak again at the same time. Alex said, "I believe that the conclusion of *Fidelismo* in Cuba has begun. I hope that we won't continue with the *Raulismo*."

After the five minutes of silence, Raúl continued, saying, "I am going to repeat what I have said on many occasions. The commander in chief of the Cuban Revolution is only one, and solely the Communist Party, as the institution that groups together the revolutionary vanguard and guarantees the unity of Cuba at all times, can be the worthy heir of the confidence deposited by the people in a leader. For that we worked, and thus it will be—any other idea is pure speculation." After a brief pause, he said, "Our nation's Constitution of 1976 dictates the procedure of succession in the case of the death of the president. It is my duty as provisional president of the Council of the State, so for that purpose I have issued orders to Ricardo Alarcón de Quesada, president of *La Asamblea Nacional del Poder Popula*r, to immediately summon an emergency meeting of that legislative body to confirm the transition of powers to the new permanent president of the Council of the State, in agreement always with Communist Party directives." He ended by saying that the process wouldn't take more than forty-eight hours.

The passengers began to discuss the meaning of this message. Some said, "Well, from *Fidelismo* we changed to *Raulismo*." Others, with a resigned tone of voice, said, "Now we are going to see what the little brother brings us." One young man said philosophically, "Well, I always have been *Fidelista* since I was born and now death took him away. What will be our future without him?" Then he himself answered by saying, "I believe that in five years Socialism won't exist in Cuba."

Another young man traveling with him said. "Perhaps you are right; I believe that we are more *Fidelistas* than Socialist."

Raúl ended his message by saying, "I have been working with Fidel for some time on a program of economic and political reforms that will be adapted to the revolution to catch up with the new realities in the world. Fidel, as a last will and desire, requested that I implement them in order to solve the difficulties that are emerging on our island. The first program's steps are already being implemented: these are the elimination of corruption within the Communist Party and the administration of the state companies. The program of reforms will include revision of the activities referring to health, education, transportation, labor policies, housing, and commerce." Moreover, after a pause, he added, "The nation will go towards an economic transformation." At the end of his exposition, as usual, he couldn't miss the opportunity to mention a few old revolutionary slogans used by Fidel to shake up the people a little.

Nevertheless, the tone of the transition speech set, very clearly, that the goal was reforms of the system. The new *máximo líder*, another Castro, continued the course of the revolution with new ideas. The remarkable thing was that he didn't mention anything about the famous economic embargo of the United States, nor did he speak much on *Yanki* imperialism, nor did he refer to the Hugo Chávez 's *Revolución Bolivariana* and his Socialism movement of the twenty-first century.

After Raúl concluded his statement, Alex said, "I believe that Raúl has accepted the reality that the government is unpopular, that only fear and repression kept it in power. On the other hand, probably he has reached the conclusion that the economic system needs changes. Perhaps he wants to experiment with economic measures similar to those established in Communist China. The sad thing is that, for saying less than what he said today, many people have been imprisoned since the spring of 2003, from the group of seventy-five who promoted the so-called *Proyecto Varela*. Raúl has taken the reformist flag; he has considered that is the best way to stay in power. He is earning time and in the near future, he will look for an acceptable successor so he can retire to enjoy his great fortune. The cosmetic changes in the system that he can make will attract reformist dissidents like Payá, Roca, and Menoyo. They can contribute their ideas to reforms that the government will sponsor, under the auspices of Raúl and his group.

"I believe that Raúl has shown great political ability because he can attract the reformist dissidents by promoting changes and reforms of the present laws," Alex continued. "Therefore, he will divide even more the dissidence against him and the Socialist regime."

Then, Alex commented, "Do you realize that the Communist Party has more power than all the laws of the Socialist constitution? This demonstrates that in Cuba there are no laws—whoever controls the Communist Party represents the law. Fidel was the one that controlled the party. With Fidel dead, the new *máximo líder* and first secretary of the party, Raúl, is the law."

The passengers were all very excited by Raúl's speech. Many said that now they felt like *Raulistas*. The reforms were necessary to maintain the revolution and with these reforms, things were going to improve on the island. Suddenly, everybody was talking about Raúl and his reforms. The people no longer spoke much of Fidel, nor of the *Yanki* invasion. Now the strong man was Raúl.

Alex reminded me that we were surrounded by regime sympathizers who, naturally, were worried about the death of Fidel and the succession for fear of losing their privileged positions in society. No doubt they also feared the possibility of a violent reaction from the common people. "The interesting thing would be to see the reaction of *los Cubanos de a pie*," he said. He said we would learn more about it in Havana.

"Now I must speak with Benito to learn about his meeting with the captain and the lieutenant. Raúl's speech could bring some changes in the lieutenant's mind, at least for the time being. Another thing that worries me is what will be the reaction of the group of leaders in the regime who don't want change, those called the *inmovilistas* and those in favor of Hugo Chávez and his *Revolución Bolivariana*."

Two hours later, at three o'clock in the afternoon, we were entering the Central Railroad Station in Havana. Two state security agents received us when we came down from the wagon and several policemen were standing around the platform. All passengers had to show their ID cards and their trip documentation. After looking at ours, they asked where we were going to stay. Alex said in a *casa particular*. The agent asked the address of the house. Alex said that the address was Aguacate 765. The agent looked at a list and said that it was good, that was a *casa particular* for Cuban travelers from the interior of the island. After he took note of our names and address in Havana, he said that we could go. We walked through a long platform and entered the station. The building wasn't well maintained, but its Venetian style was very impressive. In its lobby was a steam locomotive constructed in 1843 called *La Junta,* which was said to have been Cuba's first steam locomotive. The lobby was almost empty; we saw more policemen and security agents than passengers.

We left the station and briefly walked on Arsenal Street, then turned left towards the Avenida Belgica (better known as Egido). We walked for seven blocks until the avenue changed its name to Monserrate. We could see the ruins of the walls that had protected the old colonial Havana in this part of the city. We were in the historical old zone of Havana; the beautiful colonial houses built in the middle of the nineteenth century were neglected and dirty, and some were collapsing. It hurt me to see my native city derelict, in ruins as if it had undergone an aerial bombing.

Traffic was very light—only state security's Lada cars were running through the streets in all directions. There weren't many people walking the streets, and every two or three blocks we could see a policeman standing at the corner, just watching everybody, just waiting for something to happen. Many people were at the windows and others were standing at the doors of their homes looking out to the street. Their faces looked sad, with gloomy eyes, as if they were waiting for something. What came to my attention was a truck dragging a large trailer with windows that was carrying some passengers. Alex told me that was a *Camello*. The revolution employed those *guaguas* for the urban transportation of people. The name came from its design; it had the shape of a camel, the desert animal. There aren't many around and they provide very bad service; like the desert, they are very hot and uncomfortable. Everybody complains about them, even the so-called revolutionaries.

After walking a few more blocks, we turned right onto Aguacate Street. Alex pointed to a house and said, "There, in that two-story house that seems as if it has never been painted, we are going to spend the night. The people here are trustworthy. They don't like the regime and they don't like the Socialist system. Nevertheless, like Benito from Camagüey, they don't want to leave Cuba and they have a great ability to pretend to be sympathizers of the regime."

CHAPTER 19

▼

TREASON AND DECEPTION

"Amazing," Jones said. "You arrived in Havana the day that Fidel Castro died. But how did you end up in the U.S. Interest Section building with two hundred Americans fleeing the city?"

"Be patient, Mr. Jones," Henry said. "We are almost at the end." He took a sip of water and began to speak again.

*　　　*　　　*　　　*

I saw the number seven hundred and sixty-five scrawled above the door, and to the right of the door hung a signboard that read *Arrendador Inscripto* next to a red symbol of a camping tent. Alex explained that the red tent meant that it was a *casa particular* and that Cuban people could stay in there and pay in Cuban pesos.

We knocked and an attractive black woman, about thirty years old, opened the door. A red and white handkerchief covered her hair. She was wearing a white dress with an apron of the same print as the headscarf. When she saw Alex, she told him, "Uncle Alex, we have been waiting for you for a long time. We thought that you had gone to the wake of *el Caballo*."

She kissed Alex on the cheek; Alex called her Marilú and told her that the train was delayed for more than three hours. She replied, "As always, Uncle, here on this island, nothing works!" Then another woman came. Wearing a white blouse and a green skirt with a green handkerchief covering her hair, she appeared to be in her fifties. When Alex saw her, he kissed her on her cheek and called her Mima.

Mima welcomed us and asked for my name. Alex told her that I was his friend Henry, from Havana like them, and he asked for Euclides. Mima said, "Alex, you know your partner Euclides. He is always working when it is possible to make a couple of dollars. He went to take some Canadian tourists to Marina Hemingway in Barlovento, in the 57 Ford Fairlane 500 of Ovidio. He left in the morning and must be back soon."

Alex said, "Mima, that *fotingo* still works! I thought that it was sold as scrap iron."

"Oh, no, Alex!" Mima said. "You know that Euclides likes auto mechanics. It took him some time to fix it, but the car is now running fine. He is earning a few dollars as a foreign tour guide in his free time."

Then Mima asked, "*Chico,* what do you think about the death of that swine? What was the meaning of Raúl's message?" She herself answered the questions saying, "Raúl was making promises to swindle the people later and consolidate his power. Everybody knows how difficult is to live in Cuba because the system doesn't work and the corruption in the country is a way of life. Fidel really screwed us well; his legacy is poverty, hatred, and disunity on the island."

Alex only listened and nodded and said, "You are right, Mima, we will see more soon."

Then Alex asked her about the doctor. Mima said, "*Chico,* for the age that he has, he is doing well. He is going to be eighty-seven years next month. Would you like to speak with him? If you want, I could go see if he is awake." Alex said that he would like to greet him. Mima told Marilú to take us to our rooms while she checked to see if Ovidio was awake.

We went with Marilú to the second floor and she took us to our rooms. The room was clean but the walls needed a little painting. The floor had beautiful ceramic tiles, but some of the tiles were cracked. The room was modestly furnished with a chest of drawers and a small wooden desk with a chair. The bed was covered with a blue bedspread. The place was very clean and tidy. Pictures and engravings from Havana hung from the walls.

On the second floor, there were two additional bedrooms, a small lobby full of old furniture, and a bathroom. Marilú told me, "Here is the bathroom, Henry, but almost never do we have water in the faucet. For that reason we have those two water buckets next to the bathtub." Then she said, "These are the comforts of the Socialism system!"

Later we returned to the first floor and I noticed that, like the room on the second floor, the walls needed some painting. Nevertheless, the decor was very pleasant, although the furniture was a little old and worn. Marilú told me that the first floor had two bedrooms, one for her grandfather, and another one for her parents. Her room was next to ours on the second floor. Then we went to sit in the living room. The living room had an old television set and a radio. Oil paintings and watercolors of Cuban landscapes decorated the walls.

A few minutes later Mima came in, accompanied by an old man with dark skin and white hair who walked with a certain difficulty. When Alex saw the old man, he immediately stood up and walked toward him. Very respectfully, but with great affection, he greeted him. Alex introduced the man as Doctor Ovidio Valdés Rama and told me, "Doctor Valdés Rama has been the professor of anatomy of the University of Havana for three generations of Cuban doctors. He was a classmate of his Uncle Florentino and teacher of his brother Jose and of his own son Euclides."

The doctor told Alex, "Listen, you are adding and counting too many years, and I am not that old." Then he hugged Alex again.

Alex asked him about his health and the doctor said that he was doing fine, thanks to the medicines that Alex sent him regularly to control his blood pressure. The only thing was that he had problems when walking due to the arthritis in his knees.

Then Alex asked him, "Doctor, what do you think about Fidel's death?"

The doctor said that Fidel's hour had come, as it does to everybody else. Then he continued, saying, "Now the important thing is what Raúl is going to do. Everybody in Cuba is looking for changes. The problem is what type of change. Change the economic model. Change the electoral system. Allow political parties to organize. Recognize private property. Authorize private business. Give freedom to the press and to the mass media. Listen, Alex, if they make all these changes, Cuba won't be a Socialist country anymore, and we will need a new constitution."

Stressing his point, he said, "We are going to see what Raúl has in mind; he already said he would eliminate corruption. This could be an internal purge within the Communist Party in order to consolidate Raúl's power after the death of Fidel. The people won't benefit from that type of change. In reality what the people want is freedom, to be able to live and to breathe without having to ask permission from the government. As you know, I am not politician. I leave these subjects to the young people. But I can tell you of the chaotic situation of the health system in Cuba. It has been deteriorating with time because the government hasn't allocated enough resources to the health system and it is using the limited resources available to help other countries instead of our own people. It has more than fourteen thousand physicians in Venezuela and it is sending a great amount of medication to that country. The island has developed two parallel health systems. The common Cuban people have one and the foreigners and the government elite have another. The foreigners receive good service because they pay in hard currencies, and the government elite 'deserve' it for their 'revolutionary merits.' The health services and hospitals for the people get worse every day. There is a lack of medical equipment and drugs for treatments, a shortage of doctors to take care of the Cuban people. There are more than fourteen thousand doctors abroad because the government receives oil and money for their services. It is like the days when Cuba had armies in Africa. The government received money from the Soviet Union for the Cuban soldiers' services. Cuban soldiers were mercenaries for the Soviets in Africa; now Cuban doctors are treated as mercenaries in Venezuela."

He added, "You know, Alex, that I don't like to speak of this because it makes me reminisce on the day that my son Octavio left for Africa. He was a victim of the revolutionary government. He, as were many other military young people, was sent to Africa to fight in a foreign war as mercenaries. Unfortunately, Octavio never returned."

Alex realized the doctor was depressed by the memories of his son who died serving in Angola. Therefore, he changed the conversation to the years when the doctor was a university professor. After ten or fifteen minutes of speaking about his years of teaching and his experiences with his students, Mima came and said to him with great affection, "Doctor, I believe that you are a little tired; you'd better have a rest before dinner."

The doctor said, "Yes, I think it is a good idea." He slowly stood up, saying to us that during dinner he was going to tell us more stories from the university.

When the doctor and Mima left the room, Alex told Marilú that he had to make some telephone calls and went to his room. I stayed in the living room with Marilú. The television was off because the electricity was down, so we didn't have anything to do but chat. Marilú told me that she worked as a nurse in the Hospital Clínico Quirúrgico, located next to the Fuente Luminosa in Havana. She worked every day, except Sundays, from four o'clock in the afternoon until midnight. She earned three hundred Cuban pesos per month, about fifteen U.S. dollars. Her father, Euclides, was a doctor in the same hospital. He made four hundred and fifty Cuban pesos (twenty-three U.S. dollars) per month. That was the reason why he had to work as foreign tourist guide. She said that her father, with the tourism job, could earn two hundred and fifty dollars monthly. She also told me that Mima was dealing with the business of the *casa particular* and looking after her grandfather. Marilú helped her when she could.

The business of the *casa particular* wasn't very profitable. The license cost two thousand Cuban pesos and they had to pay the government another two thousand Cuban pesos monthly in taxes, plus a 10 percent tax of the profits. "The government allows us to operate the business, but it cripples us with so many taxes. Nevertheless, my father says that this house of my grandfather's is very large and if we don't maintain it as a *casa particular* the government may take it away or send two families to live here permanently with us."

Then she told me, with certain resignation, "Life in Cuba, it ain't easy. Look at the case of my grandfather," she added. "He is a physician who has worked in public hospitals all his life, and he was a professor of the University of Havana for almost forty years. When he retired, the revolutionary government gave him two hundred Cuban pesos monthly pension (ten U.S. dollars). Tell me, who could live with that? Thank God that he has his family and the house, as long as the government allows it, and we all live here together working very hard to sustain us and to take care of him."

Then with despair on her face, she said, "I am turning thirty next month and my mother is telling me, 'Marilú, *te vas a quedar para vestir santos,* when are you going to get married?' I always said to her, 'Mima, the day that freedom comes to Cuba.' Mr. Henry, on this island the government controls everything. Here there is no private property or private life. The state tells you what you must do, where you must live, what you must study, what you must eat—they own you. Here, we all are state's slaves. I don't want to marry another slave and bring to the world a creature that is sentenced to be a slave. The black slaves won their freedom at the end of the nineteenth century. When will we win ours?"

I realized that Marilú perhaps was considering me as another uncle and was relieving her frustrations with me. I could only say that maybe things were going to improve. Perhaps, with the death of Fidel, the Cuban situation could begin changing for the best.

While we were talking, Alex returned to the room. He seemed a little worried and I asked him if something was wrong. Alex said that he had spoken with Benito and that the captain told him that the lieutenant wanted to wait for a while, to learn more of the changes Raúl had mentioned. "I also have good news," he said. "I spoke with Julisa and she said that Genaro had returned to the house repentant; he was very sorry. She told me there are no problems from his temporary disappearance. However, you will still leave the island from Pinar del Río."

At five-thirty in the afternoon, Euclides arrived. He gave Alex a very warn greeting and asked his pardon for not being in the house earlier, saying he couldn't miss the opportunity to make few dollars. Alex introduced me to him. I immediately realized that Euclides was a good man. He was a quite tall and well-built man, with a good-natured face adorned by an ample smile of very white teeth. Euclides appeared to be in his fifties.

Alex asked him if he had heard anything new. Euclides said, "The people don't know what to say. The death of *el Caballo* after more than forty-seven years of absolute power has left all the people confused, especially after Raúl's statement. The people ask themselves if the changes Raúl mentioned are to alleviate poverty in the country or to save Socialism on the island. The people are tired of suffering due to external events of international order. They are demanding the termination of the *periodo especial*; they no longer can bear the misery in which they are living—they are demanding an improvement of their economic and social well-being."

After a pause, he added, "The people have realized that the so-called achievements of the revolution in health and education systems are myths, fables. Cuba is now behind most other countries in Latin America in these areas, when before the revolution it was ahead of them. UNESCO reveals that information, but the government doesn't publish that data on the island. On the other hand, the government's excuse for the island's economic problems is the United States' commercial blockade. That's another story the people don't believe anymore. The people realize that it is another fictitious story, a sham. Chancellor Perez Roque bragged that Cuba maintains commercial relations with one hundred and fifteen countries in the world and that the island receives preferential credits from the European banking community, but the reality, my friends, is that Cuba doesn't have anything to sell, nor any money with which to pay international debts. Instead of professional financial managers, faithful political leaders of the regime manage the island's industries. These industries are behind the times in technology and they operate under excessive bureaucracy. They are unproductive and they cannot compete with any country in the international markets."

To complete his explanation, Euclides told us, "Any scheme that Raúl could have for the future of Cuba would be unacceptable, if as a first step he doesn't release the political prisoners, reduces repression and the abuses, at least, and improve the distribution of foodstuffs and consumer goods. Perhaps the people will give him time to fulfill his promises. However, the patience of the people almost is exhausted and tempers are getting hot. I can tell you this," said Euclides, "because I take care of many patients in the hospital, walk around the street, and speak with many people. I am seeing the reaction of the people when the *Damas de Blanco* go out to march in the streets and when the paramilitary gangs at the service of the government make their *actos de repudio*. The people are scared, but they are already getting tired and eventually, they are going to explode."

Alex said there was no doubt that Raúl had shown great political ability when he delivered his statement to the people. Euclides said, "Listen, Alex, what he has demonstrated is good sense. He didn't have any other recourse than to say what he said if he wants to be able to eventually enjoy his wealth with peace of mind. For some years, Raúl has had the absolute monopoly of the *diplotiendas* and special stores, tourism, and the currency exchange business. Raúl lives in the middle of an artificial lake. The property is fenced and he has a special force unit of fifteen hundred men for his protection. He has a great fortune deposited in Swiss banks and houses in Italy and other parts of Europe. Raúl's idea is to recycle *Fidelismo* and to adapt Cuban's Socialism so that the power won't escape from his hands."

Alex replied, "Euclides, then what are the *inmovilistas* going to do? They consider themselves the guards of the totalitarian essence of the regime and the precursors of the *Revolución Bolivariana*. They can't be in agreement with the reforms. This group always has feared that any opening and reforms constituted the end of the regime."

"I don't know the answer to that," Euclides said. "It is necessary to learn the degree of the alliance between Fidel and Chávez. The affiliation of these two characters in brotherhood in a messianic planetary revolution is worrisome and represents a threat to peace for the American continents. Chancellor Felipe Perez Roque, in a speech given in Venezuela in December 2005, outlined this thesis when he said, 'The world has recovered from the collapse of Soviet Communism, which happened with Perestroika. It is now a reasonable aspiration to construct a planetary Socialist model. After the disaster and the treason of European Communism, the heart, the brain, and the muscle to carry out that task of burying the imperialist *Yanki* was transferred to Latin America. Within Latin America, the axis Cuba-Venezuela has the responsibility to take ahead that enormous adventure.'" Then Euclides concluded, "And this wasn't all. Days later, the second vice president of Cuba, Carlos Lage, added, 'Cuba has two presidents: Fidel Castro and Hugo Chávez.'" In reality, this statement postulated the creation of a true federation that had been forming during the very frequent contacts of Castro and Chávez."

Alex answered, "I believe that under the current conditions, we only have to wait and see the events. However, we must continue developing a civil society and helping political prisoners and their relatives."

When Alex finished with this commentary, Mima came and said, "Are you guys ready for dinner? I have prepared black beans and rice, a roasted chicken, and fried green bananas."

Euclides, standing up, said, "Mima, we haven't seen that menu on our table for a long time. You did that because Alex and Henry are here with us. I believe they must come more often to improve our diet." Smiling, he added, "Mima always is complaining that she can't find anything to buy in the state stores and that everything is very expensive in the special stores and black market."

Mima answered that she paid twelve dollars for the chicken in the special store and that she bought the bananas illegally from a *guajiro* that brought them from Pinar del Río. Euclides said, "Well done, lady—you have gained our admiration for your marketing ability and now we are going to prove your culinary knowledge."

When we were walking to the dining room, we saw Marilú coming with her grandfather, helping him to a seat at the table. The doctor sat at the head of the table where he gave a blessing for the food and welcomed us again. The food seemed wonderful, maybe because Mima was a very good cook, or maybe because I was very hungry after five days of little and bad food. During dinner, we spoke about Cuba before the revolution and the anecdotes of the doctor at the university. It was an enjoyable and cozy family supper.

After diner Euclides, Alex, and I went to sit in the living room while Mima and Marilú cleared the table and washed the dishes and the doctor went to rest in his room. Euclides asked Alex if the security agents at the train station had asked us where we would stay in Havana. Alex said yes, that he had told them here in the house. Then Euclides said that he needed our identity cards because he had to maintain records of the guests of the *casa particular*. He told us that in this way the government controlled who entered and left the city and where they stayed. This information went to the CDR, which controlled the movement of people and activities of the *barrio*.

We gave him our cards and when Euclides saw them, he couldn't contain his laughter. "Listen, you guys have very amusing names." He turned to Alex, saying, "One day you are going to run out of names to use. Today you are Manuel Jiménez Colón and just couple of weeks ago you were Armando Santana. Well, that is good so that the authorities see that we provide accommodations to many different people." He looked at my papers and said, "Henry, today you are José Rodriguez Pantoja. The Pantoja last name is from the interior of the island; in Havana it is not very common."

While he was recording our information in the register, Alex told him that the program was to go tomorrow evening to Pinar del Rió to leave me there. Due to recent events, the trip to Camagüey was canceled. Alex would return to Havana to attend meetings and perhaps on Thursday he would go to Camagüey. Euclides said it was fine, because he didn't have to go to the hospital tomorrow. The trip to Pinar del Río was only three hours; if we left at two o'clock in the afternoon, they could be back in Havana before nine that evening.

Alex gave an envelope to Euclides. When he opened it, he said, "Why are you giving me this money?" Alex said that it was to cover our stay and to help him to pay the expenses of the trip to Pinar del Río. Euclides said, "Alex, you know that this is your house and you don't have to pay anything to me for the stay. You and Henry are our guests. In addition, you know well that if my father finds out I received money from you as payment for your rooms, he will get very upset with me."

Alex looked at him and said, "Take the money and don't mention it to him and he won't find out. I feel among family when I am here, but I know how difficult life is in Cuba and the precarious state in which you all live. Also, I know of the taxes you must pay to the government to maintain this house as a *casa particular*. Please accept it; it will make me feel better." Finally, after several arguments, Euclides took the three hundred U.S. dollars Alex gave him.

We remained in the living room talking for a while. When the electricity came back, Euclides put on the television to see if there was any news but all that was on either of the two national television channels were programs that spoke of the life of the deceased *máximo líder*. Around eight-fifteen, the phone rang and Mima answered it. The call was from the hospital for Euclides.

When he came back to the living room, we noticed that he had a very serious face. Euclides sat down first and said to us, "Something is happening. The hospital just called me with an emergency order to report to work in the hospital in less than one hour. That is very rare. What could be happening? I am going to call a friend of mine who works in the MININT." When he came back, he said, "My friend wasn't home, his wife told me that he went to work at five in the afternoon. He is an electrician who works in the radio and communication facilities of the Ministry and his wife told me they called him because there was some technical problem in the plant." He looked at us and said, "I don't know, but something big is happening. Well, I must go now; I will call from the hospital. I believe that I will come back at dawn or early tomorrow morning because we must go to Pinar del Río in the afternoon."

Euclides left and we stayed with Mima and Marilú in the living room with the television on, talking about the hospital and the emergency call. Then Marilú had the idea to put the radio on to see if it had something different. The radio didn't have anything new, only Fidel's old speeches. Around nine o'clock, the famous *Radio Reloj* announced that Ricardo Alarcón, president of the *Asamblea Nacional del Poder Popular,* was going to give an important message to the nation at 9:30 p.m.

We all remained very quiet until Alex said, "What is this, now? What will Alarcón say? Will he inform the people when the National Assembly will meet to confirm Raúl as president? Perhaps, but he could wait until tomorrow to say that. It must be a very important thing, a new event." Alex stood up and said, "I am going up to the room to make some phone calls."

We remained in the living room listening to the radio and watching the television in search of news. We all were speculating over what could have happened, until Alex came back ten minutes later and said, "The National Police are in state of alert in the Province of Havana. All state security agents from the MININT were called to duty and security was reinforced on all radio and television stations. The traffic of people in and out of the MININT building is very unusual. The embassy guards were doubled. Benito told me that in Camagüey there were rumors that the FAR had cancelled all licenses and vacations."

Then Alex said, "Well, in few minutes we will know what is happening." At 9:33 p.m., Alarcón appeared on the television screen, seated in an office behind a desk, with a fearsome expression on his face. He announced that a group of terrorists financed by the United States had perpetrated an attack on Provisional President Comandante Raúl Castro and three of his assistants, and as consequence of wounds suffered in the attack, Raúl Castro had died like a hero of the revolution, accompanied by his three faithful assistants. Still unknown was how many terrorists had participated in the attack, but some of them were able to escape after facing the brave defense of the president's guards. The forces of the MININT and the National Police had initiated a detailed investigation and an extensive search for the terrorists. He stressed that the search wouldn't finish until the apprehension and execution of these mercenaries, enemies of the revolution. He said that the FAR was in the state of alert to defend the nation from any *Yanki* aggression.

Without more details on the attack, he said, "As president of the *Asamblea Nacional del Poder Popular* and following the constitution, I have temporarily named Chancellor Felipe Perez Roque as *presidente del Consejodel Estado* and Carlos Lage Davila as *primer vicepresidente del Consejo del Estado*. These appointments are effective immediately until the National Assembly meets in an extraordinary section to ratify or to name other members of the Communist Party to hold these positions."

The news left us speechless. Nobody was expecting this. The Castro brothers were already history. Now, the Cuban people were in the hands of the *inmovilistas*, those who always lacked their own criteria and followed the madness of the *Comandante*. The two new leaders were very young and they hadn't participated in the epic revolution against Batista. What would happen to the reforms and changes that Raúl had mentioned in his morning message?

Alex reminded us that Perez Roque had been a university student leader and former personal secretary of Fidel. He was promoted meteorically to chancellor several years ago after the crisis with the young Roberto Robaina who was in favor of Perestroika. Perez Roque, as Minister of Foreign Relations, had always demonstrated little diplomatic ability as consequence of the coarseness of his character. Nevertheless, some people considered him as the best interpreter of Fidel's ideas. Carlos Lage Davila was a little bit older than Perez Roque, but he didn't participate either in the fight against Batista. He was the leader of the *Union de Jovenes Comunistas* and went to Ethiopia as a physician during the Cuban intervention in that war. The man was incapable of having his own ideas; he had always been a blind follower of Fidel.

A few minutes later there appeared on the TV screen the image of the new *Presidente* Felipe Perez Roque. With his eyes almost jumping out their orbits and in funeral tone of voice, he said that in fulfillment of his functions as president of the council, he wanted to confirm to the Cuban people that the nation was prepared to fight until death against *Yanki* imperialism. He said the transition of power was proceeding according to the program set up by our *máximo líder* Fidel Castro. He also mentioned that the generational relay of state controls was always a concern of our leader. However, the people could be sure that the new leaders wouldn't diverge from the revolutionary line maintained by the Communist Party and legalized by the Socialist constitution. He mentioned that the government recognized that Latin America was at this historical moment the center and muscle of the great task of destroying *Yanki* imperialism and capitalism. The aspiration of the people of Latin America was to construct and develop planetary Socialism. Therefore, it was very important to maintain the close relationship with the Venezuelan and Bolivian brothers. The Cuban revolution goals would expand to accept the responsibility with these brothers in the great adventure of the *Revolución Bolivariana* until reaching the final victory against imperialism.

Later he said that, without loss of time and due to the prevailing necessities, he had named Comandante Ramiro Gómez Guerra as Minister of the MININT and General Abelardo Fontana Flores as Minister of the MINFAR. They were two dedicated revolutionary leaders of great vision and history, he said. In addition, he informed the people of the great rally the next morning at eight on Malecón Avenue. The demonstration would march in front of the den of the "murderous capitalists" in the building of the SINA (Section of Interests of North America). He concluded, "Therefore, I have decreed that tomorrow, Monday, will be a day of mourning and revolutionary fervor in Havana Province. All the people are invited to attend this great event."

Alex stood up and said, "We all know that the dissidents are disarmed; here we can see the indications of an internal conspiracy in the regime. Possibly all this has been planned with anticipation, perhaps even before the death of Fidel. The hard *inmovilista* line within the regime couldn't allow any modest reforms of the system to somehow improve the living conditions of the Cuban people. Once again, the regime has demonstrated its scorn of the people. The new leaders have committed the people again, this time in a new stage of internationalism now called *Revolución Bolivariana*. With the Venezuelan money from oil revenues, they will go abroad to intervene in other countries' conflicts. I believe that the Cuban people don't wish this new call for more sacrifices, due to the political wearing down of the revolution and due to the conditions of economic misery in which they live."

Alex remained for a moment in silence and then said, "It is difficult for me to accept that Fidel Castro, with his delirium of greatness, thought that in Cuba's history there could be another Castro as a *máximo líder*. He prepared the plot of his succession so that his brother Raúl, the eternal successor, died after him without ever arriving at the power. Fidel still wasn't satisfied at the damage and the destruction that he did in Cuba. He wanted *Fidelismo* to continue and expand throughout all Latin America. He, like all megalomaniac tyrants, dreamed that his ideas indefinitely metastasize after his death."

Alex then said, "For the Cuban people, and particularly for the political prisoners, the name of Ramiro Gómez is associated with the worse pages of the repression. This man was the one that organized the state security system in 1960; he was responsible for the firing squad executions and for the greatest crimes than were ever committed in the Cuban prisons since 1959. He is a real jackal."

He reminded us about General Abelardo Fontana Flores, who was a combatant in the Sierra Maestra and the Sierra Cristal with Raúl. He always was considered a *Raulista*. The general had been Minister of the Interior for some time years ago. He was a member of the Political Bureau of the Cuban Communist Party and a member of the Central Committee of the Party. However, during the last five years, he had been somehow marginalized from power.

Alex concluded, "If what I am thinking is certain, someday we will know the truth of what has happened today in Cuba. I believe that General Fontana acted like Judas within the group of *Raulistas*. Fidel couldn't finish his life without another treason and deception. How much harm this man has done to the human race!"

We continued for a while discussing the events of the day and waiting for Euclides' call from the hospital. Meanwhile, Alex went several times to make phone calls to his various contacts on the island. He told me that he had spoken with Benito, who told Alex that he was going to visit the captain because the situation had changed in only a few hours. The city of Camagüey was quiet, but the police were in a stage of alert. Also, Alex spoke with other people who informed him of a large mobilization of state security vehicles and trucks in the neighborhoods around Havana. When Mima got tired of waiting for Euclides to call, she called the hospital. The telephone operator told her that the doctors were very busy and that their lines were blocked.

Around eleven o'clock, we heard the engines of several cars and trucks in the block around the house. Five minutes later, somebody was striking the door of the house. Mima opened the door and suddenly three uniformed men armed with AK-47 assault rifles entered the house, followed by a state security officer and accompanied by a man dressed in civilian clothes. Mima looked at the man in civilian clothes and said, "What is going on, Esteban? What are the reasons for the deployment of this force?"

The man, looking a little embarrassed, said to her, "Mima, we are verifying the guest records of the *casa particular*. Do you have the registry at hand?" Mima went to look for the registry while we stayed facing the armed state security agents.

Mima came back and gave the registry to the man in civilian clothes. He looked at it and said, "Where are the guests Jiménez Colón and Rodriguez Pantoja?"

Alex took a step forward and said, "I am Manuel Jiménez Colón."

"And I am José Rodriguez Pantoja," I said.

Mima told us that Mr. Esteban was the president of the CDR of the block. He requested our identity cards and the trip documents. When we gave him everything, the man looked at them in detail and said to us, "I see that you are *cederistas* from Camagüey and are here receiving technical training in the organization of political and cultural acts."

Alex said, "Yes, *compañero*."

Then the security agent told Esteban, "Let me have the ID cards to check the names against the list of suspects." The agent took the cards and compared them with a long list of names and numbers. After five minutes of thorough study, he looked at us and said, "Fine." Then he asked us when we had arrived in Havana and what type of transportation we had used. When Alex gave the information, the agent wrote it in a notebook.

Later the agent asked the president of the CDR, "How many people live in this house? This is a very big house." Esteban said four people. The agent asked, "There are only two here. Where are the other two?"

Mima said, "My husband is a physician and he is at the hospital working. He works in the Clinico Quirurgico just as my daughter Marilú, who is a nurse in the hospital."

The president told the agent she was telling the truth and that the young woman was Marilú. Then the agent said again, "We are missing one person here!"

The president said, "The other person is Doctor Ovidio."

"Where is he?" the agent demanded.

The president said the doctor was in an advanced age and that he was probably sleeping in his room. Then the agent shouted in a coarse tone that he had to come to the living room or he was going to look for him in his room.

Mima said she would get him but that it would take a few minutes. Around five minutes later, she came back with the doctor. The poor man had a sleepy face and seemed to be very displeased and confused. The agent asked him for his name and the doctor said that his name was Ovidio Valdés Rama.

The agent looked at us and said, "Technically, I should take you guys into custody under investigation. My original orders were to arrest any person who had entered Havana today. However, headquarters just told me to take prisoner only the people who are on the list of suspects. It seems to me that they no longer have space to put more people. Well, anyway, you are under investigation and can't leave the Province of Havana." He wrote our names in a notebook, removed two pieces of papers from his pocket, and gave them to us. Then he said, "These are the summons. You have to appear Tuesday at eight in the morning at the MININT for further investigation. If you don't show up, an order of arrest will be issued and you will be accused of *desacato*."

Nevertheless, he said, "If the *compañero* president of the CDR invites you to attend and you guys go as volunteers to the great rally against the *Yanki* imperialists tomorrow morning on the Malecón, in front of the SINA, I could write a note in the record qualifying you as good revolutionaries. That could help your investigation process."

The president looked at us and said, "It seems like a very good idea of the *compañero*. If you want, I could do that. Outside we have the trucks to take you to the Malecón now."

Alex looked at me and we both accepted the invitation. I realized we didn't have any other choice; we had to go to the Malecón. At least we would be resolving the problem until Tuesday and earning some merits, if you could think like that. Of course, immediately I thought that all this would mix up our trip to Pinar del Río and my exit from Cuba. Then I realized, *I am already acting like the Cubans on the island.* The motto of their daily activities begin with the phrases "*It ain't easy*" and "*It is necessary to solve ...*"

Well, our fate was apparently settled, at least until Tuesday. However, the security officer had something else in mind. He looked at Marilú and said, "Listen, you are a nurse." She said she was. The agent said, "You should volunteer to go to the rally to help with first aid."

Marilú told him, "*Compañero*, I must report to the hospital tomorrow at four in the afternoon."

The agent looked at her and said, "You come with me now to work tonight as a volunteer for the revolution and tomorrow you report to work at the hospital. There is no problem!"

Marilú looking at him and said, "No problem, *compañero*."

Then he looked at Mima and said, "And you, *compañera*, stay here taking care of this old man." Nobody said anything, but Marilú's face and ours showed expressions of anxiety and fear as if we were in the presence of an evil force manifested through the abuse of power.

*   *   *   *

Henry paused in the telling of his story and told Mr. Jones, "Well, sir, you already know what happened this dawn. My friend Alex and I were taken to the Malecón by force to participate in the failed great event of the revolution. I, in the confusion produced by the shooting, had the luck of entering the building with the group of American tourists. This is my story, Mr. Jones."

With resignation, he added, "This is why I don't have a passport or any identification with me. I only have a false Cuban ID card with the name of José Rodriguez Pantoja. However, I am a citizen of the United States and my name is Enrique González Rueda, but everybody calls me Henry, as I mentioned before. I live with my wife Natalia, who also is a citizen of the United States, at 208 Ocean Drive, Point Pleasant, in the state of New Jersey."

Jones glanced at him and said that the story was very original and intriguing. He had recorded it and would send it to Washington, where a department analyst would review and process it. The department would probably call his wife to set an interview to verify his identity.

"How long will this process take?"

Jones thought for a moment before answering. "I can't really say, because there are more than a hundred and fifty people without passports in very similar conditions in the Section of Interests here in Havana. Due to the situation that has developed in Cuba, the Department of State has been very busy. At least it will take one or two weeks, maybe more."

Henry said, "I don't have any money, family in Havana, or documents to go outside of the building and I don't know where to stay."

Jones said, "Listen, Henry, your case is very difficult and different. You not only broke the law that prohibits American citizens from traveling to Cuba, you were involved in illegal transfers of cash from the United States to Cuba against the law of the Commercial Embargo. I personally endorse your cause, but I am going to be completely honest with you—you'd better get a lawyer, because you are going to pay several fines and possibly will have to go to court. The good news is that the Red Cross is going to open a temporary refuge in the gardens of this building to lodge the people who have situations like yours."

Then Jones commented, "Your friend Alex has put you in a very difficult situation, and now he has disappeared."

Henry stared at the State Department agent for a while and then said, "Mr. Jones, I know you are very young and with time and luck, you will learn the value of friendship. My brother Alex has always fought for freedom and he has taught me the value of it. In only one week, Alex taught me the value of honor, the meaning of the word patriotism, and the significance of friendship. I don't know where Alex is. However, I can tell you that you will be able to find him where there is dignity and honesty. And I am going to repeat a phrase, which I learned from him: *'Freedom is the hope of humanity, and it isn't free.'*"

CHAPTER 20

▼

THE NEW MÁXIMO LÍDER!

Henry was safe, waiting for the Washington's bureaucracy to clear up the big mess where he found himself. However, outside of the iron fence of the U.S. Interest Section building, the Cuban people were engaged one more time in another skirmish toward their ultimate goal, *freedom*!

As Henry was telling his story to Peter Jones, the rally dissolved by itself and all the demonstrators had run, terrified by the confusion of the burst firings of the AK-47s and the shouts of "Assassins" and *"Viva la FAR."* Everything happened very early in the dark dawn of Monday before the sun's rays illuminated the Malecón. Some people in Havana maybe thought the *Yanki* invasion had arrived.

The early events had triggered additional problems for the revolutionary government. The mass of scared and desperate people, taking advantage of the confusion, had sacked several nearby shopping centers. The first place to receive the impact of the crowd was the Galeria del Prado on Malecón Avenue. The stores there had all types of imported articles on sale, from footwear like Nikes and Reeboks to Japanese electronic equipment. These were some of the so-called *diplotiendas* only for foreign diplomats and tourists, where only it was possible to buy with dollars, euros, and *chavitos*. The people broke the shop windows and entered the premises that were closed at that early hour in the morning. The mob looted all the merchandise. Cimex Company, property of Raúl Castro, operated the shopping center. The police and security agents didn't show up because everything happened very quickly. The confusion and chaos of the mob didn't allow time for the authorities to react.

Later the mob reached the shopping center of Twenty-fifth Street, the one next to the Hotel Habana Libre and the Pan-American Stores located on the ground floor of the FOCSA building on Seventeenth Street between M and N in the Vedado area, near the Malecón. These stores, like those of the Galeria del Prado, were very well stocked with imported articles for the foreign tourists and businesspeople, and Cubans of the government elite who had dollars and euros. There all the stores suffered the same fate as the one in the Galeria.

The crowd walked without resistance to Coppelia Park between L and K beyond the area of La Rampa and disposed of all the ice creams and treats that the Coppelia Ice Cream Parlor, owned and operated by the state, had in its freezers. In addition, they sacked the refrigerators and warehouses of the restaurants Rumbos Café, Fiat Café, Pizzería Milano, La Zorra y el Cuervo, and the Polinesio, all only a few blocks away from the Malecón. The revolutionary government in the sixties confiscated all these restaurants, and since then, they had been operated by the state for foreigners and the regime elite.

Everything happened so fast and in such a short period of time that the authorities didn't have time to stop the sacking. The people carried away all types of articles and food that they hadn't seen for a long time. All those items, which could only be acquired in dollars or euros or that, weren't attainable by the *Cubanos de a pie* earning their subsistence in useless Cuban pesos.

A few minutes after five-thirty in the morning, Licenciado José Regalado Ruiz, the personal secretary of newly appointed President Felipe Perez Roque, took the internal telephone from the office of the president in the Palace of the Revolution located in the Plaza de la Revolución behind the monument to the apostle José Martí. The president had been preparing, until two o'clock in the morning, the stellar speech he would give during the great rally of solidarity of the people with the new horizons of the revolution. He had worked hard and it was late, so he decided to stay in the palace to sleep in one of the special suites constructed for Fidel in case he wanted to take a *siesta*.

The room was luxuriously furnished and maintained. It had a perfect computerized control of temperature and humidity to the taste of the occupant. It had been constructed to be soundproof and was reinforced with steel plates of two inches of thickness for protection against aerial bombing attacks. The suite had a luxurious bathroom and an office equipped with all types of telecommunications equipment. The door that communicated with the interior of the palace opened only with the suite occupant's electronic authorization. In reality, the elegant suite was a palace bunker built for the protection of the dedicated and beloved revolutionary leader.

The president had given orders to Licenciado Regalado to wake him at six o'clock in the morning so he could get dressed and have a good breakfast before making the short trip to the building of the SINA. He had planned to arrive only a few minutes before seven-thirty at the Malecón, riding in the well-known black Mercedes that Fidel had used. However, due to the events of the early morning, Regalado believed it was necessary to wake the president before the scheduled time.

The telephone of the bunker rang three times before the president awoke and answered with his habitual bad temper, saying, "What *carajo* is going on, José, I told you to wake me up at six and now it is only five-thirty!"

The licenciado, with a shaking voice, said, "I know, sir, but I beg your pardon, sir, but certain things have happened that I believe you must be informed of."

The president said, "Well, what *carajo* has happened?"

The licenciado began saying that the state security agents from the MININT had shot down the luminescent screen of the SINA and that they had destroyed it. The president first said, "*Coño*, I knew that eventually somebody was going to get rid of that screen of *mierda*. It was a provocation against the revolution."

The licenciado said, "Yes, sir, but the problem is that the disturbance caused by the bursts of the AK-47s sparked off an unexpected stampede of the people who were there and they all left, running towards downtown. I believe that we aren't going to have a rally because everybody fled in terror when the shooting started."

The president jumped off the bed and said, "*Coño*, José! Come to the suite. I am going to open the *cabrona* door so you can tell me what happened." And, without taking off his olive green presidential pajamas with the Cuban flag embroidered on the front pocket, he went to the electronic controls and began touching them desperately. First, by error, he touched the button that activated the music system but he finally pushed the one that opened the door. In about a minute, the licenciado opened the door slowly and with a lot of effort because the door was made of heavy steel and weighed quite a bit. The president, wanting to show his calm and complete control of the situation, was seated in a comfortable armchair of deerskin. He said, "Well, José, tell me the story from the beginning."

The licenciado, upon seeing the steady attitude of his president, felt a little calmer and began to tell the story, according to what was told him by Máximo, the Mercedes driver. First, he told the president about the accusations of Lieutenant Rodríguez Caso in Camagüey and of the rebellion of the FAR in several provinces in the center of the island.

By the middle of the story, the president already seemed to be extremely irritated. The licenciado noted it and began to stutter. This was making the president more irritated and nervous. He suddenly stood up and grabbed the poor man's neck, shouting, "*Coño, cabrón,* tell me everything before I kill you!" Thank God that the president wasn't a big man and that the licenciado was able to get away and leave the room running.

The president took the telephone and told the first secretary who answered it to call immediately the Minister of the Interior. In less than five minutes, when the president was in the bathroom, the telephone rang. The president very quickly answered the telephone next to the toilet. The secretary said that she hadn't been able to locate the minister. When hearing this, the president became infuriated and said, "*Coño,* call General Fontana Flores in the MINFAR."

While the secretary was making the call, the president dressed himself and put on his platform shoes, which made him looked a little taller, because he wasn't a very tall man. Of course, he knew that he would never be of the height of Fidel, and that reality he didn't like.

Finally the phone rang; it was the secretary saying that she had left a message in the Ministry office, because they hadn't been able to locate General Fontana. Upon hearing this, the president began to curse and swear. The secretary, with perhaps the idea of calming him down, said that maybe it was very early and that soon both would call back. This commentary sparked off the president. He began to shout and to insult the secretary and the ministers and all military personnel of the MINFAR and the MININT, describing them as gorillas, idiots, thieves, mental retards, and many other qualifying adjectives and names. After he finished his tantrum, he threw the telephone to the floor, breaking it in several pieces.

When the president was leaving the suite to look for the licenciado, one of the other phones on the desk rang. He picked up it and it was the secretary, who, with a little hoarse voice, said that Chancellor Carlos Lage Davila was on the line. The president, in a very rude manner, said, "Put him on."

The chancellor, who now was the first vice president of the council, began saying, "*Coño,* Felipe, who *carajo* issued the order to shoot the luminescent screen of the SINA? I just got a call from our ambassador in the UN telling me what had happened and saying that the *cabrones Yankis* are going to take the case today to the Security Council. They are requesting sanctions for Cuba due to the attack on the SINA." He continued saying in a reproaching tone, "*Coño,* before you order *mierda* like that, you must consult me."

The president replied, quite irritated, "*Coño*, I didn't order that *mierda*."

Then the chancellor said, "Well, if you didn't order it, then which *carajo* did order it? Did you speak with Ramiro and Abelardo?"

The president said that he had called them, but hadn't been able to speak with them. Moreover, he said, "*Coño*, you and I always have discussed the problems that these *cabrones* old soldiers could cause us. They think that they can do whatever they please without consulting with us."

Then the chancellor said, "Listen, Felipe, find out what happened and call me; meanwhile I am going to tell the ambassador that the *Yankis* shot first and that they were the ones that destroyed that *mierda*."

The president said, "Listen, do you know anything about a FAR rebellion in several central provinces in the island?"

The chancellor was very surprised to hear that. "*Coño*, I hadn't heard anything! You must talk with Abelardo; that could be a very serious problem."

Neither the president nor the chancellor knew that after the stampede, the crowd had ended up sacking several shopping centers and restaurants. The president was informed about the sackings as soon as he got to his office, when the chief of the National Police called to inform him.

Later, the president asked Licenciado Regalado Ruiz to come to his office. The licenciado came, a little fearful, with a pale face and a red neck. When the president saw him, he said that the licenciado had misinterpreted him. Due to his clumsiness when speaking of such important subjects for the revolution, he was driven him crazy. He said he did not intend to kill the licenciado.

When they were talking, the red telephone rang. This was the direct phone line with the president of Venezuela, Hugo Chávez. When President Perez Roque answered, a secretary told him that President Chávez wanted to speak to him. He held the line for about five minutes and Chávez didn't answer. While he was waiting, President Perez Roque said to the licenciado, covering the telephone with his hand, "*Coño*, this gorilla is so arrogant, he thinks that he is a god because he has the *mierda* of oil. Let's see what is the *mierda* that he has now on his mind."

After waiting for ten minutes a voice said, "Felipe, *Vale*, what type of *zaperoco* is happening there? I have been informed that you ordered the *Yanki* luminous screen on the empire building shot down. Listen, *Vale*, that wasn't in our program. I also was informed that, resulting from this incident, the great rally initiating the transformation of the Cuban Revolution into the *Revolución Bolivariana* had to be cancelled. *Vale*, that never would have happened with the *penco senil*, as you used to call Fidel. *Vale*, what did Abelardo tell you about the FAR mutinies in the provinces? What is going on in Cuba? I don't like it! You know that I don't like military revolts, ho, ho, ho."

President Perez Roque first explained that he hadn't ordered the shooting and that he immediately had issued orders to initiate a detailed investigation of the incident. The offenders would pay with their lives for treason to the revolution. Moreover, he said that General Fontana was in control of the situation with the collaboration of the MININT. Then he told Chávez that he would speak to the people through radio and television, explaining the new goals of the revolution.

President Chávez ended up saying that he was too busy to continue the conversation, but he requested that the president of Cuba should keep him better informed in the future. He was hoping that everything would return to normality, as in the good times with the old man. He then reminded the Cuban president that the continuous supply of oil to the island was conditional to the conversion of the Cuban Revolution to *internationalism* according to the program of *La Revolucion Bolivariana*. He ended up saying, "*Vale,* you guys cost me a *puyero.*"

When the president hung up, he shouted several curse words about Chávez and told the licenciado to call the MININT; he had to speak with the minister. When the phone rang, the licenciado answered it. On the line was a secretary saying that she had General Julio Cuevas Aponte on the line to speak with the president. The president said that this was another gorilla calling to complain. He shouted, "That is the *cabrón* handling the GAESA activities. As soon as I have time, I must get rid of him." This institution was Raúl's military enterprise group, which operated the convertible currency stores in Cuba and other businesses outside the island. He took the telephone and answered, "Yes, here is the president." It seems that the general was complaining of the looting of the stores and the loss of millions of dollars in merchandise. The president patiently listened to all sorts of complaints and criticism and when the general finished, he just said to him that everything was under investigation and that the offenders would be executed, and then he hung up the phone.

The president spent the next hour getting calls from the *Milicias Territoriales,* the Communist Party, the ELAM (Latin American School of Medical Sciences), from the *Oficoda,* and from many other organizations of the Socialist government, all complaining about the events of the early morning on the Malecón and asking what kind of security measures had been taken.

One of the calls came from Ricardo Alarcón, the president of the Nacional Assembly of the Popular Power. He was very worried, thinking how the delegates of the provinces in rebellion could be transported to Havana to attend the meeting to confirm the new leaders. He tirelessly asked for a quick termination of the military rebellion. After a small tantrum, he ended up saying, "What are you doing to end this mess, Felipe?" The president just repeated the same phrase to all callers: everything was under investigation and under the control of the MININT and the MINFAR. However, the reality was that with so many calls, he still hadn't been able to speak with the Minister of the MININT, nor with General Fontana of the MINFAR.

When the Minister of the MININT, Comandante Ramiro Gómez Guerra, arrived at five forty-five in the morning at the building of the Ministry, there were already waiting for him two of his closest collaborators. These were Colonel Arnaldo Luna Llano and Colonel Manuel Blanco Ochoa. The last one had waked the minister ten minutes after five in the morning with the news of the incidents at the Malecón. Colonel Luna Llano had made already a quick investigation and found that the officer who ordered the shooting of the screen was Captain Pánfilo Torquate Grande of the MININT. Before the minister's arrival, the colonel had already informed the minister of the results of his investigation. The minister had issued orders to look for the captain and to bring him to his office as soon as possible.

The colonels told the minister the details of the incident. When they were in conference in the office of the minister, the president called by phone and the minister told the secretary to tell him that she hadn't been able to find him. Then he said to the colonels, "That *comemierda* is already *jodiendo*, I will call him later," and he continued discussing the situation. Colonel Luna Llano reminded the minister that Captain Torquate Grande had been directly involved in the attack on Raúl Castro. The minister looked at him and with a whisper said, "Yes, I am very conscious of that."

Moments after that, the secretary rang the Ministry office to say that Colonel Sanchez Ortiz was here to see the minister, along with Captain Torquate Grande. The minister said that they could come in. After both officials entered the office, he thanked Colonel Sanchez Ortiz and then asked all present to leave him alone with the captain. When the three colonels were leaving the office, the minister apparently changed his mind and asked Colonel Luna Llano to stay in the office.

When both colonels left, the minister approached the captain and asked him, "*Carajo,* who issued the order to shoot the luminous screen?" The captain, with a face full of fear, said that he had ordered the destruction of the provoking imperialistic screen because it was accusing them of committing the assault and murder of Raúl Castro.

The minister, with a full glance of fury, shouted, "*Coño*, nobody can give any order here without my authorization." He then smacked two powerful punches to the captain's face. When the captain lost his balance and was trying to hold himself from the armchair that was at his side in front of the desk, unconsciously he moved his right hand to the pistol that hung from his belt. It seemed that he had intentions to withdraw the weapon. But when he raised his head in search of the minister, he found in front of him the barrel of the pistol of Colonel Luna Llano. The minister then made a gesture with the hand to the colonel, as if he was ordering him not to shoot. The colonel took a step back and lowered the pistol, but he kept it in his hand.

The minister yelled, "*Comemierda*, the bursts of the firings of the AK-47s produced a stampede of the people there and the cancellation of the rally. Do you realize the *mierda* that you have done?" Then he looked at the colonel and said, "Take him away. I don't want to see him again; get rid of him."

After they left the office and the minister sat behind his desk, perhaps getting ready to call the president, the intercom rang. The secretary told the minister that Colonel Blanco Ochoa wanted to see him. The minister said to let him come in. The colonel entered the office and told the minister that he had more bad news from the Malecón incident. When the crowd ran in stampede, most of the security agents put their AK-47s on the ground and ran with the people because the multitude was wild and would run them over. "Now, we have realized that we haven't been able to recover forty-eight AK-47 rifles," he said. "Apparently, the crowd took them."

The minister shouted a few bad words and ordered the colonel to lead an investigation to find the missing rifles. He said, "We will have to search all the houses in Havana, if is necessary, but the people can't have weapons in their hands. First begin with the houses of the apathetic and the antisocial elements and continue the search until you find them all."

The General and Minister of the FAR, Abelardo Fontana Flores, hadn't moved from his office in the MINFAR building since three o'clock in the morning. The general had been wakened by a call from General Aurelio Domínguez Roja, head of operations of the FAR in the Province of Cienfuegos. General Domínguez Roja called him, in a tone full of uncertainties and fears, with the news of a rebellion of young officers of the FAR in the adjacent provinces of Villa Clara, Santi Spiritus, Ciego de Avila, and Camagüey. He feared that his young officers and the troops in his province could join the rebels.

General Fontana ordered him to cut all telephone and radio communications with the FAR in the rebellious provinces and to block all access roads to them.

He said that he was going to call General Tino Toro Negro of the adjacent Province of Las Tunas so that he would do the same. He then stressed that it was necessary to isolate the rebellion's source before it extended throughout the island.

A rebellion inside the FAR was the last thing the new government needed. The seriousness of the situation made the general think, at least for a moment, that the attack and murder of Raúl had been a great error. He felt a little guilt and remorse, like the way Judas felt after he betrayed Jesus. He thought that it was Chávez's fault because of his urgency to go ahead towards the new stage of internationalism of the Cuban Revolution, after Fidel's death. The island had become dependent on Chávez's oil and money, and now came the hour to pay back. Well, now was too late and it was necessary to do something very quickly to contain the rebellion.

He began calling all the provincial chiefs of the FAR to make sure of their loyalty. When the president called him around six o'clock in the morning, the general was speaking with the general in charge of the Province of Guantánamo. He told the secretary to say that she hadn't been able to make contact with him; he was too busy to waste time with that *comemierda*.

Later he called the FAR in the Province of Camagüey and, instead of talking with the general in charge of the province, his call went to Lieutenant Iván Perez Vila. The general first threatened to take him to a military court, charging him for insurrection and treason to the revolution. However, when he saw the determination and the strength of character of the lieutenant, the general offered him a promotion to colonel if he stopped the insurrection. The general, realizing that nothing could convince the lieutenant, ended the call saying that eventually he would be shot in company of the other rebellious officers, not only for the insurrection, but also for the attack and murder of Comandante Raúl Castro, in complicity with the *Yanki* CIA and elements of internal dissidence. He said, "You can't escape revolutionary justice; you are a traitor sentenced to death."

In the Province of Camagüey, Lieutenant Perez Vila, in just couple of hours, had obtained the support of the officers and the troops of the provinces of Ciego de Avila, Santi Spiritus, and Villa Clara. The only government officials under arrest were the military leaders of the provinces and certain active members of the Communist Party. The statement of Lieutenant Rodriguez Caso in reference to the attack on Raúl Castro and his accusations involving members of the MININT acted like the catalytic factor that motivated the rebellion of the FAR in the provinces. Everything had taken place without bloodshed. The peaceful development of the insurrection confirmed the displeasure of the young officers and the troops in general with the chaotic situation of economic, political, and social bankruptcy that *Castrismo* had brought to Cuba.

The rebellion continued during the day and a few hours later, the FAR had the control of the civil governments of the provinces in revolt and all prominent members of the Communist Party had been put under military custody. Officers of the FAR occupied the MININT and the commanding chiefs of the Ministry were arrested. The chiefs of the National Police were replaced and the old provincial chiefs were placed under military custody. Later, the first disposition made by the military government was to order the distribution of foodstuff and essential goods from the warehouses of the special stores to the population of the four provinces. The military government said that all those articles belonged to the people and for that reason they didn't have to pay for them. The population very enthusiastically received this measurement, because the people were hungry and full of need.

Around two o'clock on Monday afternoon in the still-loyal Province of Cienfuegos, a great number of people concentrated in front of the special stores, demanding the distribution of the goods. The people had heard that the rebel provinces had distributed them, and now they were expecting the same. When the police and the state security agents from the MININT used force to break the marches, the multitude revolted and broke the shop windows of the special stores with stones. There were several arrests and injuries resulting from the incident.

The chief of the MININT in the province, worried about the situation, called the FAR to request soldiers to guard the streets and the establishments. The provincial chief, General Domínguez Roja, without consulting with the MINFAR in Havana, sent a large contingent of soldiers for such mission, thinking that in that way the people wouldn't go out that night. However, when at five o'clock in the afternoon the people saw the troops walking on the streets, they thought the FAR in the province had joined the rebellion of the other four provinces nearby. Unexpectedly, the people came out to the streets and ran towards the special stores. When the colonel in charge of the military contingent ordered the soldiers to use force to stop the people, the captains, lieutenants, and the troops refused. Instead, they joined the people in sacking the stores.

When the news arrived at the provincial FAR headquarters, the young officers and the troops seized the place and arrested General Domínguez Roja and several other officers. Before six o'clock, the Province of Cienfuegos joined the other four provinces in the military insurrection of the island.

Finally, around seven o'clock on Monday evening, President Perez Roue was able to call for a meeting in the Palacio de la Revolucion with his ministers, the first vice president, the president of the *Asamblea Nacional del Poder Popular* and two leaders of the Cuban Communist Party. The meeting took place more or less sixteen hours after the military revolt and the events of the Malecón began.

During the first part of the meeting, only complaints and recriminations were heard. Nevertheless, nobody dared to propose a plan of action to solve the precarious state of affairs of the new administration. The problem was that nobody knew what to do; the island had been for more than forty-seven years completely controlled by a single person, the *Máximo Líder* Fidel Castro. This type of situation never had been anticipated, because during Fidel's days it couldn't have happened. However, the reality was that the *máximo líder* had died. The new leaders were accustomed to following the decisions made by Fidel and they had never been able to propose changes. Experience had taught them that declaring different opinions was the way to political misfortune, prison, and in many occasions, even death. The best thing was to abdicate docilely the capacity to think and to give an opinion. This was the safest way to avoid problems and maintain the privileges that the revolution gave them in payment for their silence and submission.

The other problem was Chávez and his oil. Any proposition to solve the situation would have to be approved by Chávez. The economy of the island, to a great extent, was maintained by the large sums of money and oil that Chávez was giving to the government. The Venezuelan's aid was essential for the survival of the regime.

On the other hand, from the strategic and logistic point of view, they all understood very clearly that ground transportation between the provinces of the east and the west were cut. The five provinces in the center of the island blocked all type of ground transportation. The air and sea routes were the only alternatives for sending foodstuff, equipment, and troops. However, aerial transportation was limited by the lack of cargo airplanes. The sea route also had a problem; the Cuban merchant fleet was neglected and in very poor shape. The Cuban navy was very small and most of it was in Cienfuegos Bay in the hands of the rebels.

All reached the conclusion that the situation was very delicate. Then, President Perez Roque looked at General Fontana Flores, minister of the MINFAR, and said to him, "I believe the moment has arrived for using Division Fifty." This division of the FAR was famous because Fidel and Raúl always had said that in this division were the best soldiers and officers of the armed forces. It had the best weapons, including a large number of Russian tanks and combat airplanes. Always it was thought that Division Fifty had been trained and maintained combat-ready to even, if necessary, sweep out units and divisions of the FAR. The president, with certain logic in mind, reached the conclusion that the moment for using that unstoppable war machine had arrived.

The general looked at the president and slightly smiled, saying, "I believe that isn't possible."

The president stood up and shouted, "*Coño,* what is going on here? I order you, Abelardo, to tell me why you don't want to use the great military force of Division Fifty."

Minister Ramiro Gómez from the MININT, interrupted the discussion and said, "Because Division Fifty was a myth created by the Castro brothers. This division was the scarecrow of Fidel to frighten the people and other small countries. It was a well-kept top secret, only known by us, the top military leaders." Then he turned to the general and said, "Abelardo, tell them the truth of the Division Fifty."

The general got very nervous and in a disturbed voice responded that the FAR had a Division Fifty but its weapons, tanks, and the airplanes were kept under secret tunnels. The equipment was very old. Most of the large Russian tanks didn't run; only a few were in working condition. These tanks were only used in military parades to show off. The airplanes didn't have spare parts and they couldn't fly. The division had many soldiers only trained to march in military parades and they had no formal combat training. He said, "Raúl used to joke about the name of Division Fifty. He playfully said that all the arms and equipment of the division had more than fifty years, but it was a useful junkyard to scare people."

President Perez Roque and the other officials in the meeting remained without speech, exchanging glances among themselves. After a little while of silence, the president said, "*Coño,* what are we going to do? Anybody have any *cabrona* suggestions?"

Minister Ramiro Gómez stood up and said that the FAR wasn't reliable, and had to be blamed for the problems. He reminded everybody that almost half of the FAR was in rebellion. Taking advantage of the opportunity, he mentioned the corruption of the generals and colonels of the MINFAR in their business activities carried out by the GAESA Group. The companies' profits in hard currencies hadn't been used for the benefit of the armed forces and great sums of money were sent abroad and deposited in the bank accounts of Raúl and his group of "protégés." For that reason the FAR was badly equipped and lacked military training. All of that had created much displeasure between the young officers and was the cause of the revolt. Everybody knew that Minister Ramiro Gómez had never gotten alone with Raúl or with his team of collaborators since the competitive struggle between the MINFAR and the MININT in the sixties. Both men felt a deep mutual distrust. This harshness between these two high leaders always was latent, although kept quiet among the high spheres of the regime.

The president, realizing that Minister Ramiro Gómez was using the situation to settle old internal quarrels, said, "*Coño*, finish that story and tell us what is in your mind to fix this *mierda*."

Then Minister Ramiro Gómez very emphatically said that from that day the MINFAR should report to him. He would appoint several MININT officers to supervise the FAR operations. The minister said that he would use the special troops of the MININT to guard the streets and all the special stores in the provinces of Havana and Matanzas, where more people lived. Then he said, "It is necessary to put fear into the minds of the people." For this, he would send to prison all the dissidents and all the *elementos antisociales*. If the jails got full and there was no space for all the prisoners, then he would put them in concentration camps in the sports stadiums and arenas. He reminded everybody that he did that during the Playa Girón invasion in 1961. On that occasion, they arrested and placed in custody close to a hundred thousand suspicious people in less than three days.

He continued, saying "We must develop a campaign that mobilizes the people and keeps them in the state of fear. We can use phrases like, 'The war of all the people.' It is necessary to accuse the *Yanki* imperialists, the Cuban Mafia from Miami, and the dissidents within the island of being allies with the treacherous members of the FAR's rebellious provinces. Since this mobilization will bring more food shortages, it will be necessary to return to more lean distribution of resources in the same way that Fidel did after the fall of the Berlin Wall.

"The FAR traitors in the five rebel provinces will learn how revolutionary justice works. For them I have a surprise," said the minister. "I can't tell what it is because we have a traitor among us." After saying that, he looked toward General Fontana, and told him that he was under arrest. Then he called his guards, who immediately entered the conference room with their AK-47 rifles in hand. The minister ordered the guards to disarm the general and to take him away to the MININT building.

He turned to President Perez Roque and told him, "You call Chávez and tell him that we need two hundred million dollars immediately if he wants the *Revolución Bolivariana* to go forward. Use your deceptive ability to tell stories and tricks to convince him." Suddenly, he turned towards First Vice President Lage and to Alarcón, the president of the *Asamblea Nacional del Poder Popular,* and said to them, "And you two, make contact with the ambassadors of the Third

World countries and Arab countries in the UN so that they begin to protest *Yanki* intervention in the internal affairs of Cuba. Go speak with the politicians in Washington who supported the Cuban Revolution so that they can put pressure on the administration to end the commercial embargo. Since the Castro brothers are dead, the politicians in Washington could find an excuse to end the *cabronas* sanctions. I believe that without that law, American companies are going to give us credit, even to buy weapons. Since they never lent us money, they should be eager to do it now. We will never pay them back, in the same manner that we have done to other countries."

The meeting ended without any other incident or discussion and again, as during the good old times of *Fidelismo*, nobody had the audacity or the courage of protesting. Cuba had found its new *máximo líder*.

CHAPTER 21

▼

THE LAST DAYS OF THE REGIME AND THE BIRTH OF THE NEW REPUBLIC

It was Sunday at noon when the news of the death of Fidel Castro got to the Cubans in Miami and to the other millions of them living scattered around the world. It seemed like the planet Earth stopped turning around its axis. This time was for real; thousands of people were celebrating the news in Calle Ocho in Miami. The famous restaurant Versalles, in the heart of southwest Miami, the focal point of the Cubans in exile, was the first to invite all the people who could enter in its ample saloons to eat and drink on the house. La Carreta and most of the restaurants, cafeterias, and bars on the famous Calle Ocho followed this initiative. In Union City, New Jersey, the Bergen Line filled the streets with thousands of people who shouted, "*Viva Cuba Libre.*" The people congratulated each other and embraced themselves. In all large and small cities and towns in America and Europe where Cuban exiles lived, the news was received with great joy and celebration.

Castro always made believe to the world that he was semi-immortal; his doctors had proclaimed that Fidel would live one hundred and forty years, at least. The tyrant had challenged the world; he had insulted and made fun of nine United States presidents, the prime ministers of England and Spain, and all the leaders of the democratic nations of the world. He had even used the visit to Cuba of Pope John Paul II to consolidate his "world-wide prestige" by deceiving the good old Pope and the Cuban Catholics. Castro had declared his personal war against the free world and had always said that his battle would never end while he was alive. Well, finally the day of his defeat had arrived with the victory of his numerous enemies. The world really proved that *el Caballo*, more recently called the *penco senil*, was only a mortal. The godlike man had died of natural causes and had escaped the wrath of justice. Nevertheless, hardly would he escape the judgment of history, when he got his place in the historical latrine along with Hitler, Stalin, Ho Chi Minh, Mao, and other despicable beings that have lashed humanity.

That was why the celebrations and the joy seen in the faces of the Cubans in exile and the satisfaction that millions of people in the world enjoyed was not entirely the product of morbid joy for the death of a human being. It was the celebration of the victory of the Cubans and all the people in the free world and the end of the "personal war" of Fidel Castro.

However, not everything was happiness, nor could we say that freedom was around the corner. Power had been transferred to Raúl Castro, the younger brother and eternal successor of Fidel. He had promised changes and reforms in the regime's administration in his first speech to the people as a *máximo líder*. Nobody knew what Raúl had in mind. Everybody in Cuba knew that it was futile to try to maintain by force a failing system that kept the population in poverty and without future. Raúl would possibly uses these changes and reforms as a pretext to consolidate his power. Nevertheless, somehow it was possible to interpret that as a victory for the reformist tendencies within the ruling class, the Left, and the reform leaders of the dissidence.

Inside and outside Cuba there were more than three hundred organizations opposing the Castro regime. The ideas of Cuban dissidents were very mixed, undoubtedly fragmented. Probably, the opposition's scorn for Castro constituted the main common denominator of all groups, followed by the desire for greater participation of the Cuban people in the election of its representatives. The ideologies and strategies of the dissidents ran from the right to the left of political and economic systems. These included the traditional groups that only would accept the absolute release of all political prisoners and the creation of a new republic under a new liberal constitution in a complete democracy. There were the reformist groups that advocated changes in the Socialist constitution, with the intention to maintain the so-called achievements of the revolution. These last ones were seen in the state as great administrators and planners of the economy, when the traditional groups favored the free market economy of capitalism. The Leftist groups dreamed about maintaining the Socialist system and considered immoral and unacceptable the capitalist system.

However, without any doubts, after they listened to Raúl's statement, the reformist groups and the Leftists felt themselves as the winners. In addition, they thought they were more able to contribute to the implementation of changes and reforms of the system, whereas the so-called historical Cuban exile felt frustrated and took a skeptical attitude toward the reforms initiated by Raúl.

Nevertheless, all this conflict of ideas lasted only a few hours. When in the evening Alarcón and Perez Roque informed the people of the death of Raúl and proclaimed the names of the new leaders and the great *inmovilista* adventure of the *Chavismo Internationalism*, all the competing groups returned to their original battle positions against the regime. Only now, they didn't have the scorn for Castro as a common denominator to blame for all the miseries that the island had suffered for more than forty-seven years. Now they all would have to accept that the problem of Cuba from the beginning of the revolutionary regime always had been the misfortune of the inoperative Socialist system that promoted government corruption and is contrary to the individuality of human nature. In addition, they would have to accept that, in reality, the so-called achievements of the revolution were only mirages proclaimed by Castro to cover his errors and failures.

The news of the death of Raúl came accompanied by the revolt of the FAR in five provinces on the island. All the groups in exile received this news with great skepticism. At first, they thought that history had taught them that military regimes never had shown a great vocation for democracy. Nevertheless, after analyzing the situation and considering first the interests of the long-suffering Cuban people, the power into the hands of the military could be better option than the adventure of *Chavismo Internationalism*. The solution wasn't perhaps the ideal, but in the short and medium term, it was better than the madness of *Chavismo* with its continuous conflicts and interferences in other countries of Latin America. The price of the *Revolución Bolivariana* madness was very high and represented more miseries and sufferings for the Cuban people.

On the island, after the stampede of Malecón Avenue and the news of the rebellion of the FAR, some groups of dissidents fled to take refuge in the rebellious provinces of Villa Clara, Ciego de Avila, and Camagüey. Alex was one of them—using his underground network, he traveled to Camagüey. There he joined the rebellion leaders and with his friend Benito coordinated secret meetings between the military and the civil dissidents.

However, in Havana in just two days, only for being suspicious, maybe close to twenty-five thousand people were indiscriminately arrested and transported in trucks to concentration camps at the University of Havana and El Cerro stadium. The intention was to frighten the population, to shut up the voices of the dissidents, and to avoid the looting of the tourist restaurants and the special stores, as Minister Ramiro Gómez from the MININT had ordered. Perhaps this massive arrest of people effectively avoided the employment of the missing rifles AK-47s in the Malecón, because they were never used.

Lieutenant Iván Perez Vila met in Camagüey on Tuesday morning with several lieutenants and captains to discuss the situation and to prepare a plan of action. They all agreed that the situation in which they were controlling only five provinces was in the long term indefensible. The rebellion of the FAR would have to spread to the entire island rather quickly. All agreed that the same causes that took them to the rebellion, like corruption, abuse of power, the misery of the people, the few opportunities for promotions, and, finally, the murder of Raúl Castro, were the common evils that prevailed in all the provinces of the island. For that reason they agreed to establish contacts with friendly officers whom they knew were unsatisfied and somehow could sympathize with the rebellion. The idea was to woo these officers to join the rebellion.

The second topic on which all agreed was to release all the political prisoners. The people received this measure with joy. The FAR of the rebellious provinces gained the confidence of the people with this disposition, together with the immediate distribution of all foodstuff and consumer goods in the special stores. In addition, the third topic of discussion was to solicit the participation of the dissidents in preparation for long-term economic and political reforms. Apparently, Alex and his group participated in these conversations had convinced the young officers of the importance of the civil dissidents' participation, considering the interests of the nation after the overthrow of the regime by the military.

On the afternoon of Tuesday, the MININT gave orders to the FAR to send all MIG-29 Fulcrum airplanes available from the military airport of the Ciudad Libertad in Marianao, Province of Havana, to the rebellious Province of Cienfuegos. The mission was to bomb and destroy the four battle cruisers anchored at the naval base of Cienfuegos Bay. The government's idea was to eliminate the possibility of naval attacks on the cargo boats carrying supplies and troops back and forth from the eastern provinces faithful to the regime. The strategy was to maintain the blockade of the five rebellious provinces that divided the island and for that purpose, it was necessary to keep open the sea routes and to use the few merchant ships available to maintain the movement of supplies and personnel with the important provinces that were isolated at eight hundred kilometers from Havana.

The air force in the Ciudad Libertad had fifteen awesome MIG-29 Fulcrums, but of these only ten were in flying condition and of these, only eight were ready to accomplish the mission that had been ordered. The eight airplanes were armed with R-73E short-range guided missiles and S-24B unguided rockets. Everything was ready to destroy the rebellious cruisers in Cienfuegos Bay. The sinister secret plan of Minister Ramiro Gómez to destroy the cruisers was underway; the four warships in Cienfuegos Bay were not a match against the powerful MIG-29 Fulcrums and their sophisticated, lethal weapons. The MININT minister's victory was at hand.

The City of Cienfuegos is located three hundred and thirty-five kilometers from Havana; the MIG-29s would be over their target in less than fifty minutes of flight. Minister Ramiro Gomez was sure this attack not only would assure control of the waters around the island, but also, it would give a serious moral blow to the rebels and serve as a warning to the military in other provinces. It would show that nobody could escape the vengeance and rage of the revolutionary government on the island.

The airplanes took off and flew in formation over the City of Havana, following the instructions of the MININT. Minister Ramiro Gómez wanted to be sure that the people in Havana saw the MIG-29s flying towards their mission. Later they would fly east over the City of Matanzas, to show the military strength of the revolution there. After this show of military force, they would continue their course towards the southeast where Cienfuegos Bay is located. The mission marched as it had been planned and it was monitored by Colonel Lopez Millán of the MININT, the new supervisor of the air force, and General Diaz Acevedo, former chief of the Revolutionary Air Force.

When the airplanes were about twenty-five kilometers from their target, unexpectedly they changed course towards the northeast. From Havana, Colonel Lopez Millán and General Diaz Acevedo told the pilots through the radio that they were flying away from their target and that they should immediately change their course toward the objective of the mission. However, the planes continued northeast, and then from Havana the general and the colonel began threatening the pilots with court martial and cursing them with the worst insults and bad words of the Spanish language. Meanwhile, in less than ten minutes the airplanes were flying over the city of Santa Clara towards the City of Camagüey. Twenty minutes later, they flew over the city and landed at the International Airport of Camagüey.

When Minister Ramiro Gómez found out what had happened, he exploded in rage and ordered the arrest of all pilots of the FAR in the provinces still loyal to the government. The disobedience and desertion of the eight pilots was interpreted by the minister as a general rebellion of all the officers of the air force.

Now, the government practically had lost the control of the skies and the territorial waters. This situation isolated the important eastern provinces of Las Tunas, Granma, Holguín, Santiago de Cuba, and Guantánamo. These provinces produced a great amount of agricultural products that were very important to feed the population of the island. The provinces of Pinar del Río, Havana, and Matanzas, on the west, didn't produce sufficient food to feed themselves. In addition, Chávez could have problems continuing Venezuela's shipments of oil and foodstuff while the rebel provinces had most of the Cuban navy's warships.

Around eleven o'clock Tuesday night, Lieutenant Iván Perez Vila, accompanied by three other rebellious officers, landed a small Cessna airplane at the International Airport of Varadero in the Province of Matanzas, only a hundred and forty kilometers from the city of Havana. On the runway, two black Ladas from the FAR were waiting for them. The cars took them to Havana Province and secretly entered the FAR military base of Ciudad Libertad in Marianao at about two o'clock Wednesday morning, through the famous Gate Five on Consulado Street. This was an historical coincidence, because through the same entrance and more or less at the same hour, Dictator Fulgencio Batista had entered the base in 1952 to give the coup d'etat to Carlos Prio Socarras, the last constitutional president of Cuba.

In the assembly hall of the base, the captains, lieutenants, and sergeants met with Lieutenant Iván Perez Vila and his three companions. After a few exchanges of ideas, they decided on the immediate deposition and termination of the revolutionary government and their Socialist constitution. They swore their loyalty to the FAR and to the Provisional Military Government. Lieutenant Perez Vila was appointed the general coordinator of the Revolutionary Armed Forces and temporary head of the military government. From the assembly hall, they made phone calls to the FAR headquarters of the provinces of Pinar del Río, Isla de la Juventud, and Matanzas, who also swore their loyalty to the new military government. After these new alliances, only the five eastern provinces maintained their loyalty to the regime. In these provinces, the *Generales Empresarios* were still trying to save their privileged positions and their businesses, and perhaps preparing their escape from the island.

Without losing any time, Lieutenant Perez Vila ordered the mobilization of one thousand soldiers, ten light armored tanks, and several other vehicles armed with .50 caliber machine guns, towards the Plaza de la Revolución. The military force stood in front of the buildings of the Palacio de la Revolución, the Central Committee of the Communist Party building, and the Ministerio del Interior (MININT). In addition, he sent two hundred soldiers with two light armored tanks to the MINFAR building. In less than half an hour, the rebel troops of the FAR occupied the headquarters of the National Police, where they put under military custody the chief of police and his collaborators. With equal agility, other troops of the rebel force occupied the building of the *Milicias Territoriales* and all the state radio and television stations.

It was only four-thirty in the morning and the people in Havana still were sleeping without knowing what was happening in the city. Everything happened so suddenly and with such military precision that, until that moment, the process hadn't produced any bloodshed.

Lieutenant Perez Vila was waiting inside a military vehicle a block away from the shady building of the MININT when the first rays of light of the new day entered the square. The building had in one of the exterior walls a black metal mural with the image of Che Guevara and the phrase, "Until the Victory Always." The lieutenant was trying to convince the people inside the MININT building to surrender. The rebel forces, without bloodshed, had already occupied all the other government buildings.

The lieutenant already knew that President Perez Roque had taken refuge in the Embassy of Venezuela. First Vice President Carlos Lage was in the Embassy of Spain and Ricardo Alarcón went to the Embassy of Costa Rica. This meant that the three members of the civil triumvirate that "governed" the island had fled, terrified, after their spies in the FAR informed them of the situation.

The lieutenant didn't know how many security agents and *milicianos* were inside the MININT building. He didn't know what type of armaments they had in the building; that was a well-guarded secret of the MININT elite force. However, he could see that on the outside of the building there were more than three hundred *milicianos* armed and entrenched behind sand bag walls. Three light armored tanks guarded the main entrance, closing the way to the only outside door of the building.

The lieutenant was trying to avoid the confrontation and unnecessary Cuban bloodshed. Already the so-called *revolución* had cost many lives in more than forty-seven years of dictatorship. The revolution wasn't popular, its main authors were dead, and the revolution had failed and had lost the respect of the Cuban people. The hour had arrived to look forward to the beginning of a new phase in the nation's history. However, in spite of his arguments, the building's occupants held their position and challenged the rebel forces of the FAR to try to occupy the building. They even threatened the rebel forces with the intervention of Venezuelan troops, which they were expecting to disembark soon on Cuban shores in defense of the Socialist revolution. In addition, they accused the FAR officers of being agents of the *Yanki* CIA, responsible for the assassination of Raúl Castro.

This situation lasted for more than an hour; the people in Havana had already waked up, and rumors ran throughout the city. The radio stations and the television transmitted fragmented information of what was happening on the island. The military government declared martial law in Havana Province. The order forbade the citizens to walk on the streets; all the people would have to stay inside their homes. The army, without asking twice, could shoot any person who walked on the street. The reason for these extreme security measures was to protect the citizens.

The lieutenant reached the conclusion that the siege of the building couldn't continue for an indefinite time. It was necessary to eliminate this source of the uncertainty that prevailed in the City of Havana. Therefore, after consultations with several of his rebel officers, he issued the orders to begin with saturation bombing of the building. Five tanks that they brought from the military camp opened fire against the building. The tanks in front of the entrance to the MININT building opened fire in response. The cannonballs exploded close to or within the trenches of both parties. From the building of the MININT, two squads of agents equipped with bazooka launchers went out under heavy coverage from the building's roof and launched several rockets against the rebel tanks. Two of the tanks flew into pieces after the rockets' direct impact. The battle continued for more than twenty minutes. It seemed that the rebellious FAR hadn't expected to find such resistance. The building was a fortress and maintained an irresistible curtain of lead on its besieger. Possibly, the rebels had lost about seventy-five men since the hostilities began.

Suddenly, when the rebel forces had stopped their advance to regroup and to request reinforcements, the thunderous sound of MIG-29s airplanes of the air force was heard. They had left from Camagüey, following orders given by Lieutenant Perez Vila. Three of the airplanes sent their air-to-earth unguided S-24B rockets against the MININT building. The first explosions were deafening; when the rockets hit the outside walls and roof of the building, the ground moved as in an earthquake. Two other planes made a clean sweep of the artillery entrenched on the building roof. In less than a minute, the other three MIG-29s sent their

R-73E short-range guided missiles. This time the projectiles disappeared in the smoke coming from a large hole in one of the building's wall. The building suddenly seemed to become reddish and exploded. All the outer walls collapsed, and an intense gray smoke came from whatever was left of the building. The debris of the building continued exploding for more than an hour after its collapse. Possibly, these explosions were caused by the powerful explosives and ammunition stored in the building when these materials contacted the intense fire that devoured all the structure of the edifice.

The rebel troops of the FAR ceased fire because they couldn't see what had happened to the *milicianos* entrenched behind the sand bags around the building and to the people inside the building. The debris of the building had fallen on top of them, burying them completely after the explosion. The intense fire of the debris lasted more than four hours and the heat was infernal. It was very dangerous to approach the fire. Therefore, it was left alone, burning until its extinction. Later, when the fire was almost dull, it was possible to see that of the building nothing remained. Only ashes and the charred stones could be seen of the once-sinister MININT building.

Never was it possible to know with exactitude how many or who had died in the building. Nevertheless, it was assumed that around eight hundred people had perished, counting the strong garrison entrenched outside the building. This group died, buried when the outer walls of the building collapsed on their heads. It is possibly that General Abelardo Fontana Flores was inside the building; he couldn't escape because he was under custody of the MININT as ordered by Minister Ramiro Gómez. Nobody heard about him again. The corpses of Fidel and Raúl Castro were never found. Both corpses were kept under refrigeration in the building of the MININT, waiting for a monumental burial rally. Apparently, their mortal remains had burned to ashes in the fire of the building.

First, it was thought that Minister Ramiro Gómez. was in the building and had suffered the same fate as General Fontana and all others. However, days later it was learned that he fled the island by plane an hour before the arrival of Lieutenant Perez Vila at Ciudad Libertad military base. First he went to Haiti and later he chartered an airplane that took him to Spain, where his family lived. Everybody knew that the minister had plenty of money and properties outside Cuba, all illegally acquired by selling armaments to the drug dealers in Colombia and other dirty businesses.

At dusk on Wednesday, the rebels already had control of the island. The five eastern provinces join the rebellion after the *Generales Empresarios* who were against the revolt fled the island in a military transport airplane towards Haiti.

From there, they flew later to permanent destinations in Europe. All of them had large amounts of money abroad from the businesses of the GAESA Group.

That night, Lieutenant Perez Vila informed the Cuban people, by radio and television, of the situation and declared that in twenty-four hours the FAR would distribute to the people all the merchandise that was stored in the special stores. Also, he announced that all political prisoners on the island would be set free. Then he mentioned, without entering in much detail, that the FAR was in consultation with several representatives of the dissidence with the intention of forming a provisional government. He also promised that in less than forty-eight hours details on these decisions would be announced. He pleaded with the people to keep calm, because they wouldn't allow acts of violence or personal revenge. Any person involved in this type of activity would be prosecuted and severely punished. In addition, he said that the military courts would investigate and prosecute all the people who had committed criminal acts during the Castros' years. All these dispositions worked out well, because, although there were some acts of violence resulting from vindictive actions, these were not as much as those that were expected. The population felt confidence in the administration of justice of the FAR and the military government.

In spite of the miserable living conditions, the people were looking toward the future with confidence and hope. Abroad, Cuban exiles enjoyed the latest news and celebrated the fall of Castro's dictatorship. In Miami, people were going to the airlines to reserve their seats for the time when flights to Cuba could resume. Some people wanted to lease boats to travel to the island. Travel agencies took reservations for future vacations in Varadero Beach. Many Cuban and American businessmen formulated plans to invest in the island.

On the other hand, the Leftist groups in the United States went to rallies in front of the White House, the Capitol, and the UN with great posters that said "Keep Hands OFF Cuba" and "NO Military Coup in Cuba." The same U.S. congressmen, sympathizers with the Cuban Revolution, who were always against the economic sanctions to the Castro dictatorship, now wanted the United States to keep them and opposed the recognition of the transitional government on the island. *The Washington Post* and other newspapers in the United States maliciously implied that the White House and the CIA were connected with what was happening in Cuba. They even were saying that they had plotted everything in a secret plan called the New Star Project. Well-known movie actors from Hollywood, worshippers of Castro and the Socialist revolution, protested and blamed the CIA and the Cuban Mafia of Miami for the island's developments.

In Venezuela, Hugo Chávez immediately accused the rebellious officers of the FAR of being agents of the CIA. Chávez cut the delivery of oil to the island and demanded the payment of three thousand millions of dollars that Cuba owed Venezuela for oil and gasoline purchases. Evo Morales from Bolivia shouted that *Yanki* imperialism had planned and financed the coup d'etat and demanded that the O.A.S. prepare a declaration condemning the United States of America's intervention in the internal affairs of Cuba. Argentina, Ecuador, and Nicaragua went along with Venezuela, supporting the idea of the declaration. In Europe, the Leftist groups protested and blamed the United States. As was expected, the worldwide Socialist movement and the anti-American groups couldn't miss the opportunity to shout and to protest the fall of the Cuban Revolution that for more than forty-seven years had bravely faced the *Yanki* Empire.

The composition and the program of the transitional government was announced Friday evening at seven-thirty on all television and radio stations on the island. The provisional government would last for two years while the Constitution of 1940 was reviewed and updated. The revision of the constitution was assigned to a committee of delegates chosen by the people for this mission. The power of the transitional government was shared by a pentarchy of five people, with the objective that all factions of the dissidents and the FAR had representation in the government during the transition to a constitutional democracy. One representative from each main faction composed the political tendencies of the pentarchy: the Socialist left, the reformists group, the liberal democrats on the island, the traditional Cuban exile, and the FAR, which was represented by Iván Perez Vila, who was promoted to the rank of colonel. The main function of the FAR was to maintain public order, to protect the constitutional process, and to coordinate the functioning of the transitional government. The plan was to celebrate free general elections in two years, after the completion of the new Constitution of the Third Republic of Cuba.

In 1933, after the overthrow of President Machado, the opposition had organized a similar form of government with Sergeant Fulgencio Batista Zaldivar, who also was promoted to colonel and head of the armed forces by the pentarchy in power at that time. This form of power sharing only lasted one week in 1933. Many Cubans on the island didn't remember the historical events that had happened more than seventy years earlier. At that time, the sergeants and the troops were the ones who initiated the military rebellion against the government of Machado. It was called then "the rebellion of the sergeants." Ironically, history was repeating itself; only this time it was the lieutenants. History might call it "the rebellion of the lieutenants" on this occasion. The people who remembered history hoped that, with the will of God, on this occasion the results would be better for the Cuban people.

One of the first dispositions of the new government was to remove all the debris and the ashes left from the gloomy building of the MININT and to put them in barges and dump them onto the bottom of the ocean several miles away from Cuba's shores. With this gesture, the provisional government told the people that the rubbish of the *Castrismo,* including ashes of their main authors, hadn't been buried in Cuban soil. This garbage, ironically, rested on the bottom of the Caribbean Sea, in the same waters where thousands of Cubans lost their lives when they were desperately fleeing the island in hopes of finding freedom.

The provisional government dissolved the hateful system of the *Comité de Defensa de la Revolución* and implemented measures to finish the food and consumer goods distribution system, with the intention of eliminating the rationing *libreta.* The death penalty was being abolished because the people thought that already too many Cubans had died during the years of the Socialist experiment. The hour had arrived for a national reconciliation, after more than four decades of hostilities, treason, lies, and splits within the Cuban family. All these miseries lashed the inhabitants of the island in the name of a revolution. A damn revolution!

Benito the *bodegero* was elected to represent Camagüey on the Constitutional Committee. Captain Rodovaldo Rodriguez died of pneumonia four months after the establishment of the provisional government. The *cederistas* Aníbal and Norberto supported the military rebellion of the FAR, trying to mend with their neighbors after their long period of mean and sometimes objectionable behavior. They bragged that they were secretly helping the dissidents plotting against the regime. The Valdés Rama family continued living in their home that wasn't a *casa particular* anymore. Marilú got married six months later to a doctor from the hospital. The husband of Leonor Correa was one of the first sergeants who joined the rebellious movement of the FAR in Camagüey and Leonor left her job in the MININT and went to work in a hospital. Genaro returned to Cuba after living in Grand Cayman for six months; he was homesick. Manny and Julisa continued working with Alberto in Grand Cayman. They were looking forward to visiting Cuba and going to Varadero Beach.

Juan, Vladimir, and Captain Pombo, all disappointed sons of the Socialist revolutionary years, were looking forward to the future. They thought that finally, they might find some answers to their rightful doubts about the purpose of their generation.

Most of the Cubans who had lived just for a short time abroad returned to rebuild their lives on the island. Most of the others Cubans in exile, the ones who had been living abroad for many years, didn't return; however, they all made plans to take vacations in Cuba and to show their children and grandchildren the beautiful island where they were born. Ernesto and Yolandita were among those remaining in San Juan with Doña Josefa. They were preparing a vacation in Cuba with their niece and nephew.

Henry, after two weeks in the Red Cross facility at the U.S. Interest Section building, returned to his home in Point Pleasant, after paying a thousand dollar fine for traveling to Cuba without authorization and justification. When the State Department called Natalia, she really got very angry with Henry for not telling her the truth about his trips. However, she was in love with him and forgave him for his lack of honesy. A month later, they went together on a nice vacation trip to Italy and Spain.

Alex, after living for some time in Cuba during the constitution revision process, faded away like a good old soldier. He thought that his generation had accomplished its mission; the Third Republic was in the gestation stage. The nightmare of the Communist system and the idea of a tyrant *máximo líder* were only sad memories in the history of a nation that was coming back and opening to the free world after a long, sad period of absence.

Believe me, it ain't easy!

Glossary

Actividades revolucionarias. Actividades. Any event mandated by the government for which obligatory attendance measures the submission of a person to the regime.

Actos de repudio. Aggressive protests organized by the regime where rotten eggs and stones were thrown at people suspected of being dissidents or at persons who have decided to leave the country.

Agro Mercados. Outdoor markets at which farmers sell their agricultural products at high prices. The government allowed the markets to operate for a time, but later closed them, saying the farmers were becoming too rich.

Ajiaco. Creole Cuban dish made of meat and root vegetables.

Ajuste Cubano. Law passed through the U.S. Congress that grants legal-resident status to Cubans who were in the United States in 1966.

Arrendador Inscripto. Term used to define the so-called "Casas Particulares."

Asamblea Nacional del Poder Popular. The supreme governing body of the Cuban state, composed of delegates chosen in the one hundred and sixty-nine municipalities. The Communist Party must approve all candidates. A sort of Parliament.

Asamblea para Promover la Sociedad Civil. An organization of three hundred and sixty-five independent groups trying to promote civil society and democracy in Cuba. The Cuban government does not recognize the organization.

Avalar. A letter of good behavior or verbal recommendation from the Committees of Defense of Revolution (CDR).

Baches. Great hollows in the streets and highways.

Balsero. A Cuban fleeing from the island in a small boat or on any object that floats.

Batistianos. The name given to people who supported the dictator Fulgencio Batista.

BC. Before Castro.

Béisbol. Baseball.

Bitongo. Name given to the young people in Cuba who reject participation in agricultural works imposed by the government.

Bocadito de Jamonada. A piece of bread with a slice of unknown cold meat that is not ham.

Bodega del Estado. Grocery store run by the state.

Bolita. Illegal lottery game played in Cuba until 1959.

Boleros. Cuban romantic music.

Buró de Represión de Actividades Comunistas (BRAC). Institution created by Batista in 1955, to work in cooperation with other foreign security agencies for the defense of democracies and to prevent the Communist expansion in America. The Batista regime converted the institution into a repressive organization.

Caballo. Name given to Fidel Castro by his supporters.

Cabrón. A derogatory name used in Cuba for a person not well-liked.

Camello. Trailer of passengers pulled by a truck which looks like a camel. The main mode of local transportation in the City of Havana.

Campo Socialista. The Communist countries of East Europe, before the fall of the Soviet Union.

Cañonazo de las Nueve. The doors of the wall that protected the City of Havana in the days of the Spanish colony. People were warned of their closing each night with a cannon shot. Following this tradition, one shot goes off every night in Havana at nine o'clock.

Carajo. The basket placed in the mainmast of the sailboats, where punished sailors were sent. In Cuba, the word is used in substitution of "hell." "Vete para el carajo" means "go to hell."

Casa Particular. Family house that rents one or two rooms to foreign and local tourists, allowed by the government because of the lack of hotels.

Castrismo. Cuban Socialist dictatorial doctrine originated by Fidel Castro.

Casuarina. A common tree of the tropical Cayman Islands that grows on the shores there.

Cederista. People who run the Committees of Defense of the Revolution.

Chancletas. Slippers. Can be of made of rubber or wood.

Chapuzón. A brief dip in the sea.

Chavismo. Socialist dictatorial doctrine invented by Hugo Chávez, president of Venezuela.

Chavitos. Name given by the Cuban people to the convertible currency that replaced the U.S. dollar in the Special stores.

Cheongsam. A Chinese-style woman's dress.

Chico. A word used to get the attention of another person during conversation. Employed by close friends in Cuba.

Chismeando. Scattering rumors about other people.

Chivato. A government informant.

Churroza. A dirty and deteriorated object. A rag.

Cola. A line of people expecting to get something.

Comandante. Highest military rank of the Rebel Army, earned during the armed struggle against Batista.

Comecandela. A person fanatical about the regime.

Comemierda. A foolish or stupid person.

Comité de Defensa de la Revolución (CDR). One of the main repressive organizations in Cuba, membership of which is obligatory; there is a committee on each block on the island. The members watch their neighbor, "guard" the area, and organize "revolutionary activities," such as meetings, blood donations, parades, etc., and evaluate the contributions of their neighbors to the regime.

Compañero. Comrade

Conga. Rhythmical and fast-moving Cuban music of African origin.

Coño. Interjection that denotes surprise, annoyance, misfortune, etc., frequently used by Cubans.

Convertir reveses en victorias. To "turn misfortunes in victories"; a nonsensical slogan that tries to justify the regime's mistakes.

Cuadros. A person holding an office in the government, usually repressing the citizens and acting outside the law.

Cubano de a pie. A common citizen, suffering the poor quality of life in Cuba.

Cuentapropista. A person operating under government authorization who left a profession to sell some service or products. Cuentapropistas pay high taxes.

Danzones and Sones. Very old and traditional Cuban popular music.

Diplotiendas. Stores operated for foreign diplomats and top government officials with access to dollars and euros. These stores are the property of Raúl Castro and do not accept Cuban pesos.

Directorio Revolucionario (Directorio). Clandestine organization of students and workers created in 1956 to develop armed warfare against Batista's regime.

Divisa. Dollars and euros.

Double Moral. To live hypocritically, repressing people, while at the same time, conducting illegal operations and defending the dysfunctional system.

Durmiendo la mona. The sleep of a drunk person.

Elementos Antisociales. People who are not in agreement with the Socialist system.

Empachaos. People blindly and unconditionally supporting the Cuban Socialist system.

Esbirros. People who serve the regime and are paid to perpetrate violence.

Escoria. The same as "elementos antisociales."

Exaltación de los valores patrios. A form of brainwashing to extol the regime and confuse democratic values.

FAR. Revolutionary Armed Forces.

Fidelismo. See "Castrismo."

Fifo. An endearing name for Fidel used by the fanatics.

Figura delictiva de peligrosidad social. A person who has not committed any crime, but who the regime suspects of being prone to disobeying their edicts.

Fotingo. An old auto.

Generales Empresarios. Old generals from the FAR who manage the army's industries and companies controlled by Raúl Castro.

GPS. Global Positioning System. A system of navigation using satellites.

Guagua. A Cuban passenger bus.

Guajiro. A farmer.

Guarachas. Joyous and fast-tempo Cuban music.

Gusano. Derogatory term for Cuban refugees, employed by Castro.

Hacerse de la vista gorda. To let things happen without saying or doing much; to be apathetic.

Hay que resolver, pa'resolver. To do something in order to survive the miseries of life in Cuba; most Cuban people do this daily.

Hubert Matos. Revolutionary commander who was not in agreement with the Communist direction of the revolution; he spent twenty years in Cuban prisons.

Ingreso. A year of study before entering high school.

Inmovilistas. High-ranking officials of the regime who resist changes in the Socialist system in Cuba.

Internacionalistas. People who are sent by the revolutionary government to fight wars abroad or with the intent to export the revolution. Cuban mercenaries; in most cases the Cuban government receives monetary compensation for their services.

Jamonada. Pieces of ham, animal fat, and soybeans pressed into the form of piece of meat.

Jaque. To maintain the common people under continuous threats and pressure.

Jineterismo. To engage in illegal activities in order to survive.

Jinetera. A prostitute who hunts foreign tourists with whom to exchange sex for money, food, and other necessities. Young Cuban people become *jineteras* in order to survive and to help their families.

Joder. To bother a person.

Jodia. Bad situation. Could be political or financial bad situation.

Jodidos. People that live under poor or bad conditions.

Lada. A car made in Russia.

Largo y tendido. A very long and detailed speech or presentation, derived from baseball, when the ball leaves the infield and rolls to the fence.

Libreta. A food rationing book used in Cuba for more than forty-five years.

L'chaim. A Jewish toast meaning "to life."

Logros de la Revolución. Initially popular measures taken by the revolutionary government that have been used for propaganda in and outside of Cuba; the Cuban people have not benefited from them.

Machado. Gerardo Machado was elected president of Cuba in free elections in 1925. He became dictator in 1930 following his first term.

Malanga. A plant, the root of which is edible. Also, known as "yautía."

Malanguitas hervidas. Cuban dish made with boiled malangas.

Malecón. An avenue that runs along Havana's coastal levies.

Mambises. The Cuban militia that fought during the War for Independence against the Spanish colonial army from 1868 to 1898.

Manzana. A square block of houses in a city.

Marabú. A very aggressive legume that invades and takes over good turf grass.

Marta Beatriz Roque. A dissident economist of democratic tendencies. Co-author of the book *La Patria es de Todos*. Founder of the Assembly to Promote Civil Society ("Asamblea para Promover la Sociedad Civil").

Matorral. Wild bushes.

Máximo Líder. Maximum leader. The supreme ruler of a dictatorship.

Milicias de tropas Territoriales. "Military services of Territorial Troops." An organization created for defense of the homeland, which threatened the people with rumors of imminent invasions from North America, demanding donations for the purchase of arms and supplies.

MININT. Ministry of the Interior.

MINFAR. Ministry of the Revolutionary Armed Forces.

Mulato. A person of dark color. Mulatto.

No es fácil. "It ain't easy." A phrase repeated by Cubans on the island that implies a complaint about the system; used in place of other phrases that could be recognized as anti-regime and put the speaker in conflict with the government.

No le cabía ni un comino. To feel very proud.

Oficoda. An office that controls the distribution and rationing of food and products that are purchased with the *libreta*.

Oscar Elías Biscet. The dissident physician who founded the Lawton Foundation on Human Rights. Dr. Biscet is in a Havana prison for merely speaking publicly about human rights.

Paso doble. Very happy Spanish music.

Pasta de bocadito. A foul paste of unknown meats, fats, soybeans, and other products that is spread on bread.

Pastelitos de guayaba. A pastry made from flour dough baked into thin layers and filled with guava jelly.

Payá. Oswaldo Payá Sardiñas. A reformist dissident of the "Movimiento Cristiano de Liberacion" and author of the so-called "Proyecto Varela."

Peligrosidad social. Any type of activities done by people who are not in agreement with the regime.

Penco Senil. A name given to Fidel Castro due to his age and physical condition.

Periodistas Independientes. Cuban journalists who do not work for the revolutionary government.

Período especial. The difficult period in Cuba after the fall of the Berlin Wall, when the Cuban government lost all support from its Communist allies, and the island economy collapsed. The standard of living of the Cuban people disintegrated to near misery.

Picadillo. A mixture of soybeans and low-quality ground meat. It has a bad smell and taste.

Pinchos. Persons from the ruling class of the regime with influence within the government.

Pioneros. Child members of the UPC (Union of Pioneers of Cuba), an organization for the Communist indoctrination of elementary school students.

Plan java. A law that grants priority to persons belonging to government organizations or to the Communist Party, to avoid *colas* in the state stores.

Pollito. A pretty girl.

Por la libre. Food and articles that can be bought in quantities in addition to the *libreta* during a given time.

Plantados. People that can't be promoted or advance in their jobs, because they are not regime sympathizers.

Principios Revolucionarios. Ideas that are considered inviolable, such as a belief in the infallibility of the Socialist system, or the evil intent of the United States (the enemy).

Proceso Histórico. A term used by Castro to identify the revolution, implying that the Cuban people have no other option than Socialism and that Socialism is natural, normal, and irreversible.

Programa Barrio Adentro. A program to provide medical attention and Communist indoctrination in the poor districts of Venezuela.

Proyecto Varela. A Reformist program, prepared by Oswaldo Payá Sardiñas, which he presented with the signatures of ten thousand people to the National Assembly of Popular Power. The program proposed changes to the 1976 Socialist Constitution of Cuba; its reforms were rejected.

Puyero. A Venezuelan expression that means "a lot." The "puya" was an old Venezuelan currency.

Quedar para vestir santos. A Spanish expression that means "old maid."

Raulismo. The fanatical doctrine supporting the ideas of Raúl Castro.

Rebelión de los Sargentos. A revolt by sergeants and army troops against their officers in 1933 in Cuba. Sergeant Fulgencio Battista was the leader of the revolt, and seven years later Batista was elected president of the republic. In 1952 he led a coup d'etat against a democratically elected president.

Reforma Urbana. A revolutionary law of 1960 that enabled the government to confiscate all the island's residential properties, making the regime the sole owner of all land.

Remesa. Money sent to Cubans on the island by their relatives abroad. These transfers of hard currency have constituted the main source of income of the revolutionary government.

Revolución Bolivariana. The idea of Hugo Chavez to turn Venezuela in a Socialist country, very similar to Cuba.

Roca. Vladimir Roca Antunes, a Socialist dissident member of the Cuban Democratic Social Party and son of Blas Rock, one of the founders of the Cuban Communist Party. He is co-author of the book *La Patria es de Todos*.

Salcocho de viandas. Root vegetables boiled with pieces of meat; very similar to *ajiaco*.

Servicio de Inteligencia Militar (SIM). Repressive organization created by Batista in 1935 to maintain the security of the state and public institutions. In 1959, it was replaced by MININT, during Castro's regime.

Socialismo Planetario. The goal of the Socialist movement to impose the Socialist system throughout the world.

Solar. An urban piece of land or a lot where a house is built or is destined to be built.

Stanley Market. A famous street market in Hong Kong.

Tarjetón. A notebook issued to every citizen to control the rationing of drugs in Cuba.

Telephone STU-III. Special encrypted telephone system secure of interceptions. The system uses satellite mobile phone connections through Immarsat.

Televisor Panda. A brand of color television set manufactured in China which can only be acquired with hard currencies.

Tinajones. A large vessel or pot used to filter water. Typical in the City of Camagüey.

Tirar la toalla. A phrase used in Cuba that means to help a person to solve a problem.

Todo el mundo canta. To divulge secrets under pressure or torture.

Trabajo voluntario. To work in agriculture or any type of work without receiving compensation only to gain revolutionary merits.

Trastienda. "Back room." A room in the back of a *bodega*.

Tremenda descarga. A scolding or verbal reprimand.

Unión de Jóvenes Comunistas. "Union of Communist Young People." An organization promoted by the Communist Party of Cuba.

Van,Van. A Cuban musical group formed during the Socialist regime.

Vigilancia revolucionaria. The constant vigilance of the activities of Cuban citizens.

Yanki. Any person who is from the United States of America.

Zapatúo. Old, hard bread.

Zaperoco. A Venezuelan word denoting a disturbance by the people in the streets of a city.

978-0-595-45114-2
0-595-45114-4